The Last Road

ALSO BY K. V. JOHANSEN

Blackdog

The Leopard

The Lady

Gods of Nabban

The Last Road

K. V. JOHANSEN

Being the final novel of the caravan road

Published 2019 by Pyr®

Cover photo: Shutterstock
Cover design by Jennifer Do
Cover © Start Science Fiction
Map illustrations © K.V. Johansen

Inquiries should be addressed to
Start Science Fiction
101 Hudson Street, 37th Floor, Suite 3705
Jersey City, New Jersey 07302
PHONE: 212-431-5455
WWW.PYRSF.COM

1 2 3 4 5 6 7 8 9 10

ISBN 978–1–63388–554–7 (paperback)
ISBN 978–1–63388–555–4 (ebook)
Printed in the United States of America

This one is for Ivan, even if he does feel that humans spend far too much time in front of computers.

(And many thanks are owed to Tom Lloyd, who finally pinned down the elusive series title for me.)

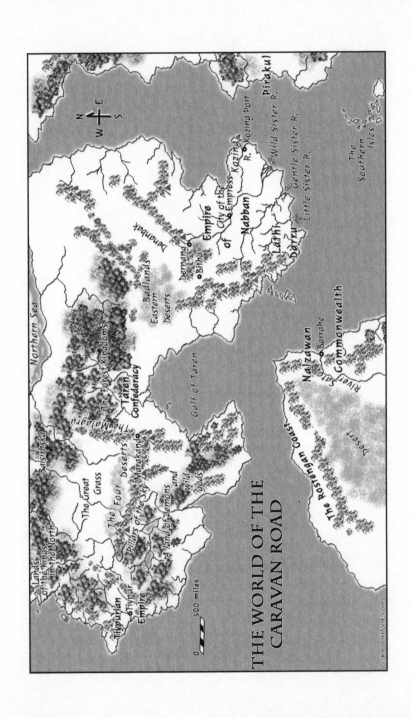

THE WORLD OF THE
CARAVAN ROAD

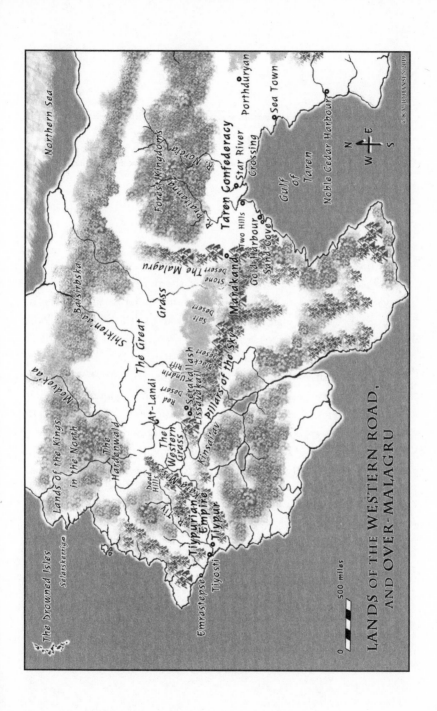

LANDS OF THE WESTERN ROAD,
AND OVER-MALAGRU

THE STORY SO FAR . . .

Long before these stories began, there was war in the heavens between the Old Great Gods and the powers known to human legend as the devils, who were defeated and sealed in the cold hells. Seven escaped and, being creatures of pure soul like the Old Great Gods, were unable to exist in the physical world for long. These seven entered in a bargain with seven human wizards to share souls and bodies; they became immortal, two-souled beings, incarnate in the world, and human songs and histories tell of ambition, betrayal, wars, conquest, and their eventual defeat with the aid of the Old Great Gods, who sealed them into earthly graves, but did not destroy them, for to destroy a soul is the greatest of sins. The Old Great Gods had no joy in their victory, for by a last desperate act of the seven devils the road to the distant heavens was barred against them, and can now only be travelled by the Gods with such pain and suffering that they rarely, if ever, reach to touch the world.

"The Storyteller"

But in time, the devil Heuslar Ogada escapes, and frees Ulfhild Vartu, killing the bear-demon who guards her grave. Ulfhild allies with Mikki, the son of Moraig the bear-demon and a human man, and makes a bargain with the Old Great Gods to hunt down her escaped fellows. To this end she is given the sword Lakkariss, forged by the Old Great Gods from a shard of the cold hells. Moth and Mikki track Heuslar to a Northron queen's hall and kill him there. Things burn down.

Blackdog

During the warlord Tamghat's conquest of Lissavakail, the caravan-guard Holla-Sayan is possessed by the Blackdog, the enslaved guardian spirit of the lake-goddess Attalissa. Incarnate as a human child, Attalissa is help-less until she comes into her powers with maturity. Although the gods and goddesses of the earth are bound to their own hills and waters, Holla-Sayan takes the girl, whom he names Pakdhala, back to his caravan and passes her off as his own daughter. He manages to find a way to keep the goddess alive even far from her own land. Tamghat is actually the devil Tamghiz Ghatai, Ulfhild's former husband. Moth and Mikki are roused from their quiet homesteading life in the northern forest by the summons of the Old Great Gods.

When Pakdhala reaches her teen years, Tamghat sends his daughter Ivah in search of her. Captured and taken to Lissavakail for a ritual which Tamghat presents as a marriage, Pakdhala/Attalissa escapes and joins a rebellion of her priestesses. She has always insisted that Tamghat means to devour her. The Blackdog, in a mindless fury, goes to try to save the goddess. Moth and Mikki, and Holla-Sayan's caravan gang, also set out in pursuit.

Tamghiz Ghatai is slain by Moth, but not before Holla-Sayan, facing death and with the Blackdog having turned on him, realizes how the spirit has been bound and releases it at the cost of his human life, then entering into a willing bond with it akin to that between the devil and wizard souls of the seven devils.

Moth reveals to Holla-Sayan that she believes the Blackdog to be the damaged remnant of a devil's soul, survivor of a much more ancient war of devils than her own. She also gives Ivah, betrayed by her father, a focus for finding her own life beyond his shadow.

The traitor chief priestess of Attalissa's temple, long ago seduced by Tamghat, had been drawn to the secret worship of a landless, bodiless god, a faith centred somewhere in the west, of which only the faintest rumours are reaching the lands of the caravan road . . .

The Leopard: Marakand Volume One, and
The Lady: Marakand Volume Two

A year after Attalissa's restoration in Lissavakail, Ivah is working as a scribe in Marakand. Gaguush's caravan has come again to the Suburb of the caravanserais beyond the city walls. The assassin Ahjvar, cursed by his goddess Catairanach to remain undying in the world to harbour the parasite soul of her daughter Hyllau, is sent to Marakand to kill the Voice of the Lady of Marakand. Ahjvar kills the Voice but is captured by the Lady's Red Masks, thought to be a militant order of priests but in truth the product of necromancy, wizards she has executed and stripped of memory to control as semi-autonomous puppets. She kills Ahjvar and makes him captain of her Red Masks for the conquest of the rest of the lands Over-Malagru—but Ahjvar has always claimed to his companion Ghu that he burned to death ninety years before, murdered by Hyllau.

The Lady chooses a new Voice but wants more than a prophet; the acolyte Zora is given a choice, to accept a bond with the Lady willingly, or to become her puppet. Zora chooses to bond with the supposed goddess, who is in fact the devil Tu'usha. Tu'usha's former human host/partner, the wizard Sien-Mor, was murdered in her prison-grave by the devil Sien-Shava Jochiz, Sien-Mor's brother, and her body utterly destroyed. Tu'usha's soul fled and found shelter with the unwitting goddess in Marakand, whom she then possessed and devoured, sealing the other two deities of the city in tombs. Zora's mind fractures under the burden of Tu'usha's soul; the devil herself suffers from Sien-Mor's mental instability, obsessed with the need to make the city a fortress and an empire to stand against a great danger she foresees coming from the west.

A revolution of the secret loyalists of the old gods is unleashed, in which Ivah plays a major role as wizard, warrior, and scholar. Moth and Mikki have come to Marakand, hunting the devil there. Moth is reluctant to kill Tu'usha; Sien-Mor was once a friend. Her depressed passivity leaves her vulnerable and she is trapped by the Lady in both the past and an underground cavern that is the source of the deep well. Ahjvar, dead and bound by necromancy, stripped of memory and will, is sent east into the Praitannec kingdoms to lead the forces of Marakand against a coalition of the Praitannec tribes. Ghu sets out east as well, to either free Ahjvar from the Lady's enslavement, or release his captive soul into death. The devil Yeh-Lin Dotemon, currently tutor to the young bard Deyandara, a descendent of Ahjvar's who is deeply enmeshed in the politics of the Praitannec tribes and the struggle of the Duina Catairna against Marakand, intends to sever Tu'usha's link with her Red Masks, destroying them to free their souls and aid the Praitannec kings and queens in their war. To prevent this and save Ahjvar, Ghu reveals himself as something other than mortal human in order to temporarily bind Yeh-Lin and save Ahjvar.

Ghu seizes Ahjvar from the midst of battle and tears him from Tu'usha's control. He and Ahjvar destroy the spell binding the Red Masks and the Lady thus loses her most fearsome weapon. Yeh-Lin Dotemon, despite viewing Ahjvar's undying state as an abomination, does not kill him, but overcoming the goddess Catairanach, buries her in a deep and undreaming sleep, leaving the mercy of Ahjvar's final death for Ghu to offer.

In Marakand, the Lady's devastating attacks on her own city destroy the goddess Ilbialla. While Holla-Sayan fights the Lady, Mikki descends to the place of Moth's captivity with Lakkariss and wakes her out of her dreaming. She ascends and fights Zora Tu'usha, who is killed amid the ruins of her temple, leaving the newly re-awakened hill-god Gurhan as the only surviving god of the near-ruined city.

Moth believes Mikki is a hostage to the Old Great Gods for her service as their executioner. To deny the Gods that hold over her, she leaves him, flying away as a falcon. Mikki is furious, devastated, and determined to search for her, however long it might take.

Holla-Sayan and Gaguush are expecting a child, and Gaguush, before the civil war erupted, had bought a share in a caravanserai in the Suburb. Holla is resolved to settle into the quiet life of a family man and caravan-master. Ivah joins a caravan to travel to Nabban.

Ghu, having revealed himself as a being growing into strange powers, tells Ahjvar that he is not yet a god, but is becoming one, and having acted to save Ahjvar from the Lady, he can no longer run from this doom, but must return to Nabban. Ghu promises Ahjvar that he won't let him be possessed to kill for Hyllau again; rather than ending Ahj's unnatural life he unravels Hyllau's soul from his and when she tries again to batten on Ahjvar rather than seeking her own road to the Gods, he destroys her. He also takes over the curse worked by Catairanach that holds Ahjvar undying in the world, making himself the power keeping Ahjvar alive. Ghu promises Ahjvar he will release him into death whenever he asks it, but asks, himself, if Ahj will try to live a little longer, to keep him company on the road he must now follow. To this Ahjvar, who yearns not for death and the road to the Old Great Gods but oblivion, agrees.

Gods of Nabban

Ahjvar suffers greatly from nightmares, a torment he cannot escape waking or sleeping. Ghu nurses him devotedly but fears he will never be whole and well again. They are joined by Yeh-Lin Dotemon, who, before crossing the Nabbani border, swears an oath binding herself to Ghu as her god.

Nabban is torn by civil war. The emperor's younger brother Prince Dan has raised his banner in rebellion. When the emperor is struck by lightning from a clear sky, Princess Buri-Nai seizes the throne and declares herself the chosen daughter of the Old Great Gods. Buri-Nai's followers begin executing priests of Mother and Father Nabban; slaves and peasants rise in revolt, promised reform and freedom by Prince Dan. The folk of the southern province of Dar-Lathi, only a generation before the free lands of Darro and Lathi, rise up against their conquerors. Ghu has no intention of accepting the Nabban in which he grew up a slave; he uses the civil war as means to seize political power for those who share his desire for reform. Many in the land, including his former master, the high lord of Choa, recognize him as something holy; others want to believe in any symbol of hope and change; still others see the proclamation of a "holy one" as a ruse of the rebels. Mother Nabban dies and Ghu takes on her role as deity of the waters. The rebellions become a revolution. Ivah recognizes in Ghu the god she has been seeking all her life and becomes his captain of archers.

Ghu and Ahjvar recognize that Buri-Nai is not acting on her own in her establishment of a new religion and suspect a devil hides behind her. During the battle in which imperial forces try to prevent Ghu's army crossing the Wild Sister River, Ivah identifies the devil as Sien-Shava Jochiz and rejects his attempt to seduce her to his service as Buri-Nai's replacement, freeing herself from the spells he has been slowly weaving into her. Ghu and his forces fight and win a great battle, but Buri-Nai, hidden by the power of Sien-Shava Jochiz, has marched near with a far larger army. Many of her followers are tattooed with a symbol that binds the person's soul, which, on their death, does not seek the road to the Old Great Gods but is drawn away somewhere else. What use Jochiz has for these souls even Yeh-Lin cannot determine. Ghu leaves Yeh-Lin in charge, entrusting her with, he says, Nabban, and goes alone with Ahjvar to confront Buri-Nai. Perhaps he hopes to convince her commanders that she is controlled by a devil; perhaps he plans to assassinate her—Yeh-Lin decides that his true intent is likely to draw the devil out into the open and that he didn't mean for her to lead a retreat back over the river after all. She and Ivah plan an assault on the empress's camp, hoping that surprise and fire will give them an advantage to withstand the imperial numbers. Brought before the empress, Ghu is unable to turn Buri-Nai from her obsessed devotion to what she believes is a messenger of the Old Great Gods; Ahjvar tells her court that the devil she worships feeds on the souls of those who are tattooed for her new faith. Buri-Nai orders her giants to kill them; they are struck down by the giants' spears, but Ahjvar's thrown knife kills the empress.

In the battle that follows between Ghu's army and that of the empress, who though obviously suffering a mortal wound continues to command like a living woman, her body a puppet to Jochiz, Ivah steals the wagon containing the apparent corpse of Ghu and the dying Ahjvar, who insists that Ghu is not dead and that he himself is not dying. Ghu's body is ice-cold, which is not natural, even for a corpse, and Ahjvar finds a sliver of crystal lodged under his tongue, the focus of a web of foul wizardry or devilry that appears intended to bind and devour his soul. He gives the splinter to Ivah before falling into a dreaming trance in which he finds Ghu at the ruined broch in which they lived before they set out for Marakand; he is able to call Ghu back to himself. Father Nabban has died defending Ghu long enough for Ahjvar to find him; this, Ghu says, was his third death, and the worst. When he wakes it is as the god of Nabban. He and Ahjvar rally their army, which had attacked under the leadership of Yeh-Lin but is being cut to pieces by the imperial forces. Many, though, of the empress's soldiers, seeing Ghu riding against them, recognize him as their true god. He calls his dogs Jui and Jiot to him, and they come as river-dragons running in the clouds, terrifying the enemy.

Jochiz in the body of the empress fights Ahjvar, but Ghu is holding Ahjvar closely, soul within soul, through their bond and Ahjvar recognizes the means by which Jochiz is putting himself into Buri-Nai and into the land of Nabban. He seizes the shard of rose-quartz crystal she wears—a piece of Jochiz's soul, perhaps, and certainly the repository of the souls the devil has stolen. Ahjvar finds the fire within him, in which he died, and the fire of light and warmth that is how Ghu sees him, and with it destroys the stone, severing the devil's path into Nabban, but he cannot contain the fire which has always waited to consume him again. Ghu leaps into the fire to seize him and they vanish from the battlefield. Yeh-Lin tells the surviving enemy commanders that Ivah, the god's captain of archers, a princess of the Great Grass and daughter of the Nabbani princess An-Chaq, will take their surrender on the god's behalf.

Later, Ahjvar wakes in the river, with Ghu, and experiences a dark, lost time, but again begins to find his way back, assured that Ghu will always hold him safe. Ghu again promises to release him whenever he asks; he again says he will try to stay longer with Ghu on his road. Yeh-Lin speculates that Ahjvar may be becoming an avatar of Nabban (the god).

Ghu wants to reform many Nabbani institutions from its government to land-holding, but Ahjvar tells him he can do no more than point the folk in the direction he would like them to go, unless he means to be emperor as well as god. Ivah becomes empress, founding the new house of Suliasra, and returning the role to its earlier sacerdotal function, instituting a senate and Ghu's plans for land reform under the temples and shrines, rather than ruling as an absolute monarch. Many other reforms come to pass, as well as unsuccessful rebellions and uprisings of various factions. Dar-Lathi is given its independence; the Little Sister River has also been waking into life in a new goddess in the Dar-Lathan queen and spy who calls herself Rat, who fought at Ghu's side in the final battle and whose lover Kaeo, who had been Prince Dan's agent and a prophet of the heir of the gods, lost his life defending Ghu.

Many years later, Moth arrives at the tomb of the Empress Suliasra Ivah. Ghu and Ahjvar meet her. She has been wandering in far lands. Ghu advises her to seek the one who helps her remember who she is, and Ahjvar gives her the clay disc in which the splinter of the soul of Sien-Shava Jochiz is sealed.

The whereabouts of two devils, Sien-Shava Jochiz, the much-feared brother of Sien-Mor Tu'usha, and Anganurth Jasberek, formerly an ally of Ulfhild Vartu, are thus far unknown . . .

DRAMATIS PERSONAE

Ahjvar—Consort and *Rihswera* or champion of the god of Nabban. Long ago and very briefly, a king of the Duina Catairna, a Praittanec tribe now forgotten and absorbed into the Taren Confederacy. Technically dead, by some lights; held undying in the world by his lover Ghu.

Ailan—Young man of the Taren city of Star River Crossing; viewed by Yeh-Lin as Ahjvar's acolyte; viewed by Ahjvar as yet another stray who has bafflingly latched onto him.

The All-Holy—A supposed holy man, a hermit who became the embodiment of the Nameless God of the west, a supposed emissary sent from the Old Great Gods. Actually the devil Sien-Shava Jochiz. See also the nameless god.

Ambert, Primate—Priest of the seventh circle, spiritual leader and one of the All-Holy's most valued lieutenants.

Anganurth Wanderer—A wizard from an unknown land, who bonded with the devil Jasberek.

Arpath—Teenage Westgrasslander wizard of the Sayanbarkash.

Attalissa—Goddess of the Lissavakail, a lake and town high in the Pillars of the Sky; once, incarnate as a human child, she was raised by Holla-Sayan as his daughter.

Aunty—Elderly relative of Nikeh gen'Emras.

Balba—A Knight-Commander of the Army of the South.

The Baobab goddess—The nameless goddess of an underground river or lake whose main physical presence in the world is an ancient baobab tree.

Besni—A child adopted into the clan of Kinsai's folk; young brother of Rifat.

Birdy—Younger brother of Nikeh gen'Emras.

The Blackdog—See Holla-Sayan.

Caro—A Marakander caravaneer captaining the lancers in Reyka's warband.

Clio, Primate—Commander of the All-Holy's sacred guard, initiate of the seventh circle, lover of Sien-Shava Jochiz.

Danil—A Marakander street-guard, serving as a soldier on the Western Wall.

Deysanal—A wizard of Kinsai's folk; daughter of Trout, mother of Iarka.

Dimas—Prince of Emrastepse; commander of the Army of the South.

Dorji, Sister—A warrior-priestess of Attalissa.

Dotemon Dreamshaper—One of the seven devils; bonded with the wizard Yeh-Lin, former empress and tyrant of Nabban.

Emras—A dead spring-goddess of Tiypur.

Enyal, Sister—A priestess and pilgrimmage-guide from the Temple of All Gods in Barrahe in the Nalzawan Commonwealth.

Floran, Sister—A Tiypurian physician of the Army of the South.

Forzra—A hill-god of the Nalzawan Commonwealth, who finds Ahjvar rather worrying.

Fury—Black Westgrasslander warhorse.

Gaguush—A Black Desert caravan-mistress and owner of a caravanserai in Marakand; late wife of Holla-Sayan, mother of Gultage.

Ghatai (Twice-betrayed Ghatai)—A devil, bonded with the wizard and Grasslander warlord Tamghiz; slain by Moth in Lissavakail.

Ghu—Personal name of the god of Nabban, who was once a human man. Lover of Ahjvar.

Gorthuerniaul—A Denanbaki horse belonging to Ahjvar, touched by Nabban's holiness, an immortal servant of the god within Nabban.

Gultage—Marakander-born son of Gaguush and Holla-Sayan; a caravan-serai master.

Gurhan—Hill-god of the city of Marakand.

Hani Jin—Lost cousin of Hani Kahren.

Hani Kahren—A caravaneer and former cavalry-trooper from Imperial Nabban riding with Reyka's warband.

Hecta—Philon's late wife.

Hezing—A prince of Nabban who stirred up trouble and was exiled to Pirakul, where he became a mercenary.

Hravnmod the Wise—One of the first three kings in the north. Elder brother of Ulfhild. Falsely said to have been slain by her; murdered by Heuslar Ogada.

Holla-Sayan—Westgrasslander caravaneer; foster-father of the incarnation of the goddess Attalissa; host of the Blackdog; now bonded with it as a devil.

Hyllanim—Ahjvar's supposed half-brother and probable son, born of his adultery with his step-mother. A king of the Duina Catairna, whose misfortune-plagued reign was the subject of many songs.

Iarka—A wizard of the folk of the goddess Kinsai, daughter of Deysanal, daughter of Trout, son of Holla-Sayan and Kinsai.

Ilyan Dan—Ambassador of Nabban to Marakand.

Iri—Suliasra Iri, empress and high priestess of Nabban.

Istva—A Westgrasslander conscript camel-driver in the Army of the South; a spy for Yeh-Lin.

Ivah—Wizard, warrior, scholar, and late empress of Nabban, nearly two hundred years previously, in the days of Ghu's advent.

Jang (Scholar Daro Jang)—Alias assumed by Yeh-Lin. (The name is taken from a former page of hers.)

Jasberek Fireborn—One of the seven devils, bonded with the wizard Anganurth.

Jayala—A river-goddess of the Western Grass.

Jiot—A shapeshifting dog/dragon, a servant of the god of Nabban.

Jochiz Stonebreaker—One of the seven devils; bonded with the wizard Sien-Shava.

Jolanan—A Westgrasslander warrior from the Jayala'arad, formerly a cowherd.

Jui—Another shapeshifting dog/dragon, a servant of the god of Nabban.

Kinsai—The goddess of the river Kinsai; patron of the ferry-folk of the Upper and Lower Castles and ancestress of many of them. Occasional lover of Holla-Sayan. (And not a few others over the years . . .)

The Lady of Marakand—A dead goddess of Marakand; an impersonation/possession of the goddess by Tu'usha.

Lark—Skewbald Westgrasslander warhorse.

Lazlan—A Westgrasslander man of the Sayanbarkash, brother of Reyka; second in command of the warband fighting the Army of the North.

The Leopard—An alias used by Ahjvar in the Five Cities in his former life as an assassin.

Lia Dur—A Marakander street-guard turned soldier, friend of Nikeh, lieutenant of the south-end tower of the Western Wall.

Little Squirrel—Nikeh's baby-name.

Melnarka—A Tiypurian demon, lover of the goddess Emras, who was said to have appeared in the forms of eagle, man, and woman.

Mikki—A demon, bear by day and man by night. His mother was a bear-demon of the Hardenwald, his father a Northron sea-rover turned farmer originally from Selarskerrig. Partner of Moth.

Moraig—Bear-demon of the Hardenwald, mother of Mikki, slain by Heuslar Ogada in the beginning of it all.

Moth—Name adopted by Ulfhild Vartu, given to her by Mikki.

The nameless god—A god long worshipped in the lands of the former empire of Tiypur; possibly a cult that arose organically out of human need in those godless lands and was taken over by Jochiz, but more likely a creation of his from the start. See also the All-Holy.

Nang Lin—Yeh-Lin's original name.

Narva—A mountain god of the Pillars of the Sky south of Lissavakail.

Nessa—A Westgrasslander of Reyka's warband, friend of Jolanan.

Nikeh gen'Emras—A child from Emrastepse in Tiypur, adopted and raised by Yeh-Lin.

Nori—Goddess of the river that flows through Star River Crossing, invoked by Ailan; probably a corruption of her older name, Noreia.

Orhan—A Malagru hillman in the army defending Marakand.

Pakdhala—Name used by Attalissa incarnate as Holla-Sayan's supposed daughter.

Pehma, Sister—Priestess of Attalissa; a wizard.

Philon—A man of Emrastepse in the former Tiypurian lands, counsellor to Prince Dimas, an initiate of the seventh circle and a devout believer in the All-Holy.

Rada—A murdered young woman of Star River Crossing in the Taren Confederacy.

Rat—The goddess of the Little Sister river, on the border between Nabban and Lathi, also called the Tigress.

Red Geir—One of the first three kings in the north.

Reyka—A woman of the Sayanbarkash in the Western Grass; warlord of the Westgrasslander band fighting the All-Holy's Army of the North.

Rifat—Teenage wizard of Kinsai's folk, originally from one of the Black Desert tribes.

Rigo, the prince of—The All-Holy's governor of the Western Grass. His proper name is not recorded.

Rose—Wizard-surgeon of the folk of Kinsai, lover of Iarka and father of her unborn child.

Rose—Name given by Iarka to her unborn daughter, in honour of the child's father.

Ruyi—Suliasra Ruyi, late empress and high priestess of Nabban, mother of Yuan, grandmother of Iri; great-granddaughter of Ivah.

Sammur—Mikki's father, a Northron human originally from Selarskerrig.

Sarzahn—An ancient being bound in service to Jochiz, who looks on him as a brother.

Sato—A river-goddess of the Nalzawan Commonwealth.

Sayid Sevanim—A young man of Serakallash.

Scorpion—A camel of uncertain moods.

Sera—Goddess of the Red Desert town of Serakallash; sometimes appears in the form of a woman, sometimes a mare.

Sien-Shava the Outcast—A wizard of the Southern Isles, bonded with the devil Jochiz. Brother of Sien-Mor.

Sien-Mor the Outcast—A wizard of the Southern Isles, bonded with the devil Tu'usha. Sister of Sien-Mor. Murdered by her brother while imprisoned after the defeat of the seven devils.

Snow—A Denanbaki horse belonging to Ghu; like Gothuerniaul, became immortal as a servant of the god within Nabban.

Spider—Another camel of rather more benign disposition than Scorpion.

Storm—Bone-horse belonging to Moth. Translation of Styrma, his Northron name.

Styrma—See Storm.

Sulloso Dur—Marakander captain of the south-end tower of the Western Wall of the Pass of Marakand.

Swift—A small sprit-rigged ship.

Tamghiz—A chieftain and warlord of the Great Grass, bonded with the devil Ghatai. Divorced husband of Ulfhild. Slain by Moth.

Tashi—A miner of the Narvabarkash in the Pillars of the Sky.

Teacher—Nikeh's term of address for her foster-mother and mistress in the scholar's and warrior's arts.

Tibor—A Westgrasslander caravaneer of the Jayala'arad; kinsman of Jolanan.

Timon—A Westron red priest and missionary of the All-Holy in Star River Crossing.

Tiy, Grandmother Tiy—Nearly forgotten dead goddess of the great river of Tiypur, once worshipped as a conductress of the dead to the Old Great Gods.

Trout—An exceptionally long-lived wizard, scholar, and ichthyologist of Kinsai's folk, Warden of the Upper Castle, son of Holla-Sayan and Kinsai, father of Deysanal.

Tu'usha the Restless—One of the seven devils, bonded with Sien-Mor. Slain by Moth.

Ulfhild the King's Sword—A wizard, sister and king's sword of Hravnmod the Wise, bonded with the devil Vartu. Partner of Mikki. Also known as Moth.

Varro—A friend of Holla-Sayan's long ago, a Northron caravaneer of Gaguush's gang.

Vartu Kingsbane—One of the seven devils, bonded with Ulfhild; bearer of the sword Lakkariss. Moth.

Viga Forkbeard—One of the first three kings in the north.

The Wolf-Smith—A demon smith who came with the ancestors of the Northrons out of the west to the lands that became known after their destruction as the Drowned Isles. The demon who forged Moth's sword Kepra (Keeper).

Yeh-Lin the Beautiful—Nang Yeh-Lin, wizard, scholar, general, empress, bonded with the devil Dotemon.

Yuan—Suliasra Yuan, late emperor and high priest of Nabban, father of the current empress, Iri.

PART ONE

PROLOGUE

. . . the early days of winter in the year in which the All-Holy came into the
lands of the caravan road, east of the Kara Mountains

There was light through his eyelids, red and warm, though he was shivering. It was that had woken him. Sarzahn blinked, found his eyes to be sticky, gritty with sleep and fever-sweat. Sunlight angling through the door of the tent, tied back for light and air. Evening, and the scent of winter, of white cold, of the wind off the grass. He lay in the antechamber of his brother's great tent, his right place, dog to sleep before his door. All as it should be. He felt very slow and tired, and, as he pushed himself to sit up, shoving the blanket aside, alarmingly weak. Every limb a log that needed dragging. He was stark naked.

Too naked. There, dropped on the carpet by the thin mattress on which he'd been laid, his amulet pouch. Soft leather on a leather thong, long carried and periodically renewed. Nothing in it but a white pebble. Meaningless. A human superstition. Token of a dead god.

But it mattered and he dropped it over his head, felt something eased at the familiar touch and rub of it against his chest. Pulled his hair through the cord, frowning. Long mane of it, curling wild, braids all undone, washed and combed loose.

What did it matter? He was no caravaneer, to bind it tight against

25

sand in dozens of braids that never knew comb nor touch of water the road's length.

No clothes. No boots. No weapon.

Had he been wounded? Ill?

Both, he thought. He remembered searing pain, something that entered him like a streak of lightning. A fire burning through him, eyes, mouth, marrow, that made his heart stutter and his eyes grow dark. Remembered a voice, calling his name. His brother drawing him into his arms, into this place of safety, of belonging.

Remembered . . .

Burning. Great swathes of green hills, burning, and words sung there by the flames, and birds made of fire painting images, painting . . . something he could not quite see . . . against the darkening sky.

A fever-dream.

There had been voices, in the darkness. In the fire.

His own voice, shouting at him. Voices.

He sat cross-legged amid the bedding a long, still time, trying to hear what they, what he, might be saying.

Long ago, in the days of the first kings in the north, who were Viga Forkbeard, and Red Geir, and Hravnmod the Wise, there were seven devils, and their names were Honeytongued Ogada, Vartu Kingsbane, Jasberek Fireborn, Twice-Betrayed Ghatai, Dotemon the Dreamshaper, Tu'usha the Restless, and Jochiz Stonebreaker.

As all should know, the gods and the goddesses of the world live in their own places, the high places and the waters, and aid those who worship them, and protect their own. And though the demons may wander all the secret places of the world, their hearts are bound each to their own place, and though they are no friends to human-folk, they are no enemies either, and want only to be left in peace. But the devils have no place, and they came from the cold hells and walked up and down over the earth to trouble the lives of the folk. And the devils did not desire loving worship, nor the friendship of men and women. They did not have a parent's love for the folk. The devils craved dominion as the desert craves water, and they knew neither love nor justice nor mercy. And the devils razed the earth and made war against the heavens of the Old Great Gods themselves, and were cast out, and sealed in the cold hells once more.

In the days of the first kings in the north, there were seven wizards. And two were of the people of the kings in the north, who came from over the western sea, and one was of a people unknown; one was of the Great Grass and one of Imperial Nabban, and two were from beyond far Nabban, but the seven were of one fellowship. Their names were Heuslar the Deep-Minded, who was uncle to Red Geir, Ulfhild the King's Sword, who was sister to Hravnmod the Wise, Anganurth Wanderer, Tamghiz, Chief of the Bear-Mask Fellowship, Yeh-Lin the Beautiful, and Sien-Mor and Sien-Shava, the Outcasts, who were sister and brother.

The devils took the souls of the wizards into their own, and became one with them. They walked as wizards among the wizards, and destroyed those who would not obey, or who counselled against their counsel. They desired the worship of kings and the enslavement of the folk, and they were never sated, as the desert is never sated with rain.

So the kings of the north and the tribes of the grass and those wizards whom the devils had not yet slain pretended submission, and plotted in secret, and they rose up against the tyranny of the devils and overthrew them. But the devils were devils, even in human bodies, and not easily slain. And there are many tales of the wars against the devils, and of the kings and the heroes and the wizards, and the terrible deeds done. And these can all be told, if there be golden rings, or silver cups, or wine and flesh and bread by the fire.

Only with the help of the Old Great Gods were they bound, one by one, and imprisoned—Honeytongued Ogada in stone, Vartu Kingsbane in earth, Jasberek Fireborn in water, Twice-Betrayed Ghatai in the breath of a burning mountain, Dotemon Dreamshaper in the oldest of trees, Tu'usha the Restless in the heart of a flame, Jochiz Stonebreaker in the youngest of rivers. And they were guarded by demons, and goddesses, and gods. And the Old Great Gods withdrew from the world, and await the souls of human-folk in the heavens beyond the stars, which we call the Land of the Old Great Gods.

CHAPTER I

. . . earlier, on the threshold of winter, following the All-Holy's crossing into the lands east of the Karas

Jolanan jolted awake at the hand squeezing hers. Silent. Straining to hear, even before her eye blinked open, what the alarm might be this time. They were behind Dimas's Army of the South on the desert road. Just another handful of refugees, creeping towards what safety was left in the world, if such a thing existed at all. There were others, caravaneers, mostly, making for Marakand. That made no more sense than running into a burning house because at least it was a roof over your head. But where else could they go, a caravan-mistress had asked bitterly the evening before. At least maybe if they fell in with the straggling tail of the Army of the South they might earn their keep carrying baggage, and so find a way home to Marakand, even if their goods would be forfeit to the plundering of the priests.

"They'll make you deny your gods and tattoo you for the All-Holy," Rifat had warned them.

The caravan-mistress had shrugged. "Small price, if it gets us home. Gurhan will forgive us words spoken to save our lives, and what's a bit of ink?"

"Time to go." Holla's whisper, close above her. "All right?" Hand brushing her face, a caress. Jolanan crawled from her blankets, rolled them, found her sabre. Hadn't even taken off her boots, that was how lightly they slept. Holla left her to wake young Rifat, and Iarka last. The four of them had lain a little apart from the caravaneers, chance-met strangers, and had set their own watch. There should be one or two from the caravan wakeful, questioning their rising.

There was not.

Their camels were already harnessed and the one they led loaded. Holla had done that before waking them, when he should have been keeping watch. Only the rolled bedding was left to strap on.

The sky told it was near the end of the third quarter of the night. The waning moon would have risen near midnight.

They managed all in silence. Even the camels were quiet, no grumbles at the early start. Unnatural. The caravan was left sleeping behind them. Not a wizard, but maybe when Holla wanted someone to sleep, they slept. Jolanan didn't know. She wasn't, she found, comfortable with asking.

Five camels, even unexpectedly agreeable ones, were not exactly tiptoeing in silence, though they wore no bells. Creak of harness, crunch of sand and stone. No one stirred behind them. "Why?" she asked softly, when they were a little distance from the camp. She wouldn't have risked that, except that she was certain no one would wake till they were well and truly gone.

"We don't want to travel with them," Iarka said. "Traitors to their gods already, in their hearts."

"You can't blame them for wanting to save their lives," Rifat said.

"I can," said Iarka.

"We don't want to travel with them," Holla said, "because we don't want them talking of us, when they do run into some Westron priest or knight. You two make sure they forget us."

As if that were an easy and ordinary thing. Jolanan did not think it was, even for a wizard of Kinsai's folk.

The two wizards put their heads together, riding side by side, voices low. Holla rode ahead, until the paleness of his camel and the baggage-carrier faded into the desert night. Iarka and Rifat followed without seeming to pay much heed to their route. Passengers. It was the camels who followed. Jolanan hung back as rearguard, for what use she could be there. Moonlight was enough to tell ground from sky, not much more. The sun would be rising in a few hours. In the meantime—Holla's nose and ears were a better watch for danger than any she could keep.

Jolanan swayed with the camel's pacing, felt it, the difference underfoot as they crossed yet another thread of the braid that was the hardpacked road, deep rutted by the passage of centuries of soft-padded feet, a flowing river of lives and hopes and goods, a pulse pumping along it, east and south to west, to north and back again . . . she could feel it like a heartbeat, but she was groggy with sleep still, dreaming. She was no wizard, no poet, no bard to think such things. But if the road held memories, its own dreams . . . maybe they drifted into hers.

Silver light on the barren slopes found a cluster of hairy saxaul marking some hidden dampness. She could see they were riding south, not south-easterly. Dry hills before them and the mountains beyond, mountains that dwarfed the western Karas, the skyline of her childhood. No one crossed the Pillars of the Sky. The lands beyond, to the south, were a silence even to the bards. One might climb into them, but only by a few tracks. There were folk lived there, folk of the gods of the mountains and goddesses of the mountain waters. But to find the road to the high lake and valley town of Lissavakail, and the folk of the goddess Attalissa, whom the Blackdog had once served, they must come first to Serakallash though the desert-edge town of the goddess Sera.

"There are ways," Holla said, looking back, as if he'd heard her thoughts. "We'll travel the tracks through the mountains' feet. No caravans, no Westron strays or outposts left to watch their supply lines, we can hope. Water, if you know where to seek it."

The murmuring of the wizards had gone silent some time before. Their magic-making done, whatever they had been doing.

"Yes," Iarka said. "Fine. Whatever. Will we come to the lake sooner, this way?"

"No."

She muttered something under her breath.

"What?"

"This camel is making me sick."

"It isn't the camel," Rifat said.

"Fine, this baby is making me sick and the camel isn't helping."

"Aren't there, I don't know, herbs . . . ?" Jolanan regretted the words as soon as they were out of her mouth. Silly to feel that as the only other woman, she ought to be the one offering advice. Two wizards—and even if one was only a boy of fifteen, he knew things, far more than she about almost everything. Except killing, maybe, and cattle. Two wizards, and a man who'd been around a very long time, with women in his life, and babies, whole lives lived of which she knew nothing, because he didn't speak of them. But her mouth persisted. "Ginger? I think I heard that somewhere. Or—some wizard thing?"

"We have no ginger left and some wizard thing is the only reason I'm not losing my breakfast all down this beast's shoulder, not that we've had any breakfast."

"Sorry," Jolanan said. "I should just shut up, right?"

"Yes. Thank you."

"Maybe we should stop, make some tea?" Rifat suggested.

"Not yet," said Holla.

"Soon," said Iarka. "Or else, old man."

"Yes, dear."

That didn't sound like Holla at all, and won a snort of laughter from Iarka.

Dawn followed as the moon sank from its height, colour seeping into the land. Red sand, red stone, frost in the hollows melting dark as the day's breath warmed it. They were climbing, and the hills, sand and red grit and flakes of stone, were held together with yellowed grass and low-growing plants long gone to seed, pods empty. She didn't recognize the shrubs, except the saxaul trees Holla had named, more of them here, growing along what she guessed must be some slough where water would gather in the spring. The Red Desert bloomed then, he had said, when the snows melted and for a brief space it turned green and scarlet, white and gold. The white-cloaked mountains seemed closer now. The Pillars of the Sky, holding up the great high blue.

They made a halt low on the southern side of a long ridge, where their little smoke might spread itself very thin before it rose against the sky. Not that anyone from the caravan was likely to come after them, if Iarka and Rifat had managed to make them forget the encounter, turn the four travellers into some boring dream no one thought worth speaking of, or whatever wizardry might do. Even if the caravaneers did remember, once they'd checked and found their own camels all accounted for and their goods unplundered they'd likely not be bothered. But enemies were ahead of them. Westron scouts might roam far from their march.

Jolanan's left eye, or the scarred socket that was all she had remaining of it, was aching again. Or her head was, around there. Hard to tell the difference. Windblown sand found its way into the seams of the scarring despite the leather patch that protected the scars.

Hideous. She still tried not to touch it, washing her face with a dampened rag, while Rifat made the smallest of fires that would boil a kettle with a few lumps of dry camel-dung and some dead twigs. Still couldn't stand the feel of it to her fingertips. A hollow, filled with scar, crossed with ridges. Being scarred across the face, as if someone had tried to take off the top of her head with an axe, which they had . . . being blind in one eye—neither of those would have given her this twist in the gut, this flinching from herself. But her eye was gone, and whatever the wizard-surgeon Rose had done, it had left no socket for a crystal eye like in the *Lay of Brued One-Eye* that the bards sang; she had no eyelid, no lashes. Just—ugliness. All that he could save.

Not dead of a cracked skull. Not dead of a festering lump of rot sunk in her face. Not dead.

"Here, let me."

"I can look after myself."

"I know. Let me?"

She let Holla-Sayan take the cloth from her hand. Childish and cranky to deny him. He meant only kindness. When he was finished, he waited for her to tie the patch in place again, but wrapped her headscarf for her. A lover's intimacy, or a sick-nurse's condescension? She leaned her face into his chest.

"I'm sorry," she said. For being cranky. For feeling as she did, still—angry, and ugly, and lost. Let the feel of him holding her deny all that. Warm, solid. Arms around her. Unwashed sweat and smoke and camels and the oiled leather of his brigandine. The man she had left her friends, left her duty to the memory of her goddess Jayala to follow.

She felt too young.

She let him go on holding her, standing there, the two of them leaning together.

"Tea?"

Jolanan twisted in Holla's arms to take the cup Iarka offered. It was black, smoky, almost syrupy. One thought of the ferry-folk of Kinsai as practically beggars, with their ragged, piecemeal looks, their collecting of the odds and ends others threw away, including children like Rifat, who had run from his Black Desert tribe with his small brother for reasons he didn't go into, but there was always sugar in the tea, and the jewel Iarka wore in the side of her nose was surely a ruby.

Holla didn't let Jolanan go, accepted a cup over her shoulder, one arm comfortably about her waist as if she belonged there, tucked against him. The fire was out again already, the remnants of the fuel to be carefully packed away once they cooled. Rifat shared out cold, oily campbread from the previous night while the camels ate a little. Jolanan leaned back against Holla-Sayan again, shut her eye. Wished this feeling of misery would stop creeping up and hitting her, this childish despair that she was—somehow no longer herself. Iarka, Rifat—they had lost family, friends—they had ridden away knowing death was going to follow for those they left behind. They didn't wallow. They rode *to* something, in anger, in love, in hate, to save something . . . all of that at once. Holla—Holla-Sayan, she had to make an effort to think of him by his true name—him, too. And Iarka made jokes about her morning sickness, and Rifat was earnest and tender with Iarka as if she were his own sister, and brotherly to Jolanan too, the stranger who'd come among them, despite all they had lost. And she couldn't shake this petty loathing of her own face.

Holla—Holla-Sayan—tipped her head back, kissed her forehead, turned her and kissed her nose and then her mouth. Not playful. Serious. Testing. She knew it. And she felt . . . nothing. Exhaustion that had nothing to do with long days and lack of sleep, which she should be well used to by now. Anything else was a distant dream, a life half forgotten.

"Into the mountain paths by nightfall, if we push it," he said, letting her go. "Ready to ride?"

They hadn't lain together to make love since the evening—the night she had been wounded. Too ill, too tired, not enough privacy, too much grief—there were many reasons and all of them good. She thought Iarka and Rifat would not have minded what she and Holla-Sayan might have done under cover of the night, but someone was always awake on watch and they slept under the open sky. It seemed a good excuse.

She didn't know what she felt, what she might feel, knowing now what he was.

Which shamed her. Maybe that was the ugliness she felt in herself. Not her scarred face after all, but her secret thought that she had lain with a monster unknowing.

Nothing had changed in him, not his kindness, his patience, not his sudden glints of humour or the passion that lurked under the weariness. He hadn't changed. Something in her had. For good? He looked like a man. She had seen him turn into a monstrous dog.

She wanted him to hold her. She didn't want him to touch her. She wished she were home, that the Westrons had never crossed the mountains . . . might as well wish papa had never been injured, that blow to the head that made him a cantankerous child again, in need of constant care, wish mama hadn't died when her little sister who never lived was born, wish she were a child again.

Wish herself the adult she pretended to be, the skirmisher and then lancer who had fought the Westrons through a summer and autumn of unending retreat, the woman and warrior Holla-Sayan seemed to think he wanted.

Wishes were nothing. Less than mist drifting on the wind.

Iarka had the first watch of the night when they had camped, as Holla-Sayan promised, in the feet of the mountains. There was even water, a little spring welling up from a crack in the rocks, shimmering away to lose itself in a dry, gravel gully, where thirsty roots drank all that it had. There was no goddess, but the mere sound of the water gave a sense of peace, at least to Jolanan.

The air off the mountains was cold, and their fire was already out. They could not go on sleeping in the open much longer, but there were not so many more days ahead of them, Holla-Sayan said, and once they were right into the mountains they could keep a fire going, or cut brush to make a shelter.

She laid her blankets down next to his, the first time she had done so since they left the Upper Castle. He looked at her. Solemn. He had such beautiful eyes. That was what she had first noticed about him, when he was a worrying stranger. The air, too, of danger, of something that might be let loose. It had drawn her, then. Matched something in herself, she had thought.

Well, she had seen that hidden danger surface, seen it wake. Found it wasn't what she had thought, whatever that might have been.

She didn't know how to say she was afraid, but she wanted his arms around her again, like this morning, when they drank tea. She wanted to have responded to his kiss.

That was all. That was all there would be, with Iarka or Rifat sitting up, watching the night.

It wasn't going to be enough for him. She felt that, when they pressed close together under their shared blankets, but what did she expect? And she . . . wanted him. She very badly wanted him and wanted not to be afraid of him, but she dreamed of a black shape laced with fire, and burning eyes, and fangs, leaping out of the night, and sometimes it was her enemy whose throat it seized, and sometimes it was herself.

He pulled her closer to him, more comfortably against him, and she settled her head on his chest. If they started kissing at this point . . . Iarka had climbed away uphill a little and Rifat had turned his back, blankets pulled up over his head. She wanted, she badly wanted, to slide a hand up under Holla's shirt, to stroke over that bare warm skin, the curling hair there, to let herself touch, as she had used to. To have his hands moving, too, to lift herself up to lie over him, face to face, mouth to mouth . . .

One arm around her, hand on her waist. The other on her cheek, cradling her head against him. He didn't move again, just held her there, whatever else he might want.

She was so damned tired. And safe. And she wanted to laugh. Rifat was snoring, and Rifat—did not snore.

She settled more comfortably into Holla-Sayan's embrace. Sighed. Fell asleep.

Woke at a hand on her mouth, a skittering of stone, a body gone tense, half rising, carrying her with him as he sat up. Jolanan rolled away, reaching for the sabre she had laid at her side. Knelt, blade unsheathed. Hearing nothing.

"Something," said Iarka, and Rifat was on his feet, a spear in his hand. Late enough the moon had risen and she should have had the second watch. The two wizards had let them lie, or someone had slept when they should not, which she did not believe of either of Kinsai's folk.

"Get out of here," Holla-Sayan said. "Go! Run! Iarka, *go!* Jo, get her away."

Because it was Iarka, Iarka of all of them, who must live.

Jolanan grabbed her boots in her free hand and ran sock-footed, nothing but a shirt between her heart and an enemy's blade, to Iarka, who still wore her shirt of Northron mail and stood hesitating by the camels, unsaddled, but restless, now. One began to heave itself up.

Nothing to be seen, nothing to be heard, but the air felt like a thunderstorm. Hopping, she pulled on her boots.

"Go!" Holla-Sayan said—snarled, as Rifat yelled and hurled his spear at a blackness that thickened out of the night. There was a flare of white, as if lightning answered. Jolanan grabbed Iarka's arm and they both ran. Camels bellowed behind. Something howled. Rifat cried out again. Iarka jerked her arm free, began muttering, tracing shapes in the air. Sparks danced along her fingers and she fell to her knees, crying out, holding her head.

Something shrieked, a high, animal sound. Lightning blazed a path into the sky and for a moment Jolanan saw it, a man, standing, a knife that trapped the light as if it were ice, and he held the dog, huge as a wolf, in the air by the throat, as if it weighed nothing. He stabbed between its clawing forelegs and into its heart even as it twisted and broke free and it fell and was a man, with the hilt of a knife standing out of his chest, but the metal—melted, like ice, in the dancing lightning's glare, and Holla-Sayan was still. And the stranger seized him up in his arms as if he were a child and they were gone.

The sudden dark was blinding.

Too fast. Too much. In the space of a thunderbolt's strike she could not have seen, have known . . .

She had, she did.

He was gone. *Again.* And this time she could not follow.

Jolanan found Rifat sprawled amid the rocks. She feared him dead, struck down by lightning, by wizardry or devil's rage. But he still breathed, though he was cold as the frosted earth and couldn't be woken. Iarka, crawling to them, felt her way over his body from head to heel and said no bones were broken, so they made a nest of all their blankets and took it in turns to lie close against him, one sharing warmth while the other kept watch. They didn't speak, beyond the few words necessary to wake each other, trading the watch. Words seemed—too much. Jolanan felt she must scream, shriek like the mad, if either of them so much as spoke his name.

Around the same time that the night began to leach out of the east, Rifat stirred and began to mutter in his native Black Desert tongue. Iarka woke him, gently, murmuring in the same speech. For a moment he clung to her like a child, whimpering, panting, that child woken from nightmare.

"What?" she asked. "Tell me, Rifat, what do you see?"

"Nothing," he said. "Nothing. Dreams—I can't—it was cold and screaming . . . I can't, Iarka. I don't remember. It's all . . . smoke. Gone." He looked around. "Holla-Sayan's gone."

Gone.

Dead.

No. You didn't murder someone and carry away their corpse. Even—

"That was the All-Holy himself," Jolanan said, her voice tight. "No wizard could have done that. It was Jochiz."

No answer. Iarka had scrambled away and was on her knees throwing up. Rifat looked like he might join her, unsteady and cautious as a hangover in moving, a black and swollen bruise on his temple.

"Holla isn't dead," Jolanan said. "He isn't." Wanting contradiction so she could argue, could yell. Or confirmation, so she could believe it. Neither wizard answered.

No tracks to follow. No wizardry of any use.

It took them four days to come to Lissavakail, Iarka guiding them, tilting her head sometimes, as if listening, or raising her head to sniff the wind. She mostly rode with a hand on her not-yet-swelling belly, as if to remind herself of what she had to protect. Sometimes her fingers tapped a rhythm. Hearing music in her head, or working some wizardry? Jolanan didn't bother to ask. Couldn't care. The older woman led them wrong only a few times, paths that disappeared, or climbed to where only goats might go. A change in the air, flurries. It was winter already, not so far above them. Feet cold, and fingers; sleeping two together and one on watch with a fire, because there was brush enough to burn and lack of a fire had not stopped the worst of enemies from finding them. On the night that Iarka

said should be their last in the open before Lissavakail, enough snow fell
to threaten the flames, and they huddled together sitting as close to it as
possible, shaggy camels turning to snow-mounds at their backs. They
broke up their camp at first light and set out, the world dull white around
them, the sky grey, threatening more. There were no shadows in that
overcast world. Too easy to misjudge a distance, to ride over a drop. Some
great black bird circled overhead, wings vast enough to dwarf an eagle,
never flapping. She thought of the devil Vartu, who flew in the form of a
bird, but she was gone to Marakand. And Vartu had already proven she
would not stand against Jochiz. The spark of hope died. Jolanan had not
till then realized it had been even been struck to life.

A halt came at noon, with a narrow lake before them. Time for a bite
to eat, time to rest the camels. Time, apparently, to consider that they
were lost.

"We want to go that way," Iarka said, pointing out over the grey
sheet of water that filled the steep-sided valley. "Old Great Gods damn,
what's wrong with—with everything? Where's the damned road?" Her
voice shook.

"That's not Lissavakail? Not the goddess's lake?"

"No! It's—there's no goddess, it's just water and it shouldn't be here."

"How do you know?" Jolanan asked. "Did he tell you?" And if Holla-
Sayan had described their route in such detail, why hadn't he told all of
them—why hadn't he told her?

"I wish he had. Why in the cold hells do you think I've been hunting
and searching and risking some bastard Westron diviner catching scent of
us all these days? This shouldn't be here. I know it, I feel it—it's *wrong.*"
Her hand was on her belly again, and Rifat edged his camel up alongside,
laid a hand on her arm.

"It's all right," he said. "We'll find a way around. Let's have something to eat, a bit of rest, and Jolanan and I can go scouting."

"Don't talk to me like I'm a child."

"Don't—"

A shout, above. No words in it, a wordless hail, meant to carry.

Jolanan set an arrow to the string and Rifat reached for his bow. Silence, then a gust of stinging snow off the mountainside. Another cry followed it, words, maybe, this time.

Iarka tipped her head, listening. Her eyes were pinched with cold, scarf wrapped to cover most of her face, frosted over.

She pulled her scarf down, cupped her hands to her mouth and called back her own name, three singing syllables. Looked over at Rifat, grinning. "Lissavakaili," she said. "And our cousins. Kinsai be thanked, we are here after all."

Figures were moving on the mountainside above them, scrambling like goats. Jolanan couldn't help but brace herself for the cry, the tumbling fall that never came.

Rifat was waving both arms shouting, asking about someone called Besni. His younger brother, Jolanan remembered, gone with the rest when the folk of the Upper Castle evacuated.

No kin or friends to welcome her here. Let them have their reunion. The wind slapped her hard, racing up over the water; it thrust icy lances under her scarves, inside her coat, stinging tears from her good eye. Her scars ached like fresh bruises.

She could see sixteen, eighteen, maybe a score of people spilling down the slope; women in blue coats, shorter than most Westgrasslanders; some taller folk among them, pale-skinned and brown and two very dark, in sheepskin or caravaneer's coats, ribbons in their hair, bright random scarves—folk of Kinsai. There was a tower up there, she saw now, a squat round thing looking like just another outcropping of the mountain, snow roofed. The people in the lead came dropping down to the track. Iarka and Rifat were afoot, engulfed in them, being embraced from all directions. Jolanan climbed down her camel's side, stood, watching, feeling a weariness, a loneliness that seemed old and entirely her own, like a coat she had misplaced, settle on her.

"Jolanan of the Jayala'arad," a mountain woman said, leaping lightly down the last drop to the track. One of the—priestesses, she supposed all the women in blue must be. Warrior-priestesses of Attalissa, guardians of these mountains. She was young, not much older than Jolanan, but spoke with the assurance of rank. She wore a circlet from which golden discs like coins dangled in twos and threes, woven through her short black hair, bright on her forehead. They chimed like little bells. Gold earrings and a collar of turquoise.

Young face, maybe. Old, old eyes. Wise. Kind. Angry.

Words failed.

"I saw the devil in my dreams," the goddess Attalissa said. She reached a hand. Jolanan took it. Was embraced. She clung, as if to a sister found.

CHAPTER II

*. . . the early spring, following the year in which the All-Holy
crossed over the Karas.*

T he sun hung low in the west. Down below in the camp, where
the roots of the mountains dug into the edge of the stony desert,
they performed the service of the evening prayers. The All-Holy prayed
apart, as was right in the eyes of his folk. He led the songs, half-sung,
half-chanted, of his seventh-circle commanders of the faith, with the
most honoured of the sixth-circle diviners summoned to weave their
words and their powers with his, in the privacy of his great tent. The
folk of the faith—soldiers and knights, teachers and followers, converts and conscripts—prayed in their marching-squads and companies,
arrayed in ragged lines, droning rote responses to the song-leaders, who
were often mere third-circle teachers, not even priests. Many of those
below did not understand more than few words of the Tiypurian dialect
of Westron that was the language of the faith. Folk of other tribes of the
west, folk of the lands east of the Karas, of the Western Grass and the
Great.

Their lack of understanding did not matter. That they mouthed the
words at all was power. It bound them, made them a fellowship, made
them kin, the chosen, beloved servants of the All-Holy, whom the Old
Great Gods had sent to save them.

Or something like that. Sarzahn didn't pay the tenets of the faith much mind. That was his brother's affair.

The singing grated on him, though. A flat drone, no true music in it. No true power.

No life.

Something else about the evening was grating on him.

There was a wrongness to the air, the scent of a stranger. Not even that alone. The taste of the colour of death, of old bone. Faint, though. Perhaps only a memory.

Memory was strange, deceitful. Sometimes he remembered . . . Sarzahn could not think what. Voices. Scents, sharp and clear as faces, but scent, face, voice—all unknown. He did not think he had ever known them, any of those mist-thin dreams. He did not think he had ever been, before. There was—now. This. All else a dream, a shadow in the water.

Now, here. A wrongness in the air, a stranger's scent, high on the mountainside, where no scouts had been dispatched. There were look-outs, yes, but they were ahead, the next ridge. Up there—broken stone, a narrow hanging valley, all stone teeth between the tree-trunks, a pale forest of still-leafless birch, bent and broken by the storms of a brutal winter. Down here, the last straggling companies of the Army of the North were coming into the camp, humans half-dead on their feet. Stink. Noise. Dust. Hard to breathe, for the dust. It was always either dust or miring muck now, as winter lost its grip. Here, there was broken stone and gritty sand in long fingers reaching from the west to the mountains, and in bands between, like valleys filled with what the steep slopes could not hold, soft and clinging clay. Water, too, shallow pools that buzzed with midges. But mostly clay, and the last weeks had been all clay, which seized the wagon wheels and would not let them go, sucked them axle deep. Clay that pulled the boots off the feet of those fortunate enough to possess boots. Few were. It made this march's return to dust seem desirable.

Over the winter they had lost many to frostbite, fingers and toes, noses and ears turning purple, black, rotting and sloughing away and the blood-poison spreading. Lost many outright, dead of cold and found frozen come the morning. Engineers and the diviners and the All-Holy himself had cut and broken stone and made a hard road down the cliffs of the Undrin Rift and up again, and they had left bodies there, too, crushed by stone, fallen from the heights. Blessed in their god's service. Such thoughts comforted a human servant.

Sarzahn didn't much care, himself. Humans were such brief things, a flash of colour, of song, of pain. Soul passing through the world in a shell of matter and gone again. Possibly it was a relief to them.

Hard to sort out the scents of the air, to think clearly. Mind wandered. He leapt down from the rock on which he had lain, padded away to a higher vantage where the ground began to climb more steeply. One might think them some desperate retreat, but they were victorious, and marching to greater victory. They had crossed the Dead Hills, barren and poisoned lands. They had climbed the Karas and spilled down onto the Nearer Grass and conquered that thinly-peopled land and the gods of that land, and the folk of those gods had given themselves to the worship of the All-Holy, or they had died. Which the priests of the All-Holy said was fitting.

Human things. Faith. Belief. He had neither. Sarzahn had his brother, and all his heart beat for him. It was not faith. It was—existence.

They had crossed the Kinsai'av—shadow-memory flickered in the water, deep in his mind. Dangerous, that river. Had he been there?

His brother had not yet found him, saved him, then. No. He had been lost, still, and dying. That flicker of—was it pain?—when he thought on the river and the long march to it was only dream as well.

The winter's skirting of the Great Grass, the engineers and wizard shattering of stone, making a road down into the Undrin Rift and up again, the bodies left buried in the rubble there—that he remembered.

The children dead, and the gods and goddesses, small powers of the grasslands, and the chieftains defeated when they came dashing their riders against the lines of spears or the ditches of the camps . . .

Kill me the chieftain of the Red Wind Banners, his brother might say, had said. Or the Blue, or the Grey-Tail, whoever opposed them. *Swift and sure, take the heart out of them, to spare our folk for the march, to save our strength for Marakand.*

And he had done this, for his brother, gone as a stalking beast in the night, to do what was murder, not war. Because it was his brother who asked, and he was his brother's faithful dog.

In his mind was a picture, such as a bard's words might make from a song. A land of low, slow hills, grass rolling in waves, green and silver, and clouds running, small, swift, white against blue, and horses below, running, and a bird unseen high in the sky, singing heartbreak . . .

A song he had heard once, perhaps. An interlude in some bard's tale. But there were no singers, no storytellers, with the armies of the All-Holy. Only the teachers and the priests, to teach and repeat the stories of the coming of the All-Holy, the hermit who became the embodiment of the Nameless God. Only the priests of the sixth circle, the diviners, the wizards, to sing the prayers of power, to weave miracles from song.

Scent drifting down the mountainside. A bit curious, beginning to be also a bit irritated, at the way his mind wandered, as if—

—as if something nudged him aside, nudged him away from paying attention to that faint betraying air, human skin and leather and oiled steel, sent him wandering into the past, other thoughts leaking . . . The voices on the edges of the mind. He pushed them down.

Wizardry. Not quite wizardry. Almost like the touch of a god, but there was no god in this region of the mountains, not even a small wild one of no folk. Wizardry, then. Something of Marakand, and it thought to hide from the All-Holy and the All-Holy's servant.

He flowed down off the ridge like a shadow, keeping to bare stone, off the snow that still lay in the hollows and the northern shade. Followed a wandering course, circling, climbing where no man could go.

The All-Holy was still with his commanders and the song-leaders of the sixth circle. There was much preparation to be done before they joined with Dimas and the Army of the South for the assault on the defences of the Pass of Marakand. This straying wizard of their enemies was not worth his brother's attention.

Dusk was falling by the time he had worked his way to where he wanted to be, uphill and, if not directly downwind, at least not where the cold night breeze rolling from greater heights would carry his scent straight to his enemy. Human. Wizard. Prey, but not an animal, to be alerted by the smell of him in turn. But it was instinct, not thought. Something in the memory of the bone and blood, the pattern he shaped, was shaped in.

Sarzahn had sight of his quarry now. A man nested in rocks among the birches. From where he lay, the camp would be in view. Had he been set there to count their numbers?

A spy and a wizard. Some divination worked on the camp. Some spell set against them. Sarzahn did not understand the working of such things, but there was, now he sought it, that faint tang in the air. Something of power, subtle in its strength. Knotted bundles of herbs and twigs scattered about, like nosegays gathered by a child with no eye for flowers, little twists of dead weeds. Not a magic he had ever seen.

Stirrup-crossbow, spanned and lying by the man's side. He should have noticed that first of all. Why leave it spanned, stretching the cord, when he could not from this height make a shot to the camp? Defence against sudden discovery—a rider's short bow would be better: swifter, more practical, lighter to carry. Sword unsheathed, too. Northron, long and ornately hilted. The man wore a grey wool shirt and trousers, a brown jerkin, high-collared, which might be reinforced with plates of horn or steel within, a headscarf in muted greys and faded green. Faded himself into the land. Made himself part of it. Was hard to see, for a moment. Rock and bark and winter-sere brush. Was lying on a long, tawny coat, settled in for a wait on the frost-bitter ground.

Maybe he hadn't been lying there long with the bow spanned. Maybe—

Maybe Sarzahn was not the only one who felt a presence by means of a sense that had no name, felt what had no words, tasted the colour of powers that moved in the world—

Sarzahn was already moving, charging to attack as the man came up on one knee, turning, the bow levelled and the trigger squeezed—

He felt the bolt; it stroked his fur, furrowed flesh, struck stone and he was leaping down the steep slope, through the trees—the man on his feet, sword in hand.

Fast. He went for the arm, to have that biting edge out of the reckoning before he took the man's throat, but his enemy—moving, striking—it was the flat of the blade smacked hard across his muzzle and he snarled rage, twisted away, turned back when the man might think he would run and seized—but the man had caught up his coat to muffle his warding arm and though Sarzahn bit into flesh he didn't crack bone, mouth full of camel-rank wool and the man clouted him with the hilt this time, top of his head, shouting something he couldn't hear, words strange and buzzing like wasps, like fainting, sound gone distant and strange, or maybe—

No!

Voice, thought, his, not his, and he had flinched away, crouching, snarling. The man moved warily. Blood stained the coat. He spoke the whole time he moved. To distract, maybe. Seeking better footing. Sarzahn watched till almost he had his ground, and then launched himself, but the man saw the movement. So swift in his movements, Sarzahn hadn't fought anyone so swift, so assured, as if he read every nerve and muscle, since—

He did not know.

But he was just as quick and the man was down under his paws—not swift enough. The man's sword, drawn back, was pressed, just biting, below his throat, the soft centre of his chest. Cold. Wet. Sarzahn was bleeding. Inches, a thrust to his lungs the man hadn't made.

The restraint could be nothing but deliberate.

Sarzahn could tear the face off him. He could survive that steel even were it pressed further, survive the blade even in his lungs. He was fairly certain. He'd known such wounds before. He thought. Maybe. The man wouldn't live.

Afraid. Of course this swordsman-wizard was. Fear of death every mortal carried, pitiable and brief. Even a wizard's life was pitiable and brief. But he spoke again and it was painful, whatever words he shaped. Some wizardry. No smell of it, no hot ash, water, stone, dust scent of a spell. Just words Sarzahn couldn't grasp the shape of, which seemed to mean something to the man, because his voice grew softer, more urgent, as he if argued, persuaded. He could not understand. He should understand, and he could not, as if some failing in his mind suddenly took comprehension of the language, of any language, from him.

Sarzahn snarled.

No. No. No!

He was bleeding, angry, growing dizzy, which he should not with so slight a blood-letting . . .

He lunged, jaws snapping, forgetting the sword on which he should have skewered himself but the blade was withdrawn—teeth met flesh but he was weak, as if something sapped his strength, denied him his own muscle and sinew. The man struck him with the hilt again and he let go, was flung off as if he weighed nothing. The man rolled aside as Sarzahn fell.

Poison on the quarrel? That first shot, wounding, hadn't been meant to kill. Disable him. They wanted to take him. Use him against his brother, his secrets, his knowledge. Poison, wizardry—he staggered splay-legged, swaying, vision swimming in shadows and flaring light, the man a tangled knot of it, ribbons, chains of light flying off him, binding him—he too himself was bound, knotted tight, he saw chains, wrapping him, wrapping something within him—

Called desperate, as the man crouched over him, sword sheathed and it was some of those bundled dead weeds the wizard held, his lower face masked with blood. Twigs, straws—they pulsed and shivered and changed their shapes, light beyond colour. The man prised open Sarzahn's jaws, though he snapped feebly and would have finished what he'd begun and ripped away his face, except vision betrayed him and he missed, clacking on air. Fingers, strong, gripping him, thumb at hazard.

He could taste sweat and his enemy's blood, and what was rough, dry—the bundle of weeds forced between his teeth, crumbling. He fought and bucked and struggled, clawing, but he was flailing like a drunk and fell into his human form, which was worse, weaker, no hope of resisting then and he choked and gagged and could not breath, throat crammed with hay, scratching, tearing, coughing, till he was the dog again and could gulp and swallow even that, too much of it—

The air tore with the sound of thunder and his brother was on them, finally, realizing Sarzahn's peril, turning sword in hand on the assassin who had come here for this, no spy but a lure and a trap. Sarzahn lurched to four feet again and staggered forward to defend the one who was life and need and heart of his world, but fell as their swords rang, his brother in rage, voice low, venomous, the assassin fighting for his life and he would die, no other outcome, though they danced as equals and it was not the swift thrust and ending Sarzahn expected, his brother—playing, surely, not pressed to hold his own, never.

They were half-dissolved in light, as if they melted, gone to colours, streaked and bleeding into stone, into sky and the white slash of birch, their twigs black cracks that webbed the sky, the searing blade-edge breaking the air. The second sword his brother bore, slung high under his arm, was a cold stillness, a solidity that resisted the dissolving fire and flow that Sarzahn's failing vision made them.

The assassin was being forced back, though—was giving ground at least—and his brother reached and began to pull to him those threads of light, those chains of fire, of power that bound the wizard and fed or were fed elsewhere. Began to gather light into fire, to burn, to destroy.

No. Again, the voice, the frantic thought, commanding, desperate. His? His, but he did not think he knew it.

Jochiz, he cried, and reached for him, clinging, clutching, a drowning man to pull down a swimmer. Not with teeth, clawing feet, grasping hands. Just reached with everything that was in him, soul to soul and held, dragged close, desperate, needing . . . It was the pain, the poison, working in him, whatever spell—it must be the poison he had swallowed, searing him hollow, leaving the terror of a howling, empty night—

His brother flinched away from the swordsman and Jochiz's cheek was opened, had already been opened by his enemy's sword when he flinched, impossibility, but he dashed blood away with a careless hand, turned away disdainful and the swordsman-wizard was in flight, dodging through the trees, making for the high rocks. Was gone. Illusion. Wizardry. Scent of him, blood and snow. His brother shouted, Imperial Nabbani, maybe, insult perhaps, and laughed, angry. Allowed the Marakander that coward's retreat. Strode down on Sarzahn wrathful at the distraction that had let his enemy escape.

Dragged his head up. Hooked a finger and cleared a painful mass of hard stalks out of his throat, face twisting at the muck of slime and blood. Let him fall, crouched over him.

Sarzahn's body was fevered, shivering, panting. Jochiz shoved at him, pushed him into a human form again, and he sweated, shivered still. Torn coat, torn skin and muscles of his back, searing, some poison at work, some wizardry, sinking threads deep into him, weaving, writing . . . burning patterns like and unlike Northron runes, he saw in the eye of the mind, painted in blood, in light, in the sky before him, in the stone, on his eyes.

He couldn't read them. Mind, memory, tried, and lost the sense.

"Nabban," his brother said, as if it were a curse. But at least he could understand speech again. "They've heard rumour of you, my dog. But the necromancer greatly underestimates you if he thinks his slave's mere wizardry will—" Laughed, not finishing his thought, and his hand was rough, stroking hard over the wound, a touch with devil's powers in it, burning out the wizardry of death. A wound which would have healed swiftly on his own but for the gnawing poison, a pain that was not— not unwelcome, a pain that promised—bitterness in his throat, bleeding, scored, scarred down his throat but it reminded him—the pain, the poison he had swallowed had a voice, a song, a whisper—

Listen. He didn't say that aloud or even for his brother's hearing. He did not say it at all. It was not his own voice and yet he knew it as he knew his bodies, the swift flow between them. It whispered, deep, *Be still, lie still, listen, wait.*

"Later," his brother said. "Later you shall kill him for me, and we will tear his necromancer god between us, and swallow him."

The fever was a darkness devouring him. He let it take him. His brother was by him. That was enough.

CHAPTER III

Ahjvar's heart still pounded; legs still had that trembling, treacherous edge of failure in the knees. Palms slick with sweat, when he gripped the edge of stone, clambering up, toe in a crack, holding himself that one moment by the toe of his boot and the grip of his fingers till this other foot found the higher hold he had scouted from below. Heaved and rolled himself over the edge, lay on his back a moment, just breathing. Stars above, though light lingered in the west. He held the pattern of the dance in his mind yet, the weaving of movement and blade's edge that wrote *almond*, to forbid, and *walnut* for secrecy, and *prickly ash*, to deny what was, or might be, worked against him. Wizardry of lost Praitan bound in twig and herb, but he had learned to make it something else long ago, held in body and blood and powers that ran in him beyond his own, strong though he had been in wizardry even when he was—that other man, long ago.

He had run. Not a retreat, not thought and planning and the best choice. Run in panic. He'd felt the devil reaching, as if Jochiz groped to seize the heart out of his chest and hold it burning, a fire that would not let him go till it was finished with him, a fire that would reach beyond him, through him, to consume Ghu—he had not cared for Nabban, in that moment, not the god of the land, his god of the mountain and the river, only Ghu, the light and warmth and heart of him, feared to know him burning in the devil's hatred till they were dead alike, ash and bone—*Not again, not again—*

Don't think it. Don't. Breathe. Find a stillness. Make the place of quiet, of roots and cold waters rising. The scent of pines. The mass of stone beneath him, not this stone, broken and shifting, tremors and fires beneath—the solid mass of the mountain that was home. Make that stillness. Cold. Sharp. Everything clear. Wizardry wrapping him, shield against the devil, thin enough, but over him too the pines, the snows, a strength not his.

Enough?

No. Not if Jochiz chose to exert himself.

Something reached, touched . . . passed on.

Or maybe? A touch, where he crouched, as if ducking down might help. Arm over him, body pressed close. Something vast. Even a god strong among the gods of the earth was not a strength to withstand a devil. But enough to be no easy prey. And perhaps the devil was not yet willing to force that fight.

They couldn't count on it.

The feeling of another by him, over him, faded, and that searching presence did not come again. The last ember-glow of sunset had faded, colour drained out of the thickening night, but a waxing gibbous moon was high overhead and he did not need even that. Owl's eyes. God's eyes. Shape of the land, making itself known. He went on, climbing, scrambling, slithering where he had not intended to, but he was still shaken and lost the path he had meant to retrace. Came, by midnight, to where he had meant to lie up to await the dawn. Not a good idea. Keep moving. Still too close, though he had come east into the rising mountains and was in a long furrow that twisted a crooked way south, high broken hills to the west, between him and the Westron line of march.

He thought he had come to the right place, at any rate. Cliff, treeless slope with towering dead stalks of fennel making what looked, all silvered and shadowed, like a dwarf forest of palms. No movement, no sound, but he could—something in him could feel—a warmth, call it life or soul or what you would. Hiding. Patience. Fear and boredom.

"Just me," he called softly, in a language a hundred years dead. The young man was picking it up, though, in overheard dribs and drabs, putting it together with what lingered in the dialect of Nabbani they called Taren now, and which wouldn't be understood at all if one spoke it in the empire, outside the ports.

Ailan stirred, uncoiling from the nest he had made himself in the grassy undergrowth, like a fawn left by its mother to wait out the day. Fennel stalks crackled as he made his way down, crawling to where the terrain turned too stony even for those to grow, the open ground by the small meltwater pool, frost-fringed. Feeling his way, mostly. He had his own pack slung awkwardly from one shoulder, dragged Ahjvar's.

"Starting to think I should come look for you."

"No! Cold hells, no. Never!"

"Don't know how I'd find my own way back."

"You shouldn't be here in the first place. And better die lost here than run into the Westrons."

"Cheerful. You hurt? Your voice sounds funny." A hand came reaching, a wary fluttering. Ailan knew better than to touch him. Ahjvar caught his wrist.

"It's nothing."

"'Course not. Let me see. Is your nose broken?"

"No."

"Let me see. Make a light."

Wretched—people didn't talk back to him. They watched him warily and got out of the way. Called him *"Rihswera"* as the Nabbani ambassador did, and bowed, and that was just fine if it gave him space.

He called up a light, a silvery moonglow in the hand. Small wizardry and not too likely to draw attention to break his shielding.

His headscarf was sodden dark where he had used it to blot his face, hold his nose, a brief pause in his flight when the dripping down his chin became demanding. Coat spattered with dark stains where he had used it to protect his arm, too. Torn.

"Nori bless, what happened? Did you find—? Here, let me."

Ailan was only trying to help and Ahjvar did not strike his hand away, when he unwrapped Ahjvar's scarf from about his neck and used a clean end of it, wetted in the pool, to dab cautiously at his face.

"It's not bad. We need to keep moving." Put some more miles between themselves and the Westron camp. They'd have moonlight through the gathering streaks of cloud for a while yet, if they kept out of the shadow of the western slopes. Some pursuit would be out after them with daybreak.

"Not till you're cleaned up. Old Great Gods, what a mess."

Ahjvar gave himself up to having his face washed, like a child who'd been brawling and gotten his nose bloodied. There was something . . . appealing in the way the young man refused to be cowed.

Or aggravating. He should have knocked Ailan around the ears and sent him straight back when he realized the young man had followed, trailing behind him, falling farther and farther back. That he was going to lose himself and die in the damned hills. Went back to retrieve him and—had been so close to striking. And that was what he was used to, Ailan, and so Ahjvar hadn't. Argued, but didn't even tell him how stupid he was being, because the Taren had a lifetime of the world telling him he was not fast enough or strong enough or smart enough, and it came down to, not lucky enough, this one. Laid out the sensible arguments, swallowing anger and frustration. Ailan had only gone sullen and angry himself, terrified all the while, which damned well hurt. In the end Ahjvar had given in to the argument that he needed someone to keep watch for him "or something"—Ailan himself hadn't been able to think of what use, precisely, he might be. Even then he'd still looked like a scolded dog, and still been shaking, inside, with the fear of what he'd chosen. He baffled Ahjvar, he really did, as not the most stubborn and over-confident imperial princess ever had.

Ailan couldn't find his own way back to the city. That had been the telling argument, in the end. Ahjvar didn't know what to do with the boy, yet if you took in a feral pup, you didn't give it a feed and drive it off the next day. But what was it with young strays latching on to him like he was some mother duck, anyway? He was hardly anyone's idea of a father-figure.

"I guess it's not broken," Ailan said. "You look—you scared me. So much blood."

"Noses bleed."

"Yeah, yours did. What happened? Did you find him? And he *bit* you?"

"Obviously."

"Lucky you still have a nose. Lucky you still have a *face*."

"How bad is it?" He couldn't see, squinting down his nose. Red smears.

"Dunno. 'S all still there. That's pretty good, really, for a dog attack. More like he was just playing, really. I think you've got a hole right through the side, though."

Forgetting himself, Ailan took Ahjvar's chin in his hand, frowning, inspecting, and that was too close, too much.

"You could put a jewel in that. Black Desert fashion. Well, for a woman. But turquoise would look good."

"No."

"Maybe your god would like it?"

"No!" He could feel the Taren's breath on his face. Feel his hand trembling. Hear—was it hearing?—the racing heart. Afraid, for all his labouring to make jokes. Ahjvar pushed him off.

"Sorry." Ailan backed away. "Maybe you'd better wash your beard? Um, I filled the water-gourds before it got dark—"

"Good."

"— yeah, so you don't have to worry about dirtying the pool if you stick your face in it . . . you want me to look at your arm, too? If he can track by smell . . ."

"Even a mortal hound could follow our scent without the blood." But Ahjvar did as Ailan suggested. It was sense. Ghu would tell him the same.

Ailan rinsed out the scarf, wrung it and tied it to the strap of a pack to dry. Sat back on his heels, watching.

Nothing but a few scratches on Ahjvar's arm. Not anything even Ghu would worry about. Ahvar clenched the light in his fist, extinguishing it. The longer he let it go, the greater the chance a wizard's searching would notice. And he was only guessing human trackers wouldn't be set loose till the dawn.

"So is he a traitor, or what?" Ailan asked.

They fell into a rhythm of walking, Ailan sticking close enough that Ahjvar could reach to steady him when the ground dropped suddenly or a stone rose to trip him. A silence that felt companionable. For all his willingness—maybe it was need—to chatter when he felt unsure of himself, Ailan could be silent. Foxes were yipping down the valley. Stones, unavoidably, clicked and clattered underfoot. The Taren's doing, not his. Patches of snow gave Ailan some light, reflecting the moon, but had to be skirted not to leave plain tracks.

"You didn't answer," Ailan said softly, when they had come into a stand of trees again, pale trunks twisted by the winds, and were picking a way around snow-patches. "Is the Blackdog a traitor?"

"I don't know. I don't know what's happened to him, what's been done. He's no prisoner."

But he did know. He felt the horror of it in his gut, growing into a smothering weight of nightmare, and if he began to brood on that—

Ahjvar had known such service. Better to be dead.

"Jochiz came after me to defend him."

"You saw the All-Holy?" Ailan's cautious voice rose, forgetful. "You *fought* him? Did you—is he *dead?*"

"Fool, no. I ran away and he stayed to try to save the dog."

"You killed the Blackdog?"

"I don't know. I didn't intend to." He had only been sent to spy, to speak if he could find the chance. To report back. Not to meddle in devil's workings that he didn't understand. Patterns of home, of finding, of a road . . . wizardry that must weigh nothing against a devil's chains. He didn't understand the shapeshifter's sudden weakness, as if he'd been struck with some poison. The arrow had been meant as a last resort; he'd wanted to talk to the Blackdog, find out what he was doing in Jochiz's train. Argue with him, if he claimed Sien-Shava Jochiz had some great cause worth his betrayal. Ahjvar might know, too well, the making and the uses of poisons; he didn't deal in such things any more, and he'd nearly missed, the dog had come on so fast. The wound shouldn't even have slowed him, unless steel itself was somehow anathema to him, a thing he had never heard of. Something had nearly undone the shapeshifter though, and given him his chance with the spells he seemed to have bound into shape, hands moving, mind drifting, dream-edge walking while he thought he watched, alert. Not quite certain what he had done, even, or what he had meant to do. Lure him within the pattern of them on the ground . . . ?

Ghu was fey and saw what his champion did not, and reached through him . . .

So what did you think we were doing, idiot boy, weaving spells against a devil? I worry when you start playing with wizardry. You don't know what you're doing.

Nothing answered. He touched the necklace at his throat, shells and acorns pierced and woven into a braid of hair, human and horse.

Ghu was very far away, and a god could not reach beyond their own land.

But they lay within one another. They made a new shape in the world. Not a braid. Two rivers that flowed into one.

Whatever had stricken down the shapeshifter, he'd better not be counting on it to last. And he did not think, whatever Ghu might hope—if Ghu had anything at all to do with it and it was not his own uneasy wizardry—that a few twists of weeds in a wish for the lost would do much good.

"It's whispered the Blackdog's a traitor," the storyteller had said. Her name was Moth, or Ulfhild, or Vartu, but Ghu had met her first the day he had also met Ivah, and she had been telling stories then, in a market of Marakand, and so she was forever the storyteller to him. Ghu trusted her, as much as he trusted any devil. Ahjvar himself found her hard to read. Still and cold. Deep water, and dark. "They've kept that rumour close, the wardens, but the spies Yeh-Lin recruited reported him as the All-Holy's most trusted companion throughout the winter. Man or dog, always there, always at Sien-Shava's side."

Sien-Shava. Yeh-Lin called him Jochiz.

"How do you decide what name to go by?" Ahjvar asked. An interruption, and rude, but he wanted to understand. Names mattered. His did. It wasn't one he had been born with, didn't even belong to his own folk, neither that of his birth nor the one of his choosing. A name of the eastern deserts. He'd taken it off a man he'd killed, another assassin employed by a rival to his then-employer. Probably hadn't been that man's own, either.

But it was the name Ghu called him by.

Names mattered, if you would hold the shape of a thing.

"Myself?" the storyteller asked. "Or him? I'm Moth, mostly. It . . . fits very comfortably. Sien-Shava, though—is Jochiz and only Jochiz, in his own mind. He despises what's human in himself and yet it shapes who he is, so strongly. More than many of us, I think. So, I call him Sien-Shava. He hates it."

"Petty."

She grinned. Always startling. She was so sombre, in manner, in dress. In mood. Mostly she smiled for the bear-demon, for him alone. He had been there too, a great golden bulk slouched between the cedars of Gurhan's hill. Opening dark eyes, at that.

"Petty," Mikki rumbled. "But a good thing for us all to remember, *Rihswera* of Nabban. There is a human soul within him yet, for all he wants to think himself a god, and it was a nasty, corrupted and corrupting little soul when he was nothing but an outlawed wizard. Holla-Sayan is no traitor."

"No," Moth agreed.

"Prisoner," the bear said. "Slave."

"The Lady did so," Ahjvar said. He could hardly find his voice. Ailan, sitting chin on his knees a little apart from them all, but where he could watch Ahjvar, frowned at that.

"The dead wizards? That was necromancy."

"But nonetheless." It was Gurhan who spoke. The god of this hill, gnarled, worm-holed stone, dwarf held in the feet of the Pillars of the Sky yet more ancient than any of their peaks. He was sole god of Marakand now, and with the devils and Ahjvar in their counsels. A committee, perhaps, preparing for war, in parallel with the senate and the wardens. Out of nowhere he was there among them, standing beside Ahjvar, looking down. His face varied. Malagru hillman, today, long brown hair knotted up in looped braids, pale skin, grey eyes. A city caftan, though, green as the cedars, grey as the stone. He settled down to sit there, put a hand on his shoulder. Ahjvar would have flinched from a human touch. Gurhan's hand was only a steadying warmth.

"Look for a collar," Mikki said.

"Speak with him, if you have the chance," Moth said. "Call yourself an ambassador of the city. Even Sien-Shava may respect that, once or twice."

"See him," the god said. "Look into the Blackdog with all that is in you. Weigh what is in him. Then we'll know. Then we can do, what we might do."

"Just don't surprise him," the demon said. "He doesn't deal with being startled any better than you claim you do. He bit me once." He rubbed his shoulder against a tree-trunk.

Moth snickered.

"Laugh, princess. He's got bloody sharp teeth." But Mikki was laughing.

"He is of Marakand," Gurhan said. "He may never have called himself one of my folk, but he fought for us and bled for us and very nearly died for us. He lived here; his descendants live here yet. I don't care that he is a devil. I find—I do not much care what kind someone's soul is. He is a good person, Holla-Sayan, and this is his home as much as any place, and I am his god, even if he does not choose to call me so. One of his gods, perhaps. I have the right, and the duty, to claim him. I do. For what strength that may give, whatever you might do."

"We can't do anything, yet." Moth sighed and rubbed her face. "I can't spare anything from your defence, god of this land. If I look away—Sien-Shava is waiting."

"Which may be why he's taken the Blackdog," Mikki said. "He lost one hostage, so he's seized another."

"But Holla-Sayan walks free. There's something more."

"Ahjvar?" Gurhan spoke.

Ahjvar looked at the god.

"Holla-Sayan is my son of this city, my adopted son of this city . . . You know there is more than wizardry in you. If he is lost—please—if you, if the two of you, if Nabban can find the way—make him a road back."

Dipped his head in a bow. "My lord," in his own tongue. Gurhan was not that, but he was lord of this hill.

Ailan was so tired he thought he might be falling asleep, only dreaming he was walking, trying and failing to move cat-silent, to be nothing but a flowing shadow. Trying to be what Ahjvar was, and, failing that, to be someone he wouldn't despise.

Missed his footing in the dark. Missed the ground altogether, a sudden drop he hadn't seen Ahjvar descend and he pitched forward, jolting fully awake even as the other man reached back and grabbed him, thrusting him upright, not letting go till he'd found his balance.

Somewhere water was burbling, but he hadn't fallen into it.

"Dark," Ailan said, stupidly, as if Ahjvar might not have noticed. Angry at himself. Clumsy. Useless. The moon had set.

"You need to rest?"

"No." He wanted to fold up to the ground, wrapped in his warm new coat, and wait for the waves of exhaustion to roll over his head and bring the safe blackness of sleep.

Ahjvar sighed. Frustrated, probably. Ailan knew he should have gotten some sleep while he was left behind by the pool, but he'd been too frightened, his mind gnawing the bones of fear over and over till he was near whimpering with it—what if Ahjvar didn't come back, what if they caught him, killed him, tortured him so he told them where to find Ailan, what if he simply decided never to come back . . .

"Lie down," Ahjvar said, and pushed him down when he just stood stupidly, words not connecting with anything. "Sun'll be rising in an hour or so. Get a little rest. We'll be climbing, come daylight. I need you awake then, not groggy as a drunk."

"Sorry."

"Don't. You haven't done anything wrong. I forget things, is all."

"Like what?" Ailan asked blearily. The ground was stony. A hollow. Out of the wind. If Ahjvar had forgotten the way back they would wander forever in the timeless mountains, like in a grandmother-tale, and come out when the wars were all over and all the folk of the land were dead.

"I forget that you can't see in the dark. That you're only human."

"I know what you are," Ailan said, which he hadn't meant to. He coiled up, head on his arm. Stones dug into him and he didn't care, hardly felt them. "I go to plays, you know. They come to the cities from Nabban, sometimes. The acting troupes. They play in the guild-courts."

"Yeah?"

"You're not just a priest. You did tell me that you're his. I know what that means. The man who gave himself to the god of Nabban—he's a foreign king who came back from the dead. The actor playing him wears a black mask, like a ghost, but with gold. Not white and black like the gods or red like live people. Black because he died once, died over and over, there's one play says, after the false empress turns into the devil and—"

"All right, never mind."

"—and gold because he's holy, like the god. He comes from the shadows with a sword, and there's a flash of light and the drums sound like thunder. Just when you think all's lost, you know." And he travelled, sometimes, with one of the seven, tamed to Nabban's service, at his side. Scholar Daro Jang, hah. The ambassador bowed as if she were the empress herself. Well, she had been. Twice. But she had obeyed when Ahjvar summoned her, so that was all right. Though he wasn't sure he liked the way she looked at him sometimes. As if he were in himself a joke he didn't see. "I knew you'd come back, when you left me there. I did. I just—I was afraid you wouldn't."

"Not going to leave a fool from the city lost in the mountains while I'm still breathing."

"They call you *Rihswera*, in the ambassador's house. Like in the plays. As if it's your Nabbani name. It isn't. I know what it means, *rihswera*."

"What, then?"

"It's the warrior who stands with the king or the queen. Their sword and shield. It's country-folk talk, from old tales. Tribal. Praitannec." That was Ahjvar's name for what he spoke, what he tried to teach Ailan, those stray words in Taren that didn't always follow the patterns, that made folk from imperial Nabban mock that they called themselves Nabbani at all. Whole lines of them, in the songs his mother had sung. "It's not a Nabbani word at all."

"Thought you didn't speak any Imperial."

"I have some. From the plays. I know whole poems. But *rihswera* was in the songs my mother sang. She used to sing. Someone broke her lute. And her hands. She didn't sing after that. Her fingers were all crooked." He was falling asleep. Thought Ahjvar said something, muttered, angry. Began to struggle awake in case it was at him. Babbling again like a fool. But the man was silent, sitting by him, and maybe there was a hand resting on his head, or maybe he was only dreaming.

The young man was asleep. He was going to break him, dragging him along so relentless, but they had to get themselves lost in the mountains, hidden from Jochiz, from whatever he might send hunting them. The Blackdog, if he hadn't died of whatever struck him down.

That worried Ahjvar still.

Didn't think he could have done anything to bring the Blackdog down so dramatically. He was a devil, Moth said, one forgotten by the tales. Didn't think even Ghu could have.

Something sidelong. Something . . .

Ailan mumbled in his dreams.

"Sleep yet," he told him. "I'm watching." Under Ahjvar's hand, he was still.

Ahjvar wondered what Hyllanim had been like, who he'd grown into, other than the cursed king of the songs. He'd only known the infant, never the boy, the unhappy man whose children had wasted the *duina* in their feuding. A solemn baby, as babies went. Ahjvar hadn't taken much interest in a brother so much younger. Had taken him up on a horse once. That had made the toddler crow happily. He'd been happy too. They'd only gone out around the walls of the *dinaz* and back by the goddess's spring. Remembered feeling, then, how small a thing a child was, how warm and alive and easy to delight. How someday he'd have a son, a daughter, and take them up in his arms . . . not even glancing sideways, very deliberately not even glancing sideways, at the thought, the shadow clinging to his heels, that Hyllanim wasn't his brother for all he was his stepmother's child, and *someday* was not the future.

Mistrust every damned distracting thought. He couldn't tell what was stirring them up.

He reached—listening, smelling, feeling the dying night . . . Nothing. Put it from his mind.

And whatever he had done to the Blackdog, it was done. If the shape-shifter were traitor, better he were dead, and if not—better to be dead than a soul enslaved, with one's memory, will, self all ripped away, if there was no road to freedom.

Be stone. Be stillness. Be stone and shadow and moonlight, even to a devil's searching. It wasn't wizardry he worked. It was . . . another heart, another hand, resting on his own. Another breath, that should never have reached to this far and alien land, and yet breathed through him.

He wished he were home, and the wish was warm against him, touch of knotted cords binding shells and acorns about his neck.

CHAPTER IV

. . . early spring, a day or so before the full moon

The prisoner had not tried to free himself, through struggle or persuasion. He had been on his knees, chained to the wall since he was brought here. Praying, ignoring Yeh-Lin as she sat watching him, waiting for Ulfhild to arrive. A priest of the fifth circle, a knight. One who had striven hard to attain rank in his faith, who had served wittingly and willingly; who had not come so far on the road from the west of the world without committing what any god would call sin, killing, knowingly, to seize what was not his, killing in the service of one who slew gods.

Deserving of a swift death, and condemned thereafter to a very long road of atonement, until knowledge of himself should make him finally fit for the presence of the Old Great Gods. Except that the faithful of the All-Holy were spared that penitential, revelatory, and cleansing journey. Snatched away—either to be with the Old Great Gods in that instant, by the grace of their emissary, the nameless god of the west made incarnate in the All-Holy, or held safe in his bosom, to be released into the presence of the Gods when their emissary should return to them. Their doctrine was unclear on some details.

"Be silent," Yeh-Lin said. She spoke Tiypurian. The priest, on his knees, ducked his head a little lower and continued his mutter of prayers. She struck him, a backhanded blow to the cheek, and seized his arm.

She had stripped him of his armour when she brought him here.

She and Nikeh had captured him as he led a patrol afoot into the hills, seeking to come around the southern tower and the end of the Western Wall. Easier than she had expected. That doomed dozen men had gotten themselves what a Malagru shepherd would call cragfast, and the hillfolk who had accompanied Scholar Jang had picked them off as if they were shooting at ripe mangos hanging from a bough, until Yeh-Lin and Nikeh, creeping near under cover of a simple working, had seized their commander before he could fling himself off the ledge.

No need to take him to the Warden, Scholar Jang had said. He was wanted for questioning in the city.

No need either to say by whom. And she had bade Nikeh stay at the south-end tower of the wall with a friend of hers stationed there. This was no business for an apprentice scholar, even one who had lived all her life as if she trained to be Wind in the Reeds, the spies and agents of the empire.

Yeh-Lin pulled the sleeve back from the man's wrist. The tattoo of the cult was a round-cornered rectangle enclosing a swirl of symbols. It was not unlike the badge of ownership that might indicate a clan's property, or be found on their banners, or a potter's or painter's stamp. Or the brands that had once marked a person a slave, she supposed. She wondered, even, if that was what had given Jochiz the idea, during his meddling in Nabban. This was not the searing of an iron but ink, though not ink only.

"You're tattooed," she said, "with the All-Holy's blood. Do they tell you that, your priests, when they mark you for the first time?"

She knew they did. The man sneered.

"The All-Holy binds his own in one blood, one fellowship. We are all brothers and sisters."

"Such a vast reserve of blood, he must have," she reflected, tracing the border with a fingernail. Not, alas, an empress's, carefully filed and lacquered. A trifle nicked, jagged at a corner. Blackened beneath. One could not expect to go clambering up cliffs like a monkey and keep immaculate.

The man shivered. She smiled and turned her attention to the pattern within. The script was both jagged and flowing. Nothing that he, nor any scholar even of the library up on the knees of Gurhan's hill, could read. The pattern expanded outward, smaller satellite designs, but those were only to denote his rise through the circles. There was no power in them.

"Your All-Holy must spend his life opening his veins, to accommodate all his many converts." She pressed a little, marking him. His breath caught. It seemed some small corner of his mind might be enjoying that.

And Ulfhild was there, slinking like a grey wolf down the stairs. Yeh-Lin had not felt her approaching through the Suburb, or over it. Stealthy.

She came to stand by Yeh-Lin. She looked . . . somewhat disapproving. Yeh-Lin smiled warmly at her, and turned back to the prisoner.

"Or," she suggested, "perhaps his blood is so holy that a few precious drops are enough for the vast jars of ink you must go through?"

Unfortunately, that seemed to be the case.

"Can we get on?" Ulfhild asked, speaking harsh Northron. "I mislike being so far from the god."

Yes, there was an abstracted air about her, a sleepwalking slowness. Even here, in this cellar beneath the burnt shell of the red priests' mission-house—boarded up by order of the Warden of the Suburb after the arson that had followed its inhabitants' flight—Ulfhild maintained a watch over Marakand's last god and a shield against Sien-Shava Jochiz. Set runes, and songs, and kept them live and thrumming with power like the notes of a harp still ringing. If she listened, Yeh-Lin might almost hear.

"The bridge and the road," Yeh-Lin said, which was the meaning of the signs, what was not mere ornamentation. "Bridge or gate. Signifying, I suppose, that he is the bridge over which their road must cross."

"I don't much care at this point," said Ulfhild. She had taken the long dagger from her belt in her hand and was turning it restlessly. Tapping the disc-shaped pommel on her thigh, flipping it, catching it by the point, tossing it, hilt again, tap, flip, catch, toss—

"Stop that." Yeh-Lin snatched it from the air. "You're as fidgety as the dead king."

Ulfhild plucked it back. "He's one of the few humans I've met I can really understand."

"You would say so. Given he's mad. He and his sweet god together."

"They've ensnared you."

"Yes, well. You don't need to mock me for it. At least I've found something to believe in."

"And that would be?"

"Hope, dear heart. The hope that one single being, one action at a time, can make things better."

"I've only ever made things worse."

"Black bile."

"What?"

"Oh, nothing. A stray remark. The dead king would understand. No, I knew Ivah well. You set her feet on a road once. A few words. A mother's talking-to, she told me, or at least an elder sister's. And that road led her to her god, and that—all Nabban, and lands that are no longer Nabban's, are the better for it."

"Says Yeh-Lin the conquerer. Those were your conquests they gave away, Ghu and Empress Ivah between them."

"Why does no one ever believe I've reformed?" Yeh-Lin sighed, as theatrically as the dead king's acolyte Ailan could manage when he was feeling hard done by. Nikeh had been tasked over the winter with improving his very haphazard literacy in the simplest Nabbani syllabic script, which was shared between Tarens and empire. Neither young person was enjoying it.

"But as you say." She resumed speaking in Tiypurian. "Is there anything we actually need to learn from this devil-worshipping killer of children?"

"I've never harmed a child!" the knight protested, finally trying to jerk his arm from her grasp. She gripped it tight as the manacle on his other wrist by which he was chained to the wall. Her nail, that jagged corner, cut red lines on his wrist, outside of the black border of his initiate's tattoo, just touching it. He winced, but then held proudly still.

Thinking she tormented him so pettily for her pleasure. "You call me devil-worshipper, when your own gods consort openly with the seven? It's no secret Vartu Kingsbane has fled to your city after the All-Holy defeated her at the Kinsai'av."

Four characters, she scratched into him. Court Nabbani, the complex symbols only a few scholars and poets still studied.

Ulfhild, playing with her dagger again, cut herself. Holding the prisoner's gaze, being certain he saw. Dipped a finger in the welling blood and traced runes at the corners between Yeh-Lin's characters. They were not the ordinary ones of Northron inscriptions or spell-casting. He whimpered. Seemed more repulsed and fearful of that than of Yeh-Lin's cutting of his own skin.

"Are we ready?" Yeh-Lin asked.

"Ya." Ulfhild stepped over behind the man, seized him by the hair, and cut his throat.

"Cold hells!" Yeh-Lin darted aside from the spewing blood. Further outrage at the lack of warning had to wait. He was still there for a moment, a breath, a roiling thing of confusion. So swift had been the execution he had hardly felt the pain grow, hardly had time to understand.

Ulfhild let him fall and stooped after him, dropping her dagger. Scooped red blood from the puddling flagstones. She knelt there and Yeh-Lin had perforce to kneel across from her, knees in the spreading pool. Her own hands under Ulfhild's, cradling them. The blood leaked, as anyone who had ever scooped up water in their hands to drink would know it must. She bowed her head—thank common sense she wore her hair short and grey as Scholar Jang and had not changed herself for this, even to annoy Ulfhild, who thought her unduly frivolous and always had. Breathed on the cupped blood, and her breath was mist, smoking over river-water.

Island, long and narrow, dividing a river. Broken pillars. Cypresses towering dark. Small roofs, peaked or barrel-vaulted, fallen. Tombs, they were, and ancient. Overgrown. Vines, even trees, thick and ancient, rooted on what remained. Ridge of stone, and stone terraces, supporting more broken pillars, one arch still standing. Foundations, crumbled. Dark water swirling past.

A town, white walled, red roofed, south over the water. Glimpsed, forgotten. Unimportant.

They rushed, dove like swallows into the darkness of a barn. Now they were in a narrow place, the walls brick, the low roof vaulted. Cold. Damp. Water pooled on the floor. They were one—an unnerving brief awareness, she and Ulfhild Vartu, uneasy sharing of soulspace. Pain, a heavy weight of it. Grief. For what? The Northron had her beloved *ver-rbjarn* back from Sien-Shava's torments—

Bones. A chamber of bones, stacked in niches where once shrouded bodies might have lain, jumbled on the puddled floor. Painted walls, bubbled with damp, flaking . . .

The walls were bright and fresh, not new but often renewed. Lamplight. No bones on the floor, only the dead decently laid out. Singing. Westron, the ear said, but not one of the languages she knew. Women's voices. Women with shaven heads, white-robed. Girls preceded them with lanterns. The grown women carried between them a byre, a linen-wrapped figure on it. Those following sang. Prayers. *Grandmother Tiy*, she heard. They passed and faded. Memory of this place, that had seeped into the stone. Then—not lamplight. These latter days of scattered bones. They rushed, flying, fleeting, themselves wrapped around the soul of the dead knight, which struggled, now. Not against them. He hardly knew their presence, faint shadow-souls trailing his flight. No, he struggled to be free of this current, this—this chain, that pulled and dragged and drew him against all the weight of the Heavens, the opening of the road. Wrong, wrong, wrong, and he fought as a caged thing fights, battering, breaking himself, mad. Futile. She would have reached, have torn him away, let him fly blessed and free to the road that reached for him and his long journey, but Ulfhild pulled her back, prevented that mercy.

Not the purpose for which they had taken him. Not mercy.

A cavern. Part of these catacombs? She had not seen. The link between themselves and the captive soul began to fray. Cavern. Soft glow of light, not the seeing of vision, a light that was truly in that place. Pearly, rose-tinged. Moonglow.

Stone. Teeth, fangs. Not the dripping spears and daggers of slow water's work. A crust of crystal. A pool of water beneath and curving from it, walls, meeting overhead, narrowing further away.

An egg. They were within an egg lined with jagged crystal. A cavern. She wrenched around, vision spinning dizzily. Black fissure, narrow, vertical.

Egg, womb of crystal.

And what might gestate there, and why such images in the mind, why such thoughts, such fear—

Within the water, crystals reflecting, crystals breaking the light they themselves cast. A stillness, there in the pool's centre. A darkness. A black stone. A shivering. There was a hollow carved in the centre of it, a basin. The liquid surface rippled. Not water. Blood. Black, in this monochrome place all pale rose and black and pearl-white glow. She did not need to strain to see it crimson, to touch, to feel the viscous, living touch, to taste or smell. It was blood, his heart's blood, living here, and the soul of the knight they had executed—even her god would not say murdered, would he, he who had once cried, no quarter, no mercy, for those who torture children—was drawn inexorably to it, though that Westron knight fought with all that was left in him, to answer the call and the demanding pull of the road, the summons of the Old Great Gods his faith had denied to him.

There was nothing that eyes might see, but the mind made a picture. A butterfly lands at the edge of a puddled rut in the road, uncoils its proboscis to drink. The water rises, a living thing, and engulfs it. But this butterfly landed fluttering wildly, beating its frail wings to pieces.

It did no good. The dark liquid swallowed it. The blood pulled, as if it were a well and she some trickle of water, rolling down its stones.

No. Ulfhild hurled them away while Yeh-Lin still strove to linger, fascinated. If she let it pull, let it take her too, just a little way—in that moment she had—not seen. Felt. Felt the vastness, the weight, the mass of what was there, growing, within that egg, that womb of crystal—

The glorious, terrible strength of it.

Not salt. Not quartz. Souls, made stone. Generations of them, bound in blood, and he had left his heart's blood there and walked half-dead, a necromancy of his own, sustaining himself—

What were souls, in the end, but the sparks that made the life of the world—

They were in the cellar of the burned mission-house, kneeling in a puddle of sticking, stinking, cooling blood.

"Old Great Gods," Yeh-Lin said. She still clasped Ulfhild by the hands. "Old Great Gods, Old Great Gods be merciful to us all. Vartu, did you see—did you taste the air of that place, that—did you *see?*"

"He steals their souls and seals them in stone." Vartu—they must be Vartu and Dotemon now, this was no human matter, though humans were very much the matter of it—Vartu shook her head. "I already suspected as much. Though not that he could have bound so many. To what end?"

And gods, Dotemon said. *He devours gods. He swallows them, in the ritual by which he destroys them. My spies have witnessed. The weight of them in the world is gone from their land. No self, no one and another. Dissolved into his blood, held in crystal, not souls but* soul. *Soul of the earth, growing and growing, as water in a cistern, drop by drop—*

Vartu agreed. *His own blood, binding them.*

Trust the Northron to focus on the blood-magic of it. And Northron magic was worked with one's own blood, most often.

Sien-Mor, Sien-Shava—they had gone north following the rumours of a new folk come over the sea, a new magic, worked in runes and blood. Admit it, so had she. Wandering, angry and outcast. Old bones aching in the bitter winter.

Not binding them, Dotemon said. *Binding it.*

He will make himself a god. In the end, when he has gathered enough souls—when they are such a weight and power in the world—he will take them into himself and become a god of this world.

Or *the* god of this world? she wondered. Oh, my horseboy, to be swallowed by that, and your bright burning king. And my lady of the baobab in her grace and patience and—every innocent babe and old man marked with his blood, witting or unwitting of what it might mean.

"I will go," she said aloud.

"We."

"No. You have work here. Gurhan still to preserve. And there is your Mikki. And—I am not a fool, Ulfhild Vartu. You never trusted Jochiz and you always loathed Sien-Shava. I do not think for a moment that you ever intended to serve out some penance here, guarding the god of Marakand until all is lost and Jochiz uses your own sword to cut the head from your neck. You are not defeated, and you are not through. I will go."

Ulfhild Vartu was still. Then got to her feet and bowed, very Nabbani in manner. "What shall I tell your apprentice, Yeh-Lin Dotemon?"

"Tell her I've gone where I must in my god's service, and she must stand tall and find her own road now. Tell her—tell her she has been a daughter to me, and she is—oh hells, tell the girl I love her and she must take care in conjugating 'to know' in the poetic form, because it does not conjugate like 'to understand' no matter how similar they seem in their root, if ever she would write good Nabbani prose. There. And tell the dead king, tell Ahjvar, to give my love to his beautiful shield-bearer, and kiss him, which I have never yet done, much as I have wanted to."

"I have no intention of kissing either of them for you."

"Not you, fool Northron. Though—"

"No." But Ulfhild's grin escaped her. One forgot, the woman had dimples when she smiled.

Yeh-Lin laughed aloud and hugged her, hard, as if they were children and sisters.

"Oh, Gods and devils and cold hells all forgive us, Vartu. We have had a strange road of it. Come, leave that Westron's body to rot. I suppose there'll be company enough for it soon enough. The Western Wall can't hold whatever you do and it won't be long. Jochiz is not prepared for a siege, whatever pretence of it Dimas has been making thus far. Come see me off."

She strode to the stairs, blood drying on the knees of her leggings. She dusted it away, and from her hands, her immaculate short nails. Shrugged her shoulders, settling her armour, the long coat of black lacquered scales and blue cord fastenings which she had not been wearing when she came into this cellar. Hair streaming back, no grey in it.

Ulfhild Vartu, behind her, sketched a rune. Yeh-Lin felt the shape of it. A simple one. Fire.

Oh well, Northrons must have their little excitements.

The ruins of the mission-house were burning bright over them even before they reached the top of the stairs.

"Perhaps you overdid it?"

"Never." Ulfhild gave her a shove. She jumped down into the street, through the boarded-up window by which, dragging her captive, she had prised her way in. A crowd was already gathering, a desultory effort being made to form a bucket-chain. No great urgency. There was little left to burn inside the mud-brick walls, and the neighbouring houses had lane-ways between.

No one noticed them walk away. Yeh-Lin turned up the first empty lane they came to, caught a window-ledge, pulled herself up, caught and swung to a screened gallery, smashing the screen in the process. And from the railing there to the flat roof. The household below slept. Ulfhild landed beside her in a flutter of feathers.

"Show-off."

"Says you."

Yeh-Lin smirked and drew her sword. Bowed solemnly, seriously. "Wish me luck, King's Sword."

"Luck, and fair winds, and all good fortune, Empress of Nabban. For all our sakes. I'll buy you a drink when you come to Marakand again."

"You'll buy me a whole jar, and it will be the best twelve-herb white-spirit, too, not the thin wine of these hills."

She settled her helmet on her head, the long ribbons, Nabban's sky blue, mingling with her unbound hair as she turned, drawing the circle in the air with her sword's point, its own scarlet ribbons and blue floating, and then began the dance.

Yeh-Lin called the winds, and the winds answered.

CHAPTER V

. . . early spring, the night after the full moon

C loud was gathering on the mountains, threatening to hide the stars and the moon, only a day past its full, all the light Nikeh needed. She could pass as Westron—which she was—and as an initiate or even a priest. She knew the prayers of the lower circles. Languages, history, arithmetic, the nature of plants and the movements of the stars, Teacher had taught her these things and many more. Sword and knife and bow . . . All that, given to her. She had wanted only to grow in knowledge and in skill, to become what her Teacher was. But there was no wizardry in her.

And Teacher had abandoned her, once she had gone to take the prisoner to the city, to the wardens or whoever had had need of him. Yesterday a letter had come, carried by a messenger of the Nabbani ambassador's house but penned by the Northron wizard who guarded the god, an unfamiliar hand. It made it far more final, somehow, to hear Teacher's words—Tiypurian words and script, which she was surprised the Northron knew, save the joke about grammar, which was in Nabbani syllabics and the ancient characters at the centre of the joke. It was proof the Northron, who looked a shabby mercenary, was a scholar of surprising knowledge, and proof moreover that the words in the letter really were Teacher's own. Hateful though they were to read.

She was loved. She was never to forget that.

She would rather have had not the words, but a summons to join Teacher wherever it was she went.

But that, like so much else, was apparently now beyond wishing for. No one even knew where or when Scholar Jang had gone.

It did make this night's work easier. She felt guilty, to be grateful for that. Nikeh's intention had formed when first they learned the name of the general commanding the desert army. Dimas, Prince Dimas. Lord of Emrastepse, wherever in the cold hells that might be, the Warden of the Western Wall had said.

"On the coast," had been her answer, from her place at Teacher's side, startling him. He had not truly meant a question. "A little place of no account. You would call it a village."

There had been something hot and hard growing within her chest. A hunger that had been in her nearly all her life, unfolding like a chick from the egg. In Marakand, all the long years—not so many at that—it had stirred, wanting to live, and she had kept it balled up tight. Not yet, she had told it. Not now. Not safe. Marakand was a city of law and of scholar-wizards, and even strangers who were not citizens could rely on the protection of the street-guards, the justice of the magistrates, the services of diviners of the ward-courts to seek out their murderers.

She never confessed this desire to Teacher. Nor to her friend, her best and only comrade her own age since the days when Teacher had been tutor to the son and daughter of a queen in the north.

Lia Dur had been a street-guard, a patrol-first. They had met when Nikeh was out wandering long after the last curfew-bell had rung, which should have cost her a fine, but she was the apprentice of Scholar Daro Jang and Lia had a fascination with travellers and travellers' tales. Which had grown into a fascination with Nikeh, or a friendship, or—it was hard to know how to be herself. She had been other people so long. Teacher's little girl, Teacher's apprentice . . . but a new person every time Teacher changed her own name. She was always Nikeh, her own name, but who, underneath, was that?

Someone who walked the streets of Marakand at night, stalking, lying in wait, for the priests she had never killed.

But now they were at war, and the red priests who had lived in the mission-house in the Suburb and strutted the city streets in arrogance, enemies and spies under the shield of the law and the god they plotted to destroy, had fled before they could be arrested, west into the arms of Prince Dimas's advancing army.

Priests of the third circle. Mere teachers.

They no longer interested her.

And Lia Dur, a soldier now, had listened to one more of Nikeh's traveller's tales, and had said, not, "You can't," or "Don't," or "The captains of the towers and the Warden of the Wall have to decide that sort of thing," and most of all not, "Your mistress won't allow it." She had said, "I'll do what I can."

The camp seemed almost deserted, but it was only sleeping. Few fires. Fuel was precious, rationed, their spies said, like grain, which followed the Westron army in camel-caravans from the Western Grass. The patrols through the laneways carried mutton-fat lanterns, dim yellow lights drifting in orderly lines, few and far between, easy to spot. People crowded together for warmth under makeshift tents. A blanket was almost worth killing for in this place, but, Nikeh guessed, there were more to go around than there had been. Winter on the caravan road had winnowed the folk.

Too many, still.

Like any town, the camp had its better neighbourhoods. Proper tents where she passed now, orderly. The priests of rank, the diviners and knights, those who could command the use of the camels of the baggage train, those who hadn't shivered with cold in the desert winter and watched their friends lose fingers and toes to it, or cough their lives away. Not a neighbourhood where a mere fourth-circle priestess and a first-circle convert, a ragged camel-driver of the baggage train, should have any business. Heads down, no haste. Istva bumped her shoulder and they turned into a narrower way. Less open, darker . . . no one had seen them. They moved slowly, wary of unexpected obstacles, guy-ropes and the like, came out behind a guarded tent, larger, grander than the rest. From the wall it could be identified by the pale banner drooping from the peak, but the camp was out of range of the trebuchets on the tower platforms.

Nikeh sank down to one knee, waiting, watching. No need for speech. She felt Istva's tension as he crouched beside her. Shivering. She didn't want him here, didn't need a guide any farther. No getting rid of him, though.

Four sentries guarded the sleep of Dimas. False prince, risen to his false god's esteem through being merely the foremost of those who licked the All-Holy's boots, or perhaps his backside.

She spent too much time with street-guards. Their vulgarity was contagious.

Four sentries. Two at the front, Istva had said, by the door, where torches burned against the night. One at each back corner.

Istva was trembling. Not fear, she thought. A hunting dog, eager to be unleashed. She herself, as well. Not fear. The guards were only an obstacle to be gotten past, as the priestess who had provided her robe had been. A woman brought by Istva into the dark beyond the watch-fires with the tale of a forager dying of a Marakander patrol's arrow, desperate for a final blessing.

The robe was a little sticky against her back, but in the dark the stain wouldn't show.

She crawled, keeping low. Didn't waste time checking on Istva. If he failed to follow, if he betrayed her now—

The sentry to the left was hers. She rose up behind him, hand over his mouth, knife slicing across his throat, all her strength in drawing it back. He struggled, briefly. Weakly. She let him down, looked, then, for Istva. Shadowy movement, that was all, at the far corner. No sound beyond a faint scuffling. Hard even to judge the direction of movement, but she thought someone moved towards her, so she went to meet him. Knife ready. But it was Istva. Good.

How long till the bodies were noticed?

Long enough, Nikeh most devoutly hoped and prayed, though her goddess was long dead.

She crouched, pulling the tent wall taut by its lower edge. Canvas, not leather, and big enough to house a family or two. Dimas wouldn't be alone, but Istva had thought there might be a clerk and a serving-man, and perhaps a couple of child message-runners.

Nikeh wiped her hand on the grass, drew the heavier knife from her boot and began slicing. Not so easy as she had hoped; it took some sawing, made a faint sound. The handle grew slick with sweat. Her boots were a flaw in her disguise; no mere fourth-circle priestess would have such good boots, or would have managed to keep them, crossing the desert after Serakallash, when the camps by night became a brutal struggle for food, for fuel, for another blanket or robe to ward off winter's bite. A nightmare, Istva had said. He didn't talk of how he had survived. Murders were done. Dimas had let it happen. Only the strong would come to Marakand, he had proclaimed. The All-Holy disdained the weak. They could not serve.

"Hurry," Istva muttered at her shoulder.

Shut up, she would have said, but enough cloth had parted and she was done. She returned that knife to its sheath, picked up the other again, long and sharp as she could make it. She slipped through the slit she had made.

Istva followed, so close she felt his breath on her neck. That wasn't what they agreed. He was to stay outside and keep watch. He had the dead sentry's short-sword in his hand and how did he think he was going to explain that? She scowled at him to say this was her affair now, leave her to it.

Greedy of her, to want this work for her own alone. Istva's wife was dead, his children taken into some work-camp where they were being taught to worship the All-Holy as the emissary of the Old Great Gods, if they even lived at all. Istva was Westgrasslander, and his conversion only words of his mouth, not his heart. It had been that or burning, for himself and his children too.

A night-lamp burned, small, weak flame. That was a blessing Nikeh hadn't counted on. A curtain divided the tent and they were in the larger half of it, the back. Proper bedstead and a man sleeping there, alone.

Dimas was devout, too devout to keep lovers, no room in his heart for a wife. All for the All-Holy. Dim dark shapes that were chests containing what might be of interest to the wardens of the wall and the city—records, if they kept such, plans, treasury—but she wasn't here to fetch and carry. Two low cots—they had come in at the foot of one. Two people in each. Servants. Soldiers. Whatever. She didn't much care. Folk of the general's service close to hand, anyway, and the rest, more lowly, beyond the curtain in the outer room. Nikeh rose to her feet, crossed to the bed, avoiding the little table with the lamp and a thick book. Devotions? It lay open on its spine.

Dimas lay likewise sprawled on his back, arms flung wide like a baby. Such a young man. Did he feel the weight of all the deaths he carried? Not only those he had commanded in the conquest of the south of the Western Grass and the desert town of Serakallash, but all those of his own following dead in the desert, hunger and sickness and cold and thirst, and the murders in the night, when love, friendship, kinship had become worth less than a piece of a blanket or a scraping of porridge.

Probably not. It was all as the Old Great Gods of his imagination decreed, the All-Holy's will.

He slept beneath a good heavy quilt, flung half off, though the night was chill with lingering winter. Nikeh dragged a fold of it up over the prince's face, pressing down to be sure of silence, kneeling over him, driving her slender knife in deep, finding its home.

"Emrastepse remembers," she hissed. Dimas jerked only the once, dead before he could twist his head away, bring an arm up to grapple. She wished she could have seen his eyes as he died.

Nikeh was off him before the welling blood could soak through. None of the other sleepers stirred, no guard called out from the other side of the canvas or the entrance.

She wiped her knife clean, wondering whether the devil knew his folk, as the true Old Great Gods knew and valued every soul they called home to their embrace, or if those tattooed for the cult were only souls, a nameless tally.

A cry, then. A man sat up on one of the cots. Istva spun on his heel and slashed as if he carried a sabre, but the blade did the job. The man fell back with a cry. Istva and Nikeh shoved one another out their rip as more cries rose.

"Get rid of the sword," she gasped as they ran.

"No!"

"Get rid of it—we're a priestess and a bondman, we shouldn't have a sword."

"Your hands are bloody."

They were. She had thought them clean.

A shout—sentries behind, giving chase. Cries, people in other tents. Little light, and the moon failing them, the cloud that had been thickening earlier in the night covering the stars now, the mountains. Istva whirled around and she should have run, she should have left him, but she wheeled back to him and wished she had the sword she had left in the fort. Hard to hide it under a priest's robe.

A soldier almost upon them—he didn't ask questions. He came sword first, a swift lunge, and Istva still fought as if he had something longer with a good edge to it, and he didn't seem any too skilled regardless.

"Give me the sword," she said, but he didn't hear, or he still thought her the clerk she had seemed when they first met, scouts bringing him in, another captured enemy forager who might be turned to their service. Eager to offer himself, it turned out. He had been foraging for fuel high on the steep sides of the valley where it narrowed to the pass. More than a few Westgrasslander converts had come into Marakander hands that way; very few had been willing to go back. The Westrons realized their mistake and began sending soldiers to guard them. It gave the slingers of the Malagru hillfolk who patrolled the mountainsides something to do.

Now the Westrons did not venture up from the valley bottom at all.

Istva was no sword-fighter. Better at cutting throats. Farmer, Nikeh decided. She watched her moment, dodged around and slashed low, knife in each hand now, and the soldier stumbled, his calf opened. Istva stabbed at last, struck armour, swore by some Westgrassland god and stabbed again at the man's face. That finished him. Kicked him between the legs for good measure. Nikeh shoved both filthy knives in the sash of the tunic beneath her robe and took the fallen man's sword, dragging Istva away.

More shouting behind them and Istva stumbled, lurching against her. She kept her hold on his arm, half dragging him. He lost his sword. There—corralled camels. Nikeh squirmed through the hurdles, tugged Istva awkwardly after her, crawling. He gave a yelp as something scraped him. Once they were in he didn't follow her among the furry mounds of the waking beasts. He just let himself down on the trampled ground amidst the dung and prickly leavings of fodder. Nikeh went back to him, grabbed him. "Come on."

"Hurts," he said, and it was more a gasp than a word. Bloody lips. Arrow in his back. Oh. It had broken off when she dragged him through the fence.

"Ah, Old Great Gods . . ."

Leave him. Run.

She felt for the wound. Middle of his back, just aside from his spine. His breath was making strange sounds now. Bubbling. Wheezing. She rolled him over on her lap.

"Istva—" Whispering. Horns were bleating an alarm. No one was paying this pen of camels any mind. Not yet. Soldiers mustering, but all the other folk too, the undisciplined, disordered rabble that was the bulk of the army, the devout who'd followed on the All-Holy's word. But there were diviners, too, and ambitious priests and priestesses of the seventh circle, the primates of the cult, who would be eager to prove themselves the prince's worthy successor, find the assassin, impose order. Present the All-Holy with a situation under control when he arrived, as rumour said he would any day now.

Istva seized her hand. "Run," he said. "Go, girl." Something more in his native Westgrasslander. Whimpering. Pain. A plea to his god, who might or might not be dead. Maybe not, if he was from the route of the southern march, but still, they were very far away. His god might as well be gone, for all the comfort he could give.

She seized Istva's left arm, turned it to the fading moonlight, pushed his sleeve back. Tattooed, first circle, of course he was, the price of his life, and he didn't know what it meant, none of them did.

"Istva," she said. "Listen, I have to—"

No time. His eyes were fixed on something beyond. But the breath yet bubbled in him, weak, his heart still labouring.

"The tattoo," she said. "I'm going to hurt you, I'm sorry."

Stupid. What greater pain could there be?

She took her fine knife, and pinching up the skin of the dark pattern on his wrist, sliced, sawing, as if she worked the skin of a rabbit free. "I'm sorry," she muttered. He moved weakly on her lap. "Old Great Gods, I'm sorry, Istva. I have to, to set you free."

He was still. He was dead. His wrist oozed and her fingers clutched a lump of skin. She hurled it away. Her gorge rose and she couldn't stop herself, but she managed to lean over and not defile him further, vomiting on the ground. That did it for the camels. Too much noise, too much strangeness, reek of blood and bile. One rose and bellowed, signal for them all to unfold, awkward and massive, threatening—she had travelled with camels when she was younger, the journey to Marakand, but she didn't understand them as she did horses. Looked like a threat. Bells about their necks clanging. Dimas's own baggage train, that's what these were. "Go to the Old Great Gods," she choked out, and the words tasted of acid and blood, which latter was her imagination. She rolled Istva off her lap and remembered what else was due, scooped a handful of dampish earth, stinking of camel, and flung it over him. "Go to the road and may your journey be short. The Old Great Gods wait for you with open arms."

She hoped they did. She hoped she had been in time.

She hoped he hadn't felt it, what she did. Hadn't hated her, in that one last breath of pain.

Camels scared her. They scared lots of people. Couldn't see a gate, but the corral was made of hurdles lashed together and she had two knives.

They surged out, bellowing, and one more small priestess among the now-scores of crowding, clamouring people, yelling of assassins, shrieking and fleeing camels . . . who noticed? And the night kept thickening.

She didn't run, except when everyone else did, and always humbly, at the back of the crowd. Let herself fall behind. Turned aside into squares where the camp still lay undisturbed.

The foot of the Western Wall was a deeper blackness in the dark, but torchlight marked its line, ancient work rebuilt in the days of the false Lady and repaired again in more recent years, barring the pass of Marakand. It was nearly dawn before Nikeh could find her way there. If the sun rose before she made it back, she would have to wait for nightfall, or very likely be filled with arrows, probably by her own side. She felt an absurd sense of safety just to be in the wall's shadow, though, when finally she made it so far. Smooth, vast blocks, like a ruin of Tiypur's imperial past. Broken stone below, and stubby bushes—Marakand had cleared all the brush and trees away in recent years, pulled down vines, built up the fallen lines of lesser walls and watchtowers that curved to the heights, the sides of the pass, relics of long-forgotten days of war with the Stone Desert tribes or the Great Grass invasions of the days of the seven devils. A little pomegranate was trying to come up from the roots here, buds showing tiny tags of pale leaf on last year's knee-high shoots. A dirty white rag was tied there, just a twist of cloth hardly noticeable. Enough to tell her where she was, a quarter mile from the southernmost watchtower.

She swallowed, tried to find some moisture in her mouth. Still tasted of acid, her throat sore with it. She whistled like a starling greeting the dawn and waited, realizing how weak, how shaken she felt.

She could feel his weight on her lap still.

It wasn't him she remembered, but her brother . . .

Whistled again. Oh Gods, if Lia could not hear . . . if Lia were not there . . . She might scale the heights, go around the wall, which was a barrier to massed horsemen out of the deserts and the Grass, not to those who could climb the mountain paths. Would she be able to persuade a patrol of hillfolk she was no enemy? She was Westron. Remembered what she wore and peeled off the priestess's robe, with its sticky, torn back—

she hardly remembered that deed, except the feeling of satisfaction, that indeed, it was easy to kill a priest, as she had always suspected. Nikeh bundled it up and buried it under some stones. She was about to whistle one last time when the knotted rope came whispering down.

Wiped her hands on the skirt of her Marakander tunic, took a deep breath. It looked a long way up, now. Started to climb. Hand over hand, foot upon foot, reach and jerk herself higher, push and catch. Sweating. Had to stop and simply cling. Hadn't been so bad going down, had it? Should have done as Lia wanted, gone by the steep sides of the riven pass as she had done on other nights, meeting Istva, but that would have cost her far more time. Just a shadow, still, but movement, above. Wake up, fool. Climb. Hand, hand, feet. A welcome face peered over the parapet, strong arms reached to help her haul herself up, and she tumbled onto Lia Dur's sandals. Shaking. Shivering so hard her teeth chattered together. Exhaustion from the climb, the sleepless night. Reaction.

"I did it," she said. "Dimas is dead."

"I knew," the Marakander said, hauling up the rope. "I could see the torches. I was afraid they'd taken you, though. I thought about throwing myself off the wall so I didn't have to tell Scholar Jang, when she comes back from whatever mysterious errand's taken her away."

"You didn't."

"I swear!" Lia offered her an arm up, pulled her into an embrace, squeezing her hard, which was not exactly comfortable, armoured as the other woman was. "A scout came in from the north," she said. "Word came just after you went down. The All-Holy's only a day's march away."

And that was an enemy against whom her knife would be no more use than a child's fantasies had ever been.

His children were long dead, and lost, their souls bereft of hope, beyond any salvation. They had gone to the road unblessed, unsigned, and the road was broken. There was no way to the Gods for them, only a slow, sad fading.

It made Philon ill, to think how many would knowingly condemn those they loved to such a horror. It made him ill, to know he had done so, and not even out of ignorance or blind prejudice, mindless adherence to the old ways and the empty worship of a long-dead goddess, but out of policy, to keep secret his own faith, so that he might continue to be a voice of quiet persuasion in his cousin's tower, counselling her against forbidding the missionaries when they came, She would not have listened to him, had he borne the tattoo—initiate, and then his secret rise to be a priest of the fourth circle. The priest who had first inducted him had counselled against it, promised him he could much better serve in secret, that the All-Holy had need of such strong faith as his to be secret in the lightless places, hidden till the time to burn bright had come. But his children's immortal souls had been the sacrifice. If he had known . . . No one could have foreseen, not the All-Holy himself. They had been meant to have been saved.

Why did he think of them now? Because Dimas had been, in some manner, like a son to him? A man he might have hoped his little one would grow into, strong in faith, in virtue, steadfast. A commander of men as his grandfather had been. Perhaps. The soul of the prince at least was safe in the embrace of the All-Holy, who was, in himself, the bridge, the true and only, to carry the souls of his faithful to the Old Great Gods, when the end of all things came.

Long ago Philon had sinned, betrayed his faith, but only in order to serve it. Killed a holy man at his princess's command so as to be later where he might do greater good. Save lives, Philon had thought. Win lives for the All-Holy, rather than deaths for dead gods. Better quick surrender, overrun, than slow dying holding their walls. Because who would not choose life given certainty of death? Too many, it had turned out. If the princess had surrendered the tower so soon as the gate of village was opened to her enemies, so many more would have lived. They would have been called upon to renounce their desperate and futile clinging to the hollow past, they would have acknowledged the All-Holy, even if, at first, only to save their lives . . . but they would have come to understand the truth, to find joy in their faith, in knowing themselves saved.

His children would have been saved. Should have been, even so. He had come to them too late, kept and questioned by the commander of the attack, who knew him faithful, and yet claimed doubts, mistrust, some trick or trap—until too late, he had come, and the house had been burned over them. The rubble was too much, stones and broken tile and crockery and charred timbers, ash, all filling the cellar. There were so many dead, and so many dying, defiant, damning themselves . . .

The body did not matter, once the soul was gone. He had not dug through the rubble for them. They were not among the living. It was enough.

His wife had survived the taking of the tower, gravely wounded, but died on the pyres, cursing him. He on his knees, weeping, cursing, begging her . . . So many chose death.

How could a man of the faith, as the Westgrasslander assassin must have been, turn his back on that, once having given himself? How could he not see, be so blind? Did he not understand the horror of a lost soul's slow decay? Did the nothingness that awaited not terrify? That assassin's body had been found, and he or his comrades had even cut away the symbol of the faith, as if to renounce it with his body as well as his heart. Such fanaticism, blind and deaf, when the All-Holy held out his hand to save.

It was consciousness of sin, of failure, that made Philon's thoughts walk such paths, brought again his children's faces, their very voices, to his ears, made him want to weep not for them but for all children yet living who were denied that salvation. It was not his duty to guard the prince's sleep. He was risen from being a mistrusted and closely watched advisor in matters related to the folk of the new-conquered town to master of Dimas's household and eventually, his counsellor, his confidant, his right hand. Almost, sometimes, he thought, a foster-father to the youth Dimas had been, and by his sacrifice an example of what faith should be.

"The sin was not yours," Primate Ambert said. Philon, clad only in his drawers, knelt at his feet, though he himself was, honour far above his due, of the lower step of the seventh circle, raised by the All-Holy's own decree after the crossing of the Karas range, before the armies divided.

His chest throbbed and he felt weak, as if he might faint, but he knelt for humility, not for weakness, and to abase himself for his failure. The wound, shallow but long, was a slash that began above one nipple and ended below the other; it was stitched and salved, bound and blessed. "You should not have slept so heavily, but it was not your duty to wake through the watches of the night, and if not for you we might not know even their number. What penance, though, for those who should have watched, and were deaf and blind?"

"They should atone with their lives," Philon said. Dimas was dead. What less could they offer? "He was among the best of us. Surely most beloved by the All-Holy. He brought all of us living—all of us who were blessed in our strength and the All-Holy's grace, across the Salt."

That had been a terrible time, worse than the crossing of the Dead Hills, worse than the mountains, and they had had the All-Holy with them then. Those who perished through their weakness at least died in the comfort of knowing their souls would be gathered safe by the All-Holy.

Even such sinners as these two soldiers, who knelt stone-faced, awaiting the primate's judgement, had that comfort.

Primate Ambert nodded. "Yes," he said, and there was sorrow in his voice. "Such a failure cannot be forgiven in life. In death, there is atonement. And there are the lives of their two faithful comrades, as well, for which they may be held responsible. Where two fell, four might have prevailed, if only they had not failed in watchfulness."

"We heard nothing, Most Blessed Primate," one man protested. "The heathen assassins came with wizardry, they must have. We heard nothing till the Blessed Philon cried out. We nearly took them, too, but by their heathen wizardry they escaped us, not just us, all the soldiers of the prince's own company, all the servants, half the camp was roused and they weren't taken."

The other said nothing, but he wept, his sobs gulping, like a child. Weak.

"Take them out," the primate told his own guards, and the fifth-circle knight who commanded them bowed, gestured. "Let the sentence be carried out straightway. Hang them."

The weeping man bolted to his feet with a yell of denial. Philon, still on his knees himself, swung a heavy arm around his legs and brought him down, a savage lashing pain across his chest his reward. He gasped and panted, curled up over his knees.

"My brother," Primate Ambert said in concern, and crouched to set a kindly hand on Philon's shoulder.

He was able to straighten up again. New blood was seeping through the bandages.

"The surgeon must attend you again."

He managed to murmur thanks. The coward soldier was being dragged away, thrashing and wailing. The other, with greater dignity, walked, though he was trembling and fell in the tent's doorway, and had then to be held up by two guards.

Ambert crooked a finger, summoning a lesser clerk to aid Philon to his feet. "Come to my tent. Sister Floran can tend you there. There are matters of which we must speak." And to other men and women of the blessed departed's household: "One of you fetch Blessed Brother Philon a clean robe."

They passed out of the tent into the morning haze. There was already a gallows. In the past days, converts had been taken trying to slip away into the mountains, and even among these blessed and desert-tried, there were thieves, mad and desperate murders. The influence, perhaps, of the wizards and gods or demons of Marakand, driving small discontent to brew up into greater sin. A priestess of the fourth circle was praying, a blessing that exhorted the condemned men to embrace their love for the All-Holy and seek his grace and forgiveness with their last breath and thought.

They stood them on a trestle, precarious balance. One fell of his own accord or weakness before the prayer was finished, and flailing, knocked the trestle away and so hanged the other. The crowd gathered beyond the barrier of soldiers to bear witness roared.

It was surely not laughter. He saw the struggle, the jerk, as someone, probably one of their own comrades, caught the thrashing legs and hung from them, to break the soldier's neck. And then the other. Did they deserve that mercy? Perhaps. Their sin had been unwitting, not willed. He did not draw Ambert's attention to it.

"A Marakander in a false robe may be difficult to find," the primate was saying. "But Westgrasslander tattoos are harder to hide or to feign. Did you see the pattern on his face?"

"Unfortunately, no. Only the darkness, enough to know he was tattooed."

"They won't have acted alone. Their allies will be found."

"Apostates," Philon said heavily. "Or heathens who have infiltrated the camp. I wish—why are people so blind? Why can they not see? To die and damn your soul to wander till it withers away to nothing, lost to the Old Great Gods—to condemn your children to such a doom—" It made him sick. Sometimes he thought he should have taken his children and gone to some place where one might hold the faith openly, seen them initiated, saved. Abandoned all thoughts of greater duty.

Selfish sin, to think so? Perhaps.

He had sacrificed his children's souls to better serve the All-Holy. He had murdered and lied, and made his life a lie. Others had been saved, by that sacrifice. Not all the folk of the village had resisted. Not all had burned. The All-Holy did bless him.

"There must be a new prince of Emrastepse," Primate Ambert said. "You were kin of the former lords of that folk, were you not?"

"My grandfather was prince, and my uncle, before my cousin."

"Did it never gall you, that the tower was appointed to Dimas, an outsider, when you were of the faith, and, by natural law and the laws of our land, its living heir?"

"I've only ever sought to serve the All-Holy how best I might. The folk would not have had me, then. They thought me traitor."

"Even though they had seen the true road to the Gods and given their hearts and souls to the All-Holy?"

"Even then."

"And now?"

"We've been long away. Only the Old Great Gods know who among us shall ever reach home. It will be as the All-Holy wills."

"Indeed," said Ambert.

CHAPTER VI

Jochiz was aware of the stir coming up the line, the courier passed along from one lesser-captain to the next, and then to Primate Clio, recently restored to her position as commander of the Sacred Guard. Restored, forgiven—humbler and more careful, one might hope, in considering what did and did not serve the All-Holy. Let the stump of her right wrist ever remind her. The emissary of the Old Great Gods did not break his given word, even when that word was pledged to a devil and the enemy of the Gods. Eagerness for approval might grow into pride, he had chastised her, while his sister's ghost whispered, *Let her die.* It was to spite ever-spiteful Sien-Mor that he had not finished what his enemies had begun, and left Clio dead with the knights who had paid the price for her folly in seeking to ambush a devil.

Only that. Not any affection he had for the woman.

Desire was not affection.

That lay at the root, therein lay the rot, of all cracks in his soul. Blood. Bone. Flesh. Filth. Flaw.

His thoughts were too easily distracted. It was the ghost of Sien-Mor, whispering into Sien-Shava's mind. But she was not, she could not. Sien-Mor was long, long dead, and whatever tattered remnant of her had persisted, an echo in Tu'usha's heart of fire, that was gone, too, murdered by Vartu, and vengeance would yet come for that, for his sister's death . . .

It was only his own human weakness to which he gave his sister's name, and had since first he started to hear her after her death, those faint traitor thoughts trying, failing, to lead him to doubt himself. He had no sister. Tu'usha had never been close to him, to Jochiz. This was the miring humanity of Sien-Shava again, confusing him.

Years he had endured such thoughts, and they had grown stronger over the winter past, much, much stronger. No doubt it was his approach to Marakand. Sien-Mor had nothing to do with that city, and yet . . . in his thoughts, in human weakness of thought, it brought her to mind.

He was stronger than that. It was only the mortal man within failed him, as ever he had.

It was Clio herself who turned her horse and rode back alongside the orderly column to him, overruling the protest the courier seemed to want to make, taking his message-case from him and dismissing him to find his own place in the march. The knights about the All-Holy saluted their commander and let her through. Their All-Holy rode alone, save for his brother; clerks, commanders, even the greatest of the primates, those who oversaw the circles or had nominal charge of the spiritual well-being of the towns back in Tiypur, were banished to let him ride in peace.

Sarzahn only did not disturb that peace; a comfort, to have him near. When Jochiz had thought, for a moment, that he had lost him . . . but he had recovered swiftly from whatever spell the assassin had tried to work against him. Weak, yes, but conscious. Exhausted from whatever fight his body had made against the wizardry, or perhaps poison, overcome before Jochiz himself could seek it. Sarzahn had only needed desperately to sleep—the weaknesses of the physical body, even for such as they. Were the rulers of Marakand such fools they thought human wizardry might truly incapacitate so great a being . . . ?

They were, yes.

The priests and primates who rode behind, outside the cordon of his knights, buzzed with their wondering at what news the courier might carry. They remained silent—they had that wit—but he felt their anxiety prickling his skin. Glanced back, swatted them with a look.

Sometimes he dreamed he struck them all down, ripped their souls away or blasted them with lightnings called from a clear sky, only to cleanse his mind of their nagging chatter, their fear and their ambition, their doglike worship, their clinging. Each thought the All-Holy a precious thing of their own, a relationship needed by the god he was. Now. For a little longer.

If the primate of the sixth circle had been among them, rather than farther back in the dust somewhere meditating on his aching bones and thinking dire loathing of his horse, the All-Holy might have summoned him up to ask why the diviners of the sixth had not known in advance if there were some disaster.

The All-Holy might ask why he himself had not.

Prince Dimas should not have pulled ahead. Such care had been taken, using the diviners to keep the marches paced to meet. But there had been too little water; in the past weeks Dimas had pushed on, defying the orders of the All-Holy himself spoken through the fire. Protesting that too many would die, if he did not reach the rising lands and wells and streams about the feet of the Malagru, where the pass of Marakand began its climb.

Perhaps Dimas now paid the price for his folly and Marakand had managed some unexpected alliance with its not-always-friendly Taren neighbours and attempted to break him before he could lay siege to their outer defences.

Jochiz should have known, if so, but he was spread so far, so many threads . . . He shut his eyes to the dust, closed ears to the muted hollow beat of hooves and feet, the noise of minds that became a babble of hope and fear and boredom and dull pain, the road, the road, the road so long . . .

Gone. Dimas was dead.

Could have cursed aloud. Might have, if he had been alone. They *dared*—

It was pointless. Dimas might have been an effective administrator of an army on the march, but he was hardly irreplaceable once Jochiz arrived himself. It was defiance. It was spite. It was—

There was a graver matter, now that he reached out of himself to notice it. There was—an absence.

There were—or were not—souls. Lost. Lost to him, in their thousands. The desert—the town of the desert—they stole what his priests had claimed—

How—?

Abruptly, he felt how the scars of his arms, scars upon scars, scars of the All-Holy's sacred sacrifice, ached. But that was humanity's weakness. His brother gave him an incurious look, alerted by his anger, but content to wait for explanation.

"All-Holy," Clio began, making as deep a bow, due reverence, as she might while on horseback. "A courier has come from the Army of the South, bearing a letter from its primate." She offered it, awkwardly, in the hand that held her reins. And she never glanced aside to his brother; she fought down, every time she must be in the presence of the two of them together, a seething brew of resentment and fear. Her virtue in doing so, her strength, did not go un-noted. It was for victory in that daily battle that he had restored her to her primate's rank. "He says—" She lowered her voice against overhearing. "—that Prince Dimas is dead. Slain in his sleep by a heathen assassin."

"This I know," Jochiz said gravely, as he took the rolled and sealed letter. Ground down anger, crushed it under his will. Deal with this. The other was beyond reach, for the time being. He should never have left the disposition of the southern road in the hands of humans who judged men by the strength of their faith.

Broke the seal and swiftly scanned it over.

Primate Ambert said nothing that Clio had omitted, only details. Traitor converts had murdered the prince; one was dead, the others were sought among the Westgrasslanders. Some were being questioned by the diviners and at the time of writing, six traitors who spied for the Marakanders had been thus revealed and summarily executed, but the other assassin—there had been one more at the least—remained unknown. He had begun the execution of every tenth Westgrasslander convert and would continue until the guilty confessed or the All-Holy commanded otherwise. The guards who had failed in their duty were dead. Blessed

Brother Philon, who had served many years in Emrastepse as Master of the Tower for Dimas and was moreover, in Ambert's most humble judgement, a man of wisdom and devotion who had been as much a father to Dimas and an example in faith and service as the high servant he was, would be taken into Ambert's household to continue to carry out his duties of overseeing all things concerned with the administration of the high command for Ambert until the All-Holy might make his own arrangements. He might also, if the All-Holy found him worthy, be well elevated to the rank of prince, since Dimas had left behind no heirs. This honour, naturally, was the All-Holy's to bestow. Ambert only sought to offer most humbly his unworthy thoughts . . .

"Fetch my clerk," he told Clio, whose rank should have spared her errand-running, but did not. "Order a fresh horse for the courier."

He would appoint Primate Ambert to command of the Army of the South until his own arrival at the Wall of Marakand. And the executions were well thought of. The killer would break, sooner or later, but more importantly, the faithful would see how their god protected his own. That the innocent died was no concern; the folk would know they went to their deaths safe in the service of the All-Holy, if they were true in their hearts, their souls flying to his embrace. He might do what he wanted with Blessed Brother Philon. A man of great devotion and sorrow, which only made his service more faithful. Let him not be made prince, though. They were far from the west; whatever governor had been left in place might carry on governing till the sea ate the rocks away, for all he cared. Jochiz had no intention of marching any of them home, and Ambert need not be encouraged to get above himself, as Clio had. A mistake to show too much favour. He would rebuke the primate, gently, for that suggestion, yes.

And today he had no patience with the stupidity of the devout. Against the cunning of the gods, devotion was useless. Attalissa and Sera would have time to regret they had tried to spit into the wind.

"Go," he said. "What are you waiting for? Go."

Clio bowed again and took her leave to obey.

Jochiz beckoned his brother closer.

"Arrogance," he said. "Do they think him irreplaceable? They could not be so stupid. A gesture of no more weight than a child throwing stones."

Sarzahn waited gravely.

"Vartu rules the Marakanders, whether the senate knows it or not. Vartu and I had an agreement. She has broken it." Yes, he would have let her go, ignored her yet, had she wandered off into the wilds with her beast and been content.

And now, with the wizards of Marakand, she guarded the god of Marakand against him, and even the city and its walls. He had reached, testing—felt the edges of his soul tear ragged on the walls of air held against him. Of no more concern than a child's skinned knee, but a warning of what might happen should he fling himself through, or attempt to, and he could not reach to Gurhan at all, though he had stone of his hill in a casket in his baggage, ready at need for the working.

Caravaneers who so thoughtlessly carried the means of their god's undoing about their necks and had come down from At-Landi begging to be permitted to carry baggage while the army was still crossing the Kinsai'av. No doubt Primate Ambert had collected such tokens too. His orders had certainly been to do so.

That would come. Vartu could not, in the end, withstand him. Not once he exerted himself. Weakened by what she had made herself. Woman. Human. Mother. Base animal. She lacked resolve. She always had.

She feared him. She always had.

She was hardly even a worthy opponent for him any longer.

"There is a devil on Gurhan's hill," he said. "Vartu. Do you remember Vartu?"

No change in Sarzahn's steady gaze. There was intelligence in those hazel eyes. No mindless animal, and yet—an emptiness that broke his heart.

"Kill her," Jochiz said. "She has betrayed us."

For a moment, he wondered if his brother had even understood. Then Sarzahn dipped his head in acknowledgement.

So.

Jochiz thought Sarzahn would likely survive, even against Vartu. He could, himself, intervene, if need be. Sarzahn might be ridden, be a path through the city's magical defences, if it came to that.

The clerk was riding up to write his orders to the primate of the Army of the South, her smallest portable desk already open and precariously balanced across her pommel, pot of ink uncorked, quill pen in hand. Admirable skill, to write so. He had raised her to the honour of the seventh circle on the basis of it.

He brought their horses together, knee to knee, reached an arm to draw Sarzahn over and kissed his cheek.

"Go," he said.

Sarzahn mutely passed the reins to him, as if he thought Jochiz might lead the horse like a groom himself, swung a leg over the cantle and leapt down. He was a dog before his paws touched the earth. The escort scattered, clearing a way for him, riders, horses, spooked, but the knights at least disciplined enough not to show their fear.

The dog cut away from their line of march, heading towards the mountains.

Jochiz turned Sarzahn's mount loose. One of the knights, catching his eye, bowed and took charge of it.

"The All-Holy has need of me?" the clerk asked, unperturbed. She had been much in his brother's presence and had grown used to his unthinking shifting between forms, which seemed to depend on the convenience of the moment and be hardly even voluntary. Grown too used, perhaps. She found Sarzahn, the man at least, attractive. He must counsel her on that failing. Sarzahn was not to be degraded so in any human's guilty imaginings.

"A letter to Primate Ambert of the Army of the South," he said.

The dog was a distant black shape, trotting, following the rising of the land towards the crags of the Malagru. Jochiz lost sight of him at last. Reached, touched, for the reassurance. Felt him respond, a flicker that was not outright irritation, more the shudder of a horse's skin at the touch of a fly.

Jochiz quashed his anger. Sarzahn had the right of it. He did not need watching. The bond that united them, the desire for the end they hoped to achieve, was stronger than any leash.

Did you give him any choice? Sien-Mor asked. She looked at him, narrow-eyed, from under her lashes, her mouth folded into a tight little smile.

No!

Sarzahn felt that cry, flinched at it.

Nothing. Go on. He pulled himself away, turned Sarzahn loose. If he might not trust his brother, his twin soul, then whom might he?

Not his sister.

She did not ride a shadow-horse alongside the clerk. He did not see her. She was not with him, not even in mind. She was nothing, traitor, justly dead. She had burned, she had been ash beyond resurrection, and Tu'usha's fugitive soul had suffered whatever doom it was Vartu had carried so long—destroyed, or devoured by the ice.

The clerk's pen scritched over her paper, dealing with the formal greetings. Dipped into the ink, paused, awaiting his words.

Jochiz cleared his mind.

"In light of the most pernicious murder of the thrice blessed Dimas, prince of Emrastepse and primate of the Army of the South, it pleases the All-Holy to charge his beloved—make that 'most beloved'—Primate Ambert with command of the said Army of the South until such time as his holiness comes to the Pass of Marakand in his own person . . ."

CHAPTER VII

Ahjvar had disappeared. Ailan didn't know how he did it. There wasn't enough cover to hide a dog, and he had seen the man climbing along the narrow ledge, seen him inch on his belly into a thin growth of some kind of green-needled bush that Ailan would probably be expected to know the name and uses of tomorrow, if they both lived so long. He could see the nearly sheer slope of broken stone rising, the bushes precariously clinging—no man lying there. It was—there, he moved, shifting position, and suddenly what had been stone, dirty grey and brown, was Ahjvar.

It wasn't even wizardry, that. It was just something about him, the magic in the man, who did everything as if he had been born to do it. Ailan tried to make himself a little flatter behind his own chosen cover— and Ahjvar had said it was a good place, where falling rocks had collected on a ledge a little wider than others, in the weird sloping edges of stone that looked as if they had been laid down like a stack of pan-fried cakes and then tilted. Probably there was a name for such a place, and such rocks. Ahjvar had names for everything, and tried to teach him, but . . . sometimes he wondered if Ahjvar even knew that he wandered from one language to another, or if he was so old, and so—so godly—that he just assumed he was understood.

A stone slipped under Ailan's hand, rattled away down to the gully below, splashing into the shallow stream. He cringed, knowing Ahjvar must be looking—not angry. He never got angry, never hit, never even told him how stupid he was. But looking, and probably thinking he'd have better left Ailan in Star River Crossing to hang, or whatever would have come to him for helping to kill foreign priests and burn their mission-house.

Another clatter of stone. That hadn't been his doing. Down the gully. In the distance, crows began some sort of conversation. He wondered if Ahjvar understood crows. If crows had words, in their cawing. If they said to one another, people are going to die; soon we can dig out their eyes.

They'd come upon a dead sheep on the hills on their fourth day out from Star River Crossing, before they'd begun following the road again. It had stunk. Something had dug out its eyes and ripped open its belly. Crows, ravens, jackals, foxes, white-headed eagles . . . that's what they'd do to a dead human, too. You'd be just bloating, stinking flesh to them.

Rada, when they hooked her out of the muck of the river's shore. He'd seen. He'd hardly have known her, but for the red gown, which was his. She'd borrowed it four days before. Well, taken it right off his back, and left him nothing but a shirt to go out in, till he found where she'd hidden her small stash of coin. She'd taken her own worn-thin gown away with her, probably to sell to the rag-woman. Seagulls and crows and stray dogs had been at her . . . No more slapping and pinching and refusing to let him share the blanket when he'd had a bad evening, anyway. He'd fled that miserable room with the money and the blanket and taken to sleeping under the bridge, when the gang who claimed it would let him, for a price, and in doorways when they wouldn't. He knew who Rada'd gone with that evening, and she hadn't slipped down the bank drunk; there'd been a cord sunk deep in the puffy, grey-brown fungus-swelling of her neck. He'd liked young men once in a while, too, that magistrate's guardsman, and ropes.

And he wasn't thinking about that sort of thing. Just—Rada, and the sheep, and the smell of both was in his mind and in his nose—

He wasn't afraid. He would not be. Just—like he was all one tight scream, and he didn't know if that was fear, or what you were supposed to feel, when you waited to see the people who came to kill you.

He tried to slow his breathing. Blood thumping in his ears. They might be wizards. Ahjvar said there was at least one wizard tracking them. They might hear. He should have asked if wizards could hear things ordinary people couldn't. Ahjvar could, but he was special.

He should have done what Ahjvar had first wanted and climbed on ahead, up what was turning into a sort of split in a cliff where the stream came down, dashing itself to white spray as it tumbled ledge to ledge.

Maybe Ahjvar should have made him go on, not listened when he had said—insisted—he would help.

He wasn't a child.

His mouth was like dust.

He had fought before. He had killed a man. He'd never won a fight in his life, even against Rada, who'd taken him over when his mother died and been only a couple of years older and no taller than he himself. Yet he always ended up the one in the dirt being kicked. Until Ahjvar, he'd never had anyone on his side in a fight. But he'd killed Timon all on his own.

He had Timon's knife in the pocket of his coat now.

The priests were coming into view. Ten of them. No dog. But the Blackdog might look like a man. Not an ordinary priest-knight, though. Would he? These were all men, no women. Most of them were knights, or at least, they had armour, scale or leather with rivets that probably meant metal plates hidden. Didn't cover their arms, though. Barely came down past their hips. Lighter for climbing through mountains. They'd mostly taken their helmets off. *Hot, poor dears,* he thought, and that was how Rada might have spoken of such men, proud in their armour that wasn't going to do them a bit of good. Especially not if they slung their helmets from their belts like that.

Didn't like hearing Rada's words in the shape of his own thoughts. What would Ahjvar say of them? Fools. Don't be like them.

One of the two who wore only a plain coat shouted something; they went from a straggle of weary men scrambling along a path of broken stones while trying not to fall into the stream to a pack of alert hunters, some settling their helmets on their heads, some setting arrows to their

ready-strung bows, some drawing short Westron swords, all looking
around, while the two plain-coated, still bare-headed, clasped hands
facing one another and began a sing-song prayer or spell or—

Ailan was already heaving his chosen stone, but a wizard was staggering into his partner's arms with a crossbow bolt through his back—
not the one Ailan had aimed for, and the stone struck before his man
could drop his comrade and seek cover. The stone-struck man went down
with a thud, a bright stain spreading over his bald head, twirling away
in the rushing water. In answer, a swarm of arrows came smashing and
skittering off the stones behind which Ailan had laid himself. He went
flat again, hurling smaller rocks over without looking to aim, heard the
more solid thunk of the crossbow striking something again, which meant
Ahjvar must have loaded the stirrup-bow lying on his back and he was in
awe, in love, maybe—anyone would be. Someone was breathing heavily,
huffing and panting, so Ailan risked raising himself and nearly got a
sword stabbing into his face. He yelled and the man slipped and had to
brace himself; that gave him his moment to bash with a sharp-edged
stone on a clutching hand. The knight cursed—sounded like cursing—
and twisted and pulled himself halfway up onto the ledge. Ailan knelt
up to smash with another trusty rock, remembered he had a knife if
he could get it out of its sheath and out of his coat—the knight was
thrashing away but not letting go. Ailan shoved and jerked his hand free
as desperate fingers clutched it. Shoved and stabbed and his hand, his eye
found their place, their swift sure striking, and the man slid in a tumble
and clatter of stones and in his fall knocked off another who'd started to
climb, no, that had been another crossbow-bolt and was he supposed to
be *bait* up here behind these stones—?

Ahjvar, leaping down the ledges like a cat. A scatter of arrows missed
or were swept aside, as if he had a god's grace in his hands, and his sword
swung and lunged and—

Ailan had lost count. He'd lost common sense, too, watching as if
this were a play, as if Ahjvar and the knights were dancers to some drum
and flute only they could hear.

It didn't take long, and they had no attention to spare for coming after him. Five—three, two and the last man running for his life. Ahjvar flicked a knife that plunged into the fleeing man's thigh and ran up to kill him while he was scrambling in the water, though from the way the man turned the stream red he wouldn't have gotten up again anyhow.

Ailan knelt where he was a moment longer, leaning on the stones. The water was dark. Three of the bodies were bleeding in the stream, and the bald wizard too, though he hadn't bled so much. The rapids over the stones were frothing pink.

His hands were dirty from scrambling up stones. Bloody, too. The man who'd made it to the top had clawed him, scratches like a giant cat had been at him, and his knife-hand was red. He'd—every damn night, on the road to Marakand. *You need to know how to use that.* Ahjvar's hands on his, gripping over his hand on the knife, gripping his other forearm. *You don't have a shield. Wrap your headscarf, a coat, anything—they're going to strike for your face, your gut.* Behind him, putting his arms where they should be, pushing down his hunched shoulders, kicking at his heel. *Relax. Don't knot yourself up, you'll be too stiff to move. Move your damned foot, you're going to trip yourself. Feel where your body is.* He'd mostly been feeling where Ahjvar's body was, like a stupid . . . Hadn't been Ahjvar's intention at all, standing so close, when all the rest of the time he was "don't touch me" and moving off when Ailan came too close, which he'd done a few times, testing, god's own beloved or not, because the wide world was terrifying and strange and he wouldn't have said no at all if Ahjvar had changed his mind—there wasn't anything wrong with wanting him . . . And then when he'd finally been able to stand to please him, and get his legs and shoulders and elbows where they should be, it had been stabbing and blocking and slashing not with the knife but sticks, like children. He'd learnt why when Ahjvar hooked the feet out from under him and he fell on his own piece of firewood.

Ahjvar had not laughed, only reached down a hand and helped him pick himself up. And said, "Try that again. And this time, don't watch only my hands."

You did the same thing over and over until your eyes and your muscles knew it, but you didn't stop thinking and planning, either, to seize what opening the other person offered, to lure them to where you wanted them, where you could strike, and you watched, feet and hands and eyes and even how someone took a breath—just like when the cranky camel named Scorpion was going to do something obnoxious, deliberately stand on his foot, maybe, and he knew it was coming by how she shifted her weight and turned her eye. But faster and harder to see and smarter.

He wasn't going to kid himself, that he'd become some knife-fighting hero of a ballad in the weeks since Star River Crossing, whatever bruises he'd borne and even if Ahjvar had started them both using dulled blades once they came to the ambassador's house in Marakand. But Ailan had survived, and the knight hadn't.

His dropped knife—there. For a moment he was reluctant to touch it. Stupid. He pulled at a tussock of dead grass, scrubbed at his fingers and then the knife. His hands trembled like an old man's.

"You coming down?" Ahjvar called.

It took him a couple of fumbling tries to get the blade back into its sheath. Almost dropped it again. Took a deep breath. Flexed his hands a few times, watched them steady. They were a man's hands, a little ridiculous, a little startling, battered and broad-knuckled at the ends of his scrawny arms.

Another breath.

He'd survived. The knight—and true enough, the Westron had been hanging off what was almost a cliff with one hand mashed to pulp—had not. But Ailan had put the knife where he meant it to go and hadn't faltered and hadn't missed and—a few weeks ago he didn't think he'd have made it climbing up these ledges; he'd have been weak and trembling in his arms and knees just getting that far, and he'd felt it, all the way up his arm, hard and controlled, when he'd stuck that final time.

"Yeah," he said, and picked his way down without knocking more than a stone or two loose. Stood with Ahjvar looking over the dead men.

"None of them was the Blackdog," Ailan ventured.

"No. Not sure either of us would have survived, then."

"You would," he said.

Ahjvar laughed. His nose had healed up over that first day and the black scabs had flaked off by the next, leaving pinkish scars against the tan of his skin, and even those were fading. He hadn't even been wounded in this fight, not that Ailan could see. He'd back Ahjvar against the Blackdog any day.

He'd still be nothing but a snack, himself. But that had always been his fate in any fight. He went to wash his hands upstream, where the water ran clean.

"If I take one of their swords will you teach me to use it?" he asked. "I don't want to be just bait next time."

"Noticed, did you? You weren't just bait this time. Two of those were yours."

"I was still bait. They didn't know where you were; they were all after me."

"Yeah. It helped."

"You're welcome."

"Check their quivers. Get as many arrows as you can. Leave any that are soaked. You might as well learn to shoot, too, with something other than my crossbow. Your aim's terrible. Probably the weight."

The sword—which Ahjvar didn't like because it was meant mostly for stabbing and that wasn't their style of fighting, he said, as if he and Ailan had some shared tradition to hold to, like their dead language—was going to be a problem with weight, too, heavier than he had thought it would be, once Ahjvar had waved around and discarded nearly all of them, making his choice. "Find you something better in Marakand," he said, which Ailan took to mean longer, and probably heavier, but maybe not; this blade was broad and thick.

But with the sword strapped to his pack—because it was only going to pull him off balance climbing if he wore it at his hip and he'd be dead if he grabbed for it in a fight anyway—he rubbed his hands over his upper arms, as if he were cold, checking, and was a little startled at just how solid his muscles were getting. Not so scrawny after all.

They ate there, by the waterfall, as if the dead were miles away. Crows circled, landed, hopped closer. Things bigger than crows, rough-throated. Ravens, Ahjvar said, when he asked. It was only noon. The sun grew spring warm. Flies gathered, summoned from rocks, from the earth, he couldn't guess where. The taste of blood in the air, maybe, like the ravens. He didn't look when the first bird grew bold enough to perch on a body. Ahjvar didn't bother to chase it away. Ailan shut his eyes, concentrated on cold water in the silver cup, the taste of the food—they were living mostly on biscuits sopped in water and Marakander sweets that were nuts and raisins and dried apricots and figs all mashed together with honey and rolled in seeds, which were marvellous but more something you'd want to share with a friend sitting on a bench in the sun with a little cup of bitter coffee and a warm evening to look forward to, not—

Three ravens began to squabble over the priest with the cracked skull.

"Time to go," Ahjvar said, washing his fingers in the stream.

"Which way?"

"Up."

Ailan, sighed, looking up the crack down which the waterfall plummeted.

"Do I go first, so I can knock you off when I fall, or do I go first so you can catch me?"

"I go first, and let down a rope. Which you will tie around yourself. And then I can catch you when you fall."

"Oh. Do we have a rope?"

"I always have a rope."

"I wish you'd said 'if' about the falling."

"Yeah, I wish I could have." But Ahjvar smiled.

Gods, Ailan almost wished he wouldn't.

No. That was stupid. He could just—enjoy that Ahjvar was good to look at, and not need to think of him that way. Because that wasn't what he really wanted from the man anyway, was it? Not really.

"We'll take a few more days getting to Marakand," Ahjvar said, testing an edge of rock, which proved to be loose. He chose another handhold. "Maybe a week. Head into the mountains first. Lose any others that might be behind. Though if Jochiz has turned the Blackdog loose on us after all . . . well, I'm doing what I can to hide our trail even from a hunting devil."

"Maybe you really did kill him."

"The more I think about it, the more I doubt I did anything to him at all."

"Someone else did?"

"I don't know. But maybe."

"Your god."

Ahjvar grunted. Well, it was a stupid suggestion, Ailan knew it. A god couldn't reach beyond their own land, or he wouldn't dare even be thinking the thoughts he sometimes had. Watching Ahjvar climb . . .

He should be keeping watch behind. There might be a second band of hunters after them.

"Look where I'm going," Ahjvar ordered. "You're going to want to know where to put your feet."

"I am. But remember I'm shorter than you."

Ahjvar looked down, up, considering. Changed where he had been reaching to.

"Alright. You'll want to move over to the left here, then, if you can't pull yourself to the ledge above . . . see?"

He killed people and sat down to eat by their dead bodies as if it were normal not to be bothered by the blood and ravens and flies, and then he was . . . kind.

Oh. This wasn't . . . it wasn't falling in love, what he felt, what was warm and safe and something he could feel wrapped around him like a blanket, like a hand resting on his head a moment as he was falling asleep, a touch in affection, not desire. It was—this was—not a father—this was a brother. What having an older brother might have been.

CHAPTER VIII

. . . spring, and it is two weeks since Ahjvar fought the Blackdog in the Malagru

Nikeh had had troubled dreams in the week since she had executed Dimas. Nothing she could remember clearly. Voices muttering in another room. Aunty, whom she had not thought on for years. A baby crying. Dreams like that. Usually she could ignore them, but she had not been sleeping well since Teacher deserted her. She should go back to the city, perhaps. Find the blond Nabbani man Teacher said was to be addressed as the *Rihswera*, though she called him something else herself and spoke to him in a language she had never taught to Nikeh and which was not any dialect of Nabbani—though that scruffy Taren servant of his seemed to get by in it well enough, and presumed a familiarity to which he had no right with Teacher on the basis of it.

Teacher was an agent of the god of Nabban, and so was the *Rihswera*, so Nikeh supposed that as Teacher's apprentice and ward, she ought to consider herself likewise a servant of that distant god. Would she be offered a place in the ambassador's house? Their quarters in the historians' college of the great library complex must presumably be given up, now that Teacher was gone. By whatever means she had gone.

She could offer to ride as a courier; that would get her back to Marakand in a single day. The city was almost fifty miles away, near the Eastern Wall of the pass.

She had no real rank or position here, though the captain of the south-end tower, Sulla Dur, was a cousin of Lia's and seemed to accept Nikeh as some kind of auxiliary of her garrison even now that she lacked Lady Daro Jang's authority to account for her presence.

She had no real rank or position in the city, either. She might be permitted to remain a scholar of the library, but scholarship seemed an empty thing at present.

Lia Dur had had command of the middle watch of the night and was still sleeping deeply, sprawled over most of the narrow upper bunk. Nikeh rolled off the edge left to her and landed softly on her feet. One of the two men crammed head to foot in the lower bunk grunted and leaned up on an elbow.

"Sorry," she whispered, groping for her boots and the plate-reinforced vest, helmet, sword, bow . . . Even on a quick visit to the latrine behind the barracks adjoining the tower proper one had to think of such things. Teacher had taught her so. Be vigilant. Be prepared, when one sleeps with the enemy near. The kitchen was awake, hot and clattering. She passed it by and climbed the stairs to the platform of the roof. The night crew of the trebuchet were scattered about like cats in an alley, not sleeping, not entirely wakeful in the light of their lanterns, ready to react at a moment's alarm. Those who kept watch on the enemy did not drowse. She exchanged a murmured greeting with Lia's street-guard comrade Danil and pulled herself up into a crenel.

"Take care!"

She ignored his fear, crouched there as if she would leap away into flight like a devil in a tale, stone tight against either shoulder. The valley was still dark, cast in night by the wall, though dawn was greying the sky behind them.

Very dark, below. She looked up. The night was clear, stars sharp. The waning moon was just past its last quarter, bright enough to cast faint light on the hills, but still high enough, too, at this hour, that there should be no long moon-shadow of the wall.

"Danil? When did it grow dark, below?"

"Uh? Sunset, I suppose? You know, when night fell?"

Street-guard. But city-bred, and never out on night patrol without a nice bright pool of lantern-light to blind him to the shades of the dark. She leaned out, straining her ears. Danil seized her belt. She ignored him, save to risk leaning a little further. Wind. Leaves rustling below. The usual sparse scatter of lights still burned in the Westron camp, well beyond reach of even the great ballista built to Teacher's design, which crouched like a lion about to spring on the platform of the gate-tower over the road. She cupped her hands around her eyes like the blinkers of a cart-horse, peered down into the nearer darkness, below, and towards the road and the fortress of the gate through which it passed. No straying lantern-light from behind to spoil her vision.

She ought to see a little. The shape, the roughness of the land. Some mottling of moonlight, grey to black.

She could hear nothing but the wind. No owl, no fox, no first chorus of birds waking to sing, as they should with thinning of the night, the creeping dawn.

She felt no wind on her face.

Illusion. All illusion. Send Danil to Captain Sulloso, ask her to send up a wizard to peer into this darkness, to listen, to ask why they heard no birds and what else they did not hear, and why the moon above shed no light west of the wall.

What if she roused the length of the wall and there was only a little fog hanging below?

Then everyone still sleeping woke early, and cursed her, and Captain Sulloso Dur sent her back to the city as a nervy clerk better off stuck among old books in the library than twitching at shadows.

Fog would show as a paleness.

Teacher would not expect her to dither, when lives were at stake.

"Sound the bells," she ordered. "Danil, go. Ring the alarm. The All-Holy's come to the wall."

"What? No, I've been on watch these four hours. They haven't broken camp."

"They're here." She pushed back past him. "They won't wait longer—the sun's rising and even you'll notice that darkness."

"What darkness?"

"Gah! Wake up!" she shouted at the trebuchet crew. "Ready your sling! They're here, they're here!" The bells themselves were so close—the belfry rising past the inner corner of the tower. Didn't do her much good. Pushed past the trebuchet crew, down the stairs to the rope-chamber, shouting.

When those charged with that watch failed to do more than ask pointless questions, she seized a rope herself. Ended up struggling with the man, kneeing him where she really shouldn't have as he tried to pull her off. Got clouted across the ear, head ringing, but so was the bell, the triple toll of warning.

Picked up at the next tower along, reverberating between the hills, the cliffs, the rising mountains. Echoing and re-echoing, swelling louder—the bells of the great tower at the gate. There were signals to be lit to pass the alarm to Marakand, fires by night and smoke by day, at stations along the heights, mostly converted windmills . . .

Old Great Gods, what had she dared?

The man she had kneed was advancing on her, limping, eyes streaming with pain, fist raised, and she couldn't honestly blame him, though she could have hit twice as hard if she'd really meant it and he should consider that he could still walk. She backed away.

"I'm sorry, I'm sorry." Gabbling. "I was—"

Two of the watch were at the bells, heaving and heaving, three and three, but now all the bells were singing full-throated, up and down the wall, tangling with their echoes. Lia in the doorway, a cutting gesture. Something thudded. She felt it through the soles of her boots more than her ears in the din. The rope-pullers stood to and the clamour faded.

"She—"

"Archers to your positions," Lia said. "Nikeh."

"I'm sorry," she offered again, as the man seized his bow from a rack and bent fumbling to string it. He scowled, but waved a hand.

Apology accepted, she hoped. The two bell-ringers were already at the arrowslits.

"Gurhan and Great Gods defend us," one said. "Lieutenant—"

Another thump. Shouts above.

"I've seen. Gods be with us." Lia turned on her heel, heading for the stairs to the roof. Nikeh went to an arrowslot, peered through. The sun had risen, lemon light touching the unfolding hills, running down towards the desert. Early morning mist smoked thinly, hiding nothing.

The All-Holy's army had shifted in the night, marching in silence, muffled in wizardry, hidden by it. Wizardry or devilry. There were wizards keeping watch at the gate-fortress, day and night. She didn't think sixth-circle priests could have worked any wizardry they wouldn't have seen through. It had been the devil.

He would not have baffled and deceived Teacher, Nikeh was certain of it. If only she had been here.

Like a tide run in over the mudflats, water where there had been land. Dark, seething with subtle movement in its stillness. Wheeled towers.

She turned and ran after Lia, out onto the tower platform.

"No ram," Lia said. "I don't see a ram—do you?"

"No." But there had been no engines, no materials for siege with the Army of the South at all, by the report of Istva and his fellows. The All-Holy, though, had brought timbers from the Malagru. They had been building engines in his camp. She had seen from the top of the belfry.

"He's not going to try to force the gate itself."

Just to overtop the walls, swarm them. Seize the gate-tower and open it from within. Or as at Emrastepse, have it opened for him, traitors in place to seize it.

Not here, where there were wizards to know the truth of a person's heart. Surely not.

The trebuchet crew were reaching high on their ropes, ready.

"And pull!" Danil dropped his raised arm, and they heaved down as one, snapping the arm. The sling flew up. Not shaped stone shot, of which they had a goodly supply, but one of the clay cannisters marked with Nabbani characters. Wizards' work.

A cheer. But, "Too far!" Danil called. They were already reloading.

Thump and shudder. Something striking the side of their tower. "Short!" Danil called jeeringly over the valley. The Westrons—Nikeh didn't like thinking of them so, when she was Westron herself and here they didn't understand how many Westron folk had died at the hands of the red priests—would be aiming for the platform and the destruction of the trebuchet, the only one at this end of the wall.

Two more of the Marakander cannisters failed to burst, or burn, or whatever they were supposed to do. Wizardry quashing them. The trebuchet switched to stone shot, scored a hit on the swaying siege-tower, shattering timbers. It leaned. The shouting carried. Oxen bellowed. Something cracked and its upper storeys fell away. People screamed, crushed by the fallen timbers. Danil called down their success and the crew cheered.

The bows had been singing; more archers were rushing up. Others ready to fetch and carry, standing by the barrels of sand and water against fire, with hooks and halberds if the enemy closed with tower or ladder . . .

At first Nikeh thought this would be the way of it as they settled to their work. The thrum and snap of bowstrings, the *ready-pull* of the trebuchet-first's voice, growing hoarser and hoarser. Trying to batter what was left of the siege-tower down past repair and smash the enemy's engine. No more cheering.

Stone smashed, chips of the coping of a merlon flying, leaving faces cut and bleeding. The devil's engineers had the range now and began to pound the battlements. A fire-pot of some kind landed next to the trebuchet, flung burning splashes of something that clung like tar and could not be beaten out till the two wizards of the tower wrote signs against it in chalk. By then there was a screaming, writhing woman, her face unrecognizable, to carry down, and one of the support beams of the trebuchet was burnt through. The burned woman, a slinger from the hills, died before the engineers got their beam replaced. Two other Marakanders died, smashed by stone shot, and half a dozen others were wounded by arrows. The enemy was closer now. Their wheeled tower was lost but they had scaling-ladders. Nikeh concentrated her shots on those carrying ladders.

The captain had come up from her post in the central chamber below the bell-ropes and was in urgent conversation with Lia. One archer more or less was going to make no difference. Nikeh traded places with one of the Marakanders. Her right hand was cramping, left arm starting to waver. She climbed the ladder to the roof of the belfry, joined Danil keeping watch there. A good vantage point.

She had thought of the ocean she had not seen in years when she first saw the army; from here the comparison seemed even more apt. The curve of the wall, down and back, the uneven motion—they were the cliff-face of the coast, and the devil-worshippers the waves curling, rushing and retreating from arrows and fire, pushing forward again.

Not much retreating.

Banners hung limp. The All-Holy's white, with the black symbols of his cult, the script that Teacher said Nikeh could not learn to read, no human could.

Marakand's banners were a tricolour, yellow over blue over white for its three gods, dead through two of them might be. The limp silk overhead stirred. Breeze touched her face.

"Nikeh, keep your head down!" Lia Dur, looking up.

"You've been told." Danil grinned. "Bossy, eh?" He dropped to his knees, tipped over. Dark fletching stood from his eye.

"Down!"

But she stayed where she was, crouched behind the belfry's low parapet. The enemy had reached the wall at another way-tower lower down, between her station and the gate, and soldiers were swarming up their siege-tower and across the bridge almost before it thumped down. Ladders ran up along that section. Some were pushed back or shoved sliding sideways, carrying down screaming dark figures that seemed hardly human. Others were made fast, defended by those who had been climbing even as they were raised. The Westrons already covered the platform of the tower, a writhing mass of human lives. Impossible to say which way it was going. Neither had any consistent uniform; there were street-guard russet tunics, but there were far more Marakanders on the wall than were street-guard, and few of the attackers had more than a red armband or a white badge badly copied from the flags to proclaim themselves. Too easy to kill a friend in that mess and she was glad of her clearly Marakander gear.

More up that tower, up the ladders, and more, and the tower seemed to absorb them. She could almost feel the terror, the fighting in the close spaces as floor by floor, chamber by chamber, the All-Holy's folk fought their way down, the floors grown slick with blood—mama must have died so, defending the princess and her little heir in the tower of Emrastepse . . .

"They've taken the halfway tower!" she called down. "We're cut off from the gate-fort."

A strong gust of wind lifted the banners. Out of the west. Like a bad omen. Could the devil control the weather? Probably. The banner of Marakand on the halfway tower was down. Something white flying from the battlements. No easy passage through, at least. Only the gate-fortress showed anything but a blank wall to the west at the lower storeys. But to spread to the other towers now the enemy had not only the track along the eastern side of the wall that ran its length from south to north, but the wall-walk, wide enough to drive a team of ponies, she had heard someone say with pride in the ancient builders. As if anyone would want to. A clear street to them, was what it was. A weakness that meant one tower taken could lose them all.

She was by the ladder to leap back to the rooftop platform, intending some warning to Captain Sulloso about barricading all the entrances to the tower, when she saw the All-Holy, the devil Jochiz himself, riding up through his lines. Even he had to go around the burning wreckage. He rode a white horse and was all in white himself. A holy man. For a moment even she felt it, his holiness, the shivering touch of the Old Great Gods. He seemed to glow, to hide starlight in his robes.

Illusion. Wizardry. Lie, forced into her emotions. Nikeh rubbed her eyes, scowled. And absurdly, her stomach growled. Past noon, and she had nothing in her belly but a swallow of wine and a hunk of bread passed around at some point in the morning.

To be hungry, when a man she knew was dead at her feet.

They were all animals. Scrambling and squabbling far below the view of the Old Great Gods.

No. The Old Great Gods saw, and reached arms to enfold all who fell. But the devil denied his own folk their sanctuary, however long it would have taken them to attain that state, and surely the Gods wept for that greatest of all sins ever a devil had committed against the folk of the earth.

She half thought the skies might open over Marakand, the Old Great Gods themselves descend in radiance, as once they had, to bind the devils. But even then they had not destroyed them, and the seven had worked some great evil, to prevent the Gods travelling the road from the heavens. Not human souls, no, that had never been said till the lies of the nameless god became the lies of the All-Holy, but the Old Great Gods—perhaps it was true, perhaps not. Certainly they had never come again.

The All-Holy's primates and commanders were around him. If the Old Great Gods answered prayers, let a bolt of the great ballista strike him, let the trebuchets hurl wizards' fire over him. Let his folk see and understand what he was . . .

He raised his arms, turned his face to the sky in an attitude of prayer. A sword in one hand. All his folk flung wide their arms in imitation, praying. As if the Old Great Gods might hear. Let them. Let them hear, and smite him down with all the lightning of every storm that yet might be, oh, let fire pour from the heavens—

He pointed with his sword at the gate-fort, and Nikeh did not at first understand what she saw, the heave and hump of earth and stone, not fire but a wave travelling through the earth, and it struck the bronze-clad gate, a great mass of earth and rubble and broken stones the size of horses, of wagons and houses, and the boom was thunder, smashing between the cliffs and crashing back again. She felt it, yelled, and the tower swayed beneath her feet.

The Marakanders had expected engines. They had expected siege. They expected to sit behind their walls, with all the lands Over-Malagru to supply them, while Jochiz battered away at the gate in the Western Wall that held the pass against him, and never an arrow to fall in even the Suburb of the caravanserais, the second city outside the circle of the city walls proper.

They would find themselves mistaken in their expectations. Senate, wardens, wizards and scholars of the library . . . even Vartu? Did she think even now he would fight this war by Marakand's rules and the limitations of human flesh, of engines and mortal wizardry?

It's a trap, Sien-Mor's voice said in his ear. *They pretend they see you for less than you are. They pretend they think it can't happen, to lead you on. But they know better. This is Marakand. I taught them to fear you, the god who would come out of the west.*

He shut his ears to his sister.

"Most Holy," Clio murmured at his elbow. "Should you ride so near the gate?"

"Do you think their stones and arrows will be permitted to touch me?"

"No, Most Holy. But I do think that they may try to insult you by killing your horse."

The earth kicked against them; he felt it smack upwards, his big Westgrasslander stallion leaping away as if it had trodden on something alarming, coming down splay-legged, snorting, reluctant to heed the rein, to stand. He forced it to turn in a tight circle. Men, horses, camels screamed. Some were fallen. Some were burning.

"All-Holy!" Clio called. She had her beloved axe in her hand, as if that might be any use here. "Come away out of range, please, Most Holy."

The smoke was grey, tinged with dirty yellow and it smelt of pitch and sulphur and wizardry. A seer failed to fight her camel out of its billowing clouds swiftly enough. She and the beast alike coughed and choked. She fell first, and then the camel. Pity. She had been one of his best, a wizard of some strength, unusual among the Westron folk, who had lost much of their wizardry when they lost their gods and demons.

And whose fault was that? Sien-Mor asked.

Sarzahn never expected the gods would involve themselves, he protested, stung.

She tried to goad him. Ignore her. She was nothing but the voice of his own doubts.

He had no doubts.

He stopped the seer's heart, stilled the screams of the burning knights and animals. Silence, save for Ambert's coughing. The smoke had caught him. That would shorten his life considerably, but it hardly mattered. Jochiz caught up the wind in his hand and swept the clouds away. They dissipated before they reached the wall. Disappointing.

The Marakanders were reloading their ballista. Jochiz watched, eyes narrowed. Sang the word in his mind alone, set fire to the timbers. They burned to ash in a breath, a roar, a ball of flame like the anger of the Great Gods. The fire did not spread as he intended, to consume all the lives on that platform. Wizardry against him.

The next tower south had been taken. Closer to the gate, the companies were pushed up against the wall if they would claw a way through with their hands. No ladders had managed to hold near the gate-fort so far, and his siege-towers were all burning.

"What god doesn't care for the lives of his folk?" Sien-Mor asked. Aloud.

His head whipped around. Movement in the corner of his eye, as if someone that moment stepped away.

Only the fluttering of a banner.

"Their lives are mine," he answered.

"All-Holy?" Clio asked.

He drew his sword. Raised it to the heavens. An attitude of prayer, of summoning, beseeching. Let the Old Great Gods hear and bless their emissary, let their will flow through him . . . something like that. Whatever pleased the folk. Those near copied him, crying various phrases of praise and prayer. He gathered himself, tasting the strength, the weight and life of soil and stone. Swallowed it and spat it out with a word, searing the air, the earth, pushed it burning with a fire that could not be seen, a wave of force, of desire and will, a shaping. The fortress of the gate, built by engineers of Marakand's brief and near-forgotten empire against the rising of a dynasty of unifying warlords on the Great Grass, rode the heaving crest of the earth like a ship rising on a swell, but as an unlucky or ill-guided ship might, it foundered in its descent. Or rather, towers heaved skyward, shook stone from stone, and fell. The bronze-faced gates twisted from their hinges and bars, crashed like thunder. Bells rang themselves the length of the wall, the wave spreading onwards, outwards, weakening, but cracking mortar and stone. Jangled to silence in a rising cloud of dust.

Silence about him, but for the thudding, the sound of ripe fruit falling.

"All-Holy . . ." It was a whisper, a breath. Lost. Clio.

Not lost. Gathered. Saved.

"She did love you," Sien-Mor said matter-of-factly. "She thought you were beautiful, and filled with the wisdom of the Old Great Gods, and strong."

She wasn't there. Only the commanders, the primates, the message-riders and signallers, the horses and camels . . . still on the bare earth. Clio. They fanned out from him, the fallen. Dead creatures, dead leaf and flower, root and stem. Dust and straw, and not a cricket, not a spider, a worm. His own horse shifted its weight nervously, snuffing the air. Hot stone and metal, maybe. No screams, no shrieks of the crushed and trapped and dying from the towers. Crushed, maybe, but dead. Those of his own who had struggled there beneath the rain of arrows, beneath the stones dropped against the ladders, dead, too, but at least their souls were gathered safe.

A necessary sacrifice. The Old Great Gods themselves could not work from nothing, not when pinioned, constrained, within the physicality of the world.

"Old Great Gods preserve us . . ." Primate Ambert, safe on the edge of the circle of dead.

The stunned pause broke in roaring, as if life returned, the dead field waking—at least aside from the gate and his path to it, where it was unlikely seed would ever spring again. Jochiz looked around—shut his mind to the woman on the red horse that shadowed his own . . . Northron horse, the tall, heavy breed that the Westgrasslanders had crossed into their own stocky herding horses, giving rise to these he so favoured for his knights, but he knew that red horse with its white nose and stockings . . . she had wept over the damned thing when she lost it in the battle at the Hill of the Claws, the last Vartu and Ghatai had fought as allies—and won, but that had been the weakness of his own chiefs and they had paid.

Sien-Mor smiled at him, sweet and secret as ever.

You are not even a ghost.

The man who killed me and burnt my bones to ash should know, of course.

His sister rode past him, towards the gate. The hooves of the red horse stirred no dust.

Sien-Shava—he was Jochiz, Sien-Shava was a vessel, no more than that—spurred his horse after her. It kicked against Clio's sprawled corpse. She should have died when she was arrogant enough to attack Vartu and Sarzahn, anyhow.

The army—most of the commanders had been too close and were dead but what did it need them, when its function was so nearly fulfilled—surged forward, as if the All-Holy's moving—his survival, as they would see it, from a vicious attack of the Marakanders and their devil-loving god, and the glorious grace of the Old Great Gods manifest in his will, the destruction of the gate—were a signal.

As it must be. He nudged at one of the commanders of the knights who had been outside the life-searing unleashing of his power, and the man—woman, one of the few to be admitted to that circle or permitted once there to rise—wheeled her horse and dismounted to prise the main standard from the hands of its bearer. It left a plume of ashy dust in the air as she rode to his side. She felt the touch of the All-Holy. He saw it in her eyes, all warmth and wonder . . .

Oh no, Sien-Mor said, in his mind, a whisper in his ear, he could not tell. *You made me yours and never let me free to find another. You are mine, now. Leave her be.*

The remaining siege-towers had found their lodging, bridges down, the defenders undone as much by their own fear as the assault, the faithful who climbed the bodies of their comrades and kin to come at them, at the heathen who defied the will of the All-Holy and the Old Great Gods. He added fuel to that fire, as he had through all the long march. He could not seize them all, ride them, but he could stoke what was there, stir it when it sank in exhaustion, wake hope in despair, quell doubt and fear. The faintest touch of them was in him, as he in them. Their god, in truth, held them all in his heart. And would more fully, soon enough.

The army of the All-Holy poured through the gap in the wall, moved out along the tracks behind it that linked tower to tower. They swarmed the ladders and the siege-towers, cleared the wall-walks, fought their way down the towers floor by floor, chamber by chamber . . .

Bells rang again, without pattern or message, only a wild alarm. From the southernmost tower, rockets screamed into the sky, shrieking like beasts in torment, bursting with colour and smoke. A desperate signal. He did not think there would be any answer, though the north tower, moments later, launched its own. So perhaps Marakand would know its wall had fallen. It made little difference. Their wizards would no doubt be aware regardless.

Sien-Mor, dismounted to lead her horse over the mound of rubble that filled the gateway, stopped and stood there where the root of a broken arch still launched itself skyward, carrying nothing. She halted, waiting for him. Smiled again, leaning back against her horse's shoulder, arms folded.

Sien-Shava rode slowly to join her.

CHAPTER IX

The night air of Marakand smelt of smoke and barnyard, but the god Gurhan's forested hill breathed the scent of cedars and ferns, water and stone and moss. There was frost in the air, cold rolling down from the Pillars of the Sky.

The horse that grazed nearby had no scent at all, save a whiff of old bone. Why Storm grazed, tearing at the grass along the edge of the path as if he had not eaten in centuries—which was the case—Mikki could not imagine. Habit, perhaps. How he grazed—that was another question. Something for the wizard-philosophers of the library to debate, if ever they had time for such things again. The shaggy-legged blue roan stallion left no piles of dung on the forest floor.

Click of hoof on stone. Sigh. Gust of air blowing Mikki's hair, and a great soft muzzle brushing over the top of his head. Nearly two centuries abandoned, a skull set carefully on a ledge in the god's own sacred cave, had given Storm time to grow sentimental, it seemed. Or whatever passed for that in an ancient, frequently contrary, bone-horse, which was to say, a creation of Northron necromancy meant to summon, for a brief period, the seeming of a horse into the world for a wizard's use. Not to recreate, in body and soul and excess of character, a particular horse, whom Moth said had not only been slain in battle under her, but cut up and thrown into a well in hatred of his rider.

"Jealous?" Mikki asked. "Don't like her playing with other ghosts? Neither do I."

He considered the burl of grey olive-wood he had been working by the light of the fire and the moon. It wasn't only the skull of the horse Styrma that Ivah had left in the god's keeping when she set out east for Nabban, but Mikki's abandoned axe and chisels.

He wasn't sure what he was making. Had made? It seemed—nearly finished. A little roughness here and there to smooth away, a little delicate detail to add: a feather's edge, a horse's eye, maybe. There. Done? He thought so. The god of the hill had asked what he did, and had nodded, understanding, when he answered that he was finding something that seemed to need discovery. He had roughed it out over the nights since finding the burl, cutting it free from the old storm-broken bough of a wild olive, years weathered. A bowl, rounded, but irregular. It looked right, so. The inside he had smoothed like the inner curve of an eggshell. The outside he carved with tiny figures, ships of the north and swans, bears and wolves, horses and eagles, all flowing one into another, circling, spiralling inwards, covering every surface save the base.

The figures he made cast shadows. In the moving firelight, they seemed to swim, run, fly. Rushing away.

The horse nosed at him again. Mikki got to his feet, taking the carving and the chisels back up to the god's cave, a well-worn path between tall grey trunks, the ground beneath cushioned with fallen needles. He had to duck to enter the low opening, a curtain of ivy hanging down, trailing over him. A holy place, a shrine, but not a home. All the hill was riddled with caves and tunnels, water-worn long ago, and all were of the god. Gurhan took human form, but he was not and never had been human; he had no dwelling-place and needed none. If his guests treated this sacred place as a shed out of the weather for their convenience, the god did not complain of it, and so neither could his priests and priestesses, who would rather, Mikki suspected, have the god's somewhat worrying friends conveniently lodged under their eye in their rambling family compound down towards the library, rather than camped like tramps within the god's holiness.

He left the bowl sitting alone on a ledge of stone. Gift. Offering.

Felt something whole in himself again, for having made it. Hands that might still shape.

The horse trailed Mikki like a dog as he went back down the hillside, crossing the track and climbing again. Like a shelled walnut, the hill was seamed with gullies and channels, little dark ravines to which the sun never found its way. Moth had laid out her ground on a small plateau, a shelf of stone across from the cave of the god, and above it, facing the east. The high moon was growing faint, the sky lightening. Sun would not find her there till nearly noon, but its still-unseen rising found him as he climbed. He was already shedding his caftan, the only clothing he wore, leaving it hanging on a cornel sapling, as the dawn this ravine did not yet see ran through blood and marrow. An ache in the bones, an old man's pain, as he went down on four legs. He was white about the muzzle now. Moth never mentioned it. White streaks in her pale hair, frost on oat-straw.

Left behind down on the path, Storm grumbled and tore mouthfuls of twigs from a hazel, dropping them, snorting, looking up to see if his tantrum were noted. Mikki did look back, to laugh. Offended, the horse plodded away.

Moth only looked up when she heard Mikki climbing through the scrub, held out a fending hand as he leapt to land beside her. Something caught in his shoulder, twinge, like someone drove a nail into the joint. Old man, old bear. He lowered his muzzle to her palm, closed his eyes a moment, just to drink the scent of her.

And of charcoal, chalk, blood. New cuts on her arms, and she had her sleeves rolled back still, healing lines of red, faded white that might be yesterday's bleeding. A devil's healing. He settled down behind her where he would not disturb the working, but could keep his head pressed to her thigh. She had been extending the pattern. It looked like a Grasslander cat's-cradle painted on the stone, with runes set at its crossings. He could feel the power that flowed in it, a barrier like moving water, like wind and the rising draft of a fire. A shield against Sien-Shava Jochiz, an armour wrapping the city and Gurhan, held against the devil's presence, his reaching power.

At her feet, though, a vessel of folded birchbark, no bigger than the cupping of two hands, half-filled with fine ash, and darker clumps of ash, too, curdled with blood. Fresh. Blood in the ashes was new. She had only whispered and sung over them, before. Telling them what she would have them be.

"What are you doing, princess?"

"Just—wondering," she said.

"Wondering in blood?"

She rubbed ashes between thumb and forefinger, breaking up a sticky clump. "Wondering, if I were to call, what might answer."

"That's not even she."

"Don't tell the runes that. Don't tell her. You don't hear him, old friend, do you? You know who you are, still and always. You remember, now." She was whispering, almost crooning the words, looking down into the ashes, not at him.

Mikki growled, softly, to himself. Flexed claws. If he thought of stretching a paw out, striking the birchbark away, scattering the ashes . . . he did not.

She had written on the outside of the bowl. A lie bound in words, a name. But Sien-Mor was dead and gone, her soul lost. Destroyed, maybe. Moth had said she thought Sien-Shava believed so, that he had thought to destroy Sien-Mor and Tu'usha together, and though the devil had fled to nest in the heart of a goddess, and it was certain he had torn one from the other and destroyed the conjoined being they were, Sien-Mor might only have died as mortal humans died, and found her long road to the Old Great Gods. Fire, like earth, and submersion in water, and salt in the mouth, was a ritual to free the soul. Even when it was also a means of murder.

Necromancy might bind the souls of the dead before they had taken the road. It could not draw back those on their journey to the Old Great Gods, nor yet pull a soul from their safekeeping. Of the dead and gone, it might only wake and use a memory, an imitation. That was a tenet of every folk's beliefs surrounding the dead, a truth of the world.

Storm—challenged that, and he was a beast whose soul ought to have faded back into the life of the world, no matter that Moth had reclaimed his skull, no matter what she wrote on it. Of Sien-Mor, Moth had not a fingerbone.

No bones left, not even a tooth, and teeth are always what remain, to go into an urn, into the earth, when the funeral pyre is cold. Only a barren little valley where nothing grows and no waters run, high on the northern face of a peak in the Malagru. The horses, Lark and gentle Fury, have been left below; Moth would have left Mikki, too, only he would not be left. Stubborn and silent, following her. He knows what she intends. They have argued it out, and she will not give up her intention. The place is still. No bird, no insect. No demon, though it had been a demon's home, once. A creature of fire; salamander, the wizards named it, though Mikki thinks it more likely that the demon had been northern dragon-kin.

There is no fire. Once this place burned undying, a crack of pale flame rising from the earth. His paws stir ash, not downy soft like wood ash, but like fine, light sand, black and white mingled to grey. Faint scent of sulphur. He sneezes. Moth gives him a reproving look. She squats down, takes up a handful of ash and blows on it.

"There's nothing of her here," he says. "This is stone, burnt stone. Nothing that was ever a living being."

"Best leave wizardry to the wizards, cub."

"Leave necromancy to the necromancers, you mean. Moth, don't."

"If there's nothing of her here, you can hardly call it necromancy." She pulls a small cloth bag from her belt. It held dried figs once, from the pantry of the Upper Castle on the Kinsai'av. He watches as she fills it with several handfuls of the ash.

"You're going to summon the memory of a fig tree, not a ghost."

"He has already summoned her, or a memory of her. It's there, that tang, that taste—like a scent on his skin. It doesn't matter if it is something of her he took into himself, unwitting, though I think that's very likely, or if it's merely a shaping of his own mind, his guilt. It's there—

she's there, already. To breathe a little life into her—" She grins, knotting a cord about the neck of the bag. "If I must fight him, cub, I want him to have always half an eye behind."

Moth stirred the ashes with a finger, breaking up the rest of the blood-bound clumps.

Down in the ravine, Storm whinnied, a trumpet of warning.

Vartu! The silent cry came with a gust of wind that tore leaves and twigs from the trees, raised a plume of ashes, till Moth clapped a hand over the container, looking up. Gurhan was with them, not in any physical form, but a presence, the heart of that agitated wind. Mikki surged to his feet. Scent in the air, there, gone, back again. Above them. He gave a grunt of laughter, unexpected joy.

Holla-Sayan? But it wasn't Holla-Sayan he touched, reaching out. Something . . . broken ice, that was what was in his mind, the image of what he met. Cold. Edged. Sharp and brittle, and fires like a devil's soul, but likewise broken, flaring and cold and flickering erratically. And chains, the touch of chains grinding over his skin, the raw tracks of them and he roared and swatted at what was no longer there, batting at the air about his head.

Moth gave him one startled look, while he still struck out and backed away, stumbling, sliding when there was nothing under his hind feet. She flung the ashes skyward and yelled, "Go, then, and be what you will." Came after Mikki, who had mastered himself, panting. Watching for movement that did not come, with Moth's hand on his head.

"He doesn't hear me," Gurhan said aloud, standing with them, something like a man, a shadow half-seen in the corner of the eye.

"Don't disturb the lines," Moth said, not to the god, and then, "Go to your priests, lord of the hill. Let them pray. Every word raised in your defence is one word more to strengthen what I've woven."

"Holla-Sayan?" Mikki tried aloud. "Hey, dog? Your horses are in the priests' stables down by the Silverward shrine. You can tell your young woman I didn't eat them after all."

Old Great Gods, and what had become of Holla's Jolanan, since he'd fallen into Sien-Shava's hands? And what of the *Rihswera* of Nabban and his fosterling, who had gone into the mountains seeking the Blackdog on Moth's word?

Stillness. Gurhan was all about them, an awareness, but he was with his priests, centred there, and they added what they might to Moth's defences. Mikki backed from under her hand, moved away, began a slow stalking sidelong up the hillside. A bear need not lumber and crash its way, forest beast in forest, soft and subtle for all his size, but he did not expect to circle the Blackdog unseen, unsmelt. Only let the dog's attention be on him, let their enemy be drawn away from the lines of charcoal and the blood-painted runes.

Holla, oh, Holla-Sayan. Can't you hear your name?

The dog came down the hillside in a rush, leaping over Mikki's head as he wheeled and snapped, fangs closing on air. It struck Moth as she rolled from its path and they crashed down together. She grappled with it, trying to seize its jaws and hold them closed, her own teeth bared in a grimace. Silent, both of them. Mikki circled, slapped with a paw, knocked the dog aside and gave Moth space to rock to her feet. Still she did not draw her sword. Mikki swatted the dog flat when it would have leapt again, pinned it down with his forefeet, but it twisted under him, nothing of Holla-Sayan in its eyes, no recognition, no fear, no struggle, only the yellow-green fire of the dog. It changed its form, growing monstrous, more bear than wolf in bulk, and it flung him off, came after him and caught him by the ruff. He felt the teeth in the loose skin there, and in the stiff scars of the devil's collar. Went limp, like a cub, a pup, unresisting.

Holla-Sayan—Blackdog . . . He tried to find something, some crack, some chink through which a word might strike. Some fleeting memory. A scent, briefly, of bruised green grass, sun-warmed dry earth. He seized on that, held it like a spark that might be breathed into flame. *Holla-Sayan!*

The dog snarled, released him, but only to turn on Moth again and he lost the touch of what he had held. Moth had Keeper in her hand, face grim; she struck with the flat of the blade, dodging aside as the Blackdog charged her, fleeing down towards the path. Leading it farther from the plateau where the spell was drawn, but the charcoal lines and the runes binding them were only a part of it, the rest an active working that took some part of her attention even when she spoke with Mikki or Gurhan or whispered over the ashes.

Mikki crashed down after them, heedless of brush and saplings, barely avoiding a stand of larger poplars. Moth had crossed the path, had her back to a cedar's bare trunk; it did not look as though she used the flat of the blade any longer. The Blackdog was bleeding. Fighting to fend it off only, though, not striking to kill.

"Holla-Sayan, in Attalissa's name, for Gaguush's memory, for Jolanan, try to hear us—"

A snarl was the only answer. Mikki bounded over the path, slammed into the dog as it turned to sink teeth into his foreleg and they all three went down, tumbling, crushing ferns. There was fire in Moth's eyes, red and silver, the flesh and bone of her become shadow over half-seen veins of flame, and she slammed the dog back when it would have seized Mikki's throat, thrust it down to the earth and pinned it, knee and blade over its ribs, her other hand gripping its throat, a strength to match its own. Mikki sat back on his haunches, breathing hard.

"Now what? Can we bind him?" Great Gods, to what end, though? "Can you see what holds him? Is he—is it Holla-Sayan at all, or is he already dead?"

Wolves, running savage in the forest, ridden by a devil's will . . .

"I can't see."

Vartu.

That whisper had not been Gurhan. Not Holla-Sayan. Mikki did not know the . . . call it voice. The touch, the colour and the shape, a stranger.

Distraction. Destruction. That was all their enemy's intent.

"Kill it," he said. "If they've killed Holla-Sayan and this is some other using his form, enslaving the dog, kill them both. The dog's something that should have been gone from the world long ago anyway."

"So am I," Moth said, which did not entirely sound like disagreement.

They were both watching for its reaction. Maybe it had not even understood the words. Maybe that mind's voice did not even belong to it. Fast, shallow breaths, as if it still struggled, or was wounded more severely than it seemed. Eyes fixed on empty space between them.

It twisted free of her grip, ignoring the sword that opened a new furrow across its ribs all unintended, and lashed up swift as a striking snake to seize Moth by the throat.

CHAPTER X

From this cloud-wrapped height, with half a waning moon high overhead, the pilgrim town of the All-Holy's cult was all shadows, a suggestion of roofs, of roads, no more, beside the silver-streaked water of the river. Once Tiypur had filled the valley and climbed the hills south of the river. By daylight, pale stone might still show what had been on the sheep-cropped turf: the lines of it, streets and walls, arcades of broken pillars, hills once crowned with some great palace or temple. Before her time, Tiypur and its empire. A rival to the Golden City, her glorious work in the lagoon of the mouth of the Gentle Sister? Yeh-Lin might grudgingly grant so. Though nothing could ever have compared with the dawn view of the city from the palace on the mainland, the water smoking, the sun rising behind, the tall houses and palaces that floated, half-seen, in the golden mist . . . But all that remained of her city were forlorn pilings and a weed-grown reef, a hazard to shipping but a good fishing ground.

Jochiz's doing, that. And to be a person who could regret the city of which she had been so proud, and not the folk who died there and the lives and works and art and hopes destroyed, was not what her young god would have of her.

She took a certain satisfaction in the fact that even viewed by night, the city of the All-Holy was a low, mean place, contrasted with what must once have been. It squatted amid the ruins on the river's southern shore and spread up the old avenues, mostly inns and hostels to serve pilgrims, she thought. More reliably above the level of spring flooding were the towers and colleges of the cult, where the administrative machinery of Jochiz's religion creaked its wheels round and ground out priests and—what, quartermasters? The whole of the land was now aimed only at feeding the army it had flung eastward, she suspected. Or had it marched, a hive dividing, swarming, and was the new swarm never to return to the old hive . . . and if so, was there some new queen, some priest or primate, or a committee of them, set to keep the faith alive after its god had marched away?

Worth finding out. Worth doing what she could to disrupt that, for the sake of the folk of this land, while there were still those alive who remembered their old way of living. Cut off the head of the cult here, now, and let the lands of old Tiypur shake off empire once again and remember how to honour memory of its true lost gods. There were those hidden folk who still preserved what little was remembered. Humans were always so.

Descend on the colleges of the circles, of the seers and teachers and priests, and go through them with the blade's edge, a storm and a fury . . .

No. She did not know over what distances Jochiz might leap, when he saw the desperate need. Folly to take the risk, so close to what she suspected was the heart of all his thought. This was not the Western Grass, a teat sucked nearly dry. This, he would defend, and she must not expend her strength on any secondary target.

The east was lightening to another dawn. To ride the winds was no easy thing, and though she had broken her journey several times, sometimes merely to linger a day in some wilderness place, to rest and renew strength and resolve, to restore that calm within that threatened, more than once, to escape her. She had broken it not least usefully, though perhaps not most restfully, at the Westron bridge over the Kinsai'av. Now, further violence against Jochiz's officers rejected, Yeh-Lin had wistful yearnings for a hot meal, a jug of wine—and the wines of the Tiy valley had been famous once, she thought, though before her time—a bath, and then to sleep in a clean, soft bed.

None of which she was likely to get over in the town, especially at this hour of the—call it morning. A hot meal and indifferent wine, perhaps, and even a tub of lukewarm water and a dubious bed if she paid enough, and if she painted again some tattoo of rank on her wrist. She might alight on one of those hills, disguise herself, walk down into the town a pilgrim from the east.

Procrastination. Below, the leaves of riverside poplars, still spring-soft, flashed silver in the moonlight and tore free. On the island, cypresses bent and hissed. Cats'-paws of wind swirled white on the water beneath the flying cloud that was herself. She dropped down, released the winds she had ridden, alighting in a small clearing on the hill of the island's eastern point, where the thin soil over the stone supported little but creeping mats of weeds. For a moment she stood in the eye of a small hurricane, a storm of wind and torn leaf and grit. The rush and rattle of her landing calmed.

She listened, but there was no sound of human activity near. Not that she expected any at this hour, or in this place, sacred and forbidden. Reached out with other senses, but no wakeful wizards probed to find the cause of the freak gale that had swept down the valley. Stillness settled about her. A blue warbler broke into sudden song, welcoming the advent of the dawn. Familiar, but one she had not heard since she took Nikeh up to the kingdoms of the north. No blue warblers east of the Karas. Such little differences, such wonders. Few even of the travelling folk marvelled as they should. Another reason to take delight in her god; he was one of the rare folk, human or otherwise, who understood how to truly see, how to *be*, in this glory of a world. She could just stand and listen. The smell of dew, the smell of bruised and broken green about her. Scent of water. Nearby. Enough of birds. Her mouth was like sand.

Yeh-Lin picked her way through the trees, a close and snaring tangle, overgrown with chance-sown grapes. No sign that any human ever came up here, this hill like a ship's prow facing upriver. The ruins of the old temple of Tiy were below, and stretching to the west, the overgrown remnants of tombs more ancient than the catacombs, where the folk of Tiy's city had been buried in an earlier time.

Somewhere under her feet, those catacombs. Somewhere there, too, the cave where it was said the hermit, the first to hear the message of the nameless god, had experienced his great revelation.

Madman. Or Sien-Shava, laying the foundations of his myth. It little mattered which had been the start.

She found her water, a little rain-fed rock-pool. Knelt to drink long and deeply, and to wash her face. Continued to kneel there, considering the reflecting surface of the water. Did not try to see beyond leaf and cloud and lightening sky, her own face, the helmet's fox-mask raised. Only paused, feeling—

Alone.

In such case, a woman should pray. Should she not?

She rose abruptly, thrashed her way back up to the hill's crest. Trees, everywhere trees. No view beyond. Smothering.

She was not the dead king, to let her environment, whether the world without or that within her own mind, overwhelm her. Only . . . she wanted to see. She wanted to look east, to see the first light break over the land, running over the world she had crossed.

She followed where the ground sloped down, wound a way through trees and came out abruptly to the clear view she sought. Finally some sign of human hand as well, although it was ancient work. A paving, a parapet on the cliff's edge. The stones of the platform were set so close no seedling had yet flung a thread of root down, to grow and lift and heave, though vines had crawled over all and were slowly burying the white pavement in leaf-mould, where young olives and figs sprouted. This had been kept clear long after the empire's destruction. A dancing place, perhaps, or an observatory. Perhaps in Tiy's day priestesses had watched the river here for the funeral boats coming down.

An edge of sun over the dark horizon of the world and a light sky: yellow, blue, scattered streaks of clouds dark. The winds she had leashed released and gone, the river gleamed like a burnished mirror.

Yeh-Lin drew a deep breath, bowed to the east. The morning was already well advanced in Marakand, and the day winding towards evening in Nabban. Did he watch, in the valley of the holy mountain's peak? Did he look west from the mouth of the cave, past peaks and forest and desert, to where the afternoon sun slid down the sky? Or did he walk among the pines by the cold rising springs and dream of his dead king, or lie in the river's depths?

Yeh-Lin went down to her knees, surprising herself. Hands spread on the stones. She bowed till her forehead touched the ground. Stone of nearby quarries. Stone that was rooted deep. The bones of the land, of the world, running, rising to hills, deep under valleys, under waters, rising to mountains, sinking again, windswept, grass-grown, and desert and mountain and . . .

"You can't hear me, Nabban. I don't pray. I don't. But hold your hands over me. I am—I find I am a little . . . apprehensive."

Yeh-Lin sat back on her heels, feeling foolish. Foolish, and comforted. For a moment, she imagined she could smell snow, and pines. Remembered kneeling on the brink of another, steeper hillside. Blood offered, words spoken. No power in them to bind her but what she gave them. She got to her feet, dusted off her knees. At least neither the dead king nor Ulfhild were here to be sarcastic.

She rather wished Ahjvar were, to tell the truth.

Or Nabban himself, she decided, halfway down the hill, and his forage-knife, to hack her a path, because clambering through the tangled undergrowth grew rapidly wearisome. The reverence with which the folk of the cult spoke of their holy island had led her to believe it some tended garden. She had never ventured into Tiypur itself in all her years in the west, not wanting to risk going near Sien-Shava, and certainly not with a child in tow. The All-Holy obviously reserved this place for himself.

The walls of the ancient temple stood higher than she had realized, hidden in what had become forest, though once it had been reverently tended groves of cypress and bay and flowering myrtle, if the old songs of the rhapsodists were true. And white paths between. She did find one such path, hint of gravel underfoot, a narrow white line, little trodden, but—definitely someone had trimmed the branches back, and kept the vines cleared away. Hardly wider than a sheep-track though, and she came on it only when the entrance of the temple was before her, a tall pillar carrying nothing, its mate fallen across her way, the drum-round sections separated like so many tipped stumps. Those that blocked the path were thickly shrouded with moss, but a little wear suggested that someone did climb over, occasionally. She followed, alert for anything—human guardian, wizard's trap, a simple deer-snare . . . Nothing prevented her, and within the walls, still high as her head in some places, and the lines of broken pillars, the trees thinned. Here once the priestesses of Tiy had sung and danced, and the dead had been blessed.

The sacred pool was dry now, a shattered curb of stone, broken chips of coloured rock visible here and there through moss and the rot of years of plant-life. Mosaic, maybe. She climbed shallow steps that ran the width of the temple, their slabs tilted and cracked. Earthquakes were not uncommon in this land. No cataclysm out of the ordinary had laid the temple low, not that any song told, only neglect and the centuries.

The songs did tell of the catacombs. Here, the dais, where the choir had sung. There, perhaps, the carved screens had stood, gilded, gleaming in lamplight, hiding the sacred mystery, the descent to the underworld.

They had believed the Old Great Gods guarded the souls of the world, the soul of all life, in an underworld of peaceful night and sleep, yes. No road to the distant heavens beyond the stars. A journey on a cleansing river, an embracing darkness, a rebirth into light, new life . . .

She had nearly forgotten.

So long ago.

Underworld of night. Heavens of purest light. They were only a little aside from the living world, a turning sideways, a veil laid over . . .

A state of being that was not . . . scratched cheek and sap-sticky hair and sweaty skin.

That was all. And everything.

She was most morbid in her thoughts this morning.

The descent was easy to find, though it had probably once been grander, a pair of circling stairways. Now a pit, a heap of rubble in which blackberries grew, canes stretching up to the light. And again, hint of pruning, a path. Not cleared in the past year, though, she guessed. The All-Holy left what he hid here to tend itself. Yeh-Lin jumped down, scrambled on unsteady stones. Down, and into night-cool air, and dimming light, to where a small hole like an animal's burrow showed the top of an arch.

Ah.

It occurred to her that she, the twice-empress Yeh-Lin, who had been a girl called Nang Lin once upon a very long time ago, did not much care for small, dark, tight spaces. A childhood nightmare, that she was buried alive. Her siblings had buried her once amid the new-planted taro, when she was very small. Dug a little pit and sat her in it and covered her up to her neck. She forgot why. Some game, no doubt they had claimed. No doubt it had been. She had begun to believe they would not stop at her neck, when already her little arms were helpless beneath the packed-down soil. She had screamed, and screamed. How they had pinched her, later, for being such a baby, getting all their backsides tanned, though the punishment had probably been as much for the destruction of the precious planting as for terrorizing her.

Oh, Ulfhild would laugh now.

"Sien-Shava," she said aloud, "is far from the fine figure of a man that the dead king presents, yet even so he is rather broader across the shoulders than you, my dear girl. If he hasn't stuck fast, neither will you. In you go."

She went head-first, like a marmot into its hole, worming on belly and elbows, and found herself slithering down a dry and leaf-drifted slope into a wider place of higher, vaulted roof—a stone-walled passageway, in fact, broad enough for four and high enough that even Ahjvar, though perhaps not Ulfhild's demon, would have headroom. A little dim light reached so far; beyond, all was blackness, to human eyes. Which fortunately troubled her not a whit.

Yeh-Lin drew her sword, sent ribbons of pale light floating and flowing ahead and beside her, like small cloud-swimming dragons, and walked on.

She might find her way by other senses, walk as surely with her eyes shut as open, but humanity would have its due. She wanted to see.

The walls had been plastered and painted once, but water had risen high enough to destroy the frescoes. Most was flaked away, leaving only patches of colour, images unidentifiable. A leaf. An eye. A splash of faded red. Arched openings showed chambers lined with niches, bones jumbled in corners, water-stirred, or where stone sarcophagi were still arrayed in ranks, with more bones about them. Like and unlike her vision. Gritty underfoot, dry river silt, and then not so dry. The walls sweated. Other corridors branched off, but many were impassible, roofs fallen, walls heaved in. This twisted and turned; she thought it might be spiralling. Walls of stone and brick gave way to tunnelling. She rather thought she must be below the level of the river. Best not to begin to wonder what kept the water out.

Here. That narrow crack she had seen from the other side. She could feel . . . not precisely an air, breathing out of it. Not warmth. The sense, though, that there was not an emptiness beyond.

A waiting.

Even she had to turn sideways to pass through, light flowing ahead of her.

The splash of her boot in water sounded loud, echoes rustling, whispering, lingering longer than they should, returning to her from all sides. And then a silence that seemed listening, and aware.

So. Yeh-Lin stood, feet apart, sword easy in her hand. The footing was uneven, dropping away beneath dark water. Her lights were caught and flung, like the sound, from facet to facet, made sharp and harsh by the crystals that lined the cavern. The pool that stretched before her was like ink, a black mirror, reflecting the light, opaque. It shivered and broke at the slight stirring of a foot, turned to a dazzling, dizzying confusion, roof and walls and floor all in motion.

Altar, she thought. The point of stillness, the black stone in the black water. It was not quite as in the vision. Smaller. Rougher in form. The hollow in its upper surface was as she had seen, though, and still it held—she could smell it—blood. Thick, old, nearly black, but still liquid, neither dried nor spoiled.

Now she let go of human vision. The cave remained, the pool, the stone . . . The blood pulsed, a faint tide. A beating heart. The dark water moved with it, which the eye alone had not seen. The crust that covered the walls, the roof, and continued under the water should have been a thing of beauty and wonder, sparkling pale white, tinged with the colours of dawn and dusk, a treasure, a wonder for pilgrimage, the holy heart of the goddess Tiy. It was not.

Not shaded quartz or amethyst, laid down in ancient fires, nor salt of ancient seas. Soul made stone. Not souls. She did not feel there were any selves that endured here, of the thousands he had harvested, bound with his blood. Only a single note of pain, of yearning, desperate: the salmon penned that would fight upstream, the shoot that should thrust to the light crushed beneath the stone, the infant life throttled in its moment of birth.

No good could come of this.

Whatever he planned—to swallow a reservoir of the souls of the earth as he had swallowed gods—however he thought he might achieve this . . . his blood was the heart of it.

Perhaps literally.

She did not suppose the cavern was without defences, but to wait, and stalk, and sniff the air, and hesitate . . . Nothing revealed itself to any sense as she stood, still, waiting, barely breathing. Assess the situation. Then strike. Think, but do not over-think, they had told the Wind in the Reeds in her day.

Yeh-Lin stepped out into the pool. Two strides, splashing, and she was up to mid-thigh in water that was disconcertingly warm, skin-temperature, like a cooling bath. She waded, hampered by boots overtopped and filling. Beneath her feet, the bottom of the pool was rough. She trod upon the stuff of souls. She was enclosed in it. Encysted. She could feel it now, feel him, all about her. An awareness on his part, not even fully conscious. Like the vague discomfort that foretold some killing inward growth.

She might hope to be so. He was vast, grown vast already. Sien-Shava—could not contain him. This was Jochiz, gestating towards some new state of being in a womb of stone.

She reached with her free hand, calling not fire from the air, but ice. Ice to swell and burst, to crack stone—

Ripples crossed the water that were not from her passage. She leapt, landed crouching by the black stone. The floor rose to shallows there, a submerged islet. Water streamed from her, leaving her leggings stained. Water tinged with blood. What lay in the black stone, thick and murky, was not the whole of it after all.

A . . . shape. Long, swimming just beneath the surface. *Long*, eight feet and two broad. Jochiz had woken some memory of ancient creatures before, shaped and used them to attack. But they had died as mortal creatures died. She struck down even as it came thrusting up into the shallows, not wriggling like a snake but pulsing forward like a worm, scaleless, glistening, pale, a fringe of tentacles tasting the air. The milky blue eyes looked blind, but it twisted aside and she only wounded it, opening a dark seam. It thrashed silently, snapping this way and that, flinging itself back to deeper water. Almost she followed, but the surface of the pool had broken into a fluttering disturbance, as if a squall of rain swept over it. Alive. Seething. A hundred, more, smaller versions of the creature. They swarmed to her and she slashed almost as if she reaped millet, cutting through pale bodies, leaving them sliced in half, sinking, but more followed, as if they bred from the water.

Eating their way out from the mother worm, which floated now, still, in a slick of darker blood. Ragged black holes, teeth like chisels, gnawing—a hideous birth, each small creature creating its own passage into the world. And they came in waves, one rolling over the last even as her blade broke its charge.

"Nabban damn you." Ridiculous, to be attacked by—by grubs. By worms. By—damned legless newts, was what they were, in their hundreds, and she gathered fire to her free hand and flung it over the surface of the water, blinding them, maybe, if they were not already blind, and blasting those uppermost to charred lumps. The pool hissed and steamed in sudden violence. And they came from beneath the surface, from all directions, till the shallows about the black stone were roiling with them, dense and slippery as the contents of a fisher's net.

Yeh-Lin formed the characters in her mind, set them carefully at the four cardinal points. A barrier—but more piled through as if it were not there. Interesting. Also annoying. She swept them away with fire again. This time, only a few were scorched.

Ah, cold hells then. If he wanted to play by those rules . . . there was nothing living here of the earth anyhow, to be stripped of life, not anything that belonged here. She opened herself to the life that did burn, the warmth, the fire that was in beast and plant and cold worm, in every gnat, every speck that lived its brief blind witless existence in the mud. Did not need even to reach for it, at first, felt it rushing into her, as water into a deep well, flowing. They died, crumbling, falling to ash that floated pale on the water and the blood that was still somehow Sien-Shava's living self, that she reached for, drawing the strength of it, the fire—

Jochiz flared into a denial, the soul-stuff of the cavern burning bright, waking towards—something. And the worms came again over the black stone, over one another, over her, piling up her legs, slithering into her water-filled boots, under the skirt of her armour, nosing under the scales, thrusting up between collar and helmet and where they touched skin— those chisel-teeth scraped cloth away, scraped and devoured leather and steel, the only sound they had made, that quiet terrible high squeaking of teeth on metal—where they touched skin they burned as if some alchemical poison burned her. She yelled and made herself fire, a robe, a skin of it, struck them from her, but her armour was shredding as if it were only a construct of lacquered paper for the theatre, its lacings destroyed, plates fallen away, worm-gnawed scales and bands shed like rotten leaves—her short gown and leggings beneath tattered as a beggar's rags and she a beggar's rotten corpse seething with maggots.

She bled. Yeh-Lin shut the pain away, which was only the human body crying out for attention and yes, she could see she was in trouble, thank you. She bled, everywhere they touched her, not their teeth, which were bad enough, but their slime breaking down the skin, so that blood oozed from every pore and they were at her ears, her nostrils, nuzzling at her eyelids, eyes squeezed shut. She could not heal herself, as if the poison of their slime that dissolved her skin were some substance antithetical to her very nature, human and devil both. It burned the body. It ate at the soul, damped fires, smothered all that she was. She reached again to feel the shape of them, their life, their creation, what thing had given them birth. Some small, innocuous creature of the catacombs, eater of slugs and worms, perverted by Sien-Shava, and he had—ah, it was not only that he made them monstrous and ever-multiplying, breeding out of the debris of a thousand years—he made them a form for himself. They were, not Sien-Shava, but Jochiz, a portion of Jochiz's will and being, a shaping of his fire and she could see it now, recognize it in them, the lines, the flow of it, cold light.

A great light. A vast and heavy strength, closing on her, without ever needing to draw on what he made here, the glowing cavern still only incubating what would be born in its ripeness into him—

A fist of stone, crushing her, Dotemon, while Yeh-Lin, skin oozing blood, fell to her knees, propping herself on her sword which alone seemed proof against the scraping teeth.

She gathered herself into herself. She was Dotemon. She was light of the stars, she was ice of the cold hells, she was fire of the heart of the earth. And he was greater, and engulfed her, and she was bound in a net she had helped to make, limited, squeezed small, as if laced tightly into some too-small armour, unable to draw breath.

It was not that the Old Great Gods could not have destroyed the seven, when they came to save the folk of the earth from the tyranny and destruction the devils had brought. It was that they would not. The Gods did not destroy the Gods. Even those they called devils.

They had held to that, in those days, even the seven, even when they flung all other law of their kind aside.

Until Vartu came by that cursed sword, to tear soul from soul and—would she had never let it from her hand.

Jochiz was watching her. Not speaking. Not even the grace to say her name, to acknowledge her as an enemy fought and defeated. Dotemon was become only a thing, an intrusion the demise of which he watched with satisfaction as Yeh-Lin collapsed, failing around her, body, self, soul . . . she had *liked* Yeh-Lin. She had *enjoyed* Yeh-Lin. She had *lived* in Yeh-Lin, angrily, enthusiastically, joyously.

She made herself an arrow, a spark, a leaping thought of light. She was the Dreamshaper, and the dead king lived half in dreams.

Ahjvar. Now would be very good. If not too late. Fool old woman.

Too late. She felt the first of them forcing itself, burning, past her teeth, down her throat.

Jochiz, with Sien-Shava's lips, smiled a moment, wherever he was. He made sure she knew his satisfaction. Corrupted, Dotemon was. Revelling in her animal humanity.

Yeh-Lin felt the worm press into her eye, and the other. Felt its slimed passage over bone, pressure growing within, burning, pain this body had never known and she was twice a mother. The world flared to white agony, and she screamed.

PART TWO

CHAPTER XI

From the Chronicle of Nikeh Gen'Emras

I was born in the lands of the princess of Emrastepse, child of a tribe of the coastal mountains who had once been the folk of the goddess Emras of the spring and the waterfall. We worshipped the memory of the goddess, and of the mountain demon her lover, who was man and woman and golden eagle in one. They had died in the wars, as had the empire of which we had been a part, almost seventeen hundred years before, when the gods perished and Tiypur fell into darkness. Few stories of those days survived, carried by the rhapsodists who travelled among the lands, from market to market and tower to tower, reciting verses grown almost incomprehensible with the wear of years. A prince's tower might preserve a collection of such tales in a scroll or two, precious things copied and recopied, but few other than the rhapsodists themselves could read them. They were the priests of our collective memory, but it was a memory worn thin like an old coin.

More recent memory held other tales. In the year that my father was born, it was said a great wave came out of the west and swept away four villages of the coast to the south. Houses, folk, boats, cattle . . . all that land was scoured to bare rock and sand and grew wild with thistles, unpeopled, in after years, and in the same great disaster the island of Corsanal, where once there had been a god's sanctuary, was split in two. Emrastepse was spared. We sat high on a clifftop. Only the fishing boats in the little harbour below were smashed to kindling.

My father said that when he was a boy, you could see the ribs of a great ship of the southlands that had been cast inland still lying in a sandbank where once they had grown grapes, but that the timbers were taken to build the new threshing-barn and other works about Emrastepse. He showed me how the roof-beams curved. I never quite believed, then, that the barn roof had been a ship.

Now I think it was true. Certainly there was a great sandy hill with the princess's vineyards about it below the cliffs, beyond the harbour, and there was a green mound where we were not supposed to play, because there were foreign sailors buried there and no one knew their names.

This was, of course, taken by some as a sign of our own state of damnation, in that we were godless, and as a warning, that we should give our faith to the teachings of the red priests. Perhaps it was even then that the seeds of treachery were sown.

My parents were folk of the princess's own household. We lived within the walls of the village at the foot of the royal tower, not in the outlying hamlets, and I remember being in the tower as often as not. My father was one of the cousins of the tower, as the nobles of the tribe were called for their descent, down to the third degree, from a prince themselves. I remember he wore a golden circlet, on some occasion, though what those occasions were I doubt I ever understood. This did not give us a manor, tenants, a swarm of serving-folk—that was not the custom of our tribe, nor anything the land could support. They worked a smithy, my parents, and Aunty, an old woman who was some kin to one of them, cared for my brother and me. My father's name was Philon; my mother's was Hecta. My brother was too young for anything but a baby-name yet. We called him Birdy. He was small and thin and lively as an eel.

It was the princes and princesses who led the tribes of the west, as once they had headed the clans of valleys and the hills, and with the magistrates of the cities, formed the council that advised the emperors. There were no more emperors and for long years, no more cities in what had been the empire of Old Tiypur, only ruins gone to green. Tiypur itself was centuries a dead place, dust and ash, foundations tracing memory amid broken pillars. It was only when the cult of the nameless god made the old island temple of the river-goddess Tiy the heart of its worship and established a settlement among the ruins on the south bank opposite it that life began to return there in creeping weeds and sprouting windblown seeds. Maybe that was the slow healing of the natural world come at last, but they claimed it to be the blessing of their god.

There were many mystery cults in the west, their secret knowledge and their rituals kept for the initiates alone. It was how we of the tribes preserved memory of our own lost gods and demons outside of the formal tales of the wandering poets, how we kept our hearts in faith, godless as we knew ourselves to be. I do not know the rites of the cult of Emras, the goddess of my folk; when my child's world ended I was still too young to be initiated. I only remember the torches carried through the village at the winter solstice, and the excitement of my mother and father, who would follow them, the reminiscent regret of my great-aunt—I think she must have been that—who stayed behind with Birdy and me and several cousins—here meaning children and kindred, not lords. There was music. It drifted down from the headland. I knew there was dancing, and that the folk wore animal-faced masks and wild, bright, ragged robes stitched all over with fluttering ribbons. My mother a hare, that one year of which I can recall such details, and my father a badger. (The masks, I think, were burnt in the hearth-fire the following day, never reused.) They returned only with the dawn, hand in hand, and maybe there were many tender-headed adults the next day and little work got done, but it was a time of joy, I remember that much, hangovers or not.

Orgy and sacrifice and perversion, the red priests taught, men and women lying with one another without regard for marriage vows or as they liked to say, the fit and natural pairing of the sexes, as though humankind are cattle to come together only for the making of children and should have no pleasure and delight in one another, or find satisfaction together where the heart leads. The priests also tell that among the heathen folk who observed such mysteries, the blood of bastard infants born of one year's rite was offered as a pledge to draw the attention of the devils at the next. Maybe there was a spate of babies born around the height of the harvest—I think my birthday fell then, and I know my little brother's did—but there never seemed any fewer of them, save from the many usual causes that mean we do not name babies with a true name till their fifth year is past.

The red priests taught lies from their very beginning. That it was a sinful empress and folk who brought about the calamitous years that broke the empire and blighted the land. That despite our great past sin the Old Great Gods had an especial love for us folk of the shattered west. That we must prove ourselves worthy of that love, win it back, by changing our lives, turning away from worship of the memories of our weak and failed and dead, so very dead, gods and goddesses, and devoting ourselves to the purification of our souls. This could only be done through living our lives according to the teachings of the nameless god, servant of the Old Great Gods themselves. At first these teachings were revealed in oracles, dreams coming to the chosen among his priests. They were set down in holy books, six of them. I have studied them. Know your enemy, my teacher used to say. They describe the torments of the long road to the Old Great Gods, which the souls of the dead must traverse. We know that the journey is not for torment, but for knowledge, and truth, for revelation and redemption, purification. We must face ourselves, and know ourselves, and acknowledge our sins and repent of them, in order to be fit to come to the Gods. But one book of the red priests teaches that it is punishment of even the least of failings. Another, the last and most recent, declares, in contradiction which they do not attempt to reconcile, that the road brings suffering because it is broken. The devils of the north, it says, laid waste to it in hatred of human-folk and Great Gods alike as they went down into their final defeat—which we know was not so final—and the road of the dead no longer brings us to the peace of the Old Great Gods. It is not a journey of self-knowledge and purification, but of unending torment and despair. It is a road without end, a hopeless journeying in which the souls of the dead are trapped, doomed, and from which they finally fade to nothing in a second death, unable to reach the Gods, more damned even than a ghost trapped unblessed and unburied in the world.

It is from this that their nameless god, who has no body, no place, no presence in the world but his voice whispering his wisdom into the dreams of his priests, was sent to save us. If the folk of the west lived true and pure lives, the red priests taught in the early years of the mystery, a messenger would come, and a way would be found to save us all, the lost of the road and those not yet dead alike. And the years passed, and two centuries. And a new oracle spoke for the nameless god. He wrote no book. A stranger in our land, a traveller who was said to have slept in the holy sanctuary beneath the ruins of the temple of Tiy one night, where the spirit of the nameless god had entered into him.

One would have expected the priests to have denied him as a heretic, or at least recognized an opportunistic charlatan, but such was the force of his presence and the power of his words that he quickly gathered many disciples, and though there are stories of fighting, both in words and with knives, their teaching after that was that his holiness had been made evident by many signs.

His immortality was not least among these.

The All-Holy became the absolute ruler of the mystery, and of the tribe of the prince of the valley folk who scraped a hard living from the sickly soil about the ruins of Tiypur. The red priests and the cult of the nameless had always been strongest there, the island of Tiy being the heart of their mystery. Now the prince gave his only daughter in marriage to the All-Holy, and died soon after. When the princess died childless, the widowed All-Holy, who had been named prince and co-ruler, continued in the rule of that folk, and folk and faith became one. Where before, the red priests had gone out among the folk of the tribes with their words and their tattooing needles—because initiates into the mystery were marked with the sign of the nameless god on the wrist—and had found welcome in some places and derision in others, now they came with warnings not only of doom to follow death, the curse of the Old Great Gods, the slow annihilation of souls on the road, but of punishment in life. The lands of the west must unite, for a great war was coming. The seven devils of the north had awoken and were gathering the sinful kings and the decadent cities and the earth-bound gods and goddesses of the east to their service, and they were moved by a hatred of the Old Great Gods, as they ever had been, and of the folk of Old Tiypur, the folk of the west, who were the beloved and chosen of the Great Gods. A prince who did not submit to the guidance of the All-Holy and his red priests condemned his or her folk to damnation, and that damnation was earthly as well as spiritual.

The army of Tiypur made it so.

They were small raids, at first. Princes and princesses who defied the priests were killed, by murder or in battle, and usually there was some cousin of the tower who had been initiated into the mystery and who would emerge as the prince of the tribe—never a princess, because following some revelation in their fourth book, the red priests taught that women were unsuited to rule, being different in nature and in mind from men, looking inward and downward to their children, not outward to the folk or upward to the Gods—a prince with a counsellor of the red priests at his side. And some of the folk would already have become initiates, because for almost two centuries there had been missionaries, teachers of the red priests, wandering all the lands west of the Kara Mountains, finding their way into every corner of the old empire. Now many more folk joined the mystery, learning to recite the answers to the ritual questions of the catechism. undergoing the ritual tattooing, forswearing their past reverence for the lost gods of their ancestors. There were punishments for those who did not: fines that must be paid, traditional rights denied, labour services that were owed to the prince and those who had the favour of the priests and new ranks within the cult.

That was at first.

Children of all stations in life were taken from their parents to be taught by priests and teachers of the cult in schools, and the parents forced to pay a tithe of all they produced, or to work in service to the prince and the priests, for their own children's support. Three years, five years, eight—it varied how long the children were kept away. But when they were returned, they were, on the whole, good and devout servants of the priests and the All-Holy, tattooed and initiated into the first or second circles of the mystery, and, if their parents were not already of the faith themselves, horrified by their heathen ways, terrified for their souls and fearing their damnation. That was if they had any love left for their parents at all. And to initiate someone into one of the old mysteries of the gods and goddesses and demons became punishable by death.

The rhapsodists were driven out of such lands, or stoned, or burnt alive.

The faith of the red priests and the rule of the All-Holy spread throughout the tribes of the lowlands of Tiypur in this manner. In the mountains of the north and the coast and among the savage, desperate tribes who clung to life in the worst-blighted lands—the Dead Hills where the soil itself leached the life from human-kind and beasts and all growing things, so that few people lived past their fortieth year, if they reached it at all before strange wasting diseases took them—the old mysteries and the old ways survived.

There came a time, twenty years before my birth, when the All-Holy declared that the war was nearly upon the west, that the devils gathered their forces and that the continued sin and depravity of the heathen tribes would deny Tiypur the blessing of the Old Great Gods when the great war came.

All the folk of the princes who acknowledged the All-Holy as their overlord and spiritual guide must devote themselves fully to the nameless god. Those who would not, and there were still, after generations, those few who kept to their old faith despite all the burdens of fines and tax and service placed on them, would be cleansed from the land. Exile, it was thought the decree meant.

It did not. Accusation or the lack of a tattoo was enough—and a tattoo was not salvation if there was accusation by one who had the ear of the priests. Sometimes there would be a trial, a tribunal of priests. Sometimes not, from accusation to sentence. Mostly, they were burned. The red priests were fond of fire. It cleansed the world.

Those were the years of terror all up and down the broad lowlands along the Tiy. There was the siege of the port Tiyosti, princeless and free and largely heathen, and the great bonfires of the living and the dead in flames called down from the heavens by the All-Holy—or perhaps it was missiles of pitch and sulphur set alight by forbidden wizardry—when finally it fell and all who had been unable to flee by sea and who survived the desperate fighting in the streets surrendered. They were not given the option of conversion.

After the massacre of Tiyosti, which left the port in ruins, the All-Holy turned his gaze to the coast and to the mountains.

All the west must serve the nameless god, the messenger of the Old Great Gods, who dwelt now in the ageless and immortal All-Holy. All the west must be his, true in their hearts and faithful, and the heathen, the perverse, the corrupt, must be purged from the land, that it might be pure and worthy of the blessing of the Gods, and stand against the terror that the devil-led hordes of the east would bring upon us.

Thus the priest-led armies of the All-Holy brought their terror to us, to save us.

CHAPTER XII

. . . some twelve years or so before the All-Holy crossed to the east of the Karas

I n the depths of the river, he dreams. A mother, a goddess searches. Children, lost.

Children, not children. Not a goddess. Only a shape made in the dreaming, a metaphor, to be understood.

It is a wholeness, and it is not whole. That which should be of it, in it, is lost.

Is taken. Held away.

Hoarded, sterile.

Ghu draws himself together. Wakes, in the deep water. Wondering.

Far in the east of the world, beyond Nabban and eastern sea, beyond the vibrant cities and the fertile plains and the broad river valleys of Pirakul, the hermit waited, empty of all thoughts but one, empty of all but the need, the message he would have understood. He lay on his bed, which was only a frame strung with rope and a thin mattress stuffed with coarse heather. Eyes were open on the darkness, hands folded on his chest. Eyes open, and soul. Every night. As the darkness thinned, dawn seeping around the cowhide curtain that was all the door he had, he would rise and kindle a new fire in the clay stove, brew his morning tea and set his barley porridge to simmer. He might walk down to the scattered cabins of the village, where he would tend the sick and receive gifts of food and the greater gift of human warmth and kindliness. Or he might walk on

the mountain, climb through the forest until he was above the highest
trees and could see the peaks unfold, blue and white to the horizon. Every
night, he lay down again and emptied himself of the day, to fill his soul
with one thought, one message, if only it might be heard, be answered.

I want to come home.

Over him, the stars turned in their cycle, and the fleeting years
passed.

Always, Nikeh remembered the fear. It never left her, marking her like
a secret tattoo, a colour sunk deep that she could not alter or scrub away.

It was, perhaps, her eighth summer. She was never certain quite how
old she was. Such things were mangled, discarded as unimportant, in
after years, and by the time they were important again, she had forgotten.
She called it her eighth and counted from there when people asked her
age. It would do.

Her parents worked dawn till dusk in their smithy that summer.
Heads for arrows and spears they made, mostly. Smiths from outlying villages brought what they could. Her father's gold circlet went, and much
of the small treasure of the princess's tower, for iron ingots off a Northron
ship. She always remembered how the big sailors fascinated her, so tall
in their bright-coloured tunics, their eyes so pale in faces ruddy from the
sun, wild and shaggy like bears, the men unshaven. Even their speech
sounded like growls and barks. There was one woman who carried her
brother Birdy piggyback all up and down the cliff-path, neighing like a
horse and making him laugh.

Aunty did not approve.

"Take the children away," she whispered to papa. "Foreigners steal
children, and Northrons trade with the caravan road. They sell children
in the east, even for . . ." and her whisper went even lower.

For what? Nikeh wanted to know. She hated secrets. Wanted to
know, to understand.

Later, she would understand that by that time there had been no
slaves in Nabban for almost two centuries. She would write that the tribes

of the west were ignorant and even among the heathen folk, it was the red priests who shaped their view of the world beyond the Kara Mountains, seeing it through fearful eyes.

"Take Birdy and go back to the house," papa said.

In her memory, she did not fuss or argue. This seemed improbable. Most likely she had. Likely she had even earned a swat on the bottom. The Northrons were so appealingly bright and loud and free of fear.

Better if that copper-haired woman had stolen Birdy away when their high-prowed ship sailed, taking with it all the remaining gold and silver of Emrastepse, and a goodly share of the last harvest's olive oil and of the year's salt production as well.

The defensive ditches were dug deeper, the earthworks built higher and new ones added, making angles and traps. Even Nikeh and the other children helped, using adzes to strip bark from tree-trunks, as ox-teams dragged in logs from the chestnut forest lower down for the building of new palisades.

Hannothana further down the coast had fallen, and its prince had been captured. They burned him alive on a great pyre, with his crippled wife. Their daughters had died in the fighting. Some of that tribe's surviving folk fled to seek shelter among the folk of Emrastepse; it was impossible to keep their stories from the children's ears. Folk of outlying villages mostly submitted. They learnt and recited their catechism under the tutelage of the red priests; they swore great oaths to serve the All-Holy, and they endured the tattooing that marked them of his faith. They gave up their children to the tutelage of the priests in the new dormitory which conscript labour began, before the ashes of Hannothana itself were even cool, to build at the foot of the new prince's tower. Folk of the prince's town themselves were slaughtered even after their surrender, in a blood-hungry fury.

Those were the stories that came to Emrastepse, like tales of long ago and far away, except that mama's own father had been a man of Hannothana. It was a real place.

"Like sharks," a woman whispered, in tears. She was sitting at table with the family of the smiths. Nikeh did not remember her, other than that one incident, as though it was a little scene carved in relief on an old tomb, a moment frozen in stone. Perhaps she was kin of mama's. "Like sharks. They tore my nephew to pieces and cried he was a devil-worshipper. I saw. I saw. This is truth."

More refugees came, hungry, dirty, desperate folk, carrying little or nothing with them. But only a few. Papa and mama spoke low-voiced and sometimes sent Nikeh out of the house, or took themselves away to the smithy to whisper together. They had frightening things to talk about in secret, which was more terrifying than if they had just told her. She imagined, every day, how the red priests would come. She had nightmares. In her dreams the red priests were red all over—their hair, their skin, their eyes red like blood. She knew that was not how it was. Missionaries of the cult of the All-Holy had come to Emrastepse in past years, usually around the time of the harvest festival, when there was communal feasting and a welcome for all. They won few converts. They were only ordinary men and women. She knew that. Muddy red was merely the colour of their robes.

There was a new prince in Hannothana, a cousin of the tower. The new prince was the puppet of the counsellor appointed by the All-Holy, and the counsellor was the real ruler. Nikeh considered, and decided for herself she understood. She was not a baby like Birdy, to think this meant the prince wore strings and sticks to move his limbs.

The other cousins of the tower had been burnt or hanged, if they survived the fighting. But some had killed themselves. They had jumped from the tower roof as its doors were forced.

Papa was a cousin of the tower of Emrastepse.

The forces of the All-Holy were coming.

An envoy, first. Red-robed priest riding a fine horse, with a dozen soldiers on foot about him, all in bronze scale shirts and leather kilts. Their helmets bore a knot of red ribbon for their god. Nikeh climbed like a squirrel up the palisade and hung there, arms hooked around a pointed log, bare toes braced against the wood, to look down on them. Her mother was with the princess and her young son, up on the watchtower by the gate. The priest spoke very arrogantly. His words did not stay with Nikeh, only his tone. *She* would never speak to the princess so. The princess would never speak so to her own folk.

He demanded the princess come with him, to learn the creed of the All-Holy and forswear the perverted worship of demons and devils and dead gods on behalf of all her folk.

Nikeh was indignant. It was right to honour the memory of the dead goddess of Emrastepse and her demon lover and they did not worship devils, nobody worshipped devils, they weren't real, only winter-tale real, story-real, not true like the goddess Emras and the woman-man-eagle Melnarka who had fought at her side and died with her in the war that destroyed the gods and the empire together. Everyone knew that, unless they were an utter fool.

The priest stood with his mouth open. His horse pranced in place, its ears back, tossed its head. The breast of his red robe grew dark, as if in drinking he had spilt his wine. Nikeh looked over to the watchtower again. Her father was there too now, standing at the princess's side. Just standing, a bow in his hands. She could see how he looked down, his head bowed, the great sigh that moved his chest and shoulders, as if he had finished some taxing labour, but he was a strong, strong man and drawing a bow was no great feat. She did not understand. The princess put her hand on his back, as if she comforted him.

Thus Emrastepse answered the All-Holy.

The All-Holy did not come himself, not for a campaign against such small tribes as lived along the coast. His divine magic was not needed to overrun Emrastepse's walls, as it had not been for Hannothana's.

Perhaps it was some traitor within the village, some secret convert to the cult who had hidden the tattoo on their wrist and had not been driven from the village when news of Hannothana first came to them. Perhaps soldiers of the All-Holy somehow climbed over the wall undetected. Someone killed the watch and the gate-guards and took their place, to open the gate in the dawn even as the alarm was sounded from the roof of the princess's tower.

Nikeh saw, as the night's dark washed away. She had gone looking for her mother. Few adults, warriors of the tower or not, had slept in their own beds that night, so the children had roamed, escaping the care of the elderly or their slightly-older cousins.

Thus she was on the roof of the princess's stone tower, which was castle and storehouse and meeting-place for all the folk. She saw how the dark thinned, and thinned, and suddenly there were dead men and women where there should not have been, on the ground all about the watchtower. Others, in plain tunics like any other person of Emrastepse, only one wearing a short-sleeved coat of dull scale armour, were pulling open the leaves of the gate.

"Go back to Aunty!" mama shouted, shoving her at the stairs. "Look after Birdy."

That was the last Nikeh ever saw of her. Mama had a place among those who would guard the princess and the little heir, who was a few years older than Birdy, not yet named.

When she thought back, trying to remember, she thought the princess's husband was killed on the wooden watchtower. Already dead. Papa may have been as well. They were close friends, he and the husband of the princess. They would have kept watch together.

Beyond the tower's forecourt Nikeh stopped in the lane to stare. There was fighting at the gate. She had never, in all the words of all the stories she had ever heard, imagined such a sight, such a sound. So many people packed so close, as if by their bodies alone they would block the way. The mass seethed and heaved and did not, to her eyes, seem to be made of individuals at all. An amorphous sea-beast, limbless, headless, writhing and pulsing.

It broke apart in a din of shout—scream—hammer-blow—thunder.

Perhaps she imagined the thunder.

She fled to the house behind the smithy.

"What's happening?" Aunty demanded. She seized Nikeh by the shoulder and shook her, which she resented greatly. She was angry, as if that might burn fear away.

"The red priests," Nikeh told her, and some of what she had seen, all jumbled, words spilling. Birdy began to wail. Nikeh grabbed him and shook him, as Aunty had her. "Be quiet," she told him. "Be quiet or they will come and kill us all."

Aunty heaved him to her hip and took Nikeh by the hand.

"Quickly," she said.

There was a cellar under the back room of the smiths' house, where oil and cheeses and wine were kept. A small, low-ceilinged, close place, dry and dusty, full of spiders. They went down, Birdy first and Nikeh following, careful and one-handed on the ladder fixed below the opening, carrying a clay lamp that Aunty must have lit at the hearth and given to her. She did not remember, only it was there, in her hand, in her memories. The flame flickered with her breath. Above her, there was noise, which made her moan in fear, but it was only Aunty throwing things about as if she had gone mad—a crash of jars, a thump as the lid of a wooden chest was thrown back, a clatter of who knew what. In the cellar were already blankets, and the smaller water-jar, and a loaf of bread. Aunty came partway down the ladder. "Sit," she told Nikeh, pointing at the blankets. "Hold your brother. Don't go crawling around and knocking things over."

Nikeh took Birdy and sat, obedient, dragging a blanket over both of them.

"Want mama," Birdy said. "Don't want Nini. Don't want Aunty."

"Nini's all you've got," she said. "Hush. We're hiding. Mama will come find us, but we have to be quiet and hide. You can do that. You're a good boy."

Aunty still stood on the ladder, her head and shoulders lost to view, doing something.

Nikeh was suddenly terrified. "Come down," she begged. "They'll see you. They'll find us. I don't want to be burned!" Her voice rose to half a scream, of which she was immediately ashamed.

"Quiet, fool child." Aunty leaned at a strange angle, dragging something up the slope of the half-opened trap door, gripping its edge. She bent almost backwards and fumbled her way down the ladder, dropped the door.

"Perhaps that's covered it," she said, not to the children, but for her own reassurance, it seemed. "If they just glance in they won't see the cellar door at once, only a disordered room. Maybe they'll think someone's already searched."

Nikeh was silent, hugging Birdy.

Aunty came to sit beside her. There was a spear on the floor, and a long knife. Aunty touched them, to be sure of finding them in the dark, and then she blew out the lamp.

In the dark, blacker than any night, they sat. The cellar began to seem cold. The air felt damp. Nikeh ached with sitting. She shivered. Aunty beside her was warm, but she shivered, too, and whispered a brief prayer. "Memory of Emras, give us strength."

Birdy squirmed and fretted. He needed to go pee-pee, he said.

Nikeh took him over to the corner behind the ladder, groping her way.

Birdy squirmed some more. He was hungry. They ate bread and cheese and water with a splash of wine in it for the warmth. She needed to use the corner herself. Aunty did. Birdy began to fuss. He wanted mama. He wanted papa. He wanted out. He was tired of hiding.

They could hear nothing from above, until there were muffled shouting voices. Not words, just the noise of them.

Nikeh hugged Birdy and put her hand over his mouth. He squirmed and tried to pull the hand away.

"Quiet," she whispered in his ear. "Quiet, or the bad men will come and kill us all."

He was still, a little. There were heavy feet on the floor above. Something fell and crashed. Birdy clung to her. Aunty dragged Nikeh close to her, whispered, "Sh!" as if she had made some noise, which she had not. Nikeh could feel the old woman shaking.

The footsteps left the floor above. Birdy was beginning to gasp, not from her hand, but the trembling deep breaths that worked up to a fit of bawling.

"Mama!" Her hand did nothing to stop that cry.

"Quiet!" A whisper like a shout.

"Old Great Gods have mercy, give him to me," Aunty said, and dragged him from Nikeh's arms, squirming and whimpering.

"Hush," she said. "Hush, hush, Aunty's got you, be still, be still."

But his gulping sobs gathered again. Nikeh heard him. She knew how he could shriek to be heard over even papa's greatest hammer, once he began in earnest.

"Old Great Gods, Great Gods, child, be still." Aunty sounded as if she would wail herself, and she seemed to be thrashing around. Trying to cover Birdy's mouth, muffle him with her body, Nikeh thought.

A strange sound, as if she swallowed a cry, or Birdy did. She panted, wheezed.

"Don't!" Nikeh whispered urgently. Don't what, she did not know, but she was suddenly terrified. She reached to take her brother from Aunty. Aunty was shuddering and Birdy was in Nikeh's arms, Aunty was letting go of him, pushing herself away.

He was warm, and heavy, and soaking. Nikeh thought he had wet himself. He was only just beyond diapering, after all, and he was afraid.

It wasn't his little bottom on her lap that was sodden. It was his torso, hugged to her own.

Wet. Hot. The smell of a headless goose. He was limp against her, and his head flopped, and his arms hung loose.

She screamed.

"Be quiet!" Aunty screamed back at her. "They'll come. They'll hear him and come."

They were not going to hear Birdy. No one was, ever again.

Hear Nikeh, all too likely. Aunty reached for her. Nikeh did not know if she meant to cut her throat as well or merely shake her into sense, but she jerked away from the old woman's grasp and flung her brother's body at her, banged into the ladder and swarmed up, banged her head on the trap door and heaved it back, and the straw mattress that had partially covered it, and scrambled on hands and knees through the mess Aunty and the soldiers of the All-Holy between them had made of the furnishings of the room. She found her feet and ran through the main room of the house, out the door, which stood open, unthinking as the hare with the hounds behind her, into the yard. The smithy was aflame, burning as though it were the heart of a furnace. Men saw her. Mouths gaped and yelled and she ran and scrambled away over the drystone yard wall. Little Squirrel had been her baby-name, because she began to climb and clamber as soon as she could crawl. Over the wall—her secret shortcut to the sloping rough ground where geese and goats strayed, behind the smiths' house and the tower, walled not by palisades but by the rising cliff against which the village set its back.

Blackthorn shrubs that even the goats did not devour. People there. Struggling. Or clutching close in screaming, wailing knots and the blades rose and fell. A man with a red surcoat over his armour who watched one such butchery wheeled his pony, whirled a hand-axe and came after her.

The pony did not like the rough ground. There were fissures and boulders and middens. Nikeh evaded it, flung herself into thorns by the cliff-foot, scrambled along behind them shredding clothing, tearing skin and hair. Later, she would find a thorn broken off in one heel and one piercing like a nail through the palm of her hand. Then, she felt nothing. Fortunate that she did not lose an eye. Along the cliff and to where a near-vertical seam rose, like a ditch climbing the cliff. Forbidden, very forbidden. In every generation, some foolhardy youngster died trying to make that climb. She had been halfway up and safely down, and gotten her bottom justly tanned for it, only a month before.

Up. No higher than the top of the concealing blackthorns. She wedged herself into the crack, perched like a swallow's nest on a ledge of stone so small even her child-toes were not supported. They curled to grip the edge.

The soldiers of the All-Holy searched along the bottom. They even looked up. The rising crack was crooked, shadowed. They did not see. Maybe a branch obscured her. They went to look for easier game.

Nikeh could not see. She could only hear. She could smell the smoke.

She could smell the blood. That was most likely her own tunic, sodden, slowly cooling and gluing itself to her skin.

She could hear, all the long day. What she heard—

She would never think of that. Never.

There was smoke. The sky, for a time, was dark with it.

Her joints seemed slowly to freeze. They ached for a while, but then they stopped feeling. Assorted cuts and scratches and punctures throbbed. Tears, silent, ran down her face, dried there. Her heel was very bad, though she did not then know why. She used her teeth to worry the thorn out of her hand when she finally noticed it. At some point as the sun lowered she had to wet herself. There was no other choice. She was bizarrely ashamed. So small a thing.

Night came, but it was not dark. It was red-lit, hungry.

She moved. Fingers first. Toes. Wiggling. Stretching, carefully. One arm, another, leg and leg, unfolding, keeping her balance. She pulled her soiled drawers off in disgust and dropped them down into the branches. To be rid of them seemed important, if irrational.

Then she began to climb.

Memory, and feel. Mostly slow, crawling, going by touch. Not caring much if she fell. It would be a clean and good death and she would find herself on the road to the Old Great Gods. Each one travels the road to the Gods alone and the innocent child is gathered swiftly into their arms, but regardless, she pictured in her mind how she would find Birdy there and take his hand. They would find mama and papa, and they would all walk the road together. Aunty would not be with them. Aunty's would be a long and grim road. She had done something terrible. Nikeh would not think of her. Nikeh would die, and Birdy would be waiting for her, and the Gods would welcome them into their land of light.

Or she would make it to the top, and the wilderness of the mountains. And she would find a weapon, and a teacher, and she would learn to kill. She would kill the red priests wherever she found them, and she would kill the All-Holy, because it was a lie he was blessed by the Old Great Gods. She would burn him in a furnace, like raw ore being smelted, till he was ash.

She slipped, more than once, and always caught herself again, though her wounded hand and her foot were burning. Little Squirrel. The cliff did not so much reach a plateau as merely become less steep, wild fig and gorse and more blackthorn growing in cracks. She went blind into unknown terrain, crawling as much as she limped, and perhaps the memory of the goddess Emras was truly with her, some ghost-shadow familiar with these mountains taken into her bones with the water of the sacred spring from which she had drunk all her life, that she did not plunge into a ravine or an old copper-pit. In the distance, human voices made animal sounds of savagery and pain. Dogs barked and howled and were brutally silenced. Farther and farther away. At some point she simply fell asleep, like an animal, unable to go on.

Light woke her. Nikeh cried, but her mouth was dry and there were few tears. Her hand was red and puffy, front and back, and she found the broken thorn in her heel, which she could not dig out. She limped onwards, lost, now, among unfamiliar stones, but keeping the sun, which was high, almost to the noon, on her right. She found rainwater held in a depression in the rock and sucked it dry. She wandered on.

Not that day but perhaps the next or the one after, Nikeh found herself in a small green valley, enclosed on all sides, but with the shadow of a track running through it, a long forgotten pack road from the days when there was still copper to be found in the coastal mountains. There was a tarn, and narrow paths showed where ibex came down to drink. There were no trees, only grass and brambles and stones. She could go no further. She had nothing. No sandals, no belt, no knife, no flint and firesteel, not a cape or a blanket to cover her back, only the sloe-dyed tunic, so pretty she had thought it, faded blue as the sky. It was brown now with her brother's blood, stiff and ragged. She was a child who had only been given her grown name and learnt her letters a few years previously, too young, too small to be any use to a great warrior even to hold their horse. Not that one would ever stumble into this lost valley. Not even in a winter's hero-tale of the ancient wars. All she could do was weep and die and with her death feed the foxes and the vultures.

To be a hero does not mean one lives, her teacher would tell her. It means that, among other things, one does not lie down and die while there is still any means of going on. But that, of course, was later.

Nikeh did not lie down and die. She drank from the tarn. She threw stones at rabbits and birds and perhaps bruised one or two, but killed none. She was not a farmer's child, to have been set to driving off birds with a sling. There were no fish in the tarn. Once she caught a frog. It looked at her from golden eyes. She looked at it. It blinked. She could not stand to kill it, to hold it dead in her hands as she had held her brother. She let it go. She ate watercress and mint from the shores of the tarn, and the leaves of dandelions and daisies, brambles and sorrel, along with other greens that were perhaps not so wholesome, because once she vomited for what seemed half the night. Her hand and her foot both swelled and oozed and were hot. She could not drink enough water, it seemed. She curled up beneath a tangle of brambles, no fruit on them yet, and did not crawl out but to drink and pee, and then not even for that. She could not stand.

Her mother came and picked her up. Mama smelt like horses and roses. She gave Nikeh drink, sweet and bitter, and cool towels for her aching head, and wrapped her in warm blankets. There was searing pain in her hand, her foot, but then much of the aching went away.

Aunty came and tried to cut her throat and she screamed and struck and kicked at her. Mama rocked her in her arms and sang, but her words were nonsense. Birdy came and looked at her and stretched out his arms to be picked up, and his head flopped over showing the cords of his neck all raw and severed, like a slaughtered sheep. She screamed and screamed some more, and mama sang.

She dreamed of the wind, roaring, roaring, and fire. She dreamed of the sea. She dreamed of snow, which came once or twice in the winter. She dreamed the shape of a woman spun of flickering pale light, white and gold and bluey-green. She woke up, because it was not her mother singing to her.

There was a fire and it was night. Nikeh was naked, clean and dry and wrapped in blankets. Her hand was stiff, and her foot, and her throat hurt. She felt all strange and hollow. Someone sat by the fire. Her singing stopped, as if she knew Nikeh was awake, though she had not moved nor made any sound.

"Go back to sleep, child," the woman said. There was a difference in her way of speaking that was foreign, but not the accent of the Northron traders. "You're safe here." She smoothed the hair back from Nikeh's forehead as her mother or father might have done. "Sleep now, without dreaming. Grow strong and well."

The next time Nikeh woke it was daylight. There was a horse grazing nearby. She lay and watched how its yellow teeth sheered through grass and dandelions, how its lips and tongue somehow avoided the daisies. It was a big horse, white speckled with brown, not one of the mountain ponies. A horse like the one the emissary of the All-Holy had ridden, tall and solid, a horse of the Nearer Grass, though she did not know it then, nor how the red priests began to build waystations across the Dead Hills along the ancient highway to the east and the pass over the Kara Mountains, nor how they brought back sometimes from their scouting horses and eastern spices and other rare and valued things for the All-Holy's favourites. She muffled her cry in the blanket, lest the priest she feared see her, but the priest was dead, papa had killed him, and the horse raised its head and gave her a somewhat wondering look out of a big purple-brown eye. And then it took a step, two, three, four, and began to snuffle over her. It started at the top of her head, great nostrils flaring, whiskers tickling over her face, and went down the length of her blanket-cocooned body to the lump of her feet. She had a confused terror it might eat her.

"Let her be, Specky."

Nikeh sat up then. She had not dreamed the woman, and she did not know her, and the stranger had a foreign horse like the priest. Nikeh was prepared to kick and scream and bite and whatever she must. She raised her arms to defend herself. Her left hand, which had been pierced by the thorn, was wrapped in linen bandages. Her arms felt strange and light, feeble as little sticks and as though they did not properly belong to her at all.

The woman squatted down by her and smiled, so kindly. Nikeh did not hit or kick, or scream. She only lay back and stared. She had never seen such a person before. The woman was not someone from Emrastepse. Nikeh knew enough to know she was not likely to be someone from the tribes of the west at all. Her eyes were narrow and thick-lashed, the darkest brown in colour, and her hair was black, black as a raven's feather, falling sleek and long about a face more lovely in its shape than any marble relic of the empire preserved in the hall of the princess's tower. Her nose was small and her cheekbones broad. She was lighter-skinned than most folk of Emrastepse but not so pink and sun-ruddy as a Northron off the ships. In truth, Nikeh thought her a goddess, though how she herself had crossed so many mountains that she had come into the land of a foreign goddess Nikeh could not have said.

The woman wore unfastened a rough, hairy coat, striped dull blue and black, but under it she flashed bright as a butterfly's wing, all rose and green and crimson.

"What's your name, child?" she asked.

Nikeh only stared at her. Tears began leaking down her face. She could never, in after years, understand why she could find no answer, only that she hurt so, and could find no way to say it.

"Well, there, it doesn't matter," the woman said. "Did you come from the village?"

Nikeh managed a twitch of her head. The woman nodded, patted her unbandaged hand and tucked both back under the blankets again. "You rest a little longer, and then you can sit up and eat some soup."

Later, Nikeh would learn how Teacher had found her curled dying under the blackberry canes as she followed the ancient miner's road through the mountain wilderness, coming by a circuitous route to spy upon what the priests did at Emrastepse, where already the surviving folk had made their professions of faith to the priests and been tattooed with the sign of the All-Holy. They were rebuilding the village to a new plan, with a great hall for the priests and a school for the children, and a tower for the new prince, who was not a traitor of their own folk but the son of the new prince of Hannothana, a boy of fourteen named Dimas.

Teacher had been to Emrastepse afoot, following Nikeh's trail by wizardly means, once she had dealt with the fever and the infection that raged through her blood. Curious where the child had come from, what she might be. She had watched, hidden by more than human hunter's cunning, from the clifftop, as the bodies were thrown into the sea off the headland where the tide might take them out into a current. She would not, once Nikeh was able to stand, let her go back.

They took the old pack-road. Nikeh was dressed in a long-sleeved smock of some fabric which was not linen, but very like it, and wrapped in Teacher's striped coat, held before her on the big horse at first, and then, as she grew stronger, clinging behind.

Teacher wore a sword on her back with a tassel of scarlet and sky-blue ribbons trailing from the pommel. Among the few burdens the horse carried was a long coat of armour like nothing Nikeh had ever seen, black, all the glossy plates fastened with cords of sky blue, blue ribbons fluttering from the shoulders. There was a helmet like a demon fox-mask with a crest of more sky-blue ribbon. Teacher put in on to show her, because she was curious, but in those days Nikeh never saw her don it in earnest.

Teacher was a warrior and a wizard. Nikeh had by improbable miracle run and limped and crawled and stumbled her way into the winter's tale of the heroic avenger she had sought. Now she need only grow big enough and strong enough to wear such armour and wield such a sword herself. Then let the red priests fear her.

Children dream. Dreams carry them on, one foot after another, when despair clings close and smothering.

"Child," Teacher called her, kindly enough. She never said what Nikeh should call her, so Nikeh thought of her as her teacher, the one she had sought. She would wonder, when she grew older, if that was why she could find no words in those first months—to speak that dream would be to destroy it in an adult's laughter, whether derisive or only gently mocking.

Teacher talked to her all the time, telling her things about the land, about the weather. Small things. Keeping the world real to her. Teacher was wise in the lore of the wilderness. Nikeh learnt to set snares and to tickle small fish into her hands in the mountain streams, to flip them out and kill them swiftly, to gut them and to cook. She learnt which plants were wholesome to eat, and which were not, and which had other properties useful to know. She learnt to brush as much of Specky as she could reach and clean his great hooves. He was a very gentle, patient horse, an intact stallion but sweet as an old pet tomcat. Once Teacher left her hidden and went away for an entire day and a night, and returned with a tunic and drawers only a little too large, an oily felt cape against rain and cold, sandals. Best of all was a knife for her very own, and a small bow with arrows, fit for a child. She began to learn to hunt. Sometimes Teacher would fall without thinking into other languages, which even Nikeh's ear could tell were not one and the same, and she began to pick out meanings. Thus she began to learn Nabbani, not as it is spoken on the eastern caravan road but the true Imperial, and also the tongue that belongs to no one folk but is the language of the western road.

It was autumn before she spoke at all herself, one evening, only to whisper, "My name's Nikeh. Nikeh. Not 'child,'" before bursting into tears. She cried for a long, long time. Teacher held her close and did not mind how the child's anguish beslubbered her silk brocade.

There had always been a hermit on the mountain. Sometimes he came to the village unasked, knowing that some child had fallen ill, some hunter had struggled home with a broken bone or a wounded dog. Dogs, ponies, men, women, the little red cattle—he was physician to them all. He knew the secrets of herbs and of the compounding of drugs. He knew the cleaning and stitching of wounds and the setting of bones. Sometimes he did nothing but lay his hands on them. There was healing in his hands. And when there was nothing else to be done, there was the easing of the unbearable pain; there was a quiet passage to the road to the Old Great Gods.

Sometimes he walked among the trees. At other times he sat in meditation, or perhaps it was in prayer, in the ruins of the old temple above the valley. It had fallen in the great earthquake, in the days of a queen only remembered because it was in her time that the great earthquake came. The fall of the mountainside changed the course of the river, which had no goddess. The royal seat moved to another valley, the farmers followed, and a new temple was built there to honour the god of the mountain. For the hunters who lived under the eaves of the forest, little changed but the distance to the queen's court and the market of the town.

The hermit had come after that. He was not a priest of the mountain god, but he was a holy man, and he was theirs. Sometimes priests or priestesses came from the king's town to seek his insight. Sometimes a scholar from the lowlands. He knew the languages of all the folk of the land. His skin was dark brown, his hair was long and black and curling, but his eyes were a brilliant green.

Once, he danced. It was a bad winter, and the snows were deep. The river in its new course—the old had been overgrown with great trees by then—was dammed by ice, and the rising waters threatened the valley. They went up the mountain to the hermit, and he danced, and in his dancing the ice shifted and cracked and stones rolled, and the river flowed, and even in the worst years it did not dam itself there again.

Stories began to come into the mountains, carried by the clans of wandering, godless entertainers who were dedicated to—and perhaps descended from—patron demons of the mountains and the plains, and carried as well by the scholars and the god-dedicated heralds of the city temples, who carried the messages of the kings and queens and were less prone to tell tall tales. The seer-priests in the temples dreamed, and the goddesses cried out at their visions. In the west, far, far in the west, maybe even beyond the rising of the caravan-road, war was coming. Not between folk and folk or land and land.

War against the gods.

And even gods may die.

CHAPTER XIII

*. . . early in the spring, a year before the armies of the All-Holy
began to move east*

They found him with the dawn. At first Mikki paid them no mind; wolves might drink at the river's edge as well as he. Almost too late he felt it, smelt it on them, ash and stone, nothing animal, nothing belonging to that forest, to that dawn. The birds went suddenly silent and the small goddess of the river coiled away hidden into her depths. He turned on them roaring, broke the back of the first to leap at him, swatting it away into the trunk of a massive chestnut like a child playing ball, tore the belly out of the next and the throat of the third, but they took no warning from that, had no thought for self—no self left to them. They swarmed him and he went into the river, cold and high with snowmelt, still striking and biting. The waters gave him what help they could; they were cousins of the forest, she and he, river-goddess and demon. Her current tore and rolled and pulled them under and he broke free of the jaws that gripped like traps, swam with that current until the scent of them was no longer in the air, before he angled towards the farther shore, clambered out, bloody water sheeting from his pelt.

No wolf-corpses broke the surface to drift past him.

Ice held her close, a web of frost grown thick. Even against summer's heat, what there was of it under the overhanging rocks of this broken hillside, it held its own, and after six months of winter it had merged and woven itself into the coiling drifts. Below, the Shikten'aa snaked its way to the northern sea, still and white, the ice not yet breaking. It divided and braided. Islands of gravel and sand shifted with every spring. She had seen them change through eighty springs now, eighty short summers when the sun barely ducked below the northern horizon at midsummer, eighty early autumns, the land painted in streaks of red and amber by the turning leaves of the low mat of dwarf willow and blueberries. Eighty long winters, when the wind howled and the drifts coiled around her, encircling like arms that did not quite dare touch, and the sun left the sky and the fires of the distant heavens danced and sang. Promises. Threats. Neither. They did not see her. She was lost. She had tried and failed to be lost, years, decades wandering purposeless, in the south, the east, even in Pirakul and the lands beyond that had no name in any language she had spoken till she came to them and went among the folk. Angry. Pointless. Drowning herself in wandering as another might drown herself in drink, maybe, and no more effective, either. Only now, in her stillness, in the ice that spread like a slow flood from the sheathed blade laid across her knees, she had found, at last, a place within herself beyond the reach of the Old Great Gods. Beyond everything.

Yet self . . . still clung to her. She would shed it too, in time, if she only stayed still, thought fading, heartbeat slow as that of the creatures that slept the winter through, fires of her conjoined souls burning low, like embers banked beneath turf and ashes. And in time, maybe, to cool, to fade.

The wolves were on Mikki's trail again by midday; they ran him, remorseless, all the long afternoon. He could outrun them for a time, but he bled and the wounds burned. They did not begin to heal, although the forest of his birth was all about him, root and branch, earth and water, stone and air. Always when he slowed to walk, head hanging, ribs heaving, he would begin to feel the wolves behind him again, a heavy presence—begin to jog again, and then to gallop. Cold behind him, and fire in the veins.

They knew him. Someone's miscalculation, that they had not come before the dawn, or maybe that was deliberate and they hunted through the day for his torment and their pleasure. For someone's pleasure. Not their own.

The Old Great Gods had damned him for the alliance he had made. He was demon, halfling demon. His father had been mortal human but it was his mother's nature came uppermost in him, soul of the earth, the Gods' ally if he chose—and he chose *not*—but either way his soul's disposition was no concern of theirs in life or death. They damned him for where he had chosen to give his love, long ago; they had held that as a weapon, without his knowing, against the woman he had chosen, but she was gone. The Old Great Gods should not seek his destruction now. She had denied him.

He had sent her away.

He was no lever to move her, no spur to force her. Not any longer. She had made that clear to all who might watch her, to the Great Gods themselves.

What hunted behind was not wolves, though it wore them, and not any will of the Old Great Gods of the distant heavens.

Dusk ran over the land, shadows spreading beneath the trees like an incoming tide. Night, inexorable, must bring an ending. The wolves were closing in. He had thought to lose them, wrapped in the forest, lost in what was, in the end, himself—a great slow-breathing life, one shaggy giant golden bear nothing but a forest soul amidst forest soul, hazed and hidden. Forlorn hope. His blood was in their mouth—they, it, pack forged to singular will—and they followed as if harnessed to him and dragged behind.

There would be no losing them. He understood that now.

Cast it aside, Mikki had said. Defy the Old Great Gods. Deny them.

She could not. They had bound her to this duty. Half she saw the need; half she defied it, and served it, and could not choose to walk away however she strove to avoid, to wait, to hope the need would, in the end, not come—she thought she would have served, to a point, and tempo-rized in her service even had there not been that threat lying over him. But there was, and he had been the last thing that mattered, when all else in her heart crumbled to dust and blew away.

She could not lay aside the weapon the Old Great Gods had charged her to wield.

Then go, he had said. Go, and don't come back. I will not walk beside that sword any longer.

And she had gone. And if she had not resumed the hunting she had so long and so reluctantly pursued, neither had she walked away from Lakkariss, which was the chain that bound her, and the prison that held her, and the reward of her service. Most of all, it was the thing that must not, ever, be abandoned, to fall into hands that might find some other use for it than that for which the Gods had set it free.

But at last she found she had come to a place within herself where she could let caring go, even caring for that—call it duty—for which she had sacrificed her last friendship. Sacrificed love. She would be bone again, and the earth would take her. What came then, if the heavens would open and reclaim the sword, if another find it and turn its edge to some worse task than what she had borne it for . . . she would not care. She would be bone, and dying embers, and dust. She willed to be no more than that. To cease.

Here, in the heart of the Hardenwald, the hill of bones, the ancient mound where a forgotten human-folk had laid their dead and the wizards of the north had bound the dead-and-not-dead devil Ulfhild Vartu in God-forged chains of song for a demon's keeping . . . here where his mother Moraig had died, the great bear-demon of the Hardenwald, slain not by Vartu but by Heuslar Ogada, the first of the seven devils to die in truth out of the world, after Mikki's own long hunting at Ulfhild Vartu's side . . . Here or nowhere, he would stand.

Here.

And too late.

Sunset upon him, too soon, too soon. He felt it in his marrow.

Halfling demon. No shapeshifter, he, not by his own will.

And he had left all human things behind in his anger, in his hurt. His axe was abandoned in Marakand long ago.

When they killed him, there would be no one even to lay his bones in the mound, as they had laid Moraig his mother.

Those ancient folk—gone long before his Northron father Sammur ever laid aside his sword and came to carve out his small farmstead in the forest's peace, to be wooed all unlikely by the song of a demon bear—had entombed their dead with their weapons by them.

Demon, yes. The bear could hold the low entryway against the pack, where the tearing fangs might come only one or two together, but the sun, the sun failed him, and the man, a giant among human-folk, could not stand upright there. Within the winding passages and low chambers, no better.

He left blood on the stones and the last light burned like dying coals scattered on the forest floor, touched the stones and faded, faded from blood and bone. The night took him, and he changed.

Wood decayed. No spear, no axe survived usable, but there was a chieftain buried here, and a chieftain's sister.

When the wolves came, soft and flowing as if they swam the night, they numbered still nearly a score, and there was a pale fire behind their eyes. Threads of fire wove one to another, as if they were one creature, one will, one soul. It was a man met them on the threshold of the gravemound, naked and painted with his own blood, but a bronze sword in either hand.

He was Northron ship-folk, or he had been, when he sailed with his cousins before ever the devil Vartu woke, and while he had strength to stand, he would fight.

Clouds raced like colts over the stars, and the eye saw, but the mind did not, should not.

Yet it did. She breathed, and breathed again, and in the stillness there was—

—an apprehension.

A waiting, a breath held, as if she caught, on the edge of the wind, some echo, so faint—

A shadow behind the wolves. A man, maybe. The night crawled over it, thick, denying the stars, as if he wore the shadows, rags over a core of cold light, scarlet and pallid fires flickering, flowing, like the dance of the northern sky. The wolves moved away, cringing, slinking. Shadows, drawing in, growing solid. A man and a blade, Mikki saw, for a moment, and the man moved, surging up the rampart he had made of the slain wolves. Mikki's thrust went home, grating on bone; he stepped back, dragging that blade free, slashing with the other at the neck, stabbed at eyes whose fire was no illusion, was the truth, and not the body—

A sweeping blow Mikki was too slow in blocking, striking deep. One sword lost, arm dead weight. Mikki stabbed with the other, all the force remaining to him behind it and felt the blow jar up his arm and yet his enemy made no sound, only jerked back a little, laughed and struck again, a false blow, and as he twisted to avoid it his feet were hooked out from beneath him and he was down, and the wolves closing in. A searing pain, jaws about his throat not ripping, only holding, closing. Choking, his own breath gone.

Mikki gasped and could breathe again, free, limp. But the wolves seized where they could, arms and legs, and dragged him out beneath the trees. The man of shadows watched.

Released again. Each breath wheezed and he rolled weakly over. Could not lift himself even to his knees. Arm under his head. One eye open, face half masked in blood and torn flesh. One sword still left to him, one hand that had still some grip left in it and would not let go, and he would take at least one more, the next, and then the man could be the ending of him.

Reek of his blood and sweat, the torn entrails of the wolves.

Scent of a devil, even through that. Fire and ash, cold stone and hot metal.

Humans, too. Rank in their terror. There, where moonlight caught among beech-trunks like pewter and the leafless oaks like ancient stones. Watching. Waiting. Hungry and afraid.

The devil spoke, hard, commanding. One of the Westron tongues, the words slipped and changed from the distant days Mikki had known the common speech of that land. Mind couldn't hold the words. Could barely hold thoughts, follow movement. The humans crossed to him, walking warily. A man and a woman. Armoured in short-sleeved scale shirts, carrying boar-spears. The woman also carried a hammer, the man chains swinging, looped over a broad shoulder. Mikki snarled as the wolves gave way, got a mangled hand on the ground, got a knee under himself, staggered up.

He went for the devil, hopeless though that was, and hopeless it was, slow and staggering in his lunge, and the humans did not stab, but used their spears like staves to strike him to the ground again. But he had not lost his grip on the bronze sword's hilt.

Last strength, last stroke, because he was the Hardenwald, because he was Northron. Because the woman he had named Moth was gone from him and there was no hope left in the world and one did not cease to hold to what mattered, just because hope was gone. He came to his knees and the sword's point did not even prick the devil's belly, caught in an uncaring hand that bled, he smelt that, and the blade was plucked from him and tossed aside. Maybe he called her, screamed her name.

Wolf—!

There was no thought, no consideration, no waking. Only the ice, the stillness, the drowned will—shattered in fire.

She was on her feet, sword in hand, and the frost that crept from Lakkariss, even sheathed, burnt away in the wreathing flames, white and scarlet and pewter-cold. It was not the obsidian blade she had caught up but the steel. Kepra, Keeper of the Hall, sword of a king's sword, till the king's sword who carried it took another road, to end in ice and despair.

—which was where this road had begun. And what did she do here, what did she wait for but a death that would not come and—

—in the silence, there was no second cry.

A boot pushed Mikki down. Feeble struggle. Could not find his feet. The wolves, his wolves, his cousins of the Hardenwald, stood and watched. *It's not your fault,* he thought, but words meant nothing to them, nor his thought. They were dead already, or as good as. The humans, given curt orders, rolled him over to his belly, reluctance in their touch, and the devil—sang.

There was sea in his voice, and stars high and cold, and fire. Human language, but alien, liquid and flowing. Words wrapped him like chains, words chained like fire, and he bucked against them and screamed, hooks of speech sinking into him, into the marrow of the soul, pulling, twisting, against all nature, and his body changed, answering not the sun that ruled his nature but the wizardry. He became bear by night and he could barely breathe, racked beyond enduring, gasping, fighting each breath. To breathe, not to breathe, to flee the pain.

The devil was silent, considering his work. Rocked him with a foot, testing, and he had not the strength to swipe with a paw, to snarl. Falling, far, far away. Drowned in the pain, twisted against his nature.

Cold, to his neck. Iron collar. Wizardry in it, and a chill that was devil's work. The devil took the hammer while the man and woman, commanded, seized his ears in fearful hands and pulled and wrenched at his head, stretching out his neck. Stone for an anvil. The devil pounded rivets, alien word with each blow, searing in his blood.

Chains.

His body vomited, as though the wizardry, the devil's working, was a poison it could rid him of. He only lay and let it do as it would.

Orders. "Wagon," he did recognize. More orders, to him. Good Northron, and not as it was spoken in this age. To get to his feet, to walk.

He lay still crumpled on his belly, legs splayed, breathing as if still running for his life, and he could not have mastered his feet even had he wanted to. The devil prodded him with his sheathed sword, kicked him in the ribs when that won no response.

He did not blink.

High-wheeled wagon, awkward, snagging on roots, catching between trees, dragged and pushed by more human-folk.

They beat him and pulled on the chains, four chains, welded to the collar, and they not could make him rise.

In the end the devil shouted at them, and the woman who had carried the hammer, and they brought the wagon close and cut branches to make a ramp of poles. They dragged him up, by collar and chains and paws and gripping hanks of blood-slimed fur, and shoved and heaved, and crammed him in.

Chained him there, and went to the pole and the wheels and the ropes again, and began to drag him away in the direction of the river.

The devil spoke. He felt the death, the deaths, the wolves discarded, the last life burnt out of them.

The night was very cold. Let cold take him, hold him deep in winter's sleep. Mikki shut his eyes at last. Opened himself up to it. Falling. Fading.

She was Ulfhild Vartu. She was Moth. She was Mikki's damned princess, his wolf, and the executioner of her fellows for the Old Great Gods, and—

Vartu raged at her. Laughed at her, at Ulfhild, at herself—she, they. Queen's daughter, king's sister, king's sword of Ulvness, wizard and traitor and devil and homesteader's wife and skald. Vartu told Ulfhild, told self, *Look what you are, what you do. What do you reach for, in the end?*

Fool.

There was never any hope of escape, in stillness.

Maybe it had not been escape she sought. Ulfhild had learnt young to hide self even from self, to be what she must and not what she would, to serve and not to seek, and so had learnt to doubt every certainty of self. Had embraced a fire of defiance, and found that road disaster, and the unmaking of all she had valued. Had lost—all. Even self, for a time. Selves, both, but only, over slow years, to find themselves anew, made new.

And yet still treading the old paths, the service owed to what she thought was duty, the safe road, the thing that she must do. Or breaking from it in rage, running from it, in stillness now, as fire and conquest then.

Neither served. Both betrayed.

The hidden heart. The truth of self.

We are the sword we were made to be. We are the singer we would have been. We are Vartu, who warred on the Gods, and Ulfhild, who carried a sword for her brother.

We are Moth.

What is she, in the end?

Let us find out.

A spring night. The mountain air was cool, but the snows were gone save from the high peaks and the spring spate of the river was past. The stars were sharp and clear, but there was a tension in the air. A storm coming. Cattle and ponies bunched together. Dogs wanted to stay in and curl themselves small. Babies cried. Flocks of russet acorn-jays were restless, circling and screeching, long in coming to roost.

Above the peak of the mountain, the blackness of the night sky was broken. Not suddenly. A seeping of light, of colour. Pale. It ebbed and flowed and eddied, greenish, blushing red. Sudden streak of fire: red, white, green. Swirling and lashing. Pouring like an avalanche down the mountainside, or so it seemed. Those folk still awake to see took in the props that held their window shutters up and fastened those shutters closed as if for winter storm, pulled their doors to and latched them tight. This did not seem a thing for human eyes.

In the old temple, the hermit blinked and stirred. He walked out among the broken stones and the high-reaching trees of the temple ruin; he stood with his arms open and his face raised to the sky, like a priest in prayer or a singer greeting the dawn. The light washed over him, till he seemed, or would have, had there been any to see, a thing of light himself, and of fire.

Mikki prayed—but his father's folk of Selarskerry had been godless and he himself had turned his back on the Old Great Gods and they would not hear—that there might be no waking.

On the day after the night of the fires in the sky, a hunter went to bring the hermit a pheasant she had taken and some herbs from her mother's garden, and also to ask, as all the village wanted to ask, what his wisdom made of the strange night.

He was not there. He was not there the next day, either, nor the next. When worry grew strong enough she was sent by her grandfather, the elder of the village, with her brother and her cousin, to venture cautiously into the still-roofed inner sanctum of the old temple, which daring childhood creeping to peep in at the door had told them was fitted out like a cabin with a little sparse furniture, nothing mysterious and godly at all, save that he slept, apparently, and they had whispered it around the village in wonder, beneath a coverlet made from the feathers of grey geese. They found the clay stove cold. The staff with which he had aided his climbing the steep mountainsides leaned in a corner, abandoned, but the coverlet of feathers was gone.

There was no doubt. Their hermit had left them.

In five generations, they had never asked his name.

CHAPTER XIV

*. . . the summer before the year in which the All-Holy marched
east over the Karas*

The ship was hardly big enough to warrant the name, a little sprit-rigged coastal fisher that could have gotten by with a crew of two, barely, but which was a struggle for one person on her own, and out on the open sea.

Moth could not have flown. She carried cargo. Oatmeal. Coarse flour. Cheeses. Sealed jars of mead and honey. Smoked herring. Line and hooks. Not to eat would not kill her. Not to eat kept her . . . half dreaming. Remote.

She would no longer be so. She reclaimed the world.

Anvil.

Hammer.

Axe. Not Mikki's.

Even a pickaxe.

She did not even think the hammer and anvil, tools of mortal making, would serve, but yet they must, so she would see they did. But to remake them to what she would need would be a long reforging of its own.

And a harp.

Long, long years since her fingers had touched such strings.

Strange, to be sailing west, alone. The circle of sea, the dome of sky cupped over her. Easier to keep her course at night, when the stars burned stark and cold above, wheeling slowly about the high polestar. Not so difficult by day. She had only a straight road to follow; she had gone up the coast, far up, till the singing sense of earth and sky thrummed with what had been, like a string of the harp calling out its sympathetic echo. And then to the west, with the polestar, the Owl-Daughter's left eye, riding high over her shoulder. Sun, for her, was warm on the eyes even when the clouds grew thick and grey; no need for a sunstone to find it.

Moth did not like this gathering of cloud. The air was warm. It smelt wet, thick with rain, and the waves began to roll into great peaks. The wind, which had for days been fair, blowing up from the south-east without any intervention of her own, was gusting again, hard and erratic, buffeting this way and that but tending over to the south-west, which she also did not like, and strengthening.

The ship was a tiny thing, a leaf, a shell.

To shift her course to the north-west would put her broadside to the waves. To turn and run before the storm took her far out of her way and into northern waters where there might even yet be floating mountains of ice, moon-pale, savage, drifting silent.

No steering oar but a tiller, a rudder beneath the sternpost. Not the ships she had known. Well, the world moved on. She had already reefed the sail to give her just enough of the oxblood-red canvas for steerage-way as the wind strengthened and gusted; now, with a rope on the tiller to keep some mastery of where the vessel headed, she hauled the sail up to its boom. She had lost the wooden sea-anchor while riding out a bad blow a week before. The fishers she had bought the vessel from—with a handful of gold more than its worth, and if the rings were plundered from a barrow, well, it was far inland; they would not be accused and Viga's reckless son was long gone to the Great Gods' road, his fingers did not need the ornament—had kept their nets, which might have served. She bundled up the waxed leather awning and knotted a walrus-hide rope about it. The knots were spells of binding and enduring, wizardry of the Great Grass. She would not lose this one. Made the rope fast at the stern and paid it out as she let the ship come about into the wind; it wallowed unnervingly at first, took the next wave under its breast and climbed it straight. Moth lashed the tiller with a turn of rope and a hitch she could free with a single tug, and took a knife. *Journey*, she cut, on the stem, which was a plain thing, unornamented. *Water.* And *hail*, for destruction, interlaced with the rune of negating. *Journey*, on the tiller itself, as the ship climbed and climbed upward, and plunged down as if it would turn whale, dive beneath the green-black wall that rolled and rolled and caught them up again, she and the ship together. *Journey*, and *sun* for protection, and *land*, which, here, in this moment, meant home. *Journey*, on the mast, and *boar* for strength, and *sun* for protection again. She cut her finger, coloured each line with blood, the ship flinging itself down another long slope. The back of the sea humped and they rose again. Moth went back to the tiller, sucking her finger. It had scabbed over by the time they climbed the next wave. No leaving nature to do its work; enough nature to contend with here.

And she did not want to exert herself, to disperse it. Should not interfere, even confining her working to human wizardry, which there were few could hope to bring to bear with any effect against such a storm, but of those few Ulfhild was one. What she set herself to do was so great a thing, an unmaking and a making . . . she wanted . . . needed, all the world about clean and pure, raw, no lingering threads of power, no stain of other thought or other desire or other will, to taint it.

And she was so close now.

Which was not a good thing.

Night had fallen in southern lands. Even here, the light thickened into a heavy twilight, the hidden sun sinking in the northwest. It would drown itself and rise again soon, but the moon was following it close. There would be no light even if the clouds were to break.

More likely to break was her hull. She might be advancing, might be holding position, might be retreating, plaything of the waves.

She could feel the wave-path to the place she sought, like a thread of warmth under her hand, when she concentrated. A pulling, as if she gripped an angler's line.

The next wave flung them skyward, and staring, owl's eyes, the dark made light . . .

A splash of white to the north-west. A darkness, thicker, harder than the waves. And another combing line of white, more darkness. Nearer.

Not good. Not at all.

At least now she knew where she was, and the ship had all the blessings she could give it. Her. All the protections, save a name.

An ill thing, not to name a ship, it had always been said in the north. She came to it a bit late.

"*Swift*," she told it, told her, and had to lean back hard, fighting some force that seemed to seize the rudder, would have flung *Swift* sidelong. To founder now . . .

Currents, beneath the waves. The water coiled and chopped.

Banks. Shoals. Reefs of savage young stone. Nothing was certain here, and no fishers ever came so far; there had been no one to question as to such things. One did not sail to the Drowned Isles, the lost lands, from which the folk of the first kings in the north had come. The songs said the land was not the same from season to season.

She should know. She had written some of them.

They had come out of the further west before that. Driven out. War in some forgotten homeland. East of Pirakul, west of the sea? Their songs had preserved that memory, till a second fleeing, their green isles broken and burning behind them, gave them new lost lands to sing of. She hadn't found any place in all her wanderings where the speech of the folk was anything akin to the language of the north. Perhaps they had all gone, sailing east to come to what she now sailed west to find, every last grandmother and child, none remaining.

White foam, a long line of it. Was that the ghost of Ertholey, and Ravnsfjell rising to the south? Ghost. Memory. Nothing there, south.

Beyond though, a flicker, more distant. Night-searing scarlet, the colour of iron heating in the furnace. Holy Ulvskerrig. Perhaps. The Wolf-Smith's isle was not the only one where the broken land belched burning stone. Lost against as the water dropped them into another black valley.

The sense of time washed away in the night, in the heave and fall, the wind-roar darkness. She was soaked to the skin and bailing, the tiller's rope around a pin for leverage and fast in her fist against the capricious roiling beneath. Gradually, that lessened. *Swift* was being pushed away, no bad thing. The glimpses of the angry white breakers over the ruins of the sunken land when they climbed to the crest of a wave grew more distant and were lost, even as the brief night thinned to a grey morning, the east burning sullen.

They rode it out, Moth and *Swift*. Another long day, another short night, and the waves calming sometime after the dawn, the wind growing gentle.

Muscles ached. Her hands felt raw, and looked it. Rope-burns, broken blisters. Shoulders felt as if her arms had been wrenched half out of them at some point. She was shiveringly cold, which was human memory. She stretched, slowly, painfully. Bent, stretched again, reaching to the cloud-hidden sun.

The wind was freshening out of the south-east again and the clouds were tearing. Flash of blue.

Laughing. A fair fight well-fought. Wrung out her hair and braided it once more. Bailed out again, the wooden pail tethered to a cleat, good thing. All she carried was secured, and the ship—a boat but for the use she put it too—had no covered deck, only the awning turned sea-anchor, which she was currently dragging behind and which had made them gradually nose around with the changing wind so that now the dawn was on her left shoulder. Moth let the waves continue to have their way with *Swift* while she took a quick inventory. Jars still intact and sealed, and waxed cheeses would take no harm from the sea. The anvil was still securely bound, had done no damage and would take little, though the last of the salt seawater still sloshed about it. Everything.

Save her boots, which she had shoved under a thwart when the rough weather blew up, thinking as it worsened there was no slight chance of her going overboard and old habit . . .

No boots. Damnation.

She might walk barefoot in snow without regard for frostbite. Didn't mean she wanted to spend six months, ten months, so. Well, she'd be caught between the fire and the ice for as long as it took, booted or bootless, and that was no new thing.

Moth hauled in the dripping rope of the sea-anchor, coiling it as it came, the awning damnably heavy in the sea's grip. Once upon a time Ulfhild, doughty king's sword though she was, would have had a struggle getting that back aboard or even hauled in close enough to grab. She might have, hah, cut her losses, cut it away. No need now. It came aboard pouring water. She spread it to dry best it might, still keeping her nose to the wind, and bailed once more. Only then turned *Swift*, slow and dead and little answer to the tiller, wave buffeted, lowering the sail from the high boom. Felt her come to life again, a tug as the sail filled, taking the wind.

Nose to the west and the sea creaming cheerfully under her bow. Turned out she hadn't been pushed so far back as she thought; it was not full dark when she saw the warning white breakers again, and this time, a black hill rising behind them. Too far north. That would be Nordholm, where the yearly midsummer gathering had been held. The god's presence was something she could feel, but he was changed, terribly changed. Something of stone, and only half-aware, like a winter-dreaming beast. No words. No thoughts. Broken by the savage breaking of his land, so many of his folk dead in so small a time, and their beasts, and the wild birds, and the very vegetable life.

Not the work of wizards or devils. Not the anger of gods or even the Old Great Gods. Only the crust of the earth cracked from within like a hatching egg. It was not a place human-folk should ever have planted themselves, to spread shape and thought and words into the half-formed god, to give him what he had not grown to hold. But even their wizards had not understood the flaws in that land, till too late.

Starlight. Enough for devil's eyes. Rocks beneath, flowing shelves and broad staircases of it, and razor-sharp ridges like the spines of Holy Ulvskerrig. Sail, or oars? Shame to lose the anvil in some channel now.

Caution was called for. Moth furled the sail to the boom again, drifting as she unshipped the rudder, then unlashed the oars and set them between their pins. Rowed without glancing over her shoulder, eyes closed, feeling her way instead. Stone, water—deep wave and shallow current pouring—like colours, woven beneath, around her, she and *Swift* one form, swimming them.

But damn, her shoulders ached.

Feeling your age, my wolf? Mikki would say, and shove a cold nose against the back of her neck, grinning. Though since it was dark night and he would be in his human form, she would point out he was the sailor born, the sea-raider's son who'd gone coasting with his cousins, not all of whom had been honest traders, and set him to the oars in her place. Put those hard muscles to good use. And they wouldn't have shipped the rudder; she'd be at the tiller, where she could steer and steer him, and if she let her eye enjoy the view and the straining of his tunic, if he had one, over his chest and belly, better view if he did not, the pelt of barley-gold curls—well, he'd be grinning at that, knowing where her eye tended, too, and all the more eager to put his back into it, to have them where they were going and free to think of other matters.

She had gone back to him. That was after Ivah had died, not her daughter but holding somehow a piece of that place in her heart. She had left her far wanderings too late and so she had gone to the empress's tomb and found there the god of Nabban, the strange and yes, beautiful creature she had first met in Marakand, not knowing precisely what he was. A vessel resonating with the distant chord of godhead, there in that city foreign to him. He had been whole, in his own land. So much more strongly of and in himself. Terrifyingly so, even though it would be she who in the end prevailed if ever they came to battle, being what she was and he only a god of the earth, however great; it nonetheless felt like standing before a mountainside of snow, knowing it might fall upon one at a wrong word, a wrong step. A mass that warped the world about it.

And his man. She knew a fellow hunter when she met one, but that one was more. Or rather, less. Predator. Missing something a sane and whole human should have. But his god made for him that missing piece, completed him, and that he was some tangled thing of necromancy and not exactly a living man did not trouble her over much. What freedom, if one did not have the disposition of one's own soul, in the end? Even to give it away to another. He was no captive bound against his will; not the Old Great Gods themselves had right to meddle there, in her opinion.

Theirs, of course, might differ.

Opinionated bastards.

"Go to the one who helps you remember who you are," the god of Nabban had said. And she had.

And Mikki had sent her away.

"I can't do this anymore," Mikki had said. "I won't follow that damned sword. Moth . . ." And he had shaken his head, naked with the first snow falling around him, slow and drifting in the dark, the Hardenwald, near the ancient long barrow, overgrown with beeches, that had been his demon-mother's den. "Be rid of it. Refuse them."

"I can't."

"And I can't," he had said, hopeless. "You never told me. You lied to me. With or without words, you did. This hunt was never your atonement, never your own will. They've made you their executioner."

"They've made you their hostage."

"They told you so. You're the one who says the Old Great Gods lie. They've done nothing while you've been gone, wherever you've been hiding. You weren't seeking Dotemon or Jasberek, were you? Or even Jochiz, who at least well deserves killing. And if they do not lie in holding some threat over me, and only wait in patience yet to see if you go back to their road, still I won't be used to compel you. I won't."

Had she said the Old Great Gods could, would lie? She did not know. She did not even know what she believed.

"I can't let Lakkariss go. To come to the hand of Jochiz? No." Sword of the cold hells. Weapon to kill the devils, to destroy them and what they had made themselves, tear them from the world. No. Not in the hands of Sien-Shava Jochiz. What else might a shard of the cold hells sever from existence?

"I won't come with you," Mikki said. "*Minrulf*, I'm sorry."

She had only stood in silence, having no arguments that had weight even in her own ears, save that one, that Lakkariss could not fall into the hands of Jochiz, and to keep it from him, she had still to carry it, and walk her road. Mikki had turned his back and walked away. She had stayed, till the snow covered his tracks in the frost. Then she had flown.

Holy Ulvskerrig, or the ruin of it. A plume of steam rose somewhere beyond, hissing like a winged dragon's warning, then died. Her keel touched. Miscalculation. She held her breath, as if that would lighten them, and *Swift* rolled forward, free. A beach, of sorts, before her. There was even sand, a thin blanket of it, the black rock ground down.

There was nothing to recognize in the landscape. Might have been the mouth of the little melt-water stream from the yearly summer ebb of the ice on the peak.

No stream. No small mountain ever-iced on its northern heights.

No wolf-demon. The Wolf-Smith—he had no other name—had come with their ancestors out of the west, following the sacred ravens. He had not joined them when they took to the ships again, fleeing along the routes they had followed east and back since ever they settled, timber being one vital thing which the green islands lacked and the great for-ested land to the east had in plenty. Ships were life.

There had always been a thought that they should follow that road over the waves anyhow, and seize some portion of the coast for their own. But the gods and goddesses of that land were not their own. An argument that ceased to hold them back, once their homes were gone.

The Wolf-Smith had remained behind when the last ship sailed, that the god of the isles not die alone. But the god had been alone, before ever they came, and some echo of him remained, while the smith was gone.

Chill reminder. Even the demons died. And Mikki was only a half-ling.

Moth pulled *Swift* up scraping over stone. No driftwood to use for rollers. She did not expect to sail her again, but she was averse to sleeping in the rain when she did not have to. She was not here to lose herself in the earth, to forget self, and that meant some acknowledgement of human needs.

"You did well," she told the ship. One did so. A ship had no soul, but she had . . . something, at least in the minds of those who sailed her. One acknowledged that.

The isle rose from the sea in black stone steps, up to a ridge like a jagged spine. A sleeping dragon curled almost nose to tail, like a horse-shoe. She unloaded the ship to spare her keel as much as possible and hauled her more than halfway up the slope, to where, Moth hoped, not even the worst autumn storms might fling the waves. Lugged up jars and sea-heavy awning, sail, ropes, cheeses, tools swathed in waxed leather, and the anvil last of all. Climbed on unburdened to the top of the ridge. The stone was rough on her feet, and warmer than it should have been. Not a wasteland, though. Some white-flowering cresses were rooted in cracks in the rocks, and lambsquarters, too. Seeds that had clung to birds, perhaps. Puffins, terns, gulls might still come to the cliffs, though the season was too late for eggs. Dawn would wake them to a raucous chorus. A little relief from a diet of fish—greens and birds both. And there would be dulse, quahogs, though not in the cove below.

Sheltered water, that cove, but not sheltering. She doubted there would be many fish down there, either. Fogs shifted, coiling like clouds, hiding and revealing.

Thread of scarlet.

Moth went back down to *Swift*. A house, of sorts, to build. And a forge. Of sorts.

Much to do.

Dreaming, beneath the pines of Swajui. Lying by the cold springs, a pair of coats over them for covering against the cool air, Ahjvar in his arms. They lay down here this summer night; it is not dream but real, and yet he dreams it, too, and in his dream still holds Ahjvar, who is lying in the true night curved against his back and a heavy arm over him, slow breath in his hair. In the dream Ahjvar is awake; he dreams, too.

"Souls go to the road," Ghu says. "To the Old Great Gods. We say, it is their proper place."

"No," Ahjvar says, and almost the dream shatters, he tenses, his sleeping hand grips hard, digging into flesh as if someone seeks to drag him away.

"Hush, no," Ghu says, and frees himself from that hand in the night, turns over and pulls Ahjvar to him, head on his chest, arms around him, a hand soothing his hair, so that dream and night are doubled, fading one into another. "I don't mean that. But why, do you think?"

"Why what?" Ahjvar is half waking regardless. The breath of his words tickles his chest.

"Why is it the proper place of human souls, to go to the Old Great Gods, when all others return again to the great world from which they are born?"

"It's the way it is," Ahjvar says, and does wake, and sits up, breaking the dream. "What's worrying you?"

"I was dreaming."

"You're always dreaming. Dreaming what?"

"That I asked you this."

Ahjvar shakes his head and laughs. Covers a yawn with the back of his hand. He's been out to Bitha, newly ridden home. A long last day of travel behind him. Takes Ghu, a hand behind his neck, pulls him down to lie head in his lap, pulls coats over him. "Go back to sleep, idiot boy."

But he doesn't sleep, warmth of a thigh under his cheek notwithstanding, and Ahjvar does not lie down to sleep, fingers playing in his hair.

"The bards," Ahjvar says at last, "have an old, old song. It's only scraps, within another tale. An old woman, a wanderer, comes to the king's *dinaz* claiming to be—the name is gone. It means nothing within the tale, but you're supposed to know that once it did, that when it was first sung, it was important, who she was, and that she was ancient, and important, in older tales. The king's own bard questions her. It's a ritual—that's what my tutor believed. Something wizards once knew, and bards, but no one remembers and it's only a strange old song that hardly anyone sings, because it doesn't make sense. She should have been a scholar, my tutor. Gone to Marakand. She was always more interested in digging into the broken ruins than in building new."

"Sing it?"

"I don't remember. I'm sorry. But there are questions about the names of trees, and stories in the stars, and one is about the journey of the dead. And it says, they walk along the river and the river flows both ways, and my tutor said, she thought, from something else she'd heard up among the forest-kingdoms, that the pieces of older songs in the song we had, told that the Old Great Gods did not hold the souls of the dead, but only—took them in. Like, like they were travellers. The dead, I mean, not the Gods. Travellers come a long and weary journey, come from long battles within themselves. Come for rest, and healing. And then they go their way."

"Where?"

"Elsewhere?"

Something wanted him to dream himself here. To this.

Ahjvar, he thinks, had never wanted that rest the Old Great Gods promised. Ahjvar had only wanted oblivion, to shed himself and be done.

Did even a good life lived happy and content, and ended in peace, did even that want to simply . . . endure? To end, but never to end, to wait, held by the Gods—for nothing, an eternity of existing without . . . living?

That pain. It has his attention now. That yearning, that desperate need. He sits up again, leaning against Ahjvar.

"Ghu—" Ahj begins to say and Ghu silences him, two fingers on his lips. Leaves them there, and smiles a little when Ahvar opens his mouth and takes them in, a tongue touching, tasting. But he is listening.

Heart reaching for what is severed from it. Open, to engulf, not to destroy, but to take back, to make whole what has been sundered, what is one life with unnumbered expressions, which cries, self to self, to be complete, an ocean living, a tide that rises and falls, a cycle, yes, of water, cloud, rain, river, sea, and the mist rises to cloud and lives again in rain and pool, in spring and stream and the great rivers and the lakes, and the ocean's pulse endures . . . and it flows life to life, gods, demons, beasts, trees, moss beneath them . . .

The Old Great Gods cannot easily touch the world, because though the souls of the dead may still pass to them, the road is broken against their returning, save with great suffering and pain. The songs of the north say this, and call it the work of the seven, as they went down to defeat and their imprisoning graves.

The souls of the dead may still pass to them. So it is said. They go to their road. He knows that much. He has felt its pull, its reaching to take Ahjvar from him, the desire of the souls of the dead to fly to it . . .

But what lies at the end of the road?

The dead are taken in by the Gods. And the songs—are they born from the dreams of the seers and shamans, or from where does this knowledge seep, rising like water through sand—changed to say, they went and did not return. But the world yearns for their return . . .

They go, and there is no return, soul into soul.

"Oh," he says, a long sigh, and gives his attention to what Ahjvar is doing.

Autumn, and the storm winds blew up from the south, warm and thunderous. *Swift* was upturned, mast removed, the hull a roof bound to the earth with walrus-hide ropes, over curving walls that were broken blocks of the raw black stone, caulked with eelgrass. A bed inside, only the folded sail for mattress and an oily woollen cloak for covering. A door of sorts, made of the bottom-boards, which could be propped in place against storm. A hearth outside, walled on three sides against the prevailing winds. There was driftwood to burn, sometimes, when she could roast fish or fish-rank bird and make porridge or bannock. Sometimes she only soaked oatmeal and the smoked fish in water till they were fit to chew. Quahogs she ate raw, and fresh fish in a pinch, with dulse and greens. She did not like to cook on the hot stones, though there were places she could have done so. She tried it for bannock. It gave the bread a foul taste and left grit in the crust.

Mikki would have joked about the food, foul and fowl and the flavour of gulls however cooked.

There was water. She had deepened one high rain-pool, hacked rivulets to fill it more swiftly. The sea for bathing, though, the warm strange water of the cove. It mattered, the bathing. She came to each morning's work clean, new with the dawn, whether that work was sweating half-naked over the heating and beating of the anvil and hammer themselves or the singing, the words building, syllable by slow syllable, what she would have be, transforming these small piece of the world, this iron of some Northron forest forge, into something adamantine.

Long weeks in the singing, the reforging. By the autumn, the fledglings of the cliffs flying away, that was done. It had been only the making of the tools.

CHAPTER XV

*. . . autumn, with winter drawing near, and Moth remains at her
forge on Holy Ulvskerrig*

A grey goose, low over the sea. Lost, for a moment, in the molten glare of the rising sun. A goose, out of season. They should have been long on their way to southern marshes, and geese, besides, did not often fly solitary. Moth stood by her hut, eyes narrowed against the light.

So.

He came to light on the stones before her, a hissing of wings shearing the air, a swirl of feathers and silk.

"Anganurth." She greeted him with a slight inclination of the head, no more.

"Ulfhild." Human name for human name. A quirk of humour at the corner of his mouth. Familiar. Missed? Perhaps. But missed so long she had all but forgotten it. The wind whipped hair across his face. He pushed it back and she smiled. He never would tie it back. Some taboo of his people, he had once confessed, that he found he could not bring himself to contravene: a wizard must not cut or bind their hair.

"I'm sent," he said.

"By whom? Anganurth, Sien-Shava has—"

"Let me take the black sword. What you intend—no."

"What do I intend?" she asked, folding her arms, but her pulse quickened. "Even I do not quite know. Listen. Did you know Sien-Shava is calling himself a god and stealing the souls of his folk?"

"Sien-Shava can be dealt with. Should have been dealt with. Weren't you charged with that very task?"

She shrugged.

"This is wrong, Vartu. What you intend—the shadows run ahead of you. The shadows of act, of consequence, are seen."

"Then you know what must follow."

"It will not be allowed. We will prevent it. We must."

"We. You speak for more than yourself, Jasberek. Who joins you in 'we'? Dotemon? Or have you allied with Jochiz in the end?"

"No. Never. Never Sien-Shava Jochiz over you. And I know nothing of Dotemon. I thought perhaps you had betrayed her and slain her as the others and still I did nothing—you know I did nothing and I could have found you any of these long years. But Vartu, what is in your mind, I cannot accept."

"You can't? Or you choose not to? Their touch is on you. The heavens—the air of them still wraps you. You are sent, you say. Are these even your own words, your own belief? What have they offered you?"

He was silent.

What? she demanded, and she was furious of a sudden. *What price your treachery?*

A thing little enough, he said. *Not even a life. I'm tired, Vartu. I'm tired, and perhaps we were right, and perhaps we were wrong. I don't even remember any more. I only want to go home. Give me the sword, to do what you will not, and then I will be allowed to return.*

They bought you with that? You?

Yes, he said. *I suppose they did. Vartu—*

No. And that was stone-hard and allowed no argument further.

He flung off the feather cloak, drawing his sword, a sweeping cut, but she was leaping back. Shieldless, unarmoured, barefoot. Unarmed; Kepra and Lakkariss both lay sheathed in the hut, and the doorway in the stones was only waist-high, like the entrance to a dog's kennel. He charged her and she leapt to the roof, stood on the keel turned ridgepole like a weathercock, wrote runes of shadows and smoke and in the moment where he blinked, summoning in mind the steps of the dance, the brief pattern with which he would have dispelled it, came down on him like a pouncing cat, to kick once and again. Anganurth Jasberek fell and rolled and never lost his sword, but she was diving through the doorway, fox to its lair, and came out with naked steel in her right and Lakkariss sheathed, held crossways in her left, catching his descending blow on its battered scabbard.

He was taller than she, his blade long, single-edged, and a slight curve to it. Wielded two-handed.

Old friends, old comrades, older in that than the human names they bore, older too in friendship than the devils they had become, Vartu and Jasberek, Ulfhild and Anganurth, doubly bound.

Doubly betrayed.

And long familiarity in their swordplay together.

Not playing now.

No wizardry now. That held between them, as if they duelled beneath the ashtree before the king's hall, and perhaps the bench-companions of Hravnmod laid bets and cried encouragement to one or the other or to both.

"Nice," he even said once, and laughed. She had laid his left arm open to the bone. But then he fought one-handed, and did not smile again. Tip caught her face, missed her eye but crossed her cheek. She was in close and Keeper thrust, and she turned aside, came back swinging for his neck and he was leading her down, and down the ridges towards the shore, where the footing was furrowed and broken and slick with bladderwrack. Lunged in suddenly and she sprang away but he kicked out and knocked her, so that she fell on her shoulder, rolling up to strike him down, kicking where she could have cut, and he landed badly, something cracking, came up again with his weight on one leg only.

"Help me," she said. "For all we ever believed, for our old alliance, help me. Don't do this, Anganurth, Jasberek—please. Don't make me do this."

He shook his head, hair falling over his face, blowing in his eyes. Red stained his shirt, a cut she had hardly noticed had touched. An underlying grey muddied the warm brown of his face, and his lips were faded. Lost his balance, that leg barely set to the ground, something grave, there.

"No. I'm done, Vartu. And Anganurth is, *we're* tired. They'll take me back, free me of him, free him of me."

"If I'm dead, and Jochiz, and Dotemon."

"Give the sword and I'll bargain for you."

He could hardly stand. But disarm him, make tea, remember old days, old campaigns, old warmth between them . . . he would heal; they did, and he would try again, and Mikki—

And Mikki.

She shook her head.

While they spoke he had been setting the patterns in his mind, behind his eyes, the dance that wove the wizardry of his folk, and the green of his eyes was washed in his fires, flame and starlight, the burning essence of him. The broken bones were knitting themselves while the spell reached into her, to pull her down to earth, to bind and hold her, rabbit-snared, choking, helpless—she felt it seizing on her, the weakening of her knees, the cord tightening about her throat.

Flung Kepra aside, drawing Lakkariss. Hilt still wrapped in old leather, dry now, brittle, hiding the silver and niello pattern. Slender blade, black. Ice. Obsidian. Its edged smoked in the air, growing a fringe of frost.

Jasberek dropped his sword, hands raised, dropped wizardry, too, gathering himself against her. Even to human eye he seemed for a moment a hollow thing, a lantern filled with flowing, liquid light, and lightning edged his hands, his speaking mouth.

Moth did not wait to hear. She thrust, following close on her blade, putting herself within his arms' grasp. His fires enfolded her. Lakkariss drank them.

She let him down to the earth, and watched the dying light, the tangled souls thinning, drawn away. Consumed, and the cold, the ice, blooming on him, frost-flowers filling his mouth, his eyes, spilling from the lips of the wound in his breast as she withdrew the sword. Frost climbing the blade, the cold's hunger reaching for her, hoarfrost over her hand.

"No," she said, and shook it away, sheathed the sword, and knelt down by him.

The body was very cold, and the little grasses, the weary end-of-autumn flowering things were crumbling to ash about him. Waves pounded the shore, the tide incoming, the weed rising to float and sway with the pulse of the waves.

Gulls cried. Only gulls, no wizard's shaping. No interest in what passed below.

He had been her friend. Her brother, her sister, before ever Ulfhild and Anganurth were born in the world. She wrapped his empty body in the feather-cloak she had taught him to make long years before and gave him to the sea where the current would take him far out, hold him for good. The ancient, razor-edged sword she threw after him.

Three days, she sat on the rocks above the tideline, where she might watch the waves run out of the east. Sat without working, without singing. Grief. Mourning. Perhaps. Perhaps only a need to be still, to let the world settle.

On the fourth day Moth rose again, took her swords and went back up to the hut, to eat and drink, and to resume what she had begun. But the first working was finished.

Now Moth changed the song to a different spell: greater, heavier, deeper. Harder to hold, and harder yet with every dawn that broke over her. The true making she had come to this place of silence and solitude to work.

The midwinter solstice came with a storm out of the north-east, and she had been singing since the equinox. Not ceaselessly, as a storyteller would no doubt have it, were a skald other than herself ever to spin this tale for the world. Only the words she needed, in the morning, bathed and fast unbroken. She sang on the shore, on the crest of the black ridge, or in the shelter of *Shrike*'s upturned keel, if the weather outside were not fit for the harp. Notes held, layered, spinning to power, a music that wound itself through and under the words, a thing of the earth, perhaps its greatest beauty. The words were not. The words were nothing of this world. They seared the air, left the scent of lightning.

One sentence, this morning. Slow. Long. Heavy. Notes scattered, a fluttering of wings. Gathered. One chord, like a great wall falling.

Strings snapped, silver—she had strung it with silver in place of the brass before she sailed—coiling wild, smoking away like hoarfrost in the rising sun.

Done.

Moth drank the last of an open jar of mead and went out into the storm, up to the height, and stood there, with Lakkariss hugged to her chest as though it were a child in need of comforting. Stood all through the day's fury, and the night's deadly cold. The sword's frost sheathed her, and the snow.

When the slow dawn came with a dying wind and a blue-torn sky, the new year's birth, she went down to the cove. No bathing. No hesitation. Nothing, now, between her and the sword and the skirling, singing shape of the power she had set.

The white fog rose to wrap her. Thick. Hot. Acrid. Water hissed.

The artery of fire had moved. It did. Sometimes it thickened, set in black scabs. It made ridges like scars, spilled over them, found a new course. The cove had changed shape noticeably since she had arrived in the summer. It might be filled and a tongue thrust out towards Ertholey before another year had passed—or there might, always that possibility, be another breaking of the earth here.

She knew it now for the deep molten heart rising. Only a weakness in the stone skin of the world, which they should never have pastured their sheep upon. Vartu's understanding, not Ulfhild's.

Vartu's vision, also, that saw the song around her, still shaped in the air, colours of deep cold and fire of the earth's heart. Fires of the stars, threads of colours that had no name, only a song.

Now the course of the molten stone crawled nearer the anvil, which stood cold, glass-glossy even in its roughness, stone risen to hold it firm, called by a song in the last of the autumn. The remade hammer lay on it, waiting. Dark, dull, eating light.

No words, now. No music. No wizardry of this earth.

Keeper was left under *Shrike*.

Moth set aside the scabbard of Lakkariss, plain and battered black leather over wood much knocked about, and with a small knife cut away the leather wrapping of the hilt's handgrip. The slender blade was black. Steel, in some lights. Obsidian. Cold. It might have been ice. The hilt was silvered, patterned all over in black niello, a scrolling design that flowed like water and was jagged like thorns. A script.

A command.

A song.

That, she could not unmake. It told the sword its nature. It made *sword*, from a shard of the cold hells, a thing that was not a thing, not here in this world, but a thought.

But she had more to tell Lakkariss, and between fire and ice, she would make it listen.

Stone, steel—both and neither. Frost was born on the blade's edge and died in the breath of the slow-flowing stone. The blade drank the heat. Molten rock grew cold and still. But the icy soul of the blade was a little warmer.

To plunge it into a smith's furnace would have done nothing. Lakkariss bore a greater cold in its heart.

No blacksmith's tongs, no bull-hide gloves. She was—there and not-there, flesh and not-flesh, making a place between worlds. Almost. A breath away from it. She felt the heat. Hair, braided back and more strictly bound than was her wont, might crisp a little where it floated free in fine pale wisps along her brow.

Or not.

It might be she was only a thing of fire herself, of cold light that would never burn, a shaping of the air.

Snow sizzled, melting as it fell.

Held in the flow, the black of Lakkariss grew red, edged in white. Heat did not deform it. The molten stone did not cling to the blade. It might have been water, rolling clean away when she withdrew the blade, drops of stone falling, bouncing. Tears of lava become pebbles.

On the anvil, the obsidian sword smoked. In her hand, a lenticular disc of clay, shaped as if pressed between two palms, scored with symbols that were just parallel lines, and angled ones. Some wizard's writing she did not know. The Nabbani god's man had made it. A spell: binding, sealing. The clay was crumbled a little at the edges. Moth held it between her two hands. Crushed. Blew dust away. A splinter of stone lay in her hand, like quartz, clear, but a milky, rose-tinged cloud in its heart, twisting, writhing . . . A fragment of a devil's soul. She laid it on the blade with a word that made the air crack like thunder and called from the air the first of the music she had made, the ringing notes, the harp strings' lark-clear cry. The words, harsh and singing. Drew one down.

Lines of fire, silver, nacre, gold. Lines of ice, tinged with the copper green of dancing light, the red of the eyelid closed against the sun.

She laid them against the blade about the shard of crystal, and they were silver on the red hot obsidian, the finest hair's-breadth filigree, and the hammer drove hard, all her devil's strength, and yet the stuff of Lakkariss and the crystal both resisted her, and the working she would make.

Heat and hammer, hammer and heat, and by day's end—a word. For those who might read it.

One word, and the crystal taken up into the silver, into the word.

Tomorrow's dawn would come.

Winter passed, and the birds returned to nest. She did not go hunting eggs, ate only in the evenings what she had brought, of which there was little now. Oatmeal soaked in water. She drank more mead than rainwater and did not fish. All was given to the work, save when she slept beneath *Swift*'s shelter or the turning stars, because the body still existed, and in this labour it grew tired as it had never been since Ulfhild became Vartu.

If the stars watched, or what lay beyond them . . . she did not any longer care.

Perhaps Mikki had been right all along and the threats of the Old Great Gods were empty. Perhaps it was only that they had lost her when she tried to put herself from the world and had not yet found her again.

A sun was setting: red, copper, rose. Not quite midsummer day. Not quite. Moth laid down the hammer. The line of lava had parted to flow either side of her anvil some time in the past weeks. The air was hot, searing-dry, harsh. Silent. She had pulled the last of the words and the music from it, the last phrase complete and hammered home, and the obsidian that was only obsidian as she was flesh and bone still held its shape, though it glowed like red-hot steel.

She carried it down to quench it in the sea.

Black blade, a lace-work of silver filigree embedded both sides of it. An edge still keen to shear the air. She did not try it.

Frost was called to its edge, and followed the silverwork, the song the made it what it would be, not a refuting of its first making, but . . . it changed. It grew in purpose. As did every living thing. Even a devil.

Moth sheathed it most carefully in its old scabbard. She laid that on the anvil, stripped—her shirt and trousers were hardly better than rags, scorched and worn thin. Hands hard-calloused, hands, arms, face, breast, thighs, shins, feet, all burn-scar spattered, a silver dappling. Flesh and not-flesh, but flesh remembered itself. This was the healing, the protection of what she was, the step aside from the world. A human woman, even a wizard, as she was, had been, would be dead.

Unbound her hair.

A white streak, falling past her face. She did not have Yeh-Lin's vanity—or perhaps not vanity, as such, but the driven necessity to shape herself exactly to what she had been, to reassure herself she was still . . . she. That, that was vanity, to care for that streak of old woman's white. But she would not remake herself to be rid of it.

Moth went into the warm water, dove and swam, out to where it was ocean-cold, and with handfuls of weed scrubbed the weariness and the heat and the feel of soot, even though there was none, from her body. Ashore, to braid wet hair again. It would dry salt-stiff. Took Lakkariss, and left her rags, and climbed over the ridge and down to *Swift*'s shelter one last time. She sat there, naked, drying, still weary, and strangely content, drinking the last of the last of the mead. Nothing else remained of the supplies she had brought. She had finished the oatmeal the previous evening.

Long shadows pooled in the twilight.

"Thank you," she said, to the memory of the Wolf-Smith, as the Westrons prayed to their dead gods. And "Thank you" to *Swift*, which would lie here until wind and storm-wave climbed high and threw her down from her stone foundation, and she bleached and cracked and went slowly back to the land.

Then Moth dressed, even to her byrnie again, and buckled on the swordbelt of Kepra, and hung Lakkariss on its baldric over her shoulder. Unfurled her feather-cloak and shook it out. That, too she had altered, over the winter, in the short evenings before she slept. A little work only, small repairs. Scavenged feathers, never prey she had taken for food. White, bright as the moon. Long-winged gull.

She flung it to her shoulders, and flew.

CHAPTER XVI

. . . early spring of the year in which the All-Holy came east of the Karas

Snow bound the mountain in sleep, and the pines bowed under the weight of it. Water still flowed. The springs of Swajui steamed; the brooks gurgled under ice. Lower down, the river too moved, hidden, the boundaries of land and water blurred, softened by snow. It sought the sea and the unending slow breath of the tides. Waves that washed the shores of Nabban, and of Darru and Lathi, his mother's lands that he had never seen but through Ahjvar's eyes, never would. Waves that swept the Gulf of Taren, that hurled themselves, high and breaking, wild, against the cliffs, where he and Ahjvar had sat on the drystone garden wall, warmed by sun or damp with fog and spray or chill with night, moonlight pouring silver over the water. Changeless, unchanging. Breath of night air, the downs behind grown with wild thyme, with lavender. The air tasted of thyme, and salt, and seaweed.

A moment, held close. He could be there. A foggy day. Damp woollen cloth. The man's knee, and he leaned his head against it as they sat in silence, the man on the wall, he at his feet. Tolerated. Maybe welcomed. In that time, he didn't know. No deeper *why*, then, but that he needed to lean there, needed that rare touch, as some kitten escaped drowning might need, more than milk or mother, to press itself into that warmth, any warmth, whatever creature it might be that had plucked it from the depths.

Ahj had taken Evening Cloud, the horse he called by the Praitannec name Gorthuernial, and ridden down the course of the river of the Wild Sister before the heavy mountain snows came. Restless. Something gnawing at him, which was never a good thing. Stories drifting in the wind, coming to them on the caravan road, like cloudy silt in clean river-water, like smoke from over the horizon, a faint stain on the sky. Rumours of war in the far west, of armies moving in the name of Old Tiypur and a new god. An empire broken and gone over a thousand, almost two thousand, years before, and a god who had no name, no place. A god incarnate and not rooted in earth, crossing boundaries a god of the earth could not cross, leaving his place, moving into the places of others.

A god who called for the deaths of the gods of the earth and waters.

A story could change, crossing the half of the world. Could be born from nothing, twisted out of all recognition, and yet . . . and yet.

So Ahjvar had gone to the City of the Empress, which had been called the Old Capital when the Golden City ruled, before typhoon and devil's malice swept that all away. Ghu might have gone himself. He might go now, move and be there, as he might be where he would, in all the land, all its hills and rivers, mountains and waters—his. But he preferred to be here, and Iri—Suliasra Iri, the young priestess-empress, daughter of the son of the daughter of the son of the son of Suliasra Ivah who had been with them when they took Nabban, did not need him under her feet. He was in all the land, and he was here. It was . . . how he was. God, heir of gods and goddesses gone, containing them all within himself. When she needed him, he would be there, or she would come to him, because sometimes the journeying was the prayer, and the empress must know her land, and be in it and a part of it, a little in the way the god was. Better Ahj went, who did not have the heartbeat of the land so strongly in him, the breath and dream of all the folk flowing over him like a thousand thousand rivers of soul. Ahj, who could stand aside and more easily look from outside, at need.

Ghu had always been confused by the noise—always, until there came a point, when need was that he was not, and all went clear and cold and clean as a blade's edge. Maybe that was just him, and not godhead. So Ahj went in his place, to see and to hear for him. Ahjvar had read what he needed in the archives of the palace, letters and reports, talked to those who had been lately in Marakand and the cities of the Taren Confederacy, which in his day had been the Five Cities with their feuding clans, rule by wealth and assassination, and the tribes of that land still, in the north at least, the free kingdoms of Praitan.

There had been little in the reports available to the palace that differed from the stories of the caravaneers. The folk of the road had their news from Marakand, after all, and Marakand was not a place for secrets. So all that they learned in the palace that the road did not say was that the senate of Marakand had decided to send agents to the west, across the Four Deserts and the Western Grass, over the Kara Mountains into the blighted lands of Old Tiypur, and that those agents had not yet returned when the most recent report from the Nabbani ambassador in Marakand had arrived. So Ahjvar had ridden down the river, the Wild Sister, and along the Empress's Canal that Yeh-Lin had built long ago to join it to the Kozing, and down that valley to Kozing Port, to talk to captains and sailors and merchant folk. He was still there, going every day to the wharves and the warehouses and the markets, among the sailors' taverns and tea- and coffeehouses, camped out by night in the rare peace of the temple garden, because Ahj did not really like to sleep under a roof, enclosed by walls.

The folk of the ships spoke of the Empire of Tiypur unified again under the rule of a holy man, maybe even a god, called the All-Holy.

They spoke of towns, Tiypurian towns burned, of crews of foreign ships seized and executed, of folk, Tiypurian folk, massacred for failing to give their allegiance to the All-Holy, for continuing to worship their dead gods with the rites of their old mysteries.

They spoke of the folk of all those lands being gathered into companies, commanded as the companies of an army are commanded, in every aspect of their lives. Of demands made of those ships of south and north which, by some accommodation of their captains, were still permitted to trade, for Rostengan iron and tin from south over the sea, for timber and hides from the kingdoms of the North.

Of agents of the priests of the All-Holy making the dangerous journey across a dead land and the high mountains of the Karas, onto the Western Grass. Buying horses of the tall, strong-boned Westgrasslander breed.

Iron, bronze, timber. Horses.

That was as much as to say, weapons.

And wagons.

And such news was already old, even the newest, whether it had travelled by the caravan road or by sea.

Ghu could reach, could touch Ahjvar . . . be with him. Now. Here. Did not. Easy to hold Ahj too close. To wind himself through him so that they became thought and thought, breath and breath, here in Nabban, in this land, his land. It was different when Ahjvar went beyond, as sometimes he did, reluctant in the going, but he went because Ghu could not and it mattered, sometimes, to see with their own eyes, hear with their own ears what the priest-emperors could not. Or need not. Or what was no concern of the palace, but must be the god's, for the sake of the land and the folk of the land. When Ahj went out of the land there was a hollowness, like a piece of himself missing. A second heart gone.

A strange god Ghu might be, different in his birth and growth and being, but still he could not reach beyond Nabban's natural borders, no more than any small god of hill or spring could stretch their awareness and will beyond their own natural reach, but Ahjvar could, and in that, he—he, Nabban—had resources a god did not. More than an agent, a priest, a witness, which any god might ask a man or woman of his folk to be in a foreign land. Ahjvar was what no servant could ever be: his own eyes, ears, mouth, heart . . . sword.

He had not asked that of Ahj, ever. If Ahjvar had killed on his ventures abroad—and he had, because enemies came upon a traveller through no fault of his own, even the Leopard of Gold Harbour, who had to work very hard not to make enemies—it had been not the reason of his going.

Ghu did not know why he thought that, now.

Yes, he did. Only he did not want to. And that was the boy in him still, who wanted to make all safe and small and hidden, and shut the world out from himself, and from Ahjvar, who was so hurt by it.

He could not lose Ahj. He could not bear it. He could not *be*, without Ahjvar. And a god had no business to let his heart be tied so into one man, one flawed and sometimes dangerous man, brittle in his scars, like a broken cup mended with lacquer. Dangerous man, dangerous to love so humanly intense what was not his to hold, what was long ago doomed to take the road to the Old Great Gods. That was the sin that had led to Ahjvar's cursing so long ago: a goddess who could not bear to let her daughter go.

He could not lose him. He would not use him.

Ahjvar would say otherwise. To both. And Ghu had promised, he would let Ahjvar go, when Ahjvar would.

But to choose the road was not to be ripped away to it by another. And he could not, he could not bear to be alone—

What might come was only patterns on water, uneasy reflections, broken, uncertain.

Eyes shut. Long, slow breath. What he must, not what he would. For both of them, maybe. Because Ahjvar surrendered self and choice and would not take them back.

In his hands—squatted on his heels, his back to the sacred stone at the heart of Swajui, beneath evergreen oaks that had been acorns once, carried from that place of cliff and downs and the unceasing breakers— shells. Small things, carried long, like the acorns. Carried much longer, now. Opened his eyes and looked on them again. Names Ahjvar had given Ghu when he first brought them back up from the shore to the ruined broch on the headland, small fascinations of colour and form. Limpet, the shade of a mouse's belly, with a contrasting ring of lavender. Already pierced. Topshell, tight-whorled snail flecked in repeating broken bands of pale blue and pink and green on lustrous white. Periwinkle, blue as final dusk. Tower shell, like the ivory-gold horn of an imagined beast in one of the palace library's bestiaries. Cerith, another fantastical horn, its spirals marked with russet knobs.

There were acorns, too, under the snow. Over-Malagru cork oak, which was not native to this place, this mountain, and lived maybe because the deepest frost was kept at bay by the hotsprings, or because he had willed it so when Ahjvar planted them. He found three by reaching for them, fingers burrowing barehanded beneath the snow. So.

From the deep pocket of a ragged caravaneer's coat, stripes faded to fawn and cream, he took a folded leather wallet carried almost as long as the shells, tools for mending. The needles were perhaps too fine, but the smallest awl would serve his purpose.

The sun climbed over the trees, pines and evergreen oaks all carrying their snow-burdened branches like clouds. The drifts glittered like restless water, breaking and flinging sparks. Shadows of the trees made depths, dark pools, and the steam of the springs added another layer of hoarfrost to twig and lip of curling drift. Patiently, carefully, he drilled with the awl, piercing the shells, the acorns. If once he slipped and pricked a finger, and blood marked them . . . that was no wrong thing for what he would work.

Rain began to patter on the road as the afternoon turned to evening. Most travellers had already sought their lodgings; only the few last home-going peasants hurried along now, returning to their villages from riverside fields. Spades and mattocks and muddy to the waist; they must have been working on some ditch or dyke, awaiting the blessing of the spring floods for the intervale land. Free folk, all, in this land they had made, he and Ghu and Ivah between them.

Yeh-Lin, too, and others long dead, remembered, always. The great council had met at Dernang, to reshape the customs of the land. An annual autumn festival commemorated it now. Ahjvar avoided going down to Dernang, the town below the holy mountain, during the week-long holy days, though he would be welcome as their god himself, who wandered the festivals of the land—all of them, in that strange and dreamlike way he had.

Ahjvar was not good at people. Maybe he never had been. He couldn't really remember. Too long ago, too far away.

Tired, deep in the bones. Too long among cities and folk and what he had gleaned had not led him to anything but a weight on the heart, chill and heavy.

Rain on the road seemed only an echo of his mood.

He could not fold the land around him, step *here* and *there* in a passing dream, and by times he enjoyed the travelling for its own sake, alone or wandering together, as they often went. Important, for him, for the both of them, to hear and see and smell and feel the land, to know the roads as well as the rivers, the folk tied together by them, the life of the villages and the city streets as well as the shrines and the palace. Sometimes. He had made a long journey of it, heading down the river valley last autumn and winter, a slow progress. Now . . . it was enough. Time to go home.

He might not wear the land like a coat. He did not need to, to find his way. Needed only to be found.

He passed a last straggling party of ditch-diggers, young men and women dallying on the road, talking, teasing. Faded out of their awareness, no more than shadow and river-fog. Laughter loud as he rode by, a bit of elbowing. Two holding hands, which was the source of the others' amusement. Lives decided. One boy turned to look after him, frowning, uncertain what and if he had seen, and a dog growled at nothing.

Ahjvar turned the dusky bay aside from the paved imperial highway, down a track between fields. The river sang in his blood. The sun was setting, turning the grey clouds a curdled rose in the west, when he came to a shrine, one of the old holy places where local folk might come to make personal prayers, seek advice, or give a gift of food to the priest. It was a grove of willows on a slight rising of the land that had probably been a sandbar or island before some shifting of the river's course. The holy ground was fenced with living willow woven together; the gate stood open. There was a bell to alert the priest to the coming of a visitor to the god's enclosure, but Ahjvar did not ring it. The ducks foraging on the green between the trees, all moss and mint, turned bright eyes to him and went back to their feeding. The priest's cabin was built of grey planks, wooden-shingled, and stood on stilts against the floods still to come. A thread of smoke rose, the smell of frying vegetables drifting from above. He headed away from the cabin, down towards the water.

Shadowy, half-seen, and then there, solid and real . . . Swan-white, black-legged Snow watched, as the ducks had, gave him a nod that was more human than horselike. He leapt down from the saddle, looped up the reins and left Gorthuernial to follow at his heels. Out in the river something stirred beneath the surface, two shapes, chasing, long and lean, one pearly pale, the other pewter streaked on gold, one rising like a whale—glittering scales, twisting, and they both swarmed ashore, changing as they came, shaking water from shaggy coats, barking and leaping.

"Sh!" He didn't want the priest down here. "Jui, shut up!" But Jui leapt and swiped a tongue at his face, and even Jiot, more reserved, flung himself up, so he got down on a knee to take two armfuls of soggy, wriggling dog. Told them they were good, told them they were wicked, and wet, and ill-mannered, and smelt like fish, which made them grin, and they went back into the river as dragons again, lengthening and changing and disappeared upstream.

Laughter, in the shadows under a big willow where the river overflowed its bank. Ghu, waiting. Ahjvar went to him.

He looked what he was, and was not: a young man. Not tall, lightly built but with an athlete's strength and assurance, grace even in the turning of his head, the lifting of his chin. Flash of a smile. Barefoot, ankle-deep in cold water, dressed in blue cotton trousers and loose white shirt, no gown over it. He could have been a labourer come to bring the priest some little gift, eggs or a handful of cresses. Black hair unruly as a Malagru hill-pony's mane, a fine-boned face of strong angles, the warm golden brown of the south provinces, eyes black as the sky between the stars, and as deep. They leaned together, and Ahjvar buried his face in Ghu's hair, in the reassuring, familiar scent of him, moss and stone, pines and horse. Held to him—Ghu thought it was good for him to go out into the world alone, to separate himself a little, but damned Great Gods, he had needed to be home—till Ghu pushed him back against the willow bole and pulled his head down to take his face in his hands, kissing him as careful as if he might dissolve to smoke and drift away at any rougher touch, which quickly turned to something more urgent. But—

"What?" he asked, because there was something of concern in that, and not merely desire.

Tongue tracing his ear, playing with the gold ring there. And words, whispered, tickling. "You were a long time away."

He slid hands beneath the shirt. Warm skin, solid muscles, heart that beat with his own. "Whose fault is that? You could have come to join me any time you chose."

"It's good to be missed, sometimes. And I was watching."

"Watching what?" Not him. No need. Ghu held his soul in his hands; what he had found was known, did not need to be said. They would only choose to haul it out to argue over conclusions. Inevitabilities.

That might come. Not tonight. Time enough.

"Everything. Dreaming, mostly."

"You'll get lost, someday. Who'll come to find you?"

"You, I expect. I was trying to see into the west."

"Was that wise?" Ahjvar asked. Old Great Gods, no, it was not. The devils might act even in dreams. Fingers busy with the fastenings of his jacket, the ties of his shirt . . .

Was this wise? He did not trust the priest to stay quiet in his house, and a priest, if anyone, would know the presence of his god. Besides, who would eat within-doors on a fine spring evening? He captured the exploring hands and held them against his chest. "Ghu—"

"I don't know. When do I ever? Necessary. I wanted to find Dotemon."

"Did you?"

"No." And that troubled Ghu; Ahjvar heard it, and it certainly troubled him. They had exiled the devil Yeh-Lin Dotemon many years back. Not for anything she had done, exactly. She had settled into the imperial family over several generations: tutor, eternal auntie, counsellor . . . even Ahjvar admitted it was not her fault young Hezing had grown so infatuated; she really had done nothing to encourage him. His ambition and disloyalty to his brother had been born of his own dreaming, not hers, and that he had made her a focus for it . . . well, she had gone, and left the House of Suliasra to sort itself out, which it had, eventually, with the god's wisdom, and without fratricide or any lethal act of Ahjvar's, though it had been a near thing, in his view. Prince Hezing had ended his days a relatively honourable mercenary captain somewhere in Pirakul, a better end than Ahjvar had ever expected for the boy.

"Dead?"

It was possible. The devil whom Ghu persisted in calling "the story-teller" was an assassin of her fellows. She may have found Yeh-Lin, though she had claimed not to be seeking her.

"I don't think so. Hiding, maybe."

"From you?"

"Would she?"

"Depends on what she's up to."

"Yes. Hiding maybe from the storyteller. But Yeh-Lin had gone into the west, the last I dreamed of her. Beyond Marakand. Beyond the western deserts."

"What's beyond? Grass, the north . . ."

"Tiypur. Ahjvar . . ."

"Not now."

"No. Alright." Ghu escaped his hold, hands sliding down his ribs, over old scars. Breath caught at nipping teeth, teasing . . . Ghu laughed at him, stepped away then, but kept him by the hand. "You're right. Not now. Come home, Ahj, before we scandalize the priest's fowl."

"More concerned with scandalizing the priest," he muttered, and let himself be drawn a step, another. Willows and the river, pines and its headwaters, the springs of Swajui where those scarred and battered in mind and soul came to find some peace and healing—all ghostly, light and shadows of mist. Then stone and storm-sculpted snow and the wind harsh, the hanging valley under the peak of the holy mountain, the tall standing stones along the track, the creeping pines and red-barked willows, low bushes here, where no true trees could grow. The shallow stream loud, ice-edged over rocks, pouring away towards the cliff and the waterfall. They were so high that spring only waited on the threshold, not yet come. The horses were there before them, heading into the open shed that some long-ago friends had built, to do them for a stable.

And Ghu, being Ghu, abandoned him to turn groom and tend to Gorthuernial, who was saddled and muddy and hungry for more than the dry winter grass beneath the snow.

The most holy sanctuary of the god, this, a high cold valley on Nabban's northern border, above the trees, below the unmelting snow, where even priests and emperors did not come unsummoned.

Their house here was only a cave, partway up the steep and stony eastern slope. It expanded beyond the narrow crack of its mouth and ran far back into the mountain's dark. The fire on the hearthstone near the mouth might be the same Ahjvar had laid at the first frost of the autumn before he left for the south, because wood had to be packed up from lower down and Ghu did not always remember that the fire should be fed—or perhaps merely did not see the need any longer and so neither did the fire. And time was anyway a strange and dreaming thing here, for all that the seasons and the stars kept their ordered turning. Sometimes it seemed to Ahjvar that he could take a breath and a year was gone. But it was home, and better than the last, the half-ruined broch they had so inexpertly repaired with a sod roof that was more often on the hearth than over their heads. The wind never found its way back so far as the alcove where they made a deep nest—juniper, hay, bracken, and camel-wool stuffed quilts—on the clean-swept floor.

He had brought coffee from Kozing Port, and a new map of the lands west of Marakand made by the empress's wizard-cartographers. Maybe would hope Ghu forgot that, for the time being. He had only put the scroll away with the other few books he kept in a chest well out of reach of any blizzard wind when Ghu came back, shaking snowflakes from his hair and laughing. Ahjvar met him at the fire, wordless. Ghu had the coat off him, and his shirt, and the sword, before ever they reached the bed.

But the shadow of the west was on him, and would not lift.

On both of them.

"I won't let go of you," Ghu whispered over him. "No matter where, how far your journey. You know I won't."

"No. Don't." It wasn't the being let go of. It was fear of being taken *from* that woke him in the night in sweating terror. But not this night, not when he was held hard and close, timeless in the dark.

Dawn just greying the world outside. Ghu sat shirtless by the fire at the cave's mouth for all the winter-cold wind, humming. An old lullaby, something from his childhood, maybe. Maybe they had sung it over him in the stables where he was first sheltered. Maybe his mother had, before she drowned the both of them. Certain it was that he had sung it over Ahjvar some bad nights when the hag stalked beneath the surface of his mind, not waking into the world, but not lying quiet, either, and the fear of her hunting and the guilt and the loathing of what he had become, ridden by her, racked him in nightmares and he feared to sleep lest it was she who woke.

Humming became words, nonsense rhyme. The moon rides in a sea-shell, Ghu sang, and the sun is carried by a golden fish.

Maybe Ahjvar woke. Maybe this was a dream. Often hard to tell. He rolled from the bed and went to Ghu anyway, wrapping a blanket over naked shoulders.

The fire blazed high. The kettle sat steaming on a stone for tea. The snow still fell, driven by the wind. Spring was not going to release their high valley yet; nor would the pass to Denenanbak and the road across the deserts and Praitan to Marakand be open soon. He was glad of it.

Ghu looked up and smiled. Turned his gaze again to what his hands did, as Ahjvar settled down by him. The dogs were curled into a single mound of fur. Jiot opened an eye to check on him, catching a gleam of firelight, a spark of jewel-tone, dragon eye. Lifted his head to yawn, curled it down again. Jui thumped his tail.

"Duck," Ghu said, setting aside what he held. There was a knife in his hand.

Ahjvar ducked, obedient. Fingers wove through his hair, found the longest lock of it, and the knife sliced, a little sawing needed. He should take that off Ghu and sharpen it, after.

"What do you want with my hair?" he asked, rubbing a stubbled patch the size of a thumbprint.

Ghu turned Ahjvar's head to face him. He did not explain the sudden need to sheer a hank of his hair. Only held him, hand cupping his jaw, fingers combed into his beard. Leaned in and kissed him.

Let him go and took up his work again. A braid, an elongated knotted web that had echoes of a Grasslander cat's-cradle spell in it. Ghu was no wizard. The framework of the thing was white and dull black horse-hair, long and strong, but braided into it was glossier black—shorter, finer. Much of that. Ghu separated the strands he cut from Ahjvar's head into several, gold and coiling loosely through his fingers, and began to braid and weave and knot. Shells were strung on the horsehair, and three acorns, pierced through, cap and nut.

Ahjvar recognized them. A boy's treasures. A place.

"Give me your thumb," Ghu ordered.

"Why my thumb?" But he offered it. The knife jabbed lightly, just enough to draw a swelling bead of blood. "What in the cold hells are you making?"

"A . . . thing." Ghu considered, still holding Ahjvar's thumb. "I don't think it has a name."

He set the knife aside and smeared the blood on his own thumb, went back to what he was doing. Now there was blood smudging the shells, the braids, hardly to be seen. "For you. For memory."

Ahjvar sucked the wounded thumb. "I remember too much."

"Not always the right things. It's also for . . . I'm not sure. Ivah would see it, I think. More akin to her wizardry than yours. Or maybe not." Ghu paused, considered again. His eyes were deep, dark as night, unseeing, at least of what lay before them. "Not a binding. A dance of edges and knots. Something we make between us, you and I."

"Also Snow." Deflecting, that. Was his god trying wizardry? Rarely a good idea, to mix human wizardry with what was power of the earth, the force and will in gods and demons, grown out of the land.

A frown. A shrug. Ghu shook his head. "No. Doesn't count." Like a child in a game, declaring rules as he thought of them. "The horse isn't part of it. I needed something strong to hold it together, is all. I could have used flax, but I thought you wouldn't want me pulling your shirts to bits for the thread."

"You can have such things for the asking down in Dernang, you know. Thread, cord, string. Or beg at the castle. They'd give you what you needed."

"True. But Snow's tail was closer. And he is mine."

Strands of gold against black. Fingers danced. Through, around. They knotted shells and acorns and bound them, black and gold, and wove a pattern. Ahjvar smelt, for a moment, the sea and the shore, the thyme-grown downs above the cliff. Memories he didn't hold close, for all Ghu did. Ghu walked the downs and the cliff and the shores of Sand Cove in his dreams, longing for that place again, as Ahjvar did not. A bad time. They were all bad times, for Ahjvar, till they came here . . . except for the sun on the stones of the wall, and the sound of the surf, and the young man sleeping on the other side of the fire, who did not have the sense to be afraid.

That was good. That was there at Sand Cove, and not to be forgotten, held in scent of sea and weed and thyme.

In the dreams, when Ghu's dreaming drew Ahjvar there, the place held no nightmares. In the dreams, when they walked in that place, there was peace, and the scent of thyme, of lavender and the sea.

"Duck again."

"What do you want this time, my ear?"

"Maybe." Ghu caught and bit him like a puppy, but was solemn the next instant. Kissed him like a blessing. The web made a crescent, a young moon, the shells caught in it, the acorns. He knotted the cords of its two tails behind Ahjvar's neck, under his hair.

It was warm against Ahjvar's skin. Scratchy, a little. He expected he would grow used to it.

The tying of it brought them to where they would not be.

"The horses can't go far over the border, can they?" he asked.

Ghu sighed. "They're not exactly . . . real and living beasts. Not entirely. Not any more. Too much drawn into what I am."

"As I am not?"

"It would seem so."

He had been east to Pirakul in the service of his god and emperor, and south over the sea to Barrahe for the god. That had not been—as Empress Iri had irreverently suggested when she was only a girl being fostered for a time by the god and his consort, as all the imperial children had been—an expedition in search of the secrets of growing coffee beans. Many times in Denanbak and Darru and Lathi, where Ghu could not go and yet had reason to send more than an imperial envoy.

"This is going to involve camels again."

Sober, then. "Ahjvar . . . I am sorry."

"Camels. You should be." A deep breath. "There's a devil behind this Westron cult of the red priests, Ghu. You know, I know—it's Sien-Shava Jochiz. He's what the Lady feared." And he said it unflinching, who could not speak of her, would not. "An empire in the west, Tiypur rising again. That's what the empress and the council of the provinces thinks, and the Pine Lady of wizards and the captain of the Wind in the Reeds. I think there's more. It . . . is it you who feels there's more? I don't know what I know. What's you knowing, what's me fearing. You were trying to find Yeh-Lin. What did you see that I can't remember the shape of?"

"I don't know. Something. I can't see. Shadows." A hesitation. "Death. For us all."

"He builds an army. He already has his own folk well under his heel, and he builds an army out of them. It sounds mad to say it. We're the other side of the world from him. But we hurt him and he hates us. Nabban, which defeated him, drove him out. The land he would have made a puppet-empire in the east. Hates *us*, you and me. *We* hurt him."

"Yes."

"Cold hells, Ghu, I don't know how we kill a devil."

Because it was hard for him not to see the world so and in this he did not understand how else to see it. When an enemy came hate-filled to kill, not in some confusion, some pain that could be eased, some wrong to be amended and the cause of hate made less—he did not see that there was any other way. But he had barely survived, and Jochiz had not even been in Nabban, not truly, only casting a part of himself into the land through a puppet, a vessel of his will.

"Go to Marakand. Speak to the god there. They are the strong point, the fortress that holds the road," Ghu said. "The Lady was right in that. By the time you come there, we'll know—we and Marakand alike—far more of what he intends. Go west and find Dotemon, Ahj, if you can. She may hide from me, but not from us, not from you hunting her. Or maybe it is only Jochiz she hides from, or the storyteller, and is hidden from us only by that, not intent."

"Yes." He wore heavy golden bracelets, the terminals leopards' heads, on both scarred wrists, warm and hardly noticed at all, but cool against the skin of his left, a braided circlet of black as well. An uncomfortable thing, a binding, even if it was not of himself. He would have given it up to Ghu, but Ghu would not take it.

"Find her. Remind her what she has sworn. Hold her to it, hold her to me, to Nabban. Whatever we can do. Whatever we can *be*, together, against this." And fierce, "You have to go. I have to send you. You're all I have against him. I said, you don't kill for me. Not my assassin, I said. But—"

"I am your champion, the *Rihswera* of Nabban. Your sword to send where you will. I gave myself to you to be whatever you would."

"Not for this." *Not to die for me.* Ghu had not spoken those words. They were only in thought, like a memory. His, Ghu's—he didn't know.

"Yes, idiot boy. Even for this." *Even for that.*

Ghu was shivering. Not cold, he who walked barefoot in the mountain winter. Shivering like that boy who had huddled forlorn on his garden wall in the rain, following—gods knew what he thought he had found. *You drew me like a fire,* Ghu had said. Ahjvar wrapped himself around him, man and god, heart of his heart, bore him down and pulled his blanket over the both of them.

"Shh," he said.

Ghu! she cries, glad. A friend, seeing a familiar figure at a far distance, and he looks for her, in this dream-place that is more hers than his, the wind-waved grass, the bowl of the sky, but his eye cannot find her.

Ivah . . .

She is dead, of course. She died long ago. He misses her. Remembers her. Horses, racing. Earnest frown over a tangle of knotted cords, a Grass-lander cat's-cradle wizardry. Commander of armies in the years of trouble, the rebellions, the attempts to deny, to resist the new Nabban they would make. Mother, in the first years of peace, to son, to daughter. He had held her so only the two times, in joy, in celebration, they took it so, of what they were, of friendship and what might be born of that love, which took nothing from any other. Well, Ahj had said so. Had found, maybe, he did not like it, not deep down, but he let Ghu go to her when they asked it. Which he would not have done, Ahjvar denying. Better a friend than a courtier who'll always be looking to gain from an imperial child, she had said, and Nour won't.

Have you asked?

Yes. He said Kharduin would beat him.

Would he?

I doubt it.

So I'm only your second choice?

She had shrugged, grinned, knowing he teased.

It was a wonder, to be a father.

He had thought he understood. He held the land in his heart; he was god. But that understanding was not complete, it woke to something more, hot and urgent. To hold a child, a tiny thing, and know it part of oneself—what would one then not do, to keep it safe?

But that was an animal's thought, right and natural, but such a need must grow and change as the young outgrew it. Eggs hatched, nestlings fledged and flew. Children, humans, souls grew, and one did not cage them.

He did understand, though, in that moment, Catairanach, who made a hell of horrors for Ahjvar in the need that had burned in her to keep her lost daughter's soul in life, and he had felt a pity he had never been able to find, pity even for her, whom he hated still with a hatred wholly human, in that perversion of her love.

But still it had been perversion, and crime, and a sin against the soul of the man and against the daughter too, made, by the goddess's desire to save her, into a worse monster than the murderer she had been in life.

But why this dream, now? It is not Ivah, truly, who calls to him, from the distant heavens. The dead do not return from the realm of the Old Great Gods. It is a world separate from the world, oil and water, which do not mix.

There is something there, that thought . . .

Holding tight what is meant to fly free . . . to return . . .

No, it is not Ahjvar's soul he dreams warning for. It is not. It is . . . He is not stolen; he is given. And that is all the difference.

But they are taken.

What is sundered must be whole. Yearns, reaching . . .

A cold wind, but it smelt of green, of singing waters, of life. The small garrison of the border fort had taken themselves back to their watch and their daily tasks, blessed by their god, and wondering, maybe, what took the *Rihswera* of Nabban—Praitannec word that had entered into Nabbani meaning not its original *king's champion* but Ahjvar and Ahjvar alone— away to Denanbak. Only the captain had lingered, to offer with her own hands the parting cup of herb-pungent white-spirit, Denanbaki custom, and now she had gone too, leaving them alone, standing face to face a few yards within the natural border, which was a little beyond the ridge where the fortress sat. A difference in the stone that Ghu felt, real and vital as the skin of his own body.

Ghu took Ahjvar's hands in his own. Long, strong hands, a soft brown that darkened with the summer sun. Calloused and seamed with pale old scars. Fingers wove through his.

"Hey."

He couldn't, for a moment, look up.

"Ghu."

He did. Ahjvar's eyes were the uncanny colour of a clear winter sky. What did one say? Travel safe, be well, come back to me?

What did one need to say?

Nothing. Ghu touched Ahjvar's face: the shape of him, the warmth, the strong bones. Let vision fade to what he was, flesh and bone, yes, made and remade living in the world, not the shadow of charred bone and ash, no, never that, but the fire and the light of him that was Ahjvar's own, bright and fierce and glorious against the night and the cold of the world. The old, old tangle of the curse Ghu had stolen from the goddess of the Duina Catairna and made his own, to hold Ahj to him undying in the world against all nature and the pull of the Great Gods' road, a snarled mess spun stronger than steel and adamant, binding them.

Necromancy. Of a sort.

Ahjvar pulled him close and he held tight, raised his face to lips that found eyes and cheeks and wordless mouth.

Let him go, last hand loosing its hold, trailing down his arm, fingers' last touch, parting, warmth of skin and skin to hold in memory. Ahjvar mounted the brown camel, which had no name, because that was Ahjvar, and it grumbled, because that was a camel, and the red one grunted. Tall, shaggy beasts, beginning already to shed their weight of winter wool, to look rather patchwork and moth-eaten. They had little to complain of, more lightly burdened than they had ever been in their previous lives in a caravan. Two, a gift from the high lady of Choa Province for the god's asking, because it was folly to cross the northern deserts between Denanbak and the lands Over-Malagru with only one mount, even for a man proven somewhat immortal, since the camel was not. And

Ahj meant to go by the badlands, through the striped and twisted stone sculpted by wind and sand and ancient waters, which was the road he knew, or at least, had travelled once before. Doubtful how much of it he remembered. It had not been a good time.

At least it was not winter.

"Ahjvar." Ghu found words after all. A word. The only one that mattered. Took from his belt at the small of his back the sheathed forage-knife. He had armed himself that morning without thinking. Instinct—Ahjvar, the road . . . of course he would go armed. The heavy crooked blade was tool as much as weapon, and since that battle in which they took the empire he had cut fodder and bedding and trimmed saplings for this use or that, but never human throats. He offered it.

Ahjvar, after a long moment, nodded. He leaned, dropped half down the camel's side to take the knife, and a last kiss in passing. A tap with the quoit to wake the camel out of the sudden doze into which it had affected to sink. A grumbling grunt and a long stride forward, a tug on the pack-beast's leading rein.

Tug on the reins binding them. The border, crossed. A piece of himself, gone from Nabban, which was himself.

The dogs stood and barked—because they might have grown up into dragons and spirits of the river serving the god, but underneath it all they were still dogs—until the camels and the rider were tiny figures indistinct against the rutted road. That was the only time Ahjvar looked back. The bay stallion whinnied after him, and then the white. Ghu raised a hand in farewell. Ahjvar returned the gesture, faced north. Did not look back again. Ghu watched nonetheless, until man and camels were out of sight, the road lost in the sinking of the land. Mounted Snow, turned him with a touch of his heel and whistled to Evening Cloud, still staring after his master, to follow.

"Shall we go to Swajui?" he asked the dogs.

Ahjvar liked it there; a place where he had long ago first begun to find the road to his peace, among the pines above the sacred springs. It was to the hotsprings that the folk came now for the healing of the soul, not the body. The pines above where the cold brook rose were quiet. Few found a way there, and chance was not what brought them. Ahjvar's place.

Ghu needed a bit of that peace himself, right now.

There is a terrible yearning, a pain. Hands, heart reaching to enfold, to hold self to self, to make whole what is sundered.

It is the dream yet again, the severed self that seeks its restoration.

Yes, he says, and, But how?

No words, only the pain. Loss, need. The urgency.

There are no demons in Nabban, no life returning in new forms, where once they lived, and fought, and died fighting a devil.

No gods reborn in the far west.

A thing known in all the world, but why, he wonders, do we accept that that should be so?

CHAPTER XVII

. . . summer, and the All-Holy has come into the lands of the caravan road

*S*ong. *Light that moves like slow flames. A pulling, a yearning . . . shed what holds him here, fall into it. Take it into himself . . .*

A voice, whispering. Can he even hear? My brother, my captain . . . is it you . . . ?

Calling. Sorrow. Desperation. Fear?

It is another voice entirely, and the first is lost, memory discarded, in its urgency.

The light shatters. The loss is pain and he wakes, crying out a denial . . .

The echo still resounds in his mind. Not his own voice, that cry. No, not the whisper that haunts his dreams, either.

Known. Beloved.

Father, long, long years dead.

No. Not his father.

His god, crying out to him.

Holla-Sayan . . .

Night would soon burn away into dawn, a clear sky in the east already thinning toward day, but clouds piled in the west, dark and starless, and the wind threatened rain. Long waves of wind rolled before it, combing the grass, colourless in the night, pewter and black like a lake. A herd of blue cattle grazed somewhere near, he smelt them, but there was no rider tending them. Abandoned. The folk had fled the land. Only scattered bands remained, harrying an advance they could not hinder. Gesture. Futile.

As, maybe, was his coming here.

He had grown used to the idea of immortality.

Time to remember he could die?

"Blackdog."

Holla-Sayan turned, turning, flowing from dog to man in the drawing of a breath. It was like breathing, now, he and the dog, one thing and not two. Mostly. Not the bone-cracking pain the change had once been. They were one, and that one remade itself, man, dog, swifter than thought. Not natural, no, he carried clothing and weapons and what he bore through the change, and the dog itself changed its form to answer need. He was only, perhaps, a thing of malleable flesh and bone, bound in memory and two souls that melted and flowed into one another like copper and tin in the smelter, making something new. Which was a monster, perhaps. A devil, certainly, and not one of the seven of whom the storytellers told.

"Sayan." The god had been all about him since he came down the last valley, a presence like a scent, here in his own land, but now Sayan was beside him. A man, like him. Or not. Sayan wore flesh as one might put on a coat, clothing himself for human eyes. He was not a god who had ever been incarnate. To Holla-Sayan he recalled, in many points, his father's face, calm and patient, always, no matter how he was tried. Wild colts and wilder boys. What others might see when Sayan spoke with them he had never asked.

A black lark took to the air, singing as it rose to greet the dawn, leaving the mottled-grey female sitting unafraid on her nest. A small owl, grasshopper in its beak, watched from the mouth of its burrow, eyes golden like twin suns.

"I'm glad you're here," Sayan said. "I don't think it will be much longer. But Holla-Sayan, why have you come?"

"You called me."

Sayan's frown was almost humanly startled.

"I . . ." he said, and shook his head. "I did. But I did not think you would hear."

He had abandoned the gang that he travelled with, a caravan-mercenary of Marakand on the desert road. Taken no leave, not even acknowledging the cry of the woman on watch. Bolted and gone, a wolf-shadow in the night. That dream, that cry.

Running, running, and coming with the dawn to the river, well below the Fifth Cataract, where ferry-folk of Kinsai's Lower Castle would have taken him across and charged him not even a song. They knew him, at the castles. Blackdog of Lissavakail. Blackdog of the Sayanbarkash. Devil whom their goddess called friend.

No need to swim.

"Go," Kinsai had said, and there had been a narrow fowler's boat but no woman or man of the ferry castle to row it. Only the goddess herself, full-figured, naked, leaning hard-muscled to the oars and not, as she ever was, laughing at him. No games, no teasing, no price to be paid for his crossing, old joke between them.

Kinsai's hair was streaked like river-water, brown and sunlit gold and her eyes, which usually shifted colour through all the shades of human and river, were the dull pewter of water under heavy cloud. She had kissed him, on the western shore, standing ankle deep in the water still, the abandoned boat drifting south. Kissed him long and slow and hard, with everything that was between them. Years and lifetimes, a child. "Run, Blackdog. Go to your god. There are shadows in the stream, nothing more. Changing every moment. A current that might be turned. Run, don't delay."

He had run, day and night with only the briefest of rests, jog-trot that had carried him across the world, into lands the young man who had left his family's holding in the Sayanbarkash for the restless road had never dreamed to see, if even he had heard their names. Run into the All-Holy's path, which was aimed, like a river's flood, at the Sayanbarkash. This last day and night he had pushed hard, no rest at all under a growing urgency, a terror. Storm about to strike. As if he raced avalanche downhill. He had cried the god's name aloud as he crossed into the valley.

But now he was here, and all was quiet. The black larks sang in the air and a killdeer cried in the distance. The Western Grass, waking. They were only ordinary thunderheads that piled on the far western horizon. Breath slowed.

Home.

"They're coming," he said. "What can I do?"

"If you don't know . . ." The god shrugged, all too human. "I don't know, Holla-Sayan. The All-Holy—I don't even know what he is. Devil?"

"His name is Sien-Shava," Holla-Sayan said. "Jochiz." A certainty. It was Sien-Shava who had lain in the west, working against Marakand, reaching even into Nabban. He had had that warning from an empress, when he was still a husband and a caravan-master out of Marakand.

"You can't fight him." Sayan did not make it a question.

"Oh, I can fight him." Hopeless. Inevitable. "And I can die. Even Moth—Vartu, fears him." And if she were here . . . would it make any difference?

Lakkariss would. Perhaps. In the right hands. Wielded by a swordsman to match Sien-Shava, yes, the sword of the cold hells would end this. But it had nearly taken him the only time he had borne it.

"We may be a devil, the Blackdog and I, but we aren't—I'm not— what the seven were."

Broken, weak—the faint shadow and last remnant of a devil's soul.

I. We.

He. It.

That he thought of himself the man and the dog the devil was, perhaps, only a trick of the mind, a way of pretending to himself that he was still human, that he did not know what he knew, had not done what he had done, did not remember . . . what he had not done, and had, in the years before Holla-Sayan was ever born not so very many miles from here.

He was not what he had been, caravan mercenary, camel-driver,

master of his wife's caravan gang in the years she stayed behind to run
the caravanserai. He had been captain, commanded armies in small wars
along the mountains, just and unjust. He had held the long thoughts,
once. Or the men who had been ridden by the Blackdog before him,
parasite soul riding soul, not the welding of two into one, had. Yet their
memories gave him no way through this.

"They are gone," Sayan said. Distress. A child's pain, facing the
unthinkable. Made small and helpless. "Brother of the hills, sisters of the
rivers, Retlavon, Jayala, Yalla of the north. Just . . . gone."

Holla-Sayan took his hands, as he would a friend, breaking. He had
sat by too many deathbeds. No easy lies, here. Not between them. No
hope in himself, none he could pretend to.

He had counted years. Counted births, lives. Deaths. Some of them.
Scratched a mark for the turning of the year in his sabre's scabbard every
spring. Because he wanted it to matter. Small mark: a year that meant
nothing, beyond another winter past. A bold, taller one for the years that
mattered. The years where there was joy. Or hurt. Gultage's birth—his
son, his wife's son, the child of Marakand. Every granddaughter: Gultage's family. His wife's death.

No particular notch to note Gultage's death. He had gone away for
good, left Marakand and the caravanserai the family ran there when those
granddaughters were young women. He had not wanted to see his son,
Gaguush's son, become an old man.

And so he had not. Regret. Nothing learnt.

No comfort to offer. No wisdom.

"I'm nothing but a weapon in the end, no different from when the
dog first took me. A beast. I was made to be, out of the wreck of this
devil. I'm no wizard; I don't have the blood. I'm no true devil. I can't raise
the powers of the land. I can't shape—whatever it is they do—out of my
will and soul. Flesh and steel I could face for you, but I don't even understand what he is doing."

Called or not, he had had to be here. To die, at last, defending his
god, or trying to avenge him.

Death stalked closer. The fading stars overhead felt black and purple as the horizon, smothering. For a moment, Holla-Sayan could scarcely breathe.

"Blackdog, I called—I don't know why. I don't want you here to die with me. I did not think you would hear."

"Maybe Kinsai carried your call over her waters, through her valley. I was with a gang on the road, coming up west. I was on my way home anyway. Listening for you, maybe. We were hearing bad things in Marakand."

"They're true."

"I know."

"I only—I wanted to see you one last time, Holla-Sayan. That's all. Strange, isn't it? You've become something strange, as well, strange to me, something I've never known. Close and dear. You know what it is to see the lives come and go. I have known you longer than any man or woman of my folk. Do you ever think of that? You are . . ." Sayan seemed to consider words, frowning, choosing carefully as a man might select a piece of wood for carving, turning each this way and that. "Brother? Yes. Become more a brother than one of my folk, a thing akin to me as no one of humankind has ever been. And so—I know I will die and leave the barkash godless. My folk are fleeing. Most are already gone over the rivers. But my thoughts went to you. My *brother*. I am sorry that I called, though. It was—the cry of my heart. I did not mean to bring you here to die. They are within the lands of the barkash. Very near to where you grew up. Very near to here. I think—I fear he prepares— whatever weapon it is, that can kill a god. I should not have brought you here. You should not have come. Go east, Holla-Sayan. Remember me and this land. It's all we have left. Remember my name, that I was, in this land."

He would have the throat out of the devil or die trying. Shatter what spell, what weapon, Jochiz would make.

And Sien-Shava Jochiz would weave it again, once Holla-Sayan was dead. The dog within him snarled. The dog—resisted his rage, and mostly the dog was rage, and reaction, and did not shape coherent thought, only emotion and that painted stark in black and the red of fire and blood.

But in all the miles beneath his paws he had found no plan, only a shadow of an idea, something he could hardly frame, could only feel in fragments—the shape of it, the way.

He, or the dog?

They. It was they. It was always they.

Yes, the dog said, and the dog had no words left in its damaged soul. Or so even gods and devils believed.

"We have *now,* this moment, nothing more, and only ourselves. Sayan, listen. I took Attalissa out of Lissavakail, and she lived. And once Sera of the holy spring of Serakallash put herself into a stone and was sheltered in the Narvabarkash."

"Attalissa was incarnate as a human child and she lived only because you found goddess-sisters to lend her their . . . life, I suppose you could call it. But I've thought on your story of Sera."

"Can you?"

"I . . . cannot feel the way. I am earth, stone. Not water, to pour myself into another way of being. Not a thing of water, to find a sleep like death through drought and winter." The god stooped and dug fingers into the turf. "I am—this."

"You are a soul of the earth."

"How can I be anything else?" The god's voice went soft and slow, a man puzzling over something. Fumbling. Like a person drunk or stunned. Holla-Sayan felt the fine hairs of his skin prickling, the dog's unseen hackles rising. "I can't . . . feel my way to it. It is not my nature . . . I think. I think . . . Holla—?"

Now he was a thing of haze, of shadows half-formed, not flesh or seeming-flesh at all, and he held out a hand to Holla-Sayan.

What he had never thought to feel from his god, that soul of deep earth and stone. Terror.

Blackdog . . .

His own terror was like ice in the heart.

The god was briefly in the world again. He clenched his teeth, an arm braced against the earth, hand splayed, eyes shut, head flung back, human form echoing human agony, and Holla-Sayan seized that other reaching hand, which was there and not-there, cold and solid as stone in his. Went down on his knees to pull the god to him, himself to the god. It was the grass, the birds hopping near, which were things of smoke half-seen.

"They are . . ." Sayan seemed almost to waver within his arms, hot and cold, near and distant. They clung like brothers washed ashore from shipwreck, and the waves still savage to wrench them apart. "They sing against me. Blackdog, hold . . ."

The dog wrenched at him. Tore through him. *Here. Now. This way. See.* Command without words. Ripped open a path for vision, and he saw. A thing of fire, of light, red and sullen dark silver, a flame bound in flesh and bone, made by that flesh and bone a thing of the earth, where it could not otherwise endure. Sien-Shava Jochiz stood by the broken ruins of a stone barn, his head raised, singing. Words in a speech Holla-Sayan did not know. Equally alien to the Blackdog; it was a tongue of the earth, but belonging to some distant land, weaving pattern as a wizard of the Great Grass would weave spells in yarn, cat's-cradles of power. Children stood in a circle about him, hands clasped as if they might dance, but they did not. They sang, high and clear, every note true, as the sun edged up out of the night. The mists in the valleys were set alight, the colour of wild roses. So earnest. So single and simple, their minds, their hearts becoming one greater thing, a unity, a vastness . . . a well to draw down a light and a mass they could never individually have contained. The dog felt this in the shape of what they made. The words were nothing to them, syllables learned in fear and awe and service of their god, in the evenings and in the wagons. He understood that, found a vision held in them, as if each were a diviner's shell and their life lay within to be seen. They knew themselves special. The blessed. The chosen. All willing, all wholehearted, and once they had promised themselves to this, all emptied of doubt and fear, of yearning for parents, for their old life, for their homes. Westron and Westgrasslander together—there were many who had come over the mountains parentless, following the army as if it made a pilgrimage, or hoping for glory in service to the All-Holy. A beautiful innocence. They offered their souls in song to their god, and their god of his grace accepted them.

No! he cried at them. *Lies. Don't. Don't sing.*

The dog quashed the urge. They would be seen, known. The children were doomed. The children were already—

Souls would fuse to one vessel, one heartbeat's space, no more, to contain even a god. Creatures of the earth and a soul of the earth made one, and made the devil's, the soul that held the centre, the hungry and devouring heart of fire, the man who sang . . . They were within him, not gods but their godhead, their potentiality, but . . . oh, the fire, the weight of them, the dark heart of stone and the roiling of waters. The earth. He, dog, man, devil began to feel its pulse beneath his own in every stillness, as if he stood there, as if he sang, as if he held himself open, to drink the god—

His own voice, smooth, weaving through them.

Not that way.

The children in his vision shivered like reflection on water, barely to be seen; it was their souls stood sharp and clear, the flame of life within, but that flame spun out in thin threads into the heart of the devil, and flowed like blood. In Sien-Shava's upraised hands, before his face, he held—only a stone.

A piece of the barkash, stone of the hills. Holla-Sayan wore a stone, a white pebble, in a soft leather amulet bag hung about his neck. Caravaneers, bards, such wanderers did so, to remind themselves they were not godless in the world. A token of his god, of his land, a stone he had taken from the crest of the barkash and the god's holiest place before he went, a young man not yet twenty, to the caravan road. It was a little magic, a small thing. A symbol only, perhaps.

Perhaps more than a symbol. Some wizardry worked so.

There were other words wound within the foreign singing, harsh, clear, shouted almost, by the devil alone. The children could not have shaped them. They were not heard but felt, a pain, a cry of longing in the marrow. A shape almost grasped, a meaning—he should have understood. Sayan cried out at his own name.

Sayan was shredding, threads of smoke pulled into a hungry wind, a burning heart. Flowing into the fire, to be consumed.

Holla-Sayan pulled himself away from the vision, felt earth, felt grass, smelt earth and grass and rain in the wind, his god.

He had no song to sing against this, no words. No wizardry. He was only a monster, a plain man made a broken devil.

No. The dog. Under the temple, dying, he called it. Dying, it came. Remember? It needed him to remember now. Flowing into him, consuming him in fire, in pain, in . . . flood of living light, filling him.

In this place he was fire—scarlet, peridot green, molten silver—two souls spun together.

Wizardry had always a shape, he knew that. Something to hold it. All he had was words, and this was not wizardry as he understood it. This was only truth, what they were, he and the dog, he and the god. This was—what was. Words made a shape. The truth did, forcing itself acknowledged.

Words made a shape. So speak them. Force their truth into the world.

"We are kin, Sayan." His voice cracked. Weak, as if every word fought through smoke and blood to shape itself. "We make ourselves kin, we do, as deep a truth as that I am my parents' son, as deep a truth as that I am my brothers' brother." He had not been. Foundling, abandoned baby, claimed and loved. Truth. "We share a name, Sayan. My mother gave me your name and you blessed it. You've let me hide in you from my enemies. Held your hands over me so many times. Hold on to me now." Words clearer now. Stronger. More certain. Feeling . . . truth, making a shape in the world. "I'm not a god, but what is a devil, Sayan? We warred against the Old Great Gods. We are powers to destroy gods of the earth. I'm not strong enough, whole enough, to stand against Jochiz. I've lost my own name. But I can be—" He hardly had words. *Friend. Love. Brother.* Where it mattered. In the heart, the soul. "You are my brother, I name you so, as you name me yours." Tightened his grip on the god, illusion though that might be. Wrapped him, pulled him close, drowning brother, kin to kin, heart to heart, soul to soul. "Hold to me. Hide in me. Let me carry you."

Shaped what he did not need to speak aloud, then. Sure and certain. *A blessing: no matter what I am, what I've become or may yet be, you are my god and my brother, you are a part of me as I am a part of you. My bones are grown from your earth. I'm stone and water of the Sayanbarkash but I am fire and ice of the stars and the hells. I can hold you, I will hold you, if you can give yourself up to me.*

The stone in the hands of Jochiz shattered. A cry of fury, of pain. Something ripped away from him. Falling to his knees, hands reaching. The singing children were silent, dead husks folding to the ground, burnt away within, as once Holla-Sayan had seen priestesses die, their life consumed by Ghatai in the working of a spell of protection as the Grasslander devil strove to possess the goddess Attalissa of the mountain lake.

Holla's arms were empty and he knelt on the dead earth. Frost edged seam and rivet of his brigandine, melted from cold-stung hands.

CHAPTER XVIII

"**D**own!" Jolanan screamed, and Tibor dropped low as the rider behind him swung—and off balance, lost his grip on the blood-slick haft of his axe. She hit the Westron, sabre slashing across the back of his neck and if it didn't cut more than the leather collar of his armour below his helmet's brim, he was still driven down, beginning to fall. Lark seized and dragged, battle-roused. The man went under the stallion's hooves and his horse swung away from Lark's lunge after it. Tibor wheeled back to her.

"Go!" she shouted. That was a knight, she'd killed a knight of the fifth circle. Lark had. "Good boy!" she sang, as if she praised a dog. "Ride, ride!"

Lazlan's horn had sounded the signal to break away and already the grey light that ran before the dawn was making them all too visible. No fog gathered to hide them. It would not. The god of this land was gone, they knew it. The young soothsayer Arpath, the closest thing they had to a wizard, had cried out, feeling that loss like physical wound, it seemed, and fallen in a dead faint the previous morning. He had not woken by the time Lazlan led his skirmishers away to make this last strike.

To show the All-Holy that even the death of their god would not break them.

Sayan had not been her god, nor Tibor's, but it didn't matter; they were all of the Western Grass.

She kneed Lark half around to meet the last pursuing rider. Tibor drew his bow to his ear and let fly. She'd thought him out of arrows, but he had one. It was enough and the pursuer fell before he closed with her. Sixteen years on the caravan road, her mother's cousin. Tibor didn't miss.

Cries from her left. Foreign. Hate-filled. It meant something like "godless," that word, and it should not be cried there; they had driven in like the thrust of a spear to throw terror into this encampment, well within the pickets before they were noticed, and she'd seized the torch that burned before an officer's tent to set it and five more alight before they'd swung away, with fires blooming all through the camp. Cries and screams as they rode down soldiers stumbling hazy from their sleep.

They'd lost contact with one another in their scattering flight. It was often so. Sometimes you never knew till days later who had gotten clear, who had fallen at the last. Deadly folly at the best of times, to ride reckless in the dark. She and Tibor hadn't shaken that last pair of knights, elite warrior-priests riding good Westgrass horses, pursuing even as night faded.

Out of the north—these must have passed close in the night, a mounted patrol, and devils damn them, that they had eluded Lazlan's company—six riding towards them on the light Westron ponies. She and Tibor could outrun the ponies, except the Westrons were close, close enough for a thrown spear—

—to miss.

Tibor had his sabre in hand now, and she saw the whites of his eyes, his bared teeth. Light spreading. Too long in disengaging, too slow, too late.

She went one way, Tibor another.

So she and Tibor would be among the lost when next they counted heads.

Jolanan had expected it every time she rode.

Something came up from the gulley, the dry watercourse they'd followed down towards the camp, a man who knew this land—it had been the grazing of his own herds—guiding them. Dog, she thought, one that must have followed Lazlan's raiders from the main band of Reyka's company that had kept pressing north.

Then she thought, wolf?

Bear?

Dog, but the size of it—not one of theirs. Did dogs grow so big? Did wolves?

It flung itself into the midst of the Westron riders with no warning. Ponies panicked, squealed, reared—riders fell. It pulled down a man and shook him, snapped his neck and flung him, bit through the arm of another as he slashed with a knife, slid aside from a spear and tore that soldier's throat—the ponies were bolting, with or without riders, and Lark was trying to turn away. She could feel the fear growing herself, something wild and howling pulsing in her belly, a cold sweat. Tibor was fighting his bay, but when the second patrol crashed upon him man and horse found their nerve again and she rode to help him. The wolf-dog came snarling among them, blood-soaked jaws closing on a Westron man's throat so close the spray arced across her face.

And then it was gone and they were free and riding hard, alone. No pursuit.

"Old Great Gods, Old Great Gods and damned devils, what in the cold hells was that?" Tibor's voice was breaking, almost a howl himself, and he clutched the amulet-bag that hung about his neck. A stone from the Jayala's bed, he had shown her once. Token of goddess and home, carried all the way to Marakand so many times. But Jayala their goddess was dead and their homeland laid waste by the All-Holy and everyone they knew . . . dead, enslaved, sworn to a foreign lie of a god to buy life. She didn't know what to hope.

It was only a stone he held now. Empty of hope.

"Wolf?" she hazarded. Her throat was croaking dry and her mouth tasted of blood. Not her own.

"You, the cow-herd, say so?"

"I don't know, then. I saw a bear come down off the mountains once. It wasn't a bear, either."

"Cross between them. Wolf and bear."

"They can't."

"Bear-mule."

"Tibor—"

He made a face. "Great Gods, look at you. What would your mother say?"

"Well done?" She hardly remembered her mother, dead when she was small.

"Probably." They didn't mention her father, wit-wandered after a bull flung him into a tree. Better he had died. When she could no longer cope with caring for him and managing their small holding, Tibor's mother had taken them on. Papa she took for charity—at least he was content to scare birds from the wheatfields, if someone kept half an eye out to be sure he didn't wander away looking for mama—Jolanan herself to ride herd. The drought years had been at their worst then, wells and water-holes drying, cattle, sheep having to range far in search of water or dying outright, and the river of the goddess herself shrivelled to pools between the stones. They'd thought better years must be coming, when the winter snows finally came heavy again, to nourish the land. But winter had opened into a black spring.

She'd been far out with the cattle when the smoke had called her home, too late, to find desolation. Luck that the Westrons had been and gone by then.

She had ridden mindless a time, heading northeasterly above the All-Holy's course until she was ahead of it, dodging Westron scouts. More by luck than any cunning. Luck and the grace of her dogs. Their sacrifice. Wrung her heart. Showed her she could still feel. Pain upon pain. The dogs had found that one patrol first, and paid the price for her flight. Bought her the time to flee.

Found Reyka's company. Found Tibor of all people among them, only family she had left.

Found a reason to keep getting up in the morning.

"Rider."

She looked behind first. No, ahead, she saw it then. Black horse. Coming up from the line of the dry stream. Tibor reached for his bow, glanced to her quiver, empty as his own, shrugged and drew his sabre.

She was tired and her shoulder hurt. Face, damn it, itched, and scrubbing at it with her arm only made her foul jacket with its few reinforcing horn plates over the breast fouler. The blood was drying, sticky and stinking. Drew her sabre—taken from a dead comrade and some approximation of skill sweated into her by Tibor when she wasn't having to figure it out with a Westron to teach her and life at stake. Arrows for hares and pheasants and the rare predators that didn't have the sense to flee a bull or a rider, her stick for the cattle—those had always been enough. Sabre was only a stick with an edge, she had told Reyka, when Tibor first brought her before the chief, and Reyka had laughed. But she had not contradicted.

Farmers, mercenaries come home from the caravan road, Jayala's folk and Sayan's, Retlavon's and the northern Yalla's. Reyka had Sayan's blessing, and the respect of those she led. She had in the beginning gathered about the core of her own cousins and herders, and she ruled them like the household of a farm. Brothers, sisters, cousins. Kin.

The rider only waited. He looked like a Westgrasslander, but a mercenary of the road, his hair worn long in many braids. Little gear. No buckler, no bow or spear. Didn't bother hailing them, didn't call to name himself. Didn't draw his sabre. Trusting they weren't converts. As they were him, she supposed, and did not sheathe her blade. He nodded as they came close enough to speak without shouting.

"Reyka's folk?" His voice was hoarse.

"Whose are you?" Tibor demanded.

The man shrugged. "Sayan's." Which his tattoos already told them, as their killdeer and frogs identified them as Jayala's, rooted them to a place. Owls curved from his temples, down around his eyes and over cheekbones, the black lines faded like the marking of a much older man. Hint, on the backs of his hands, of the entwined snakes and cheetahs in black and blue that would mark his arms. His brown face was burnt dark from the desert, paler scars seaming above and below his left eye.

Beardless, as most Westgrasslander men were. She'd been startled at the hairiness of a Red Desert man's face, partner of a caravaneer of the Retlavonbarkash who'd come from the road to join Reyka's company. Dark eyes peering out over a thicket of curling black. He had made her laugh. Gerbil peering from its burrow.

Dead, both of them, a week back.

The company had been almost six hundred, when she joined. Two-thirds that, now, and fewer fit to fight. Those so injured they couldn't ride even clasped in a comrade's arms or tied to their horse—

Better a friend's knife than to be taken by the Westrons.

"Ride with you." Not a question. The stranger looked exhausted. So did his horse.

If that savage dog-thing belonged to him, there was no sign of it. She saw Tibor scanning the horizons, too.

They could contest him joining them. Jolanan wasn't sure how it would go. He looked menacing in a way that Tibor and the other caravan mercenaries, hard though they had seemed when she first found herself among them, did not. Caravaneer's coat the colour of a brindled cat, undyed grey sheep's wool and sandy camel spun together, flung open over his russet brigandine. Indigo headscarf pulled down about his neck. His hair was very long, even for a caravaneer, and so dark as to be called black, under the dust, which was caked to him as if he'd ducked his head into some pool and ridden while still wet. It wasn't the look of the road so much as the air of him. The bull that knew the herd was his. The bitch that all the other dogs gave place to in the dooryard.

"Yeah," Tibor said wearily. "They can kill you when we get back if you need killing. I'm too tired. Want your name and gang, though. I'm Tibor. Used to ride with Hammad's gang out of Marakand. This is my cousin Jolanan. We're of the Jayala'arad."

"Holla," the man said. Shrugged. "Ridden with a few gangs, over the years."

Jolanan had been around caravaneers long enough now to know that "a few gangs" wasn't a recommendation, was a flag signalling trouble, in fact. They valued loyalty on the road. Someone who couldn't settle or who got themselves turfed from master to master was not someone you wanted standing shoulder to shoulder with you in a fight.

"Who?" Tibor demanded.

"Gaguush's gang," Holla said, and there was a smile, even. Bleak. "Long time ago. She's dead."

It didn't satisfy Tibor. "Never heard of her."

"You wouldn't have. Came up from Marakand this time with Mistress Varnouri."

Tibor grunted, seeming to recognize the name. "Kin?" he demanded. "Cousins?"

"I look Westron to you?" The man turned his horse. "No kin. No cousins. They're all dead. Whatever. Ride on my own, then."

There were even Westrons among the company, caravaneers come with their partners and spouses, folk who swore by memory of their dead gods and reviled the faith of the red priests. Not lightly trusted, but Sayan had known the truth in their hearts.

"Still want to know who your kin were," Tibor repeated, and kicked his bay up even, waving Jolanan to keep back. She ignored that, went up the other side. Holla didn't seem much disturbed, although his black didn't like it. Three stallions unfamiliar together. Lark didn't like it either. Jolanan and the skewbald were still settling into one another's ways. A spear had taken her old mare from her a fortnight back. Lazlan gave her Lark then, with the blood of a Westron commander still on his white-splashed flanks and Lark, it turned out, was no cattle-horse. He had a taste for fighting.

Holla stared Lark in his blue nearside eye and the horse settled down. The man nodded to Jolanan, as if to say, *There.* His own eyes were hazel, flecked golden-green, she decided. Warm.

Nice face. Much as she distrusted him, she liked it. Old, almost as old as Tibor, who was past thirty, but—when you were alive and hadn't thought to be, it was surely an insult to life itself not to take a moment to appreciate a pleasing face, as much as it would be to shut one's ears to the rising songs of the black larks or the bright swathe of pink a patch of campion made across the hillside.

He smiled.

Warm smile, too. Like he really saw her.

Jayala prevent he'd seen anything but proper suspicion in her scrutiny.

"I'll talk to the warlord," he said, turning from her.

"The chief, yeah," Tibor said. "You'll be talking to her, never fear."

"How about we just take all the sniffing and growling as given, Tibor, and just ride? We want to be bearing more easterly."

"No."

"We do."

Jolanan didn't quite smile herself. Too tired. But the man was right. Tibor had an appalling sense of direction.

They caught up with the spread-out straggle of the warband eventually, just as it was drawing together again around the start of a camp: a few cookfires, pickets riding out. Jolanan didn't like the way Holla frowned, seemingly noting everything. Disapproving. Assessing. Spy, she thought again, and when they found Reyka and Lazlan standing apart in some quiet consultation with the Marakander caravaneer Caro, she made sure to keep herself between the stranger and the chief, which she saw Lazlan noting, then moving to do the same.

"This is Holla," Tibor announced without dismounting. "We found him riding north after the raid. He doesn't give any good account of what he was doing there. Says he was looking for us, chief. No family, no kin, and shiftless between gangs, by his own admission."

"Looking for us, why?" Reyka demanded. A woman nearing fifty, her hair cut short, narrow face tattooed with the black larks that folk of the Sayanbarkash used for women, making a difference in pattern as Jolanan's own folk did not. Grey eyes. A necklace of mountain-turquoise about her throat, last trace, maybe of the wealthy farmer she had once been. Her younger brother was very like her. Staring up now, with eyes narrowed against the sun, at the weary stranger on his horse.

"You'd rather I rode with the All-Holy?" Holla asked. "I'm heading over the rivers. Thought I'd travel with you, lend my sabre to yours, if you're heading north or east. If you don't want me, I'll ride alone."

Wanted the relative safety of a company about him, and precious grain for his horse, probably. Or wanted them to think that his only desire.

She knew that horse. Dark stallion, white blaze. Small wonder Lark had reacted as he had. She'd killed its rider, that very dawn. The knight. She'd have known it at once if she hadn't been so tired.

"Arpath?" Lazlan called, turning away.

The young Sayanbarkashi seer was conscious again, at least. He came from the round tent the chief's household shared, a blanket wrapped over his shoulders, though the day was warm. Face wan, golden-brown eyes bruised-looking as if he'd sat unsleeping too many nights. His gaze fixed on the stranger, stayed there.

"This is Holla. Tibor and Jolanan found him after the raid. He says he wants to join us. We trust him? Won't say who his kin are."

Arpath, like Lazlan, had the men's owls of the Sayanbarkash tattooed on his face. A different style than the work on Holla's. Well, the bards who did the work when a youth came of age sometimes revived old styles, or found new of their own. Didn't mean Holla's tattooing was false. It would have been fresh and new and out of place on his weathered face in that case, anyway.

"Lose your own horse?" she asked him.

The corner of his mouth tucked up, as if she amused. "Yes. Thanks."

"For what?"

"Providing another."

"Did I?"

He shrugged, looking away now, at Arpath. "Found him straying when I needed him. Rather like I did you two."

"We found you," Tibor said.

Arpath still stared.

"Go on," Lazlan said. "Ask him."

Lies, Arpath had said, gave him a bitter taste, like bile rising.

"I'm not a Westron spy," Holla said to the seer. "I'm not any enemy of yours."

Arpath swallowed, nodded.

"You didn't grow up under a mushroom," Reyka said. "Who're your kin? What farm, what valley?"

"They're all dead," Holla said. Seemed to hesitate. "Where you from? North hills?"

"I held the valley below Dyer's Hill."

"Huh. Thought so. You've got his face."

"Whose?"

"Someone I knew once." He shook his head. "No family. I was a foundling. Doesn't matter." He looked tired, suddenly. More tired than he already had. "It really doesn't matter where I'm from. You want me to ride with you a while, or not?"

"Arpath?" Reyka asked, gentle, as she always was with the young seer. They'd come on him at his own family's execution. Father, mother, sister, cousins, grandparents already burning, beyond saving. He'd been on his knees, screaming, cursing, a sixth-circle priest, a diviner of the All-Holy, in her soot-smudged white cope pulling his head back by the hair, shouting at him in bad Westgrasslander to look, see what awaited if he did not give himself and the blessing of his talent to the service of the All-Holy as the Old Great Gods had intended.

"He's true," the young man said. "He's—" Fell silent. Took a deep breath. Eyes wide, pupils dilated, as if he were falling into vision without drum or prayer.

Did Holla shake his head, ever so slightly? Arpath blinked and looked away. "He's not a Westron spy. Trust him."

Reyka was frowning. Summoned her brother with a raised chin. They murmured, heads together. Beckoned Arpath in close. More murmuring. The seer seemed vehement. "I swear it, chief, marshal, Sayan—Old Great Gods be my witness, he's true."

Jolanan leaned over to murmur herself, "They'll kill you if they decide you're a spy anyway."

"Sensible. If I were."

"Does Arpath actually know you?"

"Haven't been back to the grass since before he was born. No."

"Are you a spy?"

"No."

He didn't seem worried. Just tired. Bored, even. The black horse stood head low, ears drooping. Holla scratched its neck absently.

"We're not bandits," Reyka said. "We're a warband. We ride in justice, with honour. We protect the folk. We don't raid them, any we find surviving. We're the rearguard of their flight beyond the rivers. We serve the folk and the gods and the goddesses—the memory of the gods and the goddesses of the Western Grass. We do as they would have us do, under the Old Great Gods. If you can't hold to this, if you think this is about brigandage, if you'd murder or steal from the folk the little they have left, if you'd abuse those weaker than you or think to make yourself a master over bondfolk like a Great Grass chieftain, you can ride away now. If you can ride on our terms, you take an oath to us."

"I take no oaths to serve any woman nor man," Holla said. Matter-of-fact, no great emphasis. "But I swear, I ride in the service of the gods of the Western Grass. Always. Take that, or don't."

"It's enough," Arpath said, as if he had authority here, and Reyka gave him a long look. He didn't seem to notice.

Lazlan began to say something, but Reyka held up a silencing hand, transferring her stare to Holla. "You an archer?"

"If I need to be."

She shook her head. "Take him to Caro for the lancers, Tibor. She's a caravaneer; she can deal with him. Jolanan, stay a moment."

Jolanan dismounted, joined Reyka, Lazlan, and Arpath as Tibor reluctantly turned his horse and led away, Holla following.

"Get Tibor alone, when you can. Let him know—you and he both, ask around among the caravaneers. See if anyone from the road knows anything of Holla."

"Yes, chief."

"He's true," Arpath said. "He's—I felt it, for a moment, Reyka. He's touched by the gods. Blessed. Somehow."

"A bard? He isn't. Nor a wizard of any sort."

"No. But—"

"I'll accept what you've seen in him, Arpath, but nonetheless, I want someone keeping an eye on him. Everyone's got cousins of some degree, by blood or adoption. Talk to Lazlan when you find out anything, Jo."

"Yes, chief."

Reyka gave Jolanan a weary smile, Lazlan a friendly thump on the shoulder as she led Lark off in search of the food and rest they both needed.

No chance to talk to Tibor alone there; he was with Caro, a Marakander caravaneer who'd followed a Westgrasslander husband to this fight and lost him to a Westron arrow in their first battle. But maybe no need.

"Gurhan grant we do get over the river," Caro was saying in the desert-road tongue, though she spoke good Westgrass. "Wish you'd brought Varnouri and the rest of her gang with you, Hol."

"They were heading up to At-Landi," Holla said, frowning over a swollen bruise on the black's neck. Lark's doing, maybe. The horse shifted its weight unhappily, turned its head, but only to rest a nose on the man's shoulder. He resumed his grooming with a twist of wiry grass. "I don't think most gang-bosses are understanding, yet, how bad things are. The Westrons aren't going to stop at the Kinsai'av."

Jolanan had to listen carefully to catch the words. Till this summer she'd never learnt any language but her own, living in the shadow of the Karas, that and a few words of Westron.

They should have killed the red priests, the missionaries, who'd been creeping down the old lost road from the mountains in dribs and drabs all her life, not listened to them, however politely, however deafly. Not given them advice on the road east, and shelter, and food, and kindness.

First folk to be overrun by the Westrons, the Jayala'arad.

"We're running north."

"I know."

Caro gave Jolanan a smile, switched languages. "You've found us a good one this time. He says the horse is yours. Can he keep it?"

Her prize? They didn't work like that. Lazlan and Reyka would assign captured livestock and supplies where they were lacking. But the man needed a mount and nobody had shown any urge to take it from him.

"Sure."

But Lark was cranky, tugging at the bridle, not liking the black any better, and she moved him off. Ate with Tibor and a crowd of fellow skirmishers and scouts. Heard who was dead and who was missing. Small stones, piling on. A weight that pressed down, day after day. Passed on Reyka's order to find out about Holla, but Tibor shrugged.

"Caro knows him. He's been with Varnouri's gang six years, she says. That's enough for me, I guess. Maybe he has good reasons to deny his family, you never know."

Even a foundling had family of some sort. Maybe he'd been heading home to look for them, and discovered them all dead, the longhouse roofless, walls pulled down. Maybe a pyre in the dooryard, and the charred bones. Maybe he hurt too much to talk of them.

As the shadows gathered into night, she left Tibor and his friends searching out their beds, such as they were. Not enough tents, and a clear night, so nobody much was bothering with cutting brush and rigging shelters of hide and blanket. Everyone slept in some order, near their own horselines. They'd had to cut and ride before. Pickets out, with dogs, and Arpath would have searched in a bowl of tea, which had made her laugh the first time she'd heard Lazlan say it, but rocking and singing, catching the sky in the dark liquor worked to bring visions for him, so what did she know?

The lancer company was over to the east, and she found Holla there. No fires, not once night fell. Reyka's rule. Folk lay close, shared blankets, not necessarily with any thought of more than warmth and fellowship.

They would be breaking camp in the first grey light of the new day, moving slowly northward, a shield to the families and herds in flight ahead, making for the Bakanav, the river that joined the Kinsai'av above the caravan town of At-Landi. The Northron ships, which came down by forest rivers and a portage between the Varr'aa and the Bakanav, gave up their cargoes there to the camel-caravans and took the goods of east and south back north. A barrier to the Westron advance, maybe. Or at least a means of getting out of his path.

Most were already sleeping and she stood staring in the dark, not able to make out hummock of body from roughness of the ground or stacked gear. She'd thought to find some cluster still gossiping with the newcomer. Many of the lancers were caravaneers, who'd come with horses and camels and years on the road behind them; they'd be wanting news of friends and gangs and even family left behind. But the days were heavy.

Hopelessness. On them all. A weight like grey cloud, unending, pressing low. This was a retreat, a withdrawal from their own land, and they left their gods and their goddesses dead behind them.

"Caro's gone out on watch." Soft voice at her shoulder. She wasn't even surprised. Turned to face him.

"I was looking for you." Jolanan shrugged, which was pointless; he wouldn't see. "I don't know—making sure you'd settled in." That was pointless, too. She wasn't responsible for the man and that wasn't why she'd come anyway. Just . . .

"Can't sleep?" Was that a question, or did Holla say it of himself? She wasn't certain. "Here, I saved the last of the tea."

Dim movement. Cup in his hand. Jolanan found it as much by the fading heat of it on the back of her hand as by sight. Took it and followed him when he walked away, off into the night, waiting for her to catch up, a hand under her elbow when she stumbled on a tussock. Found a place to sit together, bruised grass sweet about them and a nightjar calling, as if all the humans and horses and camels were nothing to worry it.

"You alone?" Holla asked her.

"Tibor's my cousin," she said. "He'd gone to the road. I found him, when—I came east. Found the warband. Everyone else is dead. You too?"

"Long dead," he said.

She drank the tea, bitter, sweet. Caravan tea, smoky as hard Northron fish.

"You should be with Caro's riders," Holla said abruptly. "I like how you handle that cranky brute of yours in a fight."

"I'm a cow-herd, not a caravan mercenary." Had he been lying up in the grass watching? Jolanan supposed he might have been; unhorsed and lacking a bow he couldn't very well have joined in when she and Tibor were fighting for their lives. Had he seen that wolf-thing?

Distracted from asking the question. He'd touched a knuckle to the back of her hand, still wrapped around his cup. Not accidental, though they both could let it seem so, if she only moved her hand away. She didn't.

"I'll teach you," he said. "They're going to have to scare up a spear or two for me somewhere, anyway, they can equip you too. You ride with us tomorrow." She didn't question how he was going to bring that about. He seemed to take it for granted Caro, Lazlan, they'd all do what he asked. Her too?

Holla wasn't asking anything. He was just . . . sitting there. Tired. Disheartened. Alone. She leaned a little. Not much. Didn't need much, to bring her shoulder to his arm. After a moment it went around her. Tucked her closer.

Heart might be beating a little too fast. Reckless and not worth worrying about, that she didn't have what the caravaneers called a maiden's friend from the glovers of Marakand or Serakallash, or the amulets a wizard more skilled in spell-crafting than Arpath might sell. Not worth worrying, because she didn't think they were any of them going to survive long enough for next year to matter. She didn't want the mere warmth of some half-known fellow archer who might be dead tomorrow snoring and sighing and breaking wind beside her, she didn't want to lie trying not to think, to remember, waiting for exhaustion to drag her down so she could sleep and forget till in the morning it all began again or the horns woke them into blind flight in the dark. She didn't want to *care*, about anything, and Holla had smiled, younger than his eyes, and even his eyes had something in them that wasn't there in Tibor, who worried over her for kinship's sake, in Arpath, in Nessa who so quickly become a friend like a sister and then was dead anyway, last week which seemed months ago now—

"You tired?" she asked, and when he looked down to answer her she could feel his breath, clean, inviting, on her face.

"Very," he said, but when she set the empty cup down and put her fingers to his cheek, thumb under his jaw, she could feel that his pulse ran hard like her own.

Jolanan found his mouth in the dark on her second try, and what was sweet, careful invitation—he could still say, *no, we need to be sensible, a Westron patrol might find us, the alarm might sound, there's someone back in my caravan-gang, I'm too old, you're too young,* or just *I'm really too tired and we should sleep*—all of that, any of that—became hungry, urgent fire burning away all the sensible arguments neither of them was making. Fingers finding buckles, ties—not quite so insensible of caution as to strip themselves utterly naked, no, but his hands were warm on her skin, fingers spreading over a breast, fingers spread on her belly, sliding down and she lay back, hooking a leg over him, tugging him down over her, her own hand going down between them where she'd never let a hand go with a man before, cuddling with Dharand who had ridden herd for some remoter cousins of the next valley, the two of them so careful, so sensible of what was right between young people who had not yet pledged their betrothal before the goddess—Dharand, like all the other people of her first life, dead or lost and only might have been, nothing to do with Jolanan who could kill a man and not even remember his face, only that his horse had a white blaze. Holla was hot down there, hard and silk-soft, and she was afraid she might hurt him, her fingers so bark-rough, ragged-nailed. He made a sound that was nothing but pleasure, though, and let her carry on with what she had begun, his mouth on her breast, till it was

his own hand exploring, fingers . . . a tongue deep in her mouth and she
was losing herself, somewhere, losing the world, which was all she asked
of the night.

Something—on the edge of his awareness. A shadow. Something . . .
slinking past, in the darkness. Like the swift-slow shadow under the
canoe, half lost in wave and shimmer. Shark. Corner of the eye and gone.

"Wake up," his sister said. "He's coming to kill you." And she laughed.

Something out there. Dangerous. Ancient. Hidden.

A shape he almost knew.

Jochiz sat up, opening his eyes, flinging the blanket back. The
woman Clio woke as well. A primate of the seventh circle, diviner and
warrior and devoted lieutenant . . . he pushed her aside, when she would
have reached for him, her words meaningless, questioning, concerned at
his alarm.

It wasn't alarm. He had not cried out.

It was only dream.

Warning.

Jochiz lay down again. Let the woman reach for him, hold him, stroke
the scars of his forearms, which fascinated her. Her mouth on them, soft,
as if she would suckle there, feed on what he had already given her, given
again and again, for all his folk in their generations. He could ignore that.
Ignore her even as her mouthing grew more insistent, teeth nipping. He
put her aside, but did not order her from the bed. He might want her
later. The body, Sien-Shava, had his needs, and her nibbling teeth . . . not
now. Later. He let himself lie, still, rocking in the waves, in the darkness,
letting the water flow through him, carrying the shape of the shadow, the
scent . . . memory.

Elusive as water, unknowable as the depths of a lake.

CHAPTER XIX

From the Chronicle of Nikeh Gen'Emras

Most of the Nearer Grass had fallen before that bloody summer's end, though a band of warriors drawn from the folk of many gods and goddesses of that land had harried the army, a small dog nipping at their heels, until the fall of the Sayanbarkash, whereupon they retreated after the folk of that land, who had fled, many of them, north over the river Bakan into lands of folk who were kin both to them and to the Northrons, and had their own customs and ways. They were not entirely unwelcoming, but neither was there any easy way for the folk and beasts to fit themselves into a land already peopled. Some found place there, others went up the Kinsai to At-Landi, the town where the caravans of the road gave up their trade to the ships of the Northrons.

The All-Holy's advance stopped at the Kinsai's western shore. His knight, Prince Dimas of Emrastepse, elevated to the seventh circle of his favour, a lord of the faith and in command of the Army of the South, on his orders established a winter camp opposite the Lower Castle, a hundred miles down river, below the Fifth Cataract. The All-Holy himself, commanding the Army of the North, did the same above the First. All across the Nearer Grass, in lands where the gods and goddesses had been destroyed, those folk who had not been able to flee and who had saved themselves from the slaughter by surrendering to the priests, swearing oaths of submission to the All-Holy, learning to recite their catechism, offering their wrists to the tattooers' needles and undergoing initiation to the first circle of the faith, laboured to bring in the sparse harvest and to supply the armies. All across the Nearer Grass, mission-houses were established that were more like the princes' towers of Tiypur, ditched and walled and garrisoned with not only teachers of the third circle, who had charge of educating the folk in their wide-scattered family

*holdings as well as the children brought in to be students—truer to say hostages—
in each tower's school, but a garrison of fifth-circle knights and ordinary soldiers.*

*There were rumours among the folk of the Nearer Grass and even among the
Westrons. They called it a lie of the heathens, the raiders, that somehow spread,
though whispering it might have the one who did so hanged. The All-Holy was
not any messenger of the Old Great Gods. The All-Holy was no oracle. There was
no nameless god and never had been.*

*The All-Holy was a devil, one of the seven, and his name, when he was a
man, had been Sien-Shava. He was the devil Jochiz.*

*The red priests killed for the hint of it. Blasphemy. But like fire in a coal-
seam, it never quite would die.*

Too many afoot, exhausted, hungry. They couldn't simply keep running
and leave pursuit behind. Caro's signaller bleated the order they all anticipated. Not too much confusion when the ram's horn blared. Holla knew
something of such manoeuvres and there were Grasslanders among them,
and one caravaneer, Hani Kahren, who said he had been Nabbani cavalry
far in the east of the world. They managed it, turning back through
themselves, first time that wasn't a drill. Jolanan kneed Lark about,
holding her place in the line. Caro came through them, moving to the
fore again, with the signaller and the man carrying the pennant ahead.
A gap formed to Jolanan's left in which they would find place. Holla was
riding up there with them, as if by right—which he had, now, since after
three days of him at her shoulder Caro had gone to Reyka and told her
to give him the damned lancers, since he had so many opinions. No, he'd
said, and ended up her second anyhow. One of the few, along with the
Nabbani man, who understood not only that they should hold to greater
order than some kind of raiding party, but how to achieve it, beyond what
Reyka and Lazlan had managed.

Jolanan wondered if Holla himself had served in the guard of Marakand or some company farther afield. Didn't ask. He didn't talk much of
where he had been, before he loomed up out of the grass on a fresh-stolen
horse. No tales of life on the road, of other lands. Didn't talk much at all,

except of each day just past. She didn't want to look back either. Or ahead. Grass and stars and a shared blanket. That was all they had.

Trotting, a threat. Fear before them. Already the Westron soldiers began to bunch together as though they would be safer so, crowding one another. If they had the sense to ground their spears, those that had them, to make a bristling wall—but they were far from their most feared captains—conscripts, probably, with little training and no armour but leather. Scouts riding far out to the east had reported the band, a hundred or so, tracking Westgrassland refugees afoot, a mass escape from one of the enslaved settlements. The fugitives seemed to be heading for the Kinsai'av.

Arguments. They were too few to split, almost to the Bakanav, which like the Kinsai at least felt as if it should be a border, a barrier. Most of the folk who had fled had gone that way, into the hills north of At-Landi at the rivers' meeting. In the end, they had divided, some to go with Reyka north, hoping to gather more folk over the river, form some plan of defence to hold that as a line if the Westrons turned that way, but a company of mixed lancers and skirmishers under Lazlan and Caro to overtake and protect the folk fleeing east. So few, they were, once they split. Nothing but raiders, brigands, the delusion that they were a warband, an army, revealed as nothing but a bard's dream, ten riders for every one when the ride came to be song. But who would sing it, when all who survived were slaves and their children raised to worship a devil?

Didn't matter. Now. Here.

The Westrons nerved themselves, a jogging charge, shouting the praise of their false god. The lancers surged into a canter, and the troop of archers flashed past, shooting, whooping, wheeling away. Noticeable gaps in the Westron formation, if you could call it a formation when it was breaking apart, each man abruptly a rabbit running in terror of his own life. Hunting exhausted folk armed with a few scrounged tools—that was one thing. Facing a cavalry charge, apparently, another, and Jolanan found she was laughing. Lance lowered on the captain's sign, the bright pennon ahead dipping, and they were up and around Caro, making her one of the line. They struck the Westrons with a roar. The shock was still strange, for all her weary evening drilling; this was only her second fight as a lancer, if you could call the patrol they ran down two days ago even a fight. Her force and Lark's made one, and the dead man dragged her lance down; couldn't free it so she let it go, drew her sabre as their own line spread, and the butchery began.

Behind them, men and women, some few mounted, others afoot, were running, running now for their lives, a company of Lazlan's skirmishers making a shield of bows and steel about them. Half a mile more, that was all—they were nearly to the Kinsai'av, the farthest east Jolanan had ever been. Nearly the whole of the camp. No children. The adults had given their promises to the red priests and were marked for the false god—because, the woman who spoke as their chief had said, it was better to live and find their children again and keep memory of the true gods in their hearts. They served by tending the ill-managed fields, vast ploughings of virgin grassland on hills that had been grazing since first ever this land was settled, stony and dry. Their children were gone. To other settlements, it was alleged, where they might attend school under the red priests and learn to be good and true servants of the All-Holy.

The Westrons weren't people, behind the faces. Jolanan didn't let them be. Just eyes and mouths, just intent and movement. Slashed and shoved and Lark struck, hoof and tooth, savage. For every lost father, lost mother, stolen child. Every man and woman and child torn from home, from god or goddess, or dead in their purging fires. A man kneeling, no weapon but a long knife which he dropped before him, hands over his head, defensive, and she leaned and slashed at his throat as Lark plunged on by. No mercy, no quarter. If the Westgrasslanders escaped from the camp were retaken, they would be killed as apostates, and not swiftly. Back when she first joined, when she was riding a patrol with Lazlan himself, so young, in the spring, they had found the aftermath of one such execution. No wood for burning, the usual punishment, so the prisoners had been pegged to the earth through their wrists and ankles and gutted alive, left to die.

They had buried them in the clean earth, and then she had been sick.

In the back of the mind, always, in those first days—would they find her father, Tibor's mother and elder sister, the folk of that farmstead, among the prisoners, among the dead . . .

Never did. Never any word. She and Tibor and every other West-grasslander among them, every time, searching, afterwards—asking among the survivors, hoping, fearing . . . most of them didn't even look any more. Didn't let hope take root.

Their own line had lost its shape, broken into solitary fury or smaller bands, scattering. Holla was standing in his stirrups at Caro's side, roaring at them to close up. The signaller's horn echoed him and Caro's pennon whirled.

"They'll try to make you scatter," he had said. "They'll want to break your line. You're a wall. Remember that. Each rider, each horse, a stone in that wall, interlinked. Weakened, the whole line of you, if there are gaps. You're not children. You're not puppies, to go chasing what catches your eye. If they run, let them run. Wait your signal, watch your five-leader, watch your captain. Don't lose yourself in the fury. Don't lose yourself in the fear. Strength in the line, remember that."

Man on her right, woman on her left. This was no longer any charge, no pushing front. They were circling, turning, closing around their enemies.

Fewer and fewer. One of their own unhorsed and down before her, his eye-framing tattoos of coots saying he was of the Darya-Kinsai. Occu-pied by the Westron Army of the South now, she had heard. The man was wounded past saving or already dead, his lower jaw slashed away. She tightened her legs, jumped Lark over him. The last Westrons were on their knees, not even begging, just crying out for death, crying the name of their lying god, arms reaching out, as if to embrace him and the miraculous translation they expected in their dying.

"Devil-worshippers!" she shouted at one as she struck him down. "Die damned and godless—your road will be lifetimes long!" They didn't understand her. Didn't matter. She smashed a man's face with her shield when he tried to scramble up Lark as if she and the horse were some tree to be scaled, hand groping to seize and pull her down. Someone who still had their lance speared him as he struck the ground.

Some had dismounted, were methodically beheading the kneeling men. They made no resistance, these last, and she reined Lark back. Chest heaving. Face wet. Sweat. Tears. Spat, wiped her mouth on her glove. Mouth bleeding. Nothing worse than a split lip.

How had she even ended up here? She was a cowherd.

The river-crossing was a slow affair. Some miracle—a settlement of a few families who lived by fishing and fowling. A handful of boats, and the families, their faces tattooed with fish, calling themselves Kinsai's folk, but not any connection to the strange clan of the ferrymen. They had boats, far too few, and had already been packing up their meagre possessions, rounding up their geese and driving and dragging their cattle, ropes about their horns, to swim the river, in fear of the Westrons. Whether they were entirely pleased to find themselves folded into a West-grasslander flight was doubtful, but Lazlan gave them little chance to object to their boats being taken over.

Jolanan grew cold, muscles stiff, sweat drying, as they kept their watch over the ferrying. The current buffeted them, unfriendly. Fear seemed to have infected the horses. Some, when it came time for them to swim, did not want to enter the water.

Holla hung back, watching to the south, downriver. He always seemed the first to notice anything amiss in the landscape, Westron scout or bad weather or a passing fox. Jolanan walked over to him, leading Lark. He gave her a look like a sleeper waking, cold, almost not recognizing her as anyone who mattered, she could think.

Something in his hand, held against his chest. His amulet pouch. Blinked, warmth returning, seeing her properly. Tucked the token of lost Sayan away inside his shirt again.

He looked worse than that first time she had seen him. A greyness to his face, and lines—eyes, mouth—that she had never noticed before, ageing him. She remembered that brown-haired woman who had worked the harvest with them that bad year, coming to her where she struggled with an overloaded basket of wet linens she'd been spreading on the hazels to dry. *Your papa's hurt, Jo. You'd better come . . .* The woman's face had been like that, with the news she carried.

Had he taken some hurt . . . ? Before she could ask, Holla said, "Kinsai's dead."

Jolanan felt . . . not nothing. Weight, pressing down. More. And more. She had thought, had hoped—Kinsai was so vast a power, compared to the gods and goddesses of the Western Grass with their small lands. Dark tales even said she had long ago devoured the lesser gods and goddesses of her shore to make herself greater, perhaps in wars against the devils. And her folk, though so few, only the two communities of the Upper and Lower Castles, numbered so many wizards among them, and scholars and seers . . .

The horses knew, reluctant to enter the water. The river was turned godless.

And Holla . . .

Gods, was he one of those Kinsai had taken as a lover, or was it only that he felt, like the horses, some pain she could not? Not the first time she had wondered if he were secretly a wizard himself. He twitched and muttered in his dreams in a language she couldn't even name.

What could mortal folk say to comfort one another, when a goddess of the earth ceased to be? And what could she? Kinsai was only a name, a story. The wild spirit of the river, mother of many mortal children, lover, seducer of travellers male and female alike.

"Come on, then," Jolanan said. "I—there's nothing we can do, and we're on the wrong side of the river. Rearguard's one thing. Having to swim myself because they've made the last crossing without me isn't what I intended."

"Yes," he said, as if it didn't matter very much. "All right."

The river seemed no different than before to Jolanan. She dipped a hand in the water, mid-stream. Only water, which was all it had ever been to her.

But it had been in all of their minds that to the All-Holy it must be a barrier, a live and active enemy his folk would not dare to engage. Great Kinsai, their salvation, a force to resist the evil that destroyed the gods of the hills and the goddesses of the grassland waters.

No respite, no sanctuary now on the eastern shore, or in the hills about At-Landi. No sure safety beyond the Bakanav, where Reyka intended to build a fortified camp, with or without leave of the scattered folk of that land and the guild-council of At-Landi.

They camped that night on the eastern shore of the Kinsai'av. No jubilation in their victory, or for the Westgrasslanders who had escaped enslavement, in their freedom. Too much lost, too much unknown.

At least there was fire. Warmth. Jolanan sat close against Holla's side, not caring who saw. Tibor, who knew, frowned at her nonetheless. Holla wasn't quite old enough to be her father but he didn't approve. Kinless, even if not entirely friendless.

"Will he cross?" Lazlan asked, meaning the All-Holy. "Will he turn north, do we think, or go south down the caravan road? Or is the Western Grass enough to content him?"

Throwing out questions to lie between them all, this fire where the commanders, informal though they were, gathered. Smoky tea, rich with milk from the fisher-folk's cattle. Holla sat withdrawn, staring into the fire.

"He'll cross," he said to the flames. "It's Marakand he wants."

"The wizards of the library will put an end to him," Kahren said.

"It's not rumour. The All-Holy is the devil Sien-Shava Jochiz." Holla looked up, the firelight gleaming in his eyes, a flare of almost green. "Nothing will stop him, whatever it is he wants, wherever it is he's going, except—" He shrugged, didn't finish his thought.

"There was a mountain demon killed two devils," Lazlan said. "But they say the Blackdog died at Marakand, defeating the false Lady."

"My god fought the servant of a devil," Kahren said. "When first he came into the land, there was an empress possessed by a devil, and Nabban and the *Rihswera* defeated her."

"The what?" Jolanan asked.

"The priest of the god. An immortal warrior from—I don't know where. I think maybe he was Northron, or maybe Taren? A king, who gave up his kingdom and was killed and came back from the dead to follow Nabban, for love of him. He fought the false empress and drove the devil out of her, and left his body to fight the devil soul to soul. There are songs. I could—"

"Nobody here speaks Imperial, Kari," said Caro. "No, don't translate. If Reyka guesses right, and if we stay beyond the Bakanav—if the All-Holy, whether, he's truly inspired by a devil or not, is intending to march on Marakand—we'll be safe for a while."

"Till the folk of the north hills drive us out of their pastures," Jolanan said. She had no place at this fire, only that she trailed after Holla and they all accepted that.

"He'll cross the Kinsai'av and head for Marakand," Holla said. "I thought she might hold a time, but—he'll cross before winter. And once he controls the desert road, he can deal with the folk between the rivers—At-Landi and Varrgash and all the hills between—whenever he has a mind to. And all their gods as well." He got to his feet, fastening his coat. Something in his face. Grim. A stranger. He'd never been anything but. Yet she caught at his coat-hem.

"Where are you going?"

"To the castle," he said. "To see the Warden of the ferry-folk. Lazlan, Caro—listen. Believe me. There's no 'if.' The All-Holy is a devil. I don't know what he wants, but he's killing, devouring gods, enslaving the folk—he's not going to rest content with the pastures of the Western Grass even if he does make a winter camp, and I don't think he will. I wouldn't. Not if Marakand were my aim. Better to keep moving, keep my momentum, keep the harvest being carried with me, after me, than to leave it sitting garnered for the conquered folk to raid and spoil and burn. You should get these folk moving, come the dawn. Head up to At-Landi, beg the mercy of the folk there for them, join Reyka. Build your camp and your walls if you think you can, but don't consider there's any lasting safety in it."

"You've got a place here," Lazlan said. "You can't just ride off."

"Desertion," said Kahren, and his tone was only half joking.

"Never said I was staying long," Holla said. "Just across the rivers. Rode with you longer than I intended."

"You're not serious, Holla."

"Sorry, Caro. Admit I'm leaving you in better state than I found you, anyway."

"You *bastard.*"

Lazlan rocked to his feet. "You're going nowhere. We're—"

"Talk to you alone," Holla said.

"What?"

"I need to talk to you alone."

"I want not to have some damned traitor riding south into Westron reach knowing where we are."

"Come on." Holla detached Jolanan's hand from his coat, gently— but he always was gentle, in his words, in his manner, as if he felt the world to be fragile as an egg. "Just you, Lazlan."

"Great Gods damn . . ." But Lazlan followed him off into the dark. Kahren poured them all more tea. Silence. They listened, of course they did. Only the camp. Talk. Singing. Someone playing a fiddle. A dog barked, once, not an alarm, just bored. One of the fisherfolk children was crying.

No exclamation, no outcry. Well, they weren't expecting for the two of them to come to drawn blades. Were they?

Lazlan came back alone.

"Well?" asked Caro.

"He's going down to the ferry-castle. We can do without him. Kahren, you'll take his place as Caro's lieutenant."

"But—"

"Just leave it, Caro."

"Mistress Varnouri always called him a fey bastard," Caro said. "He'd up and leave without a word and be back a week later, out of the desert, no warning."

270 The Last Road

"You could have mentioned that," said Lazlan. He sounded angry. Found his cup and wrapped both hands around it.

"I liked him," Caro said. "Stupid bastard. What's at the ferry castle? Nothing to help us. The Westrons'll take it before long. What's he going to do then?"

"His son's there," Lazlan said. Laughed, still with anger in it. "Gods, I—" Shook his head, dumped the dregs of his tea hissing on the fire. "Are the watches set?"

"Yes, marshal," Kahren said, sudden formality.

"Good. I'm going to sleep." And abruptly, looking down. "Jolanan. Jo. Oh Sayan, Jo, I forgot. He said to tell you—he was sorry. That's all."

Jolanan hunched up, pulled her coat close. Cold. Nothing to say. She wasn't going to shout or weep. Just another blow, another piece of what was hers ripped away. Of course it was. Nothing endured. A breath, no more. Each day its own thing, nothing to follow, each gift, every shaft of sunlight, broken, swallowed in grey cloud. She couldn't even complain, rail of seduction, abandonment. If anyone had been doing any seducing—

Son. Well, why not? A man might have a child and still take a lover. Lazlan didn't say wife, partner. Just a child. Of course he would ride to take the boy out of harm's way. Wherever that might be.

He could have asked her to come.

No place was safe.

Lazlan's hand on her shoulder. He stood there. Squeezed it, then, and walked away without speaking.

Pity she didn't need. Nothing endured. They were all just leaves, battered in the wind, tearing free one by one to fall and rot and go back to earth.

"Jolanan . . ." Caro began.

"I'm going to see Tibor," she said, cutting her off. Angry at the shake in her voice. Furious. Stupid, traitor, childish voice. Walked off into the dark. Tripped on a saddle left where it should not have been.

Holla'd be at the horselines, saddling the black stallion he had named

Fury. His idea of a joke. She wouldn't follow. What would she do? Shout? Cry? Curse him? Beg?

Maybe he was hoping she would follow.

Then he should have asked.

She wandered the scattered fires. A few greeted her. Most were already rolled in their blankets. Tibor . . . she found the patrol group he usually rode with, nearly all asleep. He and another lying close, sleeping, but the woman's arm was over his chest. Did she really want to be crying on his shoulder, anyway?

Wanted something to kick, to scream at. Wanted to be home. Wanted to make a fool of herself. Back to the lancers' horselines, and of course Holla was already gone.

"Who—? Oh, it's Jolanan," the young man on watch there said. "Looking for the lieutenant? You just missed him. I don't know what the marshal's thinking, sending him south in the dark, and after the day the horses have had."

"I know," Jolanan said. "I wasn't supposed to go, but second thoughts . . ." Lazlan's, hers, she didn't need to say. "He'll have to stop to rest the horse, at least, in an hour or two. I'll catch up then. Can you give me a hand with Lark?"

She had nothing but her sabre and buckler, which no one set aside even at the campfire. The heavy brigandine and the bulky sheepskin vest over it. Not even a blanket, a water-gourd.

At least Lark was easy to find by the white splashes on him. The moon, just about full, was climbing in the east.

"You know where you're going?" the boy asked. She couldn't remember his name. "I guess if you head down the river, you'll pick up the road where it swings over around this hill. It's more a lot of cow-paths, not a wagon-road, from what the caravaneers say."

"Camelpaths," Jolanan said.

"Yeah. Well, take care you don't break anyone's leg, yours or the horse's. Don't fall in the river."

"No."

"Shouldn't be any Westrons over this side of the water, anyway."

"No."

Lark was reluctant to be saddled up again. She couldn't blame him. Thanked the youth and rode away, around the camp, aiming for the deepest darkness. Any watch should challenge—

Movement.

"Jolanan?" Woman's voice in the night.

They were so few, and Lark so recognizable a horse. Even by moonlight.

"Did you see which way the lieutenant went?" Jolanan asked. "We've missed one another in the dark."

"Right down the track along the river. Was he going to wait?"

She made her voice rueful. "He's expecting me to overtake. Thanks."

Urged Lark on before she had to explain anything. Was anyone going to miss her, come after her? If they thought she'd gone off to her friends among the skirmishers, maybe not, till it was too late.

Deserter.

She didn't have a son to worry about. Or a partner. He wasn't hers. He and she were just—something that had happened. Obviously. Nothing more. He could have mentioned he had a child. Could have said. Could have asked her, could have at least said, I don't want you, or, stay here where it's safer. Just to leave, without a word—

Might as well die following him as die following Reyka and Lazlan. The Westrons would come, either way. This month, next season, next year . . .

There was a hollow, ripped, hurting place in her chest, that was what it felt like. Like someone had died. Again. And she didn't want it there.

She wanted to know why it was there, for a man she'd just wanted— the way sometimes you just wanted to be drunk. She had thought.

Now she wanted . . .

She wanted she and Lark not to fall in the damned and goddess-less river, for starters.

The road a rutted, lumpy darkness between the paler grass of the rolling land, the water distant to her right a different darkness, moon-flecked, whispering.

No glimpse of Holla, no sound of a horse's hoof. No point, either, to dismounting to scour the rutted paths that crossed and recrossed, braiding themselves into confusion, for hoofprints. No scent of recent horse's passage, but Lark was less contrary that she would have expected, so perhaps he smelt what she could not.

Put her faith in that, and let him walk on, slouched and swaying. Don't sleep. Not quite.

She had to stop after a few hours. Tired, hungry-sick, afraid. Her journey east from the Jayala'arad all over again. Numb. Like a lost dog, heading mindless for where home should be. Except it wasn't, and he wasn't. If she thought he was . . . she only imagined it.

But she could shut her eyes and feel him by her. The way he smiled, and his eyes, as if she mattered, when he looked at her. Which she didn't. Not to anyone. Her goddess was dead. To Tibor, a little? Not to matter as if her absence would change the world.

Which obviously it wouldn't, not for Holla. He hadn't even come back to the fire to say farewell.

After midnight, the moon past its height. Lark had halted, sleeping on his feet, and she hadn't noticed, sleeping herself in the saddle. Way to ruin a good horse and break her own neck. Caravaneers might drowse in the saddle, it was said. She certainly didn't feel safe doing so. Let Lark drink, leading him down to the river, feeling her way. It was very still— water, air. An owl called somewhere, another answered from across the river. Faintest whisper of water against the stones. Then Lark's splashing, slurping. She shouldn't drink straight from the river but though she had flint and firesteel, she had no kettle. Cupped water in her hand, upstream of the horse. Tasted mud. No food. Lark was peevish. Not even a handful of grain to appease him. A rope in the gear she did have, at least. Tied him to a twisty little bush and let him sleep or graze as he chose. She curled up, cold in her brigandine and over-large vest inherited from Nessa, arm pillowing her head. Woke stiff and with her hip aching, damp through with dew and the sun rising, the river breathing out fog.

Warmer than it had been.

Smell of smoke.

Warmer because there was a blanket over her.

Fire. Battered iron kettle.

"Porridge," Holla said.

He hadn't crossed the river again, running to the Westrons. She hadn't thought it. Not more than once or twice in the night. Not really.

She couldn't tell if he was angry, or pleased, or just resigned. Nothing at all. They might have set off together. Except he didn't say anything more, while they shared the porridge, which was oats and lentils with a lump of salt butter thrown in at the last. She couldn't find words to speak herself. Blame or apology—she didn't want to offer either.

"I'm not a good person to be standing next to, Jo," he said, as if they had been having that conversation anyway. "I like you." He shrugged. "Care about you. So I didn't want you there. I've been having bad dreams and—something's looking for me. I'm not even sure what. Nothing good. I shouldn't have let you—"

"You didn't even come back to the fire to tell me." That burst out in anger, deciding her. No apology. "I know we weren't—I never expected— I wasn't looking for you to marry me or anything, but Jayala damn it, you just rode off!"

"I know."

"Of course you need to go to your son," she said. "I'd have understood that. Great Gods, of course you have to go to him. No matter how well-fostered he is, he's your child, with an army moving on where he's housed. But you could have—"

"My—is that what Lazlan said? That I was going to the castle for my son?"

"Aren't you?" She was a fool and it had been a lie for her comfort . . .

He shook his head, a hand over his face. Laughing. He was laughing. "I suppose I am, at that . . . Oh, Jo. Things I didn't want to have to tell you. I'm sorry."

"What?"

"Well, all the scowls I got from Tibor—he's quite right. I'm too old for you."

"I'm the one gets to decide that. You're not that old."

"Reyka and Lazlan are my kin. My brother . . . he and his wife were the first to take the pastures at Dyers' Hill, where the alkanet grows."

"What do you mean?" Was he some late-sired child of Reyka's grandfather? Old men did get up to such things, and a bastard born long after a man had adult grandchildren, heirs, yes, such a child might end up adrift, rejected, estranged, taking the caravan road.

"Wait till you meet my son." Something was amusing him. But then he sobered. Shook his head. "Go back to the warband, Jolanan. Really. You'll be safer."

"No."

"You don't know anything about me."

"I know—you."

"You don't."

"All that matters, I do." Kind. Gentle. Passionate.

Patient in teaching. Wise in war.

All secrets. Maybe lies.

She didn't care, just wanted . . . him. Touching her. To feel his warmth to her fingers, skin, muscle, the strength of him.

The way she felt she was real, when he looked at her. That he saw her, though she was half a ghost to everyone else. To herself.

"I'll come with you. What does one lance more or less matter? One less mouth to feed through the winter, that's all, and they'll have a hard enough time of it as it is." She added, which sounded childish the moment the words left her mouth, "You can't make me go back."

"No." He looked old, then. But when she took his hand, his fingers coiled around hers. Didn't look at her, though. "Better pack up and ride, then."

Not that she had anything to pack. She took the kettle down to the river to scrub it clean.

The day grew almost summer-hot as the sun rose, and they didn't push hard, sparing the horses, who had had too hard use and too little rest these several days. Their noon rest in the shade of a solitary spreading poplar, its leaves flashing silver in the sun as a light breeze stirred them, turned into half the afternoon gone, slow and sweet and . . . an apology, maybe, on both parts. Water and stale flatbread, with blackberries that were growing along the riverbank, unravished by birds. By evening they had not yet come to the castle, though it was near enough. The hills here were dry, stony, the thin grass between the barren bones grazed short, though there were no sheep or cattle to be seen. A jackal was yipping, somewhere farther east, a lonely sound.

"We could push on," Holla said, reining in. "But . . . if you don't mind porridge again. One last night?"

"Before what?"

"You might look at me differently tomorrow."

"No."

"Don't promise what you don't know you can keep, Jo."

"You're being annoying."

"I know." He drew a deep breath.

"Don't," she said. "Nothing changes. Don't say anything. I want you. I don't know why. I like the sound of your voice. I like the way you smile when you look at me. I like the way you make me feel."

That smile, then.

"I didn't mean—" Well, actually, she did. "Not just that. If you really don't want me, tell me, and I'll ride back. Say it and I'll leave you alone. If not—you're stuck with me till the Westrons kill us."

"We might just get fed up with one another," he suggested.

"At this rate it won't take long."

He grabbed her. Hugged her, hard, mashing her face into his neck and she didn't mind. "I am sorry I didn't come back to tell you I was going," he said into her hair. "I am a fool, and I hurt, you have no idea. People keep dying. I didn't want to be hurt, seeing you hurt by my leaving. I'm a coward, and how could we hurt each other so much when we hardly know one another, a few nights between us? And I am going to hurt you more, things I need to tell you, and I want you, too, I do."

"Don't tell me."

"Cold hells, Jo, you need to know—"

"No. Tomorrow. Whatever it is, tell me tomorrow, deal with it tomorrow, at the castle. One last night in the grass like you said, alright? Like it's the harvest festival or the midsummer races, and we've gotten clear away from our fathers and mothers and aunties for the first time ever among the tents and the corrals—"

"—and brothers," he said drily.

"And brothers, with a flask of ale—"

"—and a blanket."

"You've done this before."

"It's been a long time."

"Was she much like me?"

"Mm. Shorter. Plumper. Not so—" He held her off, far more sombre than his words. "I don't even remember her name. Shall we make a fire, eat?"

"Not hungry. Later."

She was ravenous, but it could wait.

"Fire," he said. "There's only the last rounds of bread. I wasn't expecting to take quite so long on the way. But a fire. There'll be frost tonight. Find good dry wood, though. We don't want smoke. The Westron army's not so far distant, over there."

"How do you know?" She stared west, west and south, shading her eyes against the low sun. Nothing to see but the rolling land. It might hide much. A haze in the sky. Smoke. The cookfires of a great camp, somewhere folded into the grass.

"What if they're patrolling on this shore?" A night in the grass wasn't quite so appealing with that to consider.

"They aren't, yet." He answered as though he could know. Stood with his head raised, like a horse listening, smelling, testing the air. "We're safe enough, another night."

An eagle circled overhead. He watched it, squinting into the sky. "Long way from the mountains." Shrugged. "Seriously, Jo. All your wicked temptations aside—no, I'm not going to argue you should go back. But camp or push on? Up to you. Food and fire and a bed with a feather mattress, at the castle."

"Camp," she said, because she would believe him if he said there were no Westrons this side of the Kinsai'av yet. One last night in the grass. She wasn't suddenly afraid of what the morning would bring. She was not.

But as darkness spread over them, they only lay holding one another close, nothing more.

CHAPTER XX

Moth wanted night for this, and night was coming. The Kinsai'aa, Kinsai'av the folk of the road called it, was like a mirror holding fire where the setting sun was caught. On the eastern shore, scattered stands of poplar. On the west, where black shadows should have hidden the water, only stumps. In the east, the full moon was rising behind a bank of towering cloud. Lightning flared distant there, silent. Weather brewing over the far hills.

Moth leaned on the wind and circled, a great wheeling turn over the towers of the ferry castle of the First Cataract. The folk of the goddess Kinsai lived there, children of the goddess or their descendants, or waifs and strays come by chance and folded into them, whatever they were. Extended family. Village. Fishers and wizards, scroungers and scholars who carried folk over the river for whatever they could spare, a coin, a song, a bolt of cloth, a baby. The stories told of them had not grown any fewer or any less fanciful over the years. She did wonder what they saw, what they planned, that they had not yet fled.

She did not think them so fey as to choose to die following their goddess.

The waters were empty of any presence of Kinsai, lifeless, for all they teemed with fish and insect, snail and weed. Gone. A great life stilled. She had thought Kinsai might fight. She was one of the great rivers and these only her upper reaches; she ran around the rising of the Pillars of the Sky, through strange southern forests and lotus-filled wetlands where the swans wintered, spread to a great lake, an inland sea. A great goddess there in the lake, sister to Kinsai, one of the mighty, at least in her own land. A silence, waiting, watching . . . But Sien-Shava must choose, south or east, and Moth thought it was the peopled east and the small gods along the caravan road that would pull him, not the sparsely settled wildernesses below the Pillars of the Sky, where demons outnumbered the human-folk.

Another wheeling circle, eagle spread on the air, hardly a wingstroke needed. Travellers on the road, two riders making a camp . . .

Well. That was . . . interesting.

Almost she dropped down.

No. She had no right to put him at risk, to draw the devil's eye to what he might, so far, have missed. A twist of a feather, the slightest shifting of weight, a long glide and she spiralled lower, narrowing her turn above the camps on the western shore. Holding herself close, silent. Unnoticed by the burning presence below. So far.

Tents and huts both, orderly rows and squares. Main encampment more or less a vast town; others its satellites. Rutted wagon-tracks led to its gates from north and west and south, the arteries that fed it from the new manors that oversaw the conquered Westgrassland folk. Did they think of themselves as bondfolk now, or enslaved? Or did they find something that drew them in the promise of a swift flight free of suffering, to carry them to the Old Great Gods?

She circled, waiting. Watching.

Searching.

Fires burned throughout the camp, brightening as the last sun fled, and she flowed from eagle to owl in a stroke of her wings.

Still she circled. What she sought . . .

Sien-Shava's presence burned. He made no attempt to mute himself, to bank his fires. Any wizard would know him, any god. He did not care. He drowned out all else, as if she listened in a gale for the quiet song of some hidden bird.

No hope that she would find Mikki guarded only by soldiers. A hostage would be no use if she could, in any way, put herself between him and the devil.

The patience of the hunting cat. The silence. Hiding. Reaching.

Low, low, silent, feathers whispering against the air. A spider's web. Chains, human wizardry and devil's power, iron and blood and song and fire, threads of Jochiz himself, circling and binding the demon, sinking into him, every thread a thousand curving needle-fangs, as if Mikki were swallowed into the mouth of a horror-fish of the deep ocean.

He was caged, a wagon of iron bars and filth. Night, and he was in his daylight form, caught there, an agony that would last till dawn, body wrenched against its nature. A bear, a giant of the forest, pale as straw, claws of ivory torn and broken and bloodied. Iron collar about his neck, inscribed with the binding of his form and sunk into his flesh, chains running to the four corners of the cage. It was not they that truly held him, though.

Gaunt, bones jutting beneath dull and dirty fur, clumped and shedding, matted. As if in a winter's deep sleep, he hardly breathed. Embers of life burned low. There, a breath, slow and rasping. Stillness again.

To cut those threads, those chains physical and devil-woven—there was death set in them, death rooted in his heart. She felt it in her own, a searing fire, waiting, watching, ready to rise, to consume him from within, body, demon earth-soul.

She came down beside the wagon, landing lightly, barefoot, drawing Keeper as she touched.

Guards in leather kilts and scale shirts covered by red tabards at the four corners, token, symbol, or to keep the prisoner from doing some harm to himself if he woke, she supposed. No use to her.

Except as the horn blown at the hall's door. Declaration and summons.

She killed the first as he turned towards her, mouth opening, and went the circle of the wagon sun-wise. Took the second's head as he lowered his spear. The third was running for her. She stepped aside and caught his thrusting spear, jerked him to her and onto Keeper's blade, went over him to the fourth, who had fallen to his knees.

She split his skull, helm and all.

The air ripped.

She stood with a foot on a wheel's spoke, cleaning her sword on the tabard she tore from the dead man.

"Sien-Shava," she said and sheathed Keeper, dropped Lakkariss in its scabbard into the cradle of her left arm.

"Jochiz," he snarled in correction. And that was a spark of light in her heart. Whatever he did, whatever he planned, he was still the same mind. Despising the human soul that made him and the human name he had borne.

She knew the shape of him, still.

"If you will." She spoke Northron. People gathered, running up in pursuit of their abruptly translated All-Holy. Men and women in formal robes, red and white. The colour of the Lady of Marakand. Not, she supposed, a coincidence. Though perhaps a lack of imagination. A court of priests. Officers, knights in scale shirts enamelled red, bare-legged save for their greaves, sandalled, in the Westron fashion that had been a thing of statuary and tomb-relief even when she was young in the world.

"He will die if you even draw that," Sien-Shava said.

She shrugged. "And you will still die, regardless."

"You were never my match, King's Sword."

"Oh, Islander, I've been many long years on the road, and not peaceful ones. What have you done? Made yourself a priest and the voice of a false god, hiding in a cave? And besides, when did we ever try ourselves? You only hope yourself my better with the blade."

"You were always afraid to fight me, even for the entertainment of the hall. Afraid to test yourself so far before your brother's eyes."

She shrugged. "You can tell yourself that. I didn't come to fight."

"Proud Vartu will ally herself with the All-Holy messenger of the Old Great Gods? Am I a fool?"

"Shall I answer that, Sien-Shava? Shall we trade words till we drive ourselves to blows and the sword's edge after all? I came to make a bargain."

"For what?"

"You know what I want."

"You are perverse. That's a beast. An animal, no matter that he speaks like man. No matter that he sometimes takes the form of one. You disgust me."

"You really mean that." Which was startling. "You've listened to your own priestly rantings too long, Jochiz."

"Humanity has perverted you."

"Humanity has perverted us all. Some more than others. Tu'usha learnt that."

Mikki flinched and moaned. Careful.

"A bargain," she said flatly.

"You have nothing to bargain with, no threat to make. You see I hold him in my hand. All I need do is close it, and he is gone. All you can do is stay out of my way, until—we shall see, in the end, what use your black sword is."

"That," she said, "is my bargain."

"What?"

"Give me my man. My bear, my lover, my *husband*, Jochiz. Free of your chains and your spells and all your bindings. Give me Mikki, and let us go over the river unhindered and out of your way, and I will give you Lakkariss."

"Lakkariss?"

"The sword."

"Northron name. It's nothing of the north."

She shrugged. Almost a smile. "It's bloody cold, though. You've got to admit it suits."

He gave a bark of laughter. "I admit I envy what you've crafted. What price did your soul pay to summon that from the darkness and the ice? How did you dare even set hand to it?"

"Those secrets I keep. It's something I could never shape again."

The priests, the officers, watched, and frowned incomprehension. Foreign words, and not an educated folk. Whispered behind hands, heads together. A woman armed like a soldier—almost the only woman so—was edging around through the crowd. A man likewise, going the other way. She raised her free hand, pointed. Swept it down. Dropped the woman to her knees. Then the man.

"All-Holy!" the man cried out.

"Be silent!" Sien-Shava roared in Tiypurian. "I speak with a devil. Do not presume to interfere. Such matters are beyond your understanding."

She might as easily have stopped their hearts. Maybe should have.

"It's something you should never have shaped at all," Sien-Shava said to her, conversational and in Northron again. "You've murdered Ogada. You've murdered Ghatai. You've murdered Tu'usha. Dotemon, Jasberek, where are they? I reach to them and I find nothing. Emptiness. Dead at your hand as well?"

"Perhaps. Or perhaps they hide from me as well. It might be they have allied against you. Or me. Or against us both. You are drawing great attention to yourself, Jochiz, and Jasberek never did like—"

"I fear Jasberek no more than I fear you. You, Vartu! You made this thing and set out with it to make yourself the only great power on this earth—and now you'll give it up for the sake of a demon beast you used to rut with? I find it hard to believe."

"I'm serious."

"You think I'll release him, while you hold that?"

"You think I'll surrender Lakkariss to your hand while you hold him bound? We were kin, once. Allies. One fellowship."

"You never trusted me."

"No," she agreed, because that was true. "I did not. But you never swore any oaths to follow me, either."

"You never asked it."

"Would you have so sworn?"

"No. Not to you, Vartu."

"So. You would not have sworn falsely? And so I never asked. I didn't seek an oath you couldn't keep. But this—this does not run against your nature. I ask nothing you cannot give. Not submission, not loyalty. Only that we deal faithfully with one another in this one thing, from which we both gain, and give up nothing of ourselves. In that, I would trust you, as I hope you would trust me."

"Let me see the sword."

"It's dangerous. It's hungry. It's long since it's fed."

"Let me see it, Vartu."

Moth, holding the scabbard in her left hand, drew the blade halfway. The moon had cleared the cloud. Silver edged the blade. Frost. Moonlight caught the silver tracery.

Sien-Shava almost held his breath. She felt how he tightened his hold on the demon's life. Felt how Lakkariss reached, hungered . . .

She rammed the blade home again.

"You don't think I could forge a substitute."

"No," he said. "I do not."

"Were I you, I would not draw it except in direst need. It is a hungry thing, as I said, and not overly particular whom it takes. To wield it is not to escape its attention."

"So you say."

"To tell the truth, it would be a burden gone, not to have it ever whispering at my back."

"I remember Vartu. I remember how you led us to this place, and why. What happened to your resolve?"

She only shook her head.

"Ulfhild," he said, and each syllable spat disdain. "Human. Mortal. Woman. No wizard, no warrior—only a whelper of children, after all. She has unmade you, Vartu."

Moth stood in silence, head bowed. "Maybe," she said at last.

He laughed.

"You have your bargain—Ulfhild. Give into my hand that blade you have made from the stuff of the cold hells for the murdering of our kin, and you may take your beast and go free, unharmed, over the river and out of my lands."

Deep breath. She held it out, slowly, reluctant, at the end, across her hands. Fingers still closed around the scabbard and the grip. Jochiz crossed to her. Not a tall man, half a head shorter than she. His curling near-black hair was worn long, dressed in ringlets, now, beneath a cap of gold brocade, and his beard was similarly dressed. Not the Westron look of the men about him, bare-headed, short-haired, clean-shaven. He assumed the air, the authority of an ancient Tiypurian prince or magistrate, a statue such as their lords had treasured in their impoverished halls in the days when the kings of the north first began to trade with them. His eyes were golden brown; the fires within roiled close to the surface. She let the physical world fade. Fire met fire. They were light and fluid light, and the sword between them, like lightning frozen in the world. He closed his hands over it, hand touching hand. She could feel his mortal warmth. A shiver up the spine that was purely animal.

"Let Mikki go," she said. "You have my word. I have yours. But Jochiz, as we once were kin, be very wary of drawing that sword. There is no mercy in it."

The chains binding Mikki were wrapped into Sien-Shava's own heart. Iron. Fire. Death.

One of them had first to trust. She would trust Jochiz no further than his own advantage led him, and Sien-Shava not at all.

A breath from disaster. He might kill now, wrest the sword from her, or try to. And they would die, and every living thing about, because she would unleash all that she had in her to destroy him—

Chains shattered. Threads of light, of fiery soul, unravelled. Contempt, maybe, he as prepared as she to unloose a wrath to destroy this land they stood on. But his grip on the scabbard tightened, bone clothed in fire, and Mikki's howl of agony wrenched her unthinking away, releasing the sword, heedless.

"Take him," Jochiz said. "And get out of here."

She was already gone, spun away to the wagon, and the red-armoured warrior-priest who flung himself in her way was already dead, falling, fool, when she had been called a devil before them all. Struck aside with the back of her hand. She had not drawn Kepra. She did, now, and it burned in the air with her fury as she struck the bars of the cage. Iron shattered as icicles from the eaves when a child hurls snowballs against them. Mikki was twisting, crying out, an animal sound high and senseless, claws tearing at the floorboards. His eyes were white, jaws snapping. The iron collar crackled, sparking like a cat's fur in winter, but the chains were broken.

"Leave her!" Jochiz roared. "I have disarmed her. She does my bidding now, and goes in fear of the messenger of the Old Great Gods. Leave her to do as she will with the demon. It was the price of her surrender. Pity even such a monster, to be a devil's slave."

Mikki!

She went through the gaps she had torn, dropping her sword. Down behind him on her knees, where his flailing could not strike, arms around the massive neck. Not so massive as it should be. All bone and loose skin. Fur came away in her hands. He stank.

Mikki! she called, but he was blind and deaf and his mind a roiling sea of pain.

"Mikki . . ." Whispered, leaning over him. Holding tight, holding fast, never to let go.

And he was still, and human in her arms, lying head and shoulders on her lap, encircled, arms and body, sheltered, gripped tight. Still a giant, seven feet, or near it. Naked, filthy, scabbed and brutally scarred—those were the bites of wolves or dogs, the lashes, too, of a whip, and he tried to coil himself up, but he was not struggling against her. She let go one hand's grip on his arm, seized the collar. The last remnant of the spells in it seared. Devilry and wizard's working fused into one foulness. There was ice in her grip. The iron shattered. She picked it off him, threw it away, shard by shard. And he caught her arm and clutched it to him.

He shivered, but he was fever-hot.

Night, she had wanted, because she had not known in what condition she might find him, and human, at least, she might support him away, if he were wounded. She had not expected this, even from Sien-Shava. Why, she did not know, but that his cruelty had always been a subtle thing, in the past. This was just . . . humanly vile, as only the mad, and the godless mad at that, might dare to be. Gaunt as a bear after its winter fast, worse, and no fur to hide it.

His ragged nails dug into her arm.

"We need to get out of here, cub," she said softly. "Think you can stand?"

No answer at all, but tightening of his grip again. Then a shifting of weight. He rolled over onto his knees, still curled up, head in her lap still, but turned the other way. Moth ran a hand over his back, spine a chain of knobs, ribs harsh. Old Great Gods stand witness, she would kill Jochiz and take pleasure in doing so.

Later.

"Up, cub. Before he changes his mind."

Sien-Shava had gone, he and his disciples, or whatever he might call them, and his soldiers too. Had he given orders, or did he hold some leash on their souls, to tug them after him? Not her worry, just now. Best to be gone before any returned. Maybe she merely hadn't heard when he spoke.

"Come now. Hold on to me."

Moth got to one knee, pulling Mikki up that far, leaning on her, head bowed on her shoulder. Held him there a moment and his hand came wandering, faltering, to touch her face.

"Up now, all right?"

She stood, and he—almost climbed her, groping his way. Swaying, leaning his weight, which was still not inconsiderable, the great bones of him, hands braced on her shoulders. Found her eyes at last. His were black, and they slid away almost at once, as from a stranger's gaze.

"Shh," she said, though he had made no sound at all, and did not speak in the mind's silence, either. Noise one might make to comfort a nightmare-woken child. "I'm here. Safe now. We're going to walk out of here."

Almost he fell, when she stooped to catch up Keeper and sheathed it. She wanted both hands free. Got an arm around his waist, and on his own he fumbled an arm over her shoulders. Not witless, though his silence began to frighten her.

"Come," she said. "Step, and again."

He was unsteady, walking upright. Weak. Shivering, still. No warmth in her feather cloak.

"Careful. The edges are sharp."

Ducking, twisting through the shattered bars of the cage. "And down, let me go first to steady you."

He fell more than jumped, and she was braced to catch him or they would both have gone over.

Straightest line through the camp, the main street north. Eyes watched from whatever safety they thought a tent would give. Mikki began to fall, weight sliding, dragging on her. She let him down. *Just wait a moment. I'll be right back.* No answer but he didn't clutch after her. She wished for Storm, faithful dead horse. He might have carried Mikki's weight without complaint, wasted as he was. She could, if she must, carry him outright. Awkward burden, bigger than she. Into the nearest tent, humans fleeing out under the back edge. She took a blanket, and if it was someone's only bed against the winter, well, she did not much care. No clothing that would fit him. The Westrons were not a tall folk. A hemp shirt, laundered thin. She went back to find him down on his knees and crawling.

"Mikki, here, wait for me." With her knife she ripped a slit in the blanket's centre, worked it over his head. Tore the shirt to a few strips, knotted them, and wrapped that for a belt, with her woollen cloak she wore beneath the one of feathers and silk over that. "Keep you warmer," she said. "All right?"

He had never had much concern for notions of modesty. Teased her with his not caring. A glorious nudity, cream-skinned, gold-curled. She did not think he should endure all those staring enemies naked, who had watched his degradation. He leaned on her. Said nothing. They walked.

His shivering was perhaps lessened. His balance a little better. Maybe?

Leaving the camp they were not challenged, but she snuffed the torches with a thought and flung the gates wide, bars breaking, so perhaps the watch found common sense, or perhaps some of those scurrying shadows flitting tent to tent had carried word from their supposed god. They had, after all, a bargain, she and he. She and Mikki passed through, unchallenged, and Moth drew the dark around them, wrapped them in night.

There was the river to cross. Of a certainty, he could not swim it. She would not have tried to swim it herself, if Kinsai were there, though the goddess would likely have given Mikki what aid she could, demons and gods being kin in the nature of the world.

Boat? When she flew over, she had seen them upturned, rank upon rank of them, along the shore. They must have collected every small rowboat and scow from every lesser water they crossed and given up wagon-space to dragging them along.

A watch there, of course, and the gang of a dozen men stood shaking, on the edge of turning to flee. Armed with spears and clubs, not against attack from over the water, but against escape from the camp. She made no effort to cloak her menace. Cold fire edged every gesture, a frost-ghost of light.

"Your All-Holy bids me be gone," she said, her Westron more that of Tiyosti than Tiypur, and that some centuries old. "Bring me a boat."

Mikki leaned on her. Flung up his head at some sound, a scent—only a fox yipping, far away.

Hush, cub, hush. We'll be gone from here soon. Safe and gone.

They brought her a boat, Westrons in terror. But the armed woman was there; she must have passed by during their slow staggering progress. She stood back where she thought she was unseen in darkness. A witness.

So now Ulfhild Vartu crept away shamed, defeated, broken by the All-Holy, the Old Great God's messenger, an Old Great God incarnate— ran without a fight. No threat left. Begging transport. A great victory; let it warm them through the winter. They did not understand the cold, the folk of Tiypur. Though she doubted that their god would care.

It was a flat-bottomed scow the Westrons brought, one that was already in the river, with a little more water washing about in it than she liked to see, but it was only a river to cross, and they were well above the cataract. She could hear its roar, though.

You want to row, Mikki?

No answer, no. He waded out, rolled in while she held the square prow. She pushed off, leaping in at the last, while he with shaking hands actually did try to get an oar between its pins.

"Leave it. I'll scull."

It was a slow crossing over the unhallowed river, the current trying to draw them downstream. Mikki ended up curled in the bilge-water, an arm over his head, undoing all the good of the blanket's warmth.

Mikki, it's all right. We're away. Sit up out of the wet, cub.

He was in there. He did hear. Didn't respond, though, save maybe to coil a little tighter. And Moth had the oar to work and all her attention held over them, shield and darkness thicker than night. Did Jochiz reach after her? No. Not so mad and child-curious that he would play with the weapon he had won, either. He would give it long, careful thought, test it with many spells, expecting some deceit, before he unsheathed it fully in this world. Study it, taste the shape of its song in the air.

Get Mikki safe away. Steal it back? Maybe.

Leave it to fate, a coin cast to the sky. Would he, would he not . . . and what might follow, either way.

There was only stillness from the camp, a waiting. Or he dismissed her, truly, as no longer a threat, no longer even of interest.

The scow grated on rocks, stilled and swung, grounded in the shallows.

Cast her mind out, a shout, a summons.

Blackdog! Get down here! I need you!

CHAPTER XXI

Flames rise above the broken roofs. Smoke, thick, black, rolls in heavy clouds, obscuring, revealing. The wind pushes it down the valley. The city is empty. The island in the river, the great temple of the goddess, the tombs that spread about it, beneath the dark cypresses, all still. No priests and priestesses, no folk seeking refuge. No boats on the river.

Bodies, yes. Abandoned where they have fallen. No ghosts to linger in fear. All safe, all drawn to their long home, taken into the embrace of the Old Great Gods.

Whether they will or no.

Who thinks to ask?

Night falls, but the smoke hides the sunset. A shimmering light lies over the low western hills nonetheless. Not the flaming glory of the sun's going down. Pale, elusive. It is not the eye that sees it; the eye he borrows sees only smoke, and darkness, and death. To call it light is a word of this servant who bears him here, this acolyte of light. Light grows. They come.

He rises to meet them.

Holla-Sayan fell out of a troubled, sweating dream, in which someone, a voice he knew, was calling, calling, but he could not understand—it was his name they called and yet he could not answer because he did not know it—

Fell. Crashed, more like.

Blackdog!

Moth, such desperation, urgency, and he did not stop to think, to wonder, to remember, not even the woman lying close against him, did not reach for his sabre or boots, just launched himself and went, answering like an arrow in flight, nothing to turn him aside. The dog, running.

What? he demanded, when he could think, when mind woke and caught up with body, or when man woke enough to master the dog, who had no cause to run when Vartu called, save that they were kin, and allies, and Sien-Shava camped across the river.

Mikki, she said, as if her attention were elsewhere, and he could hear beneath what she maybe would not have had him know, hear, smell—she was afraid. Not of any active threat. No fear of that in her, ever, that he could imagine. A deep human fear, and Old Great Gods forgive him, damned Old Great Gods, he had left Jolanan sleeping alone by a dying fire.

Long loping strides. Outrun a horse, the dog could. He could see the fires of the Westron camp now, and the tents, and a darkness on the water.

Unease pressed on Jolanan. In her dreaming, it was horns, alarm, the stir, the rise and arming . . . That was dream, but her back was cold. She turned over, half-waking. Then entirely so. Cold, yes. Silence. The moon was high, enough to see Holla wasn't sitting by the dim remains of the fire. She felt for her boots. Stirred up the fire, put a last few sticks on. Called softly, "Holla?" because if he had gone off for a moment, he should have been back. Boots. She stared at his boots, his sabre, lying by their sleeping-place. He would have woken her at any disturbance. He wouldn't have gone to investigate anything at all without his boots, unarmed.

Both horses were there. Awake. Restless.

"Holla?" More loudly.

Only the night.

No. He hadn't gone off again. Not without his boots. Not—that was madness.

Monster from the river, dragging him from beneath the blanket. Without disturbing her.

No.

She fastened her brigandine, shrugged on her sheepskin vest again. They had been using it as a pillow against the cold earth. Belted on her sabre, and using a burning branch as a torch, circled the camp. Frost, he had been right. Not down by the river, where the mist pooled, but on this higher ground above the road, every blade of grass was edged white. There was a track, dark in the moonlight, like a spattering of blood. The trail of—

—something.

It had gone from the camp in great bounds.

Grass brittle with the frost, black and bruised, crushed and broken, holding a print like snow.

She spread a hand by one. Dog, she would have thought. Bigger than her splayed fingers.

Lion? This far from the desert? Cheetah, wandered east, disturbed by the Westron army crossing the grass?

Dog. Wolf. Bear-wolf, Tibor said. Jolanan stayed so, crouched, hand spread by the paw-mark, till the icy chill made her fingers ache. The burning brand smouldered and went out.

She went back and made up the fire with the last wood. Packed up by that little light, methodical, forgetting nothing. Saddled the tractable black stallion first, tying on Holla's boots, his sabre, the blankets and kettle. Lark, fidgeting and trying to avoid her, last.

Put out the fire, covered the hot ashes. Mounted and headed down to the road again, leading the black horse. The tracks had aimed south. Nothing to see on the road, not by moonlight. The marks of paws, of nails digging in to hurl the beast forward, might be visible by daylight, maybe.

She turned the horses, faced the north, the high moon throwing a stubby shadow under them. The river quiet, muttering. Its goddess dead. A devil led the armies of the west and killed the gods.

The Blackdog of Lissavakail, demon of the mountains, was a dog that might be the size of a bear. It possessed men, and killed devils, and had died at Marakand. The songs all said so.

She turned Lark's head. He pranced, objecting. She was implacable. He gave in. Jolanan rode south.

Holla-Sayan smelt them before anything else, human, animal, disease, filth. Turned and plunged through densely growing willow scrub and dogwood.

"What took you so long?"

But Holla-Sayan was human and down on his knees. "Old Great Gods, Mikki . . ." Gaunt as if he had been starved, and filthy, wrapped in a torn blanket and Moth's old grey cloak. He was hunched as if cradling some injury; he had cringed and whimpered and tried to crawl away at Holla-Sayan's crashing appearance.

"Don't touch him, he's—Mikki love, Mikki, it's all right. Look, it's the Blackdog. Holla-Sayan. You remember."

"Sayan bless."

There was a battered old scow nose-in to the bank, twisting in the current, trying to pull away. It slipped, even as he looked, and slid out.

"Great Gods damn—"

"You want it?" Something he could do, of use.

"Let it go. It's sinking, anyway. I didn't want to risk it, going down to the castle. He can't swim, the state he's in. And I don't like having him out on the water. Too exposed. There's something watching, still."

Mikki was crouched now, not crawling. He tried to push himself away when Holla again reached a hand to him.

He sat back on his heels with an indrawn breath at the demon's flinching. "What in the cold hells—?"

"Sien-Shava's had him prisoner. Over a year," Moth said wearily. "He's been in chains, chained hostage to the devil's heart, and bound in his daylight form. And the Old Great Gods know what other abuse. For which I will call them to account." Vicious, that.

"Jochiz is dead, then?" Hope, irrational, waking. All over, it was all over—but such a battle, so near, he would have known, that great fire torn from the world—

"No."

"Moth—"

"No."

Holla put a hand on Moth's shoulder. Turned her. She let him, all bone and lean muscle and taller than he. Sat back on her heels, meeting his eyes in the night. Fire in her own, flicker of red, of silver.

"*Lakkariss,*" he said. Hissed, as if it were a curse. Maybe it was.

"Ya."

"Old Great Gods damn—"

"All of us. Yes. It bought Mikki free."

"Vartu!"

"I had to choose," she said. "I chose him. Will they help, at the Upper Castle? If you speak for me?"

"Yes," he said, because Kinsai's folk would not turn a demon of the earth away, even a demon who had given himself to love a devil, and besides . . . they knew the Blackdog for what it was, there in the castle. Kinsai had known. Maybe even before he and the dog between them understood it themselves.

"Good. I don't know how to—he won't speak. Or he can't. I don't know what best to do." Almost whispered. Unnervingly human despair.

"He needs food and fire, to start with. We're not all that far. Mikki, can you walk, if you put your arms over us? Friends of mine, close by. Trout and his family. I told you about Trout, do you remember? That winter after Gaguush died and the two of us went up to Baisirbska, looking for Moth?"

They hadn't found her. Hadn't spoken of her, just roaming, with that between them. Memory of cold, frost that cracked trees, froze your breath . . . the taste of flowers in the black nights. They'd drunk too much, too often. Northron *meadu* that the settlers of Swansby and such places offered, honouring Mikki, the demon carpenter of their grandparents' tales. And the crisp, spruce-flavoured beers that the hunter-folk of the forests brewed.

A night. Out in the forest, far from human roof-trees. Some word-wandering discussion filling the darkness. The nature of demons, and gods, and devils in the world. Mikki, who was shapeshifter by his birth, called Holla-Sayan unnatural, a thing that made and remade itself, and so carried clothing and weapons and what he bore with him through the change that was his own will and his own transformation of his self, whether he or the dog within him understood what they did or not. Proof he was a monster, a magic, and no thing of the world as Mikki was.

Envy, Holla-Sayan had said, grinning.

"Naked envy," he had added, and Mikki, who had not a rag to his name then but a long sheepskin coat they'd—acquired—somewhere, and Holla's horse—it was a dun Malagru hill-pony he'd had in those days—to carry it during the daylight, had swept him from his seat on a saddlebag and headfirst into the snow with an arm like a lashing paw. Held his head in the snow, too, till he'd come up with a leg hooking around and brought Mikki down.

The first time he'd seen the demon laugh since Marakand, lying there on his back in the snow. Laughing far harder than the joke was worth. A jar of mead at their winter fire and in their brief wrestling then they nearly spilt the one and buried the other. They had gotten very drunk, after that, as he recalled, and Mikki had talked not about Moth— he never talked about her, in that time, for all that their wanderings were a searching—but about sailing with his Northron cousins along the western edge of the world in some vague time after the seven devils were sealed in their graves.

He was not left with the impression that those human cousins had been honest cargo-carriers.

Holla-Sayan didn't remember the headache, but probably there had been one. Hard to wake Mikki the next morning, but then, in winter, he had discovered, it always was.

That was the winter of the endless snows.

No reaction at all.

"Come on, cub. Give Holla-Sayan your arm. Good. Now me . . ."

Sound, out on the river. Creak of rowlocks. They froze. But it was upriver. Not good, no, definitely someone crossing from the west.

They went quietly, stumbling like a party of drunks who'd lost their way between tavern and caravanserai. Mikki was a giant and a weight sagging between them. Kept his head down, though not looking where he put his feet. Holla-Sayan discovered he was bootless himself, wearing coarse wool stockings, and unlike Mikki he did not customarily go barefoot. Like a bad dream, not quite desperate enough for nightmare, but something that would not end. He was about to tell Moth that he would run ahead, rouse someone in the castle to come up with a horse or a boat, when a human cry shattered the night.

"*Holla!*"

"Jo!" he said, and Mikki tore himself free of them, flung away into the darkness. Moth went after him.

Holla-Sayan was already racing back up the road. She had woken and followed him, of course she had, and that boat had landed . . .

They came rushing out of the darkness between road and river, shapes in sudden motion, not bushes. Lark reared, striking out with a hoof and bringing down the first to close with her. No time to tug the knot to free Fury; sabre drawn and Jolanan was fighting for life, too many to count, swarming in the dark, short-swords and axes and the helmets of Westron warrior-priests. She shrieked his name, a warning, because he had been wrong, the Westrons were over the river and she had run blind into them. Fury was trampling at her side, an angry killing shield to her left, but one had him by the bridle, knife slashing, not to kill but to free his reins—made the mistake of trying to mount him and went down, screaming, under his hooves. Lark unencumbered but now she had them on both sides and another had scrambled into the black's saddle, yelling, swinging. She saw from the corner of her eye, ducked down alongside Lark's neck, striking, too, blade grating on armour, weight on her, heaving, leg twisting, pulled down and she kicked her foot free before her ankle gave, landed half on her own feet, staggering, recovered and sliced up a man's thigh, left him to die bleeding and swung desperate, two-handed, at a woman with an axe, Lark bolting away after the black, out of the mob—bodies on the ground but six still standing, reaching to seize as if they'd take her alive and Westron shouting, "Not the one!"

She was fighting two of them, men with short-swords, the woman with the long-hafted axe standing back, looking away, looking for someone, something else—Jolanan had nothing to set her back to—she was struck from behind, falling to her knees, right down flat with a boot in her back, trying to twist up, to stab with a blade not best meant for it. Something howled—howl broke jagged into snarling, a human voice shrieked, a horse whinnied—she kicked and rolled and got to a knee, still keeping her grip on her hilt. Swung from her knees at whatever was near, legs, hands, and a man screamed, the woman turning, the axe sweeping—the Westron turning yet, someone behind kicking and Jolanan fell even as the axe came slashing round and bit, and the night burst into red and pain and nothingness.

Jo! Ride! But she did not hear, mortal human, and the dog had no voice. Human cries, many voices shouting. The first men before him, shouting, a pair with axes, and human cries turned to animal shrieks as he leapt and ripped and threw them aside, felt in his jaw the crack of bones parting. Snarled and flung himself at the seething knot in the roadway, the horses bolting at the scent of him, but neither had a rider and she was a hare being ripped by a pack of hounds. Woman with a long axe, stooping to see what she had done, half-lifting something by—scarf, hair—he roared rage and as she let the limp body drop bit through wrist and haft and dropped hand after the thudding axe, blood spraying, even as Moth came down on them like lightning, vast shadow wings and silver veins of fire, crimson, dark as blood and burning in her eyes. Not eagle, not owl. Swirling in the midst of them, long blade of demon-forged Northron steel singing as it cut the air, cut bronze scale and flesh and bone beneath, devil's strength and devil's will and the hand of the king's sword of the Hravningas.

He was human, trying to gather Jolanan into his arms.

"Don't. Don't! Leave her lie till we see—"

Moth skewered the last man to the earth where he struggled, broken, trying to push himself up. Waited till he was still, stepped around, shaking gore from Kepra's blade. Holla-Sayan snarled, halfway to the dog again, as she dropped down to her knees beside him. Light flared within her, anger too close to the surface. Her hand closed on his arm, grip hard as a beast's claw and he saw naked bone a moment—

She was listening, head flung up like a horse, ears straining, or sniffing the wind.

Mikki. She had left Mikki unguarded to come to him.

Let her breath go.

"That's all of them," she said. "Dead or dying. And that one, the woman—one of Jochiz's lieutenants. She was watching when I crossed the river. But there's no touch of him, here. Didn't believe him when he called me a devil? Thought she'd win praise and finish me, maybe." Her hands were moving as she spoke, touching, assessing. "The girl's still breathing. Make me a light."

Holla-Sayan did, without thinking, something he rarely tried. Not quite a wizard's working, just a sourceless moonlight glow, which maybe she needed to see flesh and bone as they were, not swamped by the colours and flow of the soul within.

"You know her."

Her hands kept busy, using the silk lining of her feather-cloak to clean away the blood, to find a face, to find what horror the axe had left. He held Jolanan on his lap. So small, suddenly, and light.

"Jolanan of the Jayala'arad," he said, hoarsely. "She's—Sayan forgive me, I left her sleeping, when you called."

Moth glanced up then. "Ah."

Jolanan still breathed. A body might, even when the brain, the mind's seat, the self, was wounded. He'd seen it, he'd, they'd, known it. Women, priestesses, injured in battle past saving, but not yet dying, and the goddess's only mercy left to give them was the Blackdog's knife or the physician's cup.

No devil to hand, in those days. Moth was muttering to herself, Northron, the old form, words Holla-Sayan barely recalled if ever he'd known them, and other speech twisting through that set his teeth on edge, almost understood, but slithering aside.

"Her skull is mostly whole," Moth said. "I think the blow was weak. She was moving away, maybe."

"Mostly whole." Dry-mouthed. Words a whisper. But that was good. Not what he'd feared.

"Chipped," she said. "Like the rim of a pot. Here beside her eye." Her hands were slick and red with blood, bathed in it. "But there's no fracture any further. Not of the skull. The bridge of her nose is broken. A hard head, your young woman." She was tracing runes on Jolanan's face as she spoke, on her brow, her cheeks. Jo's blood, not her own. He didn't know their meanings. Trusted.

Bone white, the flesh gaping, swelling, but the blood had ceased to flow. Her eye was a dark pool, red and shadows, not the fire of a devil. A mangled mess.

Moth began to unwrap the scarf from about his neck. Jo might have had something cleaner in a saddlebag; he didn't know, didn't want to waste time searching. Better even this than the dust of the road, he supposed. He had washed it out in a brook a few days' ago, at least. Moth wrapped it loosely over Jolanan's face, knotting it, leaving mouth and the tip of her nose free. Not that she was breathing through her nose.

"Now we have two to carry down to the castle. I'll get the horses for you, then I go. I'm not leaving Mikki alone any longer." Moth stood and shook out her cloak. Blood stained it. She didn't go in search of the horses. Reached, touched, forced them to her will. A rough handling, and they came sweating, afraid, eyes rolling.

"I'll hand her up. Let me take her."

He gave Jolanan into her arms carefully, as if she might break. Soothed the horses. Black Fury's reins were slashed and dangling short, but he wasn't taking Jo up on Lark in this state. Cut a length from the rope Jo had carried in her gear to lengthen the reins, looped more through Lark's bridle, just tucked through a strap, so he could be turned free in a moment. A relief when he was on the horse with Jo cradled against his chest, right arm wrapped around her.

The horses shied, released, as Moth flew, owl-silent. He whistled and chirped and settled them, and got the black to give him a nice, smooth amble, Lark following, sulky, maybe, but not wanting to be left alone. Jolanan stirred and moaned.

"It's all right," he told her. "You're safe. You're hurt. I've covered your eyes, that's all. Just rest. You're going to be all right." Lies, maybe, some of it, but he was guessing that in the lake of pain which must be drowning her, it was the sound of his voice that would matter, not the words.

Clouds were creeping over the stars, out of the south, off the mountains, rags hazing the bright moon. The first spits of angry rain began, a wind tasting of autumn.

CHAPTER XXII

Mikki was not a rider, but she got him up on the big brown and white horse when Holla-Sayan overtook their halting march and was able to stride out at a decent pace, keeping at the horse's shoulder, prepared to steady Mikki if he started to fall. Holla didn't wait. There were wizards among the ferry-folk, and physicians more skilled than she. The woman should live, now. Strength and healing set on her. Moth owed her that.

The highest tower of the castle was alight, not candles behind windows or torches on what she had always assumed was a star-viewing platform—the folk of Kinsai being philosophers of nature, in their own strange way, not warriors—but a cold white wizard-light, throwing the crenellations into stark contrast, pale and black. That the castle was built like the defensive towers of Marakand seemed, it suddenly struck her, strange. Or something out of foreknowledge. When she turned down the lane to the bridge over the moat, the gates beyond were already opening. Just as well. The bridge raised would not have stopped her, nor the bronze-riveted gates. Two women came out, carrying more wizard's lights. Older and younger, mother and daughter, maybe, and with the streaky hair and mismatched eyes so common among Kinsai's folk. These women had light brown faces and the elder, with grey in the blonde and brown of the braid that fell from beneath her scarf to her waist, a blue fish tattooed on her cheek. The younger woman wore a red gem in the side of her nose, as a caravaneer might pierce her earlobes. Both were dressed in a random mixture of clothes, loose trousers, one a long Northron tunic and a silk headscarf, one a scrap of a shirt nearly transparent, with a Mara-kander caftan throw over, unbelted. Blue and red beads knotted into her uncovered hair.

Something of Holla-Sayan, a bit, in the nose, the jaw, of both.

"My father dreamed," the elder woman said. "A devil, a demon, the river rising . . . He bade me welcome you, Ulfhild of Hravnsfjell, and Mikki Sammison of the Hardenwald." She spoke good Northron and didn't say, in Kinsai's name, which would have been correct courtesy, but the goddess was dead and not so likely to have welcomed Vartu as was her . . . granddaughter, Moth guessed. Daughter of the current warden, who was the son of Holla-Sayan and the goddess. The woman was older than she looked.

"Thank you," she said. No blessing of the gods to offer in return. "Mikki is—"

"The Blackdog said." It was the younger woman spoke now. "I'm Iarka, this is my mother Deysanal. Come within. Will he let us help him down? Holla-Sayan said he didn't want to be touched."

Iarka was taking the horse's bridle, leading him through the gate-house. Into an inner bailey that looked more like a farmyard than any-thing—empty pens, a dung-pile, trampled feed, a few camels. Strange absence of any other animals. She didn't sense that there were any else-where, either, not the goats and asses, swine, cats and dogs, one would have expected even in a fortress at war. Poultry, somewhere, still roosted with heads tucked under wings.

Very few human souls. She had thought each of the castles, Upper and Lower, a village sufficient unto itself.

Moth coaxed Mikki down. He leaned on her, shivering. Eyes—not empty. Fixed on the ground, and unseeing, though, as if he were driven far back, deep inside himself. Lost.

He flinched from the older woman's offered hand, but then, hesi-tantly, took it. Good. That was good.

A boy had come out of a dark archway to take the horse. Not a servant, not in this place. Dark eyes, dark skin, black hair, thin gold earrings, and no tattoos. Wizard, cook, gooseherd, boatman? He might be anything on any day. Another of Kinsai's folk, one way or another. Certainly a wizard, as the two women were. The look he gave Moth was wary, bordering on fear, but he made a noise of pity when his eyes rested on Mikki. "Great Gods bless," he said, Black Desert tongue, and she didn't snarl at him. He means well, Mikki would have said.

"Come," Deysanal said.

The chamber they came to was warm, a fire burning high on the hearth, a bed already prepared on the floor, mattress, blankets, a basin of water, clean cloths. Two beds. A thin, dark man who moved like a bird, a bit hunched, one shoulder twisted higher than the other, but not much impaired in his movements by it, all darting hands and eyes—he knelt by the young Westgrasslander, humming to himself. An old man held an ordinary clay oil lamp close. Bloody rags cast aside. Holla-Sayan, all too clearly told to stay out of the way, crouched to the side. Jolanan, the girl's name. She lay limp, deep in spell-bound sleep, and the humming wove some pattern Moth would hear, if she were curious and concentrated, but she was not. Let the physician, or surgeon, work his wizardry however he wished. He glanced over to nod at her.

"Nicely done," he said, and sketched a rune in the air with a bloody finger. Not power in it, only an echo of what she had worked, to stop the bleeding and fix the broken, grating edges where they should be before the brain took some damage. Showing he saw and understood what she had done. She was so startled she almost laughed. Long time since anyone had condescended to treat her as a mere equal in wizardry.

Wizard-surgeon at his own art. She could only bow, awkward incline of the head, leaning under Mikki's weight, in acknowledgement.

"Let him down here on the floor, lady," Deysanal said. "Better we get him clean and see what harm he's taken before the sun comes. I don't like the look of those sores on his neck."

"No," Moth agreed. "I can tend to them."

The younger woman, Iarka, went without a word to take the lamp from the old man. She must have been forty, Moth thought, wizard-blood, goddess-blood, lengthening her days and her youth even in a third generation. A new life burned within her, glowing like the warmth of a lamp. New kindled, and yet so strong. The physician looked up, smiled, the two of them bound in that one look. Affection, friendship, pain . . .

There were strange undercurrents in this place, patterns in the river water, shade and sunlight falling deep, and secrets. None she need concern herself with.

"I dreamed of devils," the old man said. "Devils, and a sword made of stars, and the sky breaking. And here you are, Ulfhild Vartu. But where is the sword of the cold hells?"

He sounded as if he were still dreaming. A stocky, white-haired man, with Holla's hazel eyes. Old. Old for even a wizard. Dressed as if for the day in trousers and shirt and jerkin—none of them had the look of folk roused unexpected from their beds in the small hours. His long hair was braided like a caravaneer's. Warden of the castle.

"With Sien-Shava," she said. "I can't and won't fight him for you. Not here, not now. I have no weapon against him. Sword to sword he would likely best me. To fight him otherwise—you of all people should know the cost of that. There are dead lands between here and the Fifth Cataract, and those are ancient, from long before ever I walked in this world. And the Dead Hills over the Karas."

His gaze lingered on Mikki. He nodded. Almost smiled, eyes sharp now, the clear gaze of a much younger man. "I'll fetch some soup. We seem to be living on soup, these days. There's always a kettle in the kitchen. Blackdog—" and when Holla-Sayan didn't react, *"Father,* you can do nothing here. Come lend me your arm on the stairs."

"I am sorry," Moth said. "Sorry for the loss of your goddess. Sorry I can do nothing for you."

Stiff words, maybe, but the warden bowed his head, accepting them. "We—were prepared. We had said our farewells. And no, we do not ask you to fight for us here. We do what we must, ourselves, as do you. The tide, as you Northrons say, races to engulf us all. Strange thing, a sea. I always hoped one day to travel the river-road, take the Varr'aa and come to the shores of the sea. Well, we save what we can. Our time comes when fate above the Gods decrees, doesn't it? To young and old alike. And now we'll fetch that soup, lady. You look like you could use a decent meal yourself."

The warden went off, not leaning noticeably on his staff or on Holla-Sayan, silent, obedient, at his side.

No one to run their errands.

No children. No truly elderly, either, beyond the warden himself.

They stripped Mikki, she and Deysanal, and washed him while he knelt on the floor, shivering, in a growing puddle of water. Washed even his matted hair and beard, best they could, warm water and soap that smelt of lavender. The water in the deep basin grew quickly brown and was renewed, once, three times. A pair of men come from somewhere, not speaking, but fetching hot water, more rags and towels, for both the physician and Deysanal. Going to build up the fire again. Wizards, both.

They worked their way down from Mikki's face. He was a mess of scabs and old, festering wounds, especially about his neck and shoulders. Many scars, too, but some were open and seeping. The livid red ring of the collar was weeping. Moth began a song of healing for body and mind alike, one that wove itself in words, in poetry that had been old even in the Drowned Isles, and it did take, settling on his skin, seeping in to wrap his heart, a fine warmth, and his shivering tension lessened. He leaned his head against her. Deysanal left the more intimate washing to her, busied herself wringing out his hair with a towel.

He looked better when they were through. A little stronger, even. That was the song and the runes she had set earlier. One of the nameless men had brought bandaging and a loose gown, but she glanced at the growing grey in the narrow window above and shook her head. Such things would only be pain and encumbrance when his body changed beneath them.

Holla-Sayan and the warden had returned by then, and the soup was chicken and vegetables. Moth coaxed some into Mikki, and once he had a taste of it he would have drunk a kettleful, gulping like a dog, but she kept it to a single bowl, taken slowly. Then he was falling asleep, sagging against her, gone, finally, slack and trusting, so Deysanal rescued the bowl lest it spill the last broth and Moth laid him down and covered him in blankets.

He stirred, just to pull them up over his head.

If that was what he needed, well then.

And dawn broke in the east they could not see out this riverward window. A much greater bulk under the blankets. She sat down on the floor, sword laid aside, legs stretched out before her—perhaps they could lend her some socks and boots—and a hand on the hump of blankets that hid Mikki's head. Shut her own eyes. The warden, the physician, Iarka, the other men who had lingered to mop up the floor, had all gone away sometime at the last. Even Holla-Sayan; she had heard the physician ordering him away, saying that the girl would sleep, that he could do nothing, hovering over her, and the warden needed speech with him . . .

Deysanal brought a quilt and spread it over her lap, startling kindness, as if she needed looking after.

"There's soup, still, lady," she said, "in the kettle on the hearth. Eat when you've a mind, and let him eat again, too, when he wakes."

Ulfhild had been "lady." Sister of the king. Ulfhild Vartu was—not deserving of that. Nor of this care.

Well, it was for Mikki's sake they offered it, not hers.

"Thank you, lady," she said. There were no hierarchies among the ferry-folk, only elder and younger and the warden respected by all, but she gave the title anyway. It seemed fitting.

Deysanal gathered up the last rags—no, that was her old woollen cloak—and carried that away, closing the door softly behind her. Silence, then. Only the fire, and ducks on the river out the window. Grey daylight and rain, soft spattering on the broad ledge.

Mikki's paw came out from under the blankets. She stroked a finger over the back of it, wary of seeing him jerk from the touch, but claws flexed and the paw pulled away only to be laid again over her hand, heavy, rough. Coarse hair between the pads prickly. Warm.

She sighed. Squirmed around so she could lie down, cold hard floor beneath her hip and shoulder, but her head on a pillow by his, blanket-shrouded though it was. Shut her eyes.

Slept, maybe. Almost. Drifting into the edge of his dreams. Running, running, and the wolves, dead already though their hearts still beat, shaped to madness, to hunger, and the burning collar, the parasite chains, fangs of lampreys anchored in his heart . . .

Sleep, cub, she said, and made a different dream, a place of birches white against a sky so blue, and the first bright golden-green of spring, the birds singing silver-gold ecstasy, the tapestry of small flowers, nodding bells and open stars, rolling out over the moss, blue and white and pink, between the first uncoiling ferns. A wolf walking there, along the bank of the brook, lean and grey, and a golden bear, and the light on the water . . .

Jolanan, waking, to a room of dim light, and pain, but a dull, remote sort of pain, that felt almost as if it belonged to someone else. Someone beside her, her hand loosely held in theirs. Couldn't see anything clearly. Couldn't breathe except through her dry mouth. Smacked her lips and tried to swallow and at once there was a hand under her, helping her sit up, a bowl held to her, a voice.

Holla's. Reassuring her, she was safe, she was in the Upper Castle of Kinsai's folk. She was hurt but would get better, there was a wizard-surgeon here named Rose, who had tended her and promised she would recover. Broth, not tea, in the bowl. She drank. She slept again.

Dreamed there had been a bear in the room, dim and blurry, stretched on its side on a white mattress opposite her, with blankets over it like a sleeping man, only a paw, the tip of a nose, an ear, sticking out.

Waking, sleeping, eating, carefully. Her face hurt, a constant grumble of thunder-pain, with jagged searing flashes like lightning whenever she made any careless movement—yawn, smile, frown, or laid her head down on the pillow. A confusion of memory. Night. A ferocious roaring. Shapes like monsters swarming out of the dark to pull her down, to kill, and the monster, roaring, come out of the darkness to her aid.

The scabs, when Jolanan untied the bandage that covered the loose dressing, were gut-twisting to touch, thick crust that devoured her left eye, her nose. At least it wasn't sticking to the linen any more. A thing on her, a growth like fungus on a log, a hideousness. No pain until she pressed, fingertips flinching away. She breathed through her mouth. Couldn't do anything else. Her nose was still thick, filled as if with dry clay. Bled if she tried to force air in or out. She had nearly passed out the day before when she sneezed.

Let the wound have some air. It was quiet here, no wind, no flying grit. Warmth. A fireplace. Holla was off with the warden of the castle, they all were. Mysterious talk, mostly in languages she didn't understand well. Usually it was the desert tongue dialect of the caravaneers, but sometimes Holla spoke Northron with the tall pale-haired woman he called Moth, who kept a vigil on the other side of the room, by the bed where the shapeshifting demon lay.

Jolanan had thought the bear a dream, but he was there, in daylight at least, a vast golden-furred bulk with eyes black as charcoal, who lay and looked into nothing, and did not speak, though he could. His name was Mikki and he slept, most of the time, or shut his eyes and pretended he slept, made sleep a wall against—Jolanan couldn't guess what.

By night he was a man. A creature of a winter's tale.

Moth coaxed him up to pad heavily around the castle, but he followed her as if giving in were easier than resisting, and came back to lie down again looking at nothing. Stirred though, and looked around for her, if Moth made to leave his side. So she did not. She sat by him, lay on the bed by him, arm over him, pressed to him, man or bear.

It ought to have been . . . uncomfortable, that closeness witnessed, an embrace better kept for an enclosed bed and the decent blanket of the dark, but it only made Jolanan feel . . . lonely.

Moth was not merely a wizard. The devil Ulfhild Vartu. The young Black Desert-born wizard Rifat had told her so.

She did not seem particularly fearsome.

Neither did Holla. Yet he was the Blackdog. Not a demon, Rifat tried to explain, in awe, in admiration. Shapeshifter, dog, two-souled, immortal and yet not quite a devil.

And the songs were wrong. He had not killed devils. Only fought against them, in wars long before she was born.

Going to his son at the castle. A joke. Such a joke. The warden of the castle, who was a true son of the goddess Kinsai, not merely her child by virtue of being of the ferry-folk. A wizard, long-lived beyond human years, but mortal. An old man, very old, almost two hundred. Holla's son and Kinsai's. Holla-Sayan, his proper name, but he hadn't told them it, because Holla was common enough but Holla-Sayan was the brother of an ancestor of Reyka and Lazlan, and the name, and his history, known to them. A family secret. Lazlan had known, when he came back to the fire, and he had not told her.

Holla-Sayan was old, ancient, immortal in the world.

And she was only a cowherd, and her twenty-first birthday had passed sometime in the summer, when she was riding with Tibor, with Lazlan's skirmishers, hunting straying scouts of the Westron army.

She wanted, like Mikki, never to leave her bed. But that was— childish. Not on the demon's part, no, she didn't mean that, the moment she thought the word of herself. Childish because she was only wounded, the fate of battle. Whatever had come upon him was something else. His silence, his sleep, his shutting out of everything, even the devil who hardly ever left his side . . . maybe, in time, he would heal, the wounds no one could see growing scabs, that would fall away as the scabs of his body had in a short few days, and leave clean scars. She hoped so, for the devil's sake. The woman looked as if her heart were breaking.

Jolanan remembered how it had felt, sitting by her father's bed, waiting for him to die. Better if he had. He would have said so.

She brought tea for Moth, and a dish of it for Mikki, too. The castle seemed more like a camp than a household. In the kitchen, she might do as she pleased. They took it for granted when she started to tend the fire and the kettle of soup or stew that was always kept going for whoever needed it. Something she could do to help whatever it was they did. Whatever they worked at, in the rooms of closed doors, they did not often take regular meals together. Rifat or one of the others would wander by to tell her where something might be found or to bring her a fish or a freshly plucked and drawn fowl. She found the pantry store, a crock in which yeast still bubbled, made bread.

They stood on the edge of something, all this castle.

The army of the All-Holy waited over the river.

Jolanan woke in panic, something near, claws on stone . . . black shape, by the dim light of the fire that never went out. Not huge and frightening, no, just an ordinary dog. But not. Coiling into a knot on the slate-flagged floor to sleep, as a dog would. She had heard his toenails clicking. Dog. Moth even called him that, often, speaking to him, as if it were a nickname. Sleep-mazed, Jolanan reached over, rubbed his head as she would have, one of her own herd-dogs coming to lie by her bed. Froze, then, her hand there. Realizing what she did.

Eyes opened. There was light in them. Not reflection. A faint and shifting yellow-green.

She took her hand away. He had felt like an ordinary living thing. Warm. Soft-furred. If he had been a real dog, she would have stroked his ears next. He hadn't touched her, hadn't held her hand, kissed her, since she woke properly—but he crept in to sleep by her.

She turned over, face to the wall, lying on her right side, so that everything, fire and shapes and the gleam of his eyes, was shut out.

Click of toenails as he padded away again. The devil, keeping her vigil on the other side of the room under the window, spoke softly. Holla didn't answer.

The bread was rising. She had found a sack of split peas, added them, with more water and some dried herbs that smelt like food, not medicine, things from far Over-Malagru, she thought, to the big soup kettle. In another, water was kept just simmering for whoever might want tea; it was filled from the well, fresh and clean and free of the taste of river, somehow. She had been to see the horses, finally getting the rest they deserved under Rifat's care. The wizard boy had found her eggs, laid by the hens they had not yet eaten. She would beat them up, cook them with onions and some of those herbs, find Deysanal or Iarka to let them know, to let the others know, there was a good hot dish ready. She was not even certain how many people there were in the castle. Less than a dozen, perhaps.

She poured hot water onto the shaved curls of tea in a bowl for herself, dropped in a brown lump of sugar. Watched the tendrils of darkness flow out from the tea, the scent of smoke rising. She could smell again. She could breathe. The bones were in their right place, pushed and pulled by the surgeon Rose's cunning, maybe, or by his wizardry, flesh and skin stitched. Her feet on the threshold of the road, an axe across the face like that; her eye burst, pulped, slashed open like a half-cooked egg—her mind offered visions, each more gruesome than the last.

She could see her reflection in the tea, like Arpath, looking for knowledge of the future. A dark-mirrored truth.

"Divining?" Holla-Sayan asked, behind her. She hadn't heard him come in. Didn't look around, as if freezing there might make him leave.

A failing swing. Such a blow with a sharp edge and someone's full strength behind it could have taken the top of her head off. Old Great Gods, she was alive. She was alive.

Face floated in the tea. Hers, she supposed. Tattoos dark, scabs darker. She was all shadows, drifting there. Hollow. One eye peering out of darkness, as if it were all that were left of some shattered painting on a broken jug.

Hideous. Her head ached.

"You've got the knack of caravaneer's tea, now," he said, peering over her shoulder. Voice gentle, as if he thought she might bolt like a half-wild horse. "Thick enough to bear a mouse."

She shook her head.

"A small mouse," he protested. "Maybe a shrew?"

She didn't mind Moth, Rifat, Deysanal and Iarka, none of them. They didn't know her. They didn't matter.

Someone's face looked back at her. Not hers.

"Hey." He came around before her, hands over hers. "Don't," Holla-Sayan said.

She frowned. Mistake. Face hurt. "I want to see." See her own face. See, not half a world. Not see the great livid furrow that would still cross half her face when the scabs peeled away, the hollow, scar-filled socket.

Wanted not to be seen.

She had never thought she was vain.

It wasn't vanity, that sick turn in the stomach when you didn't recognize yourself.

Her hands were shaking. She let him take the tea away, set it on the table. Scalding, and she was going to spill it down her shirt. His hands on her shoulders. Hands cupping her face, careful of the scabs. Didn't force her to look up, just held there, cool fingers growing warmer.

"Jo, you're alive." Hands stroked down her arms, to enfold her own again. Her hands were still her own. "I keep losing people, Jo. I thought they'd killed you and you're here. Please. Your face will heal. It's healing already." His thumbs caressed the backs of her hands. "Won't you look at me?"

She shook her head.

She didn't look at him. She never did. She looked at the floor, the soup-kettle, the platter of bread, her hands, whenever he was near. Turned over in the night to face the wall.

She hadn't realized . . .

"You want me to stay away, leave you alone?" He'd not quite released her hands, but his grip was light, hardly touching.

Her one eye could cry. Watery. It wept in the slightest breeze, when she went out into the courtyards. It wept now. Made her nose run. Thin, bloody snot, draining tears. Something not quite healed yet.

"No." That was a choked whisper.

Fingers tightened on hers again. Carried her hands to his mouth, pressed them there. Great Gods damn, she needed to wipe her face.

"Jo," he said. "Oh, Jolanan. It's gruesome now. It'll be better."

He could say so. He must have come close to losing an eye himself, once, those ancient scars—but he was not human, and anyway, he had not.

"Better, how? It won't grow back. I can't see, all that side. There's just this—this lump, in the way."

"That's your nose."

"How can I fight?" As if she cared. She should. She didn't.

"With practice," he said. "Adapt. Make sure you've always got a friend to be your near-side shield. Is that really what you're afraid of?"

He had a handkerchief, clean rag, at any rate. He was wiping her face for her as if she were a snivelling child, and he had so much practice with that, didn't he, with snivelling little girls and cranky children who bawled over nothings, as children did—father, grandfather, great-grand-father . . . She was crying, stupid choking coughing sobs, and she couldn't seem to stop. So tired, so devils-damned tired and papa, child-simple, mind-addled papa dead, lost, but not the peace he deserved, only more pain and uncomprehending horror for his last moments a summer and a life ago and now, now she cried, and—and she didn't even know what she was crying for, only she was tired and her head hurt and—

So childish. So ungrateful of this gift of the Old Great Gods, of fate, of chance, of Rose's skill and wizardry. She could so easily be dead.

Made herself stop, somehow. Made herself be still, and this time he put the handkerchief into her hand, let her clean herself up, but his hands held her by the shoulders and when she looked up—she could look up, and for a moment he wasn't some old man, some legendary monster-hero, he was only a good-looking man a bit too old for her, maybe, but not even old enough to be her father, and it was a friend's face, a comrade's face, as it had always been, and unchanged, not flinching away. But there was a flinching in her, still. She tried to hide it. She was wrong to feel it, to be

. . . afraid. To have that thought, that he was a beast and a monster and an alien soul was alive in him, a thing neither human nor demon nor god of the earth . . .

She pressed herself to him, carefully, wounded side turned away, and he wrapped his arms around her. She tried to make herself relax there, as she wanted to.

"It's not your face," he said. "It's all of you, you know. It always was. And all of you is beautiful, body and soul. Still and always."

Alone with Trout on the roof of what they called the observatory tower, where deep-scored grooves in the parapet stones marked the rising and setting of particular stars, particular dates. All over his head, such matters. No scholar, not in himself, and what the Blackdog's hosts might have known, men like the Tiypurian Hareh, he didn't chase.

Already in the fading light the fires of the Westron camp made their own constellations, red and threatening. There had been no further foray over the river. Not yet. A small, unauthorized excursion, not something, it seemed, that Sien-Shava Jochiz meant to retaliate for. They had a bargain, the All-Holy and Moth, and it had been Jochiz's own folk who broke it. He would have extracted a price for that, she said, if she had not.

But she did not trust him to leave her be, if she lingered here.

"Time you were going, too, Blackdog," Trout said. Not wizardry. They had spoken of this already, though not to say, tomorrow, the next day.

"You should all leave."

"We can't. You know why. He may follow, if we leave. If we stay, we can obscure the trail."

Holla-Sayan shook his head in denial.

"Yes, father. Leave the understanding of wizardry to those of us who are wizards. I've seen . . . what comes. It's enough."

"What do you see?"

Trout smiled, an old man's smile in the twilight. "For you? A road east . . . a road through shadows, the darkest of all . . . a fierce and valiant young woman."

"For us all."

"The long road and the stars and the blade of the ice . . . I can see, Blackdog, but . . . as if in a smear of smoke, shadows deep in the current. They . . . give me hope, but to name them, pin them in words . . . I can't."

"Wizards.

"Indeed. Ride with the dawn, Blackdog. Take your fierce young woman, and my fierce Iarka, and make certain that Rifat rides with you. Persuade him Iarka needs him to attend her, when she goes among the folk of other goddesses. He has ideas of serving Kinsai with a noble death."

"I'll make sure he stays with Iarka."

"Good.

Only five camels in the stables. Four to ride, and one for baggage. And the fierce young woman was not his.

Moth came out onto the roof, silent as a ghost, and Mikki padding after her. Jolanan behind. She might have been walking with them. He'd never seen her speaking long with Moth, but she seemed comfortable in the Northron's presence. Seemed to care for Mikki. She had taken over much of the cooking, making vast dishes to tempt the appetite of an invalid giant. Grown easy with strangeness, with walking among legends. Easy with some. Himself—not so much. Not always. Which hurt. Let him hold her, sometimes. Flinched away, others. Wouldn't meet his gaze, too often.

Still found reflection to trap herself with, when she thought there was no one else to notice. He hurt for her, didn't know any way to help, but to wait. To be there, when she did want an arm about her, a warm body to lean on. A friend, if nothing else.

"The Blackdog and his *noekar* are leaving with the dawn, Ulfhild Vartu," Trout said. "My granddaughter Iarka and Rifat ride with him to Lissavakail in the mountains. And you?"

"No. I go to Marakand, and the Salt Desert made Mikki too ill, last time we tried to cross it. Ended up spending almost a year in the mountains while he got his strength back. Better to travel the edge of the Great Grass and cross the Undrin Rift, this time. He doesn't like the heat."

Mikki didn't react, but he watched them all, listening.

"Is *that* what took you so long?" Holla-Sayan asked, deliberately light.

"Ya. Also there was a god in the Salt who took a dislike to me."

"I wonder why?"

A shadow of a smile, and Mikki, Mikki, wonder, showed his teeth, not a snarl but a dog's grin. Her hand, resting on his head, tightened in his fur. But she glanced at the horizon, not the fires but the last sliver of sun, hot red copper.

She was already handing him a quilted winter caftan as he shook himself and stood up, human. Even Jo was so used to this she only glanced away a brief, polite moment, while he shrugged it on, tied the sash. Moth kept an arm around his waist.

"The farther we are from Sien-Shava when he crosses the river, the better for all of us, and Mikki's fit to travel, if we take it easy. We'll meet again."

"Marakand?"

"Ya. Lend me your horses, dog. I'd rather travel by night, for the first while, and those brutes they breed in the Western Grass these days can carry him."

No protest from Mikki, whom Holla might have expected to protest that he could walk on his own four feet. He spoke rarely, quietly, and mostly to Moth. He would smile. He would meet Holla's eyes, which in the first days he would not. But speech . . . mostly he just slid away into silence or away altogether, so that Holla-Sayan had begun to feel any attempt on his part an intrusion.

They needed space, and a fire, and a jar of mead. Silence and the stars, to see what followed.

"What happened to Styrma?" he asked instead.

"I lost him, long ago."

"One of the horses is Jo's."

They had already spoken of this—the need to leave the horses behind, at any rate.

"Yes," Jolanan said. "Of course. But you'll look after them?"

"Don't let the cub eat them," Holla-Sayan said, with a sidelong look at Mikki.

"I don't know, he gets hungry, sometimes."

Mikki—Mikki shook his head and rolled his eyes. A bark of laughter. Moth—at that she might have seen the dawn, after a sunless Baisirbska winter. Mikki said nothing more, but he smiled at Jolanan.

"We won't eat your horses, Westgrasslander. Warden of the Upper Castle . . ." And Moth drew her sword, bowed her head, touching it to the hilt, a salute Holla-Sayan had never seen before. Mikki gave a grave nod. She slid into Northron. ". . . We take our leave. Thank you. We needed shelter. We needed—" a hint of a smile, "reassurance. I did. I've spoken to Lady Deysanal and Master Rose much these past days. They've been of great comfort. We've already taken our leave of them, but—what blessing can I give you, short of what I won't, to fight Jochiz in this place and lay waste to the life within this land so beloved of you?"

"None," Trout said. "We serve the road. You are of the road, and you are my father's true friend. And never would we have turned a demon of the earth away. What blessings are left to us to speak, go with you, and safety on your road, and healing, and . . ." He shrugged. "What I see, perhaps you do. Go well Ulfhild Vartu, Mikki Sammison. Come safe to where you need to be."

She nodded, bowed, Mikki did. Spoke, deep voice rough with disuse, "Thank you, Trout."

Moth gave Holla-Sayan and Jolanan a more casual nod.

"We shall meet at Marakand, Blackdog," she said. "Come on, cub. The moon will rise before we leave the road for the hills."

Holla-Sayan watched them down the stairs, till they were below the level of the rooftop.

"I want to see Lark one last time," Jolanan said, and ran after them. Hand out to feel where the wall of the stairwell was, going down. She began to learn to judge distance again. Awkwardly. Not often successfully. Felt for cups, before she poured. Rifat had made a patch for her eye, working with soft leather. Protection for the scar against what she could not see coming, and blowing dust and grit as well.

"You should all leave," Holla-Sayan said again.

Trout came over to him, leaning on his stick, which he so rarely did. Hugged him close.

"I'm glad," he said, "to have known such a father."

CHAPTER XXIII

From the Chronicle of Nikeh Gen'Emras

Within days of the death of the goddess Kinsai, the warband of the Westgrasslander chieftain Reyka had crossed the river of the goddess Bakan, abandoning their own land. Far to the south, the Lower Castle of the ferry-folk by the Fifth Cataract had burned and stood an empty shell, its folk travelling east on the caravan road while a second caravan followed them, with all the books of the Upper Castle's library in its care. It passed the ruin of the Lower Castle while the All-Holy's army of the South was still building its camp on the western bank of the river there.

Above the hundred miles of white water, the army of the North began to cross, a flotilla of small boats, and then there, too, the work of quarrying the hills of the eastern bank and bridging the never-tamed Kinsai began, and many men and women, eager Westrons and captive Westgrasslanders, died in the quarrying and in the building, as if there lingered still some hostility towards them in Kinsai's waters and the valley that had once been hers.

Travellers on the caravan road had this news at Serakallash, and found themselves marooned, as it were, in that Red Desert town, their road to the north grown too perilous. Some sold at a loss; some turned back for Marakand. Others went on, thinking that the traditional neutrality of the caravan road would be their shield, or that they might find some route farther east of the river valley in the bare hills. In this they were mistaken, and few came through with their goods to At-Landi, or at all.

The All-Holy crossed the river with the seventh- and sixth-circle priests of

his mystery, his highest officers and his seers, and determined to make his winter
residence in the Upper Castle of the ferrymen, in which, his scouts and spies had
reported, a few of the elderly and ill of Kinsai's folk had remained, abandoned
by their kin.

A thin skin of snow lay over the hilltops and in the dawn the river smoked. Ice fringed the rocky shore. Cat-ice, the children called it, though it would need to be a venturesome and lightweight cat that would risk it. The river never froze over, not this far south. This was only a warning of winter. The Kinsai'av stormed down the falls of the First Cataract in braids, chains of white, all foam and fury. A mile above the castle, on this eastern shore, men broke stone, gnawing a quarry into the hills. Women loaded stone. Carts hauled stone. A great company of labourers had crossed in boats. Footings were rising above the water. The piers of a bridge began to take shape.

The river's shores were black with boats, east and west. They crossed and recrossed.

The Upper Castle was built within Kinsai's embrace, its foundations in the water, a moat crooked around its landward side like an arm encircling. Their bridge was gone, the gates closed. They were watched, of course. The watchers might see, sometimes, candlelight, behind narrow high windows. Let them. No wizard-lights burned.

Westron labourers and Westgrasslander conscripts hauled stone to the moat, and a causeway advanced. The warden watched, every day, from the roof of the north tower. Deysanal didn't like him climbing up there, but he wanted sun, wind, and sky while they were still his to claim. To lurk furtive at a window—no. No one shot at him. He had laid a small pattern over the tower roof, nothing of great power, though he suspected such a working was beyond the capabilities of the Westron priests without their false god lending them a thread of his powers. Few wizards among that folk; even their seers were weak. They did not notice him watching. He was shade and cloud-shadow, only that.

Footsteps on the stairs. Deysanal. She came to his side, leaned there.

Confident in his spell's obscurement for herself, for all that she would rather he were below.

"They're nearly over."

"Yes."

"Papa . . ." Long since she had called him that. She said nothing further. He put an arm around her.

Below, a man among those wrestling an unhitched cart into place slipped, but others were already heaving. Stone fell. The man screamed. Two women rushed with spade and pick to try to lever up the boulder crushing him, but there were shouts, orders—the cart was pushed away, another already backing into place. A man in a red tabard went down to him. He shrieked and was silent. Silenced. The work went on. Smaller rubble filled the gaps, making a surface.

Others kept watch on the river. The warden and Deysanal left the roof, took a meal in the kitchen. They were mostly living in the kitchen these days, and the great dining hall next to it. Eating together, sleeping there, the one fire kept burning. It was too grim, elsewhere: the library where generations had gathered the fragmented thought and dreams of the world, the study where he himself had worked, meticulously documenting the fish of the river in coloured inks and piecing together scraps of memory teased from songs and broken histories, the tales of the coming of the Westgrasslanders out of the east. What point, that work? Who could say? Gone with the caravan, racing to be ahead of the Army of the South's crossing at the Lower Castle. The shelves and pigeon-holes and cupboards were bare. All gone, or buried in the hills, sealed in lead and wax.

Someday . . .

"Warden? The devil's crossing."

They went, nearly all, to what windows faced upriver. He to the tower roof again. Yes, the devil himself, no feigned double. Priest-knights at the oars, and banners flying, mottoes to be read, for those who knew the Tiypurian characters. He had hoped Jochiz might wait for the completion of his bridge, which would surely not be till the spring.

Threefold blessings of the Old Great Gods.
The All-Holy, Beloved of the Heavens.
He is the Bridge where there is no Road.

Strange, how human he seemed. A man, nothing more. But Vartu had seemed so too, against all his expectation. A woman, ageing, tired, fighting her grief to keep a strong face to her beloved, to hold him to some road back into the light. Not at all what he had thought a devil might be, for all of the stories he had heard of her, servant to the Old Great Gods though she might be. Expected something more angry. More arrogant. More careless of all about.

There was a horse brought over for Jochiz. He rode, for his dignity. Robed in white, his hair and beard long and curled in ringlets. They had carved faces and little grave-gift figurines of such men, princes and magistrates, in odd corners about the castle. Folk brought them sometimes out of the west, knowing how the children of Kinsai were pleased by such oddities of the world.

Jochiz rode to the causeway, and an array of clean-shaven priests walked at his back. Many were of the sixth circle, wizards. They wore pleated red robes, white copes, caps of crimson and white, some even ornamented with golden thread. Trout judged most to be mere diviners, not true visionaries to whom dreams might come unsought. Weak in power, worse educated.

Jochiz left his horse and crossed the causeway afoot.

So.

It came.

One always thought one had tomorrow.

Jochiz had no rams, no engines of war at all. Armoured priest-knights likewise afoot waited, in orderly ranks, behind the vanguard of seer-priests. Their attention was fixed only on their All-Holy, the very spear's point of their assault. If the folk of the castle had had any defence to make, would the Westrons even have raised their shields, down there, the warden wondered? Or would they have stood, reverential, and died, as arrows fell?

It didn't matter. Perhaps none of this mattered, perhaps they should have fled with the caravan. Perhaps he should have stayed alone. It had been he who wanted this. Break all threads. Hide all trails. Make an end, that no faint spoor of what might come to be remain, to come to a devil's notice.

Too late to change course. The river flowed.

Jochiz raised his arms and began to sing. Trout felt the force of the spell. For a moment, he could almost see the shape of it. Taste of salt, and burning sun, white sand and palm-green hills. Gulls crying. Song, wizardry, of a distant land.

"Time to go down," he said, and Deysanal took his arm.

He could feel it when the ancient timbers of the gate, oak gone iron-hard, flared and crumbled. There was no resistance, no wizardry in them. Just good stout planks, swiftly consumed in the wizardry. Did it disconcert their enemy, that lack of resistance?

They would have a choice of ways within. Trout pictured them, advancing through the ashes, the high officers, the devils' commanders, those who followed and who led, the seers who aided him in his song-weaving death, consuming the souls of children to devour those of the gods. Those who glorified him, and basked in his glory. Ash, dust from the ruin of the gates, might rise to smudge their robes. Seers, minor wizards, spreading out through the castle to recite small bindings against the rejected, the elderly, those left behind. Perhaps to seek out whatever of value or historical interest may have been overlooked. The priest-knights following, to do the butchery, or to take prisoners for later execution. Edifying, no doubt, for the Westron devout. Jochiz himself—what would he be seeking?

Any lingering echo of Kinsai.

And thus—

This.

Trout and Deysanal waited in his study, the top chamber of the north tower. The physician, who had once had another name but had been Rose since he drifted up at the castle, a stray of the caravan road,

joined them there. No words needed. Rose and Deysanal interlaced their
fingers, briefly, but then Deysanal moved away to look a last time out
the window, stepping carefully over what was prepared. They could hear
sounds from elsewhere. Cries. Small battles. Priests dying, and knights.
And sometimes wizards of Kinsai. They were few, those who remained.
Enough, though. Perhaps too many. But it mattered that nothing linger,
no faint memory of the goddess, that might otherwise . . . draw attention.

They had all agreed. Best to be thorough.

The door, latched but not locked, smashed open, kicked. A dramatic
gesture, not needed.

Jochiz strode in, alone. Smiled.

The floor was a maze drawn in chalk, in charcoal and river-silt, laced
and knotted around vessels of water: beaten copper, cast bronze, plain
earthenware, fine coloured glass. Silver. Gold. Carven wood. A pattern, for
those who knew the reading of it. Unlikely the sea-island devil did. Small
stones, river stones, rounded and flattened, were scattered throughout the
room.

Not random.

Jochiz frowned, hesitated to step.

Too late.

The warden had been leaning on his staff. He straightened up. To his
left, the physician drew a deep breath, tucked his bony, nervous hands
into his sleeves. To his right, Deysanal smiled at Rose, at him. At Sien-
Shava Jochiz.

She held a cup, red-glazed, chipped on the rim. There was nothing in
it but water. River-water. Kinsai's water.

His daughter's eyes fixed on his again. Trout nodded. In the distance,
there was another cry, another death. Deysanal parted her hands, let fall
the cup. It smashed, spilling water into the pattern, and the warden swept
his staff in a low arc, like a man scything hay. He struck nothing, but
the fire Rose had kindled on the hearth roared out into the room as if a
Northron firedrake had plunged down the chimney. Every vessel in the
room cracked or shattered.

And the walls. And the roof. And the floor.

The castle fell.

The river came rushing, churning, roaring eager, to hurl itself through the ruins, sweeping all away.

Water, sky, stone. Trout had always known the manner of his death.

Sien-Shava Jochiz stood on the hill of the quarry, breathless. Angry. Not afraid. Had they thought he could drown?

His robes were wet to the waist. Clio, a handful of others of his close court, were on their knees, sodden and gabbling prayers.

Fools.

On the road south, Iarka wept.

CHAPTER XXIV

. . . late in the summer, and the All-Holy has conquered
the Western Grass

T he young man was watching him.

He had been watching, lounging against a wall, when Ahjvar rode in the gate. A group of youths stood there, idling away a warm evening, talking, laughing, a play-scuffle that ended in arms draped over one anothers' shoulders, sharing an apple . . . he wasn't one of them. Apart. Even shabbier. He had turned to follow Ahjvar with his gaze, a flash of copper-bright hair. Ahjvar had been looking back and had seen. Looking only because that red-haired young woman he had called his grand-daughter had been in his thoughts, here deep in the heart of what had once been Praitannec lands, where he had been hearing the language still spoken among the country folk.

The scrawny youth's look, for that instant, was intent, fixed. Dog, its whole being pointed at what it would hunt. Then it was gone and he was watching the others again; a wariness, as if their friendly scuffling might turn on him and be not so friendly. Ahjvar looked away.

The Heron had been recommended by the cook of a caravan he'd met heading east and had camped with two nights previously. Not a caravan-serai but a decent inn for a traveller with only a few beasts to put up, and fair enough in its charges. Said cook's wife's cousin's father-in-law . . . the usual sort of thing. But it was as good a recommendation as any.

Star River Crossing was changed. It had never been the most prosperous of the Five Cities, not a sea-harbour but a hundred miles inland on a river, the Noreia. It had grown larger, busier, an important node on the eastern caravan road No rival to Marakand in itself, though the weight of the Taren Confederacy was that, these days. There had been war a mere thirty years earlier. Taren tolls and taxes on the road, the caravan road that had always been free, belonging to no folk and to all. Settled, eventually, when the Five Cities began to quarrel between themselves and some of the outlying regions, the old tribal kingdoms that had lost their queens and kings a century or so before, grew restless, threw up pretenders . . . that hadn't lasted. The clan-fathers and -mothers who ruled the cities settled things between themselves in their traditional manner, which meant assassination, and in their new, which meant negotiation, and in the end the Confederacy had endured and come to some agreement with Marakand that seemed to please everybody but the caravan-masters, who paid tax on what they carried between east and west at Star River Crossing, as the shipmasters did at the four seaports. Not that distant Noble Cedar Harbour was more than a nominal part of the Confederacy. It had its own ways and kept to them.

Memory of Praitan might be fading and the folk of the many gods of the lands Over-Malagru all one now, tribes and cities all Taren whatever god or goddess they held to, but not so many more days' travel and it would be Ahjvar's own hills the road passed by. His horizons. The shape of the sky you never forgot, and the wind with the scent of the earth and the green of home . . .

He could wish for a devil's powers, to be ride the wind and be gone from all this land, whatever it called itself these days. Get to devils-damned Marakand and have done with.

He had a stronger yearning to take the road to the southwest, cut down to Two Hills, where once Ghu had stolen horses—abandoned not long after in a harried few days they'd been hunted through the hills by bodyguards of a dead clan-father, and then he'd taken Ahjvar's purse and spent the entirety of it on better beasts, having a taste well beyond their means—before ever a red-haired bardling came to drive them from their strange—it had not been peace. Their waiting. It had only ever been that.

Ride to Two Hills, and down the coast to Gold Harbour where the Leopard had been a name to fear, even by the clan-fathers who hired him, unchancy, uncanny, unkillable, they said, with more truth than they knew. And beyond, south again, to a fishing village where a stone cliff, wave-battered, overlooked the little cove, and the air on the high downs smelt of thyme and lavender.

Not his impulse, and no, he would not. Better to let it live in memory, anyway, than to taint it with seeing what no longer was. It would be changed. All changed. Their broch had been a ruin when they lived there, the path that joined them to the land narrow. Probably an island now, or washed away altogether, the ancient stone tower and the garden, the plum tree and the wall where they had sat to watch stars and storms and sunlight . . .

Changed and gone. Let it live in what Ghu had made of it. His peace.

He was lonely. He had been on the road six months. Six months out of Nabban, where air and stone and water held him, ran through him, breathed in him.

Here he was something else, caught between life and death, out of place, out of time, an uneasiness on the edges of the awareness of the gods and the goddesses of the land.

The bones of his father and his son alike were lost, forgotten, long gone back to the earth. The name of the goddess who had once been his was equally unknown on the road, in the villages. A bard might remember her: Catairanach. Remember the ill-fated kings Cairangorm and Catairlau and Hyllanim, the songs and the curse of the Duina Catairna. If he found one. If he asked. He would not.

No music in this inn, which was rougher than he'd been led to believe, but the stabling, at least, was adequate, the food blandly over-cooked. He was low on funds. They always were, he and Ghu. What coin he had came from the imperial treasury, which would provide for his camels in Marakand too, once he came to the ambassador's house there, but meanwhile the beasts had to eat and the barley and beans he had bought them in Porthduryan were running low. He would rather have slept rough and avoided the city altogether but for that, and the feeling that a wise man would try to gather some news of the road ahead.

This place between the old wall of the city he had known and hunted in, and the new, encircling its growth, provided that. Nothing of great concern. Risk of brigands, outlaws, in the wild places. "Out along the tribal lands, beyond the Praitanna River."

His lands, his folk . . .

Brigands were a useful way of replenishing a thin purse. They invited their fate. Shouldn't think that way. Desperate ordinary folk more often than not, lost, their place in the world slipped away from them. Still.

A lone traveller, someone who didn't belong to the road like a bard or a soothsayer, ought to join a caravan or one of the parties that clubbed together to hire city-licensed guards to see them safe to the pass, the old man who oversaw the stables told him.

Indeed, that was wise.

Advice repeated by the woman who took his coin for the high attic room. They were wary, the stabler and the mistress of the place. Polite, but not entirely welcoming.

Possibly he looked more a brigand than an honest guest.

Possibly he should seek out a bathhouse. Cold water washing had its limits. But why bother, before he came to Marakand? Still eight hundred miles of mud and dust before him.

They couldn't place him. He spoke what was now called Taren Nabbani, but found, after so many years, that accent and words kept straying into Imperial; the two hadn't been mutually comprehensible to most even in his day. Another, younger woman, bringing the mutton and carrots and bread that was the evening's dish, with a cup of beer, asked his god, an effort to pin him down to a place, and he said Moyugh, who was one of the four deities of Noble Cedar Harbour and had been when it was the Duina Moyughan before ever a ship of defeated rebels came west fleeing Empress Yeh-Lin's first reign. No reason to lie, but he'd said his name was Strath, which was a good Praitannec name, unlike Ahjvar; he vaguely thought he had used Strath before, maybe when he was in Sea Town. Just habit, the lie.

Except that the red-haired youth had slipped in not long after he had. And had got himself a cup of something and was leaning back against the long counter, watching again.

A man who'd seen twenty, maybe, but barely and no more. Too thin for his height, which wasn't great. Not armed, that Ahjvar could see, not even a knife for eating. Short wrapped gown a faded yellow-brown, too broad in the shoulders, too long in the sleeves, old tears mended, fraying at the hems. Narrow-legged trousers that were the style in these lands now. Mended carefully, but much, both knees patched, mismatched. Sandals. Washed and shaven, hair still damp, in fact, and curling on his shoulders. Necklace of glass beads, red and blue. Praitannec enough—they'd say tribal, here—to wear earrings, only the thinnest of wires, which few among the Tarens did any longer. Finery that mattered something more to him than the few days of comfort selling them might have bought?

Nervous. Carefully not being nervous, leaning there, so casual, cup in his hand, looking like he waited for a friend, but the hand of the elbow that propped him on the counter was almost a fist, and the thumb fretted against the fingernails, then fingertips over the heel of his hand, fidgeting, fidgeting . . .

No one else there who had that alert air, not even anyone who was better, more professional in their watching, who might have set the man to it as a distraction. No one too careful in not noticing him. Ordinary, all ordinary. Only awaiting some friend—he had looked friendless, there by the gate—more likely an assignation he was doubting would be met and Ahjvar was a curiosity; there could be nothing more ominous than that in his eyes, which were elsewhere, now. On his cup, on the two grey-haired women talking low, heads together, laughing. Anywhere but on Ahjvar's corner. Flicking back, and he took a deep swallow of his drink.

Watching. And scared.

Ahjvar didn't like the city, and he ought to take himself up to the private room he had paid for, and lie quiet, if he could not sleep. He was starting to get the frantic, thought-killing urge to keep moving, keep moving no matter what to have it over with, and the camels couldn't stand such use.

Practice for Marakand, that was what this night here was. For when there would be no escaping. Endure it. People and noise and the press of bodies all about. Eyes. Hands. Couldn't watch everything. Couldn't feel he didn't need to, still, after all these years.

The youth hadn't needed to risk being seen following. Just asking along the street after Ahjvar had gone by would have been enough. He wasn't exactly not noticeable, a lone traveller with two camels, ancient Northron sword, bright pale hair.

The youth crossed the room, weaving around the tables. Other travellers, mostly, judging by dress and the accents, not locals. The food wasn't such as would bring the neighbours in. Nor the beer. Ahjvar was eating with torn bread and a knife that looked like what anyone might carry for dining, but was far too sharp. Wiped it absently on the bread, waiting, sitting back, his shoulders against the wall. Corner table Ahjvar had successfully kept to himself so far. The youth slid onto an empty stool with the other wall to his back, not facing him, too near, knee brushing knee. Flinched away. Ahjvar did. So did the stranger, which was—odd. He didn't look . . . unused to the game he seemed to be playing.

Set down his cup of wine, not yet emptied, like an invited friend. Smiled at Ahjvar. He was flushed, a little drunk already. Strong unwatered wine on an empty stomach, Ahjvar guessed. Thin face, sharp bones. Hard living. Sweet smile, younger than his eyes. Neither necessarily lying. Actor on the stage, and a brittle veneer of courage his only mask.

"Go away," Ahjvar suggested, watching the hands more than the face. The hands were very nervous.

"You want company? I can buy you a drink." The young man waved a hand vaguely in the air, not looking around, but it brought over the older woman who tended the barrels behind the counter, a pitcher in either hand. She gave the redhead a raised-eyebrows look, familiar, disapproving—shrugged when he flourished a pair of copper coins at her, poured wine, raised the other pitcher with an enquiring look at Ahjvar.

"No," he said, and put a hand over his cup. The woman shrugged again and left them.

"I paid for that, you know. You might as well've drunk it." But the hand clutching his cup trembled.

"No."

The redhead didn't protest. Eyes widened as the woman came back with another plate of food. "Eat," she said. "Better use of your coin." Left them.

He hesitated. He certainly hadn't handed over enough for that heaped plate. Ahjvar ignored him, resumed his own meal. Didn't mean he stopped watching, though. A bit curious, be honest, to see what happened next. The man finally tore bread, sopped it in the gravy. Stopped pretending he didn't care after the first bite and ate as if it were the first food he'd seen that day, tearing at the meat with teeth and fingers, scooping up vegetables and gravy with the bread, even his fear forgotten. Ignored the wine.

First meal he'd seen, yes, and maybe in more than a day, yet he'd gone to the bathhouse and paid for a shave, unless he had a razor up his sleeve.

Gone, or been sent.

"Who paid you?" Ahjvar asked, when the plate was nearly as clean as Jui or Jiot would leave it and the man was licking his fingers, trying to wipe them on the hem of his robe and pretend he had better manners than to have torn into his food so . . .

"What?"

"I'm not interested in what you're selling. You're not wanting to be here, however much effort you've put into making yourself presentable. Anyway, buying me drinks? I thought it was meant to go the other way."

Dark, narrow eyes. Staring. He licked nervous lips, took up the wine. Drank. Took a breath, then; found courage to speak.

"Could show you around the city," he suggested. "Maybe . . . there's a nice tavern by the south gate. They bring their wine from Gold Harbour vineyards, better'n anything around here. How about we go there?" Smile. "I'd let you pay."

"I've seen the city." Not in a couple hundred years, give or take, but he didn't suppose it was any more worth seeing now than it ever had been.

Nobody here who wanted to kill him. Not any more. The Leopard was long forgotten, and any earlier hunting name he'd ever worn as well. He'd worked for a clan-mother of the Thuya once. Generations dead. Even if that hadn't been so, someone sending the man to, what, seduce him— kill him? Surely not. Lure him off somewhere, for whatever purpose— who? Why? They'd left the lad terrified, whatever they'd asked of him, or expected of him, or told him, and he wasn't new to his miserable game; the serving-woman had been surprised he was the one paying, not that he was cosying up to one of her guests.

"Not interested," Ahjvar said, and to see what would happen, put a hand over the redhead's, as one might, maybe, taking leave of a friend. It felt awkward. "Sorry," he said, equally awkward, because he wasn't. Was damned angry, not so much at the unfortunate young man as at the city, maybe for existing at all. But the lad tensed up at the touch, didn't try to make it any kind of second thought, attempt to hold him, to persuade, which he ought to have done if that was his game. Ahjvar let him go. Got up and left the table himself. Went out to the back, with a pause at the counter, where the woman rinsed cups in a basin. "Don't let him up to my room," he said, with a jerk of his head back towards the redhead. "I'll throw him down the stairs if you do."

Her lips thinned, but she nodded.

Good.

Didn't go up to his room, though. Nothing up there he needed. Had left everything in the loose box he'd seen his two camels into. Scorpion's distrust of strangers would keep all safe, probably better than the wiz- ardly knots he tied his bundles with. Just pulled his plaid headscarf up from his shoulders, wrapped it to hide hair and beard, drifted through the stableyard to the street, unnoticed, night and shadows. Not taking on Ghu's nature, here, walking unseen. Maybe he could draw on that, maybe not, so far from Nabban. Didn't want to be drawing other attention, though. Goddess of the river. Other things that might watch. Found a dark corner. When the young man came out the street-door, though, he didn't even look. Walked slowly away, head down. Reluctant in his destination?

Ahjvar followed.

They ended up near the southern gate of the city, where the man did get nervous, looking over his shoulder. Full night by then, and waxing moon just setting. The few people out and about had been like the redhead and Ahjvar, intent on their own affairs. The streets here were utterly deserted. Warehouses, mostly, and a few workshops standing within their own walled compounds. The young man knocked at a gate in a stone wall. It was opened at once, spilling lamplight. Someone had been watching for him.

The gate was painted white. Something on it. A design . . .

He'd seen that before, tattooed over a dead assassin's heart.

What had the devil Yeh-Lin said? *A calligraphy you would not know . . . the gate and the bridge . . . it means nothing to me.*

Voices. Ahjvar moved closer, keeping close to the wall.

"No," the redhead said. "You just tell Timon yourself. I'm done with his games. I'm going." Sudden venom. "Tell him to go try himself, if he wants the man that badly."

A yelp as someone seized his arm, jerked, and he vanished within. The gate slammed shut.

Ahjvar leapt, fingers just making the top of the wall. Swung himself up, on fingers and toes till he saw there were no spikes set. Lay flat then, studying the ground. An open yard, ordinary enough. What could have been workshop or warehouse with living quarters over it, long building, the first storey stone, its few narrow, horizontal windows set high against thieves; the upper wooden, with a gallery running all the way along, and a wing running away to meet the southern wall. Smell of horses. Stable. A man in a long gown was marching the redhead across the yard, his arm twisted behind his back. No one else about. Ahjvar flowed down the wall. Knife in either hand. He was close behind when the man opened the front door of the building, dragged the captive within.

Waited, listening. Silence. Long enough for them to move beyond the entryway. He tucked the left-hand knife into his belt, lifted the latch, pushed the door open just a crack, listening. Still silence. Darkness. He slipped in.

A bigger space than he had expected. He waited, until the faint light behind him, from the window above the entrance, became enough to make out what he faced. Looked like a dining hall, strange thing to have at your front door. Long tables with benches, what he guessed was a serving hatch in the far wall, a closed door to either side.

Left or right? Investigation proved the right opened into a kitchen, the left a dark passageway. He followed it. An open doorway, stairs leading up to silence. Living souls above. Living souls ahead. Shut his eyes, listening—call it listening. Wondered, Ghu, can you tell? Where is he?

Ignored the stairs. Not sure if he knew, or only imagined he knew. Trusted and went ahead.

Door, open, to the left. Light. Suddenly raised voices.

"That's all you had to do, get him here! Seven devils damn you, how hard can it be?"

"You were wrong. He wasn't interested. I can't make someone want me. Nori knows, if I could don't you think I'd be more choosy than to take up with—"

A thump and a yelp. Angry words. Beyond anger—deathly rage, but a language he didn't know. Several voices, others shouting what sounded like orders.

He needed his sword, not knives, in this space. Slid around the doorpost.

A large, square room. Closed door in the far wall. One window over it. Candles burning either side of it, two clusters of three set on the floor. Three also lit in the centre of the room. Unfamiliar white script ran from each grouping of candles to the others, crossed the threshold, the blocky whitewashed characters running between two guiding lines that were not painted on the floorboards but poured, thin ridges of yellow dust.

The young man huddled on the floor, arms wrapped around his head. Small red-robed man, kicking him. Men—all men, no women—were gathered around, voices a babble. Nine of them. Three armed with swords and one a spear besides, armoured, plain helmets, short scale shirts, leather kilts reinforced with riveted plaques, greaves . . . blurring, long red-lacquered scale hauberks, tall boots, faceless masks the colour of blood and flame—fire seared across his belly . . . there was water, dark and deep, her breath in his mouth, and the taste of his own blood—

No.

He was drenched in sweat, and yet the cold of icy water cut to his bones.

No.

Here. Now. He touched wrist against the necklace beneath his coat. This was . . . not even his nightmare. It pushed at him, that memory—from outside himself.

Oh, Jochiz, would you? He grinned, teeth bared at the shadows.

Three armed, three in plain red robes, three with sleeveless white over-robes setting them apart, and none of them had heard anything, none turned to see. One of the white grabbed the kicking man, pulled him away, threw him to his knees, then struck him backhanded across the face. Followed up by kicking the redhead himself as he tried to crawl away.

"Leave him!"

They saw Ahjvar then. A moment's silence, beyond startled. Knee-melting terror. One of the red robes dropped to the floor, hands over his face, gabbling what sounded like prayers, intense, rhythmic, circling back to the same words over and over.

"The devil you worship can't hear you," Ahjvar growled, but didn't care if they understood, and for all he knew it wasn't true. "He can't help you." Of that he was more certain. Jochiz wasn't here, not riding any of them with even a fragment of his soul. No possession. Just dreaming tools.

The three in white fled to a far corner. The cowering priest gave a strangled sort of scream and scrabbled away backwards. One of the armed mastered himself and rushed forward, drawing a short stabbing sword, shouting at the same time. Some command. The three in white crowded together, began singing, hands clasped together, facing one another, voices unsteady, which wasn't going to help their working any . . . Ahjvar stepped aside and hooked the warrior-priest's leg out from under him, stamped on his hand and kicked the sword away.

Pointless mercy, letting him live. Pointless asking what they wanted. The song gathered strength, wrapped him. Words to hold and bind, to pull him to his knees . . .

He didn't bother with any wizardry that might counter their working. Felt it crackling over his skin, uncomfortable, not even pain. As if they had taken a fine bird-net to catch a stag. Spear and sword moving to take him from either side, and the spearman lunged. Swayed aside and took the man's head, turning back. Killed the man on the floor who was coming up with a knife. Went after the third armed man, who leapt back—he followed—the sing-song unknown words battering, stifling all thought, an assault on its own, a din of noise, a hundred carts stampeding over a bridge. Foot had crossed the line of script. The surge of wizardry laid in the spell woke, answering—fire waking, the sulphur burning but not smouldering, not sulphur alone, a wildfire hunger, and it was him it reached to feed on, seizing him, burning within, sightless flames unseen. On the floor and he did not know he had fallen, but he rolled away and to his feet again, unsteady, sword in hand, and couldn't see, a drunken confusion of light and shadow melting, running, something clubbed him down but he didn't lose his sword this time, twisted and slashed at sand-alled and fleeing ankles, missed his distance. Shut it away, what pulled at him, flames, needle-teeth, peeling at what felt like his heart. Up on one knee, blinking, blur of white. There. Yelling. The redhead was struggling with one of the men. Later. Went in a surging rush upright, swinging, into the wizards. Laid one's throat open, swept back into the belly of another, man folding over. He staggered himself, struck from behind, the heat of a blade, but in anger he found his balance, whatever their song had fed into their lines of spell fading. Fires still burned, choking, lung-searing fumes of sulphur all too real now, but the burning that raked at him within gone, and it was only his tearing eyes distorted vision, nothing more. Ran the last wizard through hardly even looking, letting go his sword, spinning away as the man fell, the forage-knife in his hand, to catch the warrior-priest turning to flee, jerk his head back, slash his throat and throw him down. Ghu's knife to his left, pulling his sword free. Could feel the blood hot on his back; couldn't tell how deep the priest's blade had bitten. Didn't matter. He was still standing. It would heal. Coat would need mending, though. He tried to avoid growing too ragged and beggar-mad. Ghu didn't like it. His young man on his knees, hands bloody, panting, wide-eyed, one arm across his face against the smoke. Priest on the floor before him, blood pooling across the words of the snare on the floor.

He'd lost count. No. Two were missing. The unarmed priests. Fled.

A word, a shape, could extinguish the flames, spreading now to the floorboards, burning cheerful, clean orange and scarlet, and the smoke was waking nightmares on the edge of mind, whispers, feather-touch of dead hands grasping—

Stop it, stop it now, he had the power—

Had the power to walk out of here, too. The smoke was nothing, the fire barely had hold yet. He did not need to lose himself to the terror of the flames. They—Jochiz would have burned him again, and again. Leave it to grow.

Not a thought Ghu would approve? Ghu wasn't here. Shoved the blood-sticky forage-knife into his belt, seized the coughing redhead by the upper arm, heaved, dragged, kicked the outer door open. Cold air like a draught of clean water.

Dragged the young man away to the compound wall, dropped him there and crouched down beside him. Burning sulphur. That could be deadly. The man coughed and coughed, doubled over, eyes streaming. His own were. Throat, lungs felt hot, sanded. He'd survive.

The Taren's wheezing was lessening. For a moment Ahjvar thought, dying, but he coughed some more, scrubbed a sleeve across his face, propped himself up.

Shouting within the building now. That one window and the open doorway bright, and firelight flickering above, flames spreading up through the wall, along posts, rafters . . . Good luck saving any of it.

He cleaned his sword, the forage-knife, while the redhead coughed and wheezed some more, and cut the signs of alder, the male holly, and yew in the hard-packed earth with Ghu's knife. Fire, death, and what was fear and death and devils, or the fear of them. A curse, of sorts, and he should have given up curses, but there was some deep anger within that he could barely see the shape of it, only that it was there, red molten stone beneath the black crust, and he would have them all dead.

You dare set your servants against me with fire? You dare do that to Ghu? Or was it for the echo in another boy, friendless and undefended in the world?

Well, at least he wouldn't go back in to kill them all. Let them take their chances with the fire. Which was not now going to be easily extinguished.

"Come on." Tugged the Taren to his feet. There were shadowy figures out running about now. Bucket chain forming from the well. Little good might it do them. Cries in the street beyond the wall, the clanging of a watch-bell. He didn't think it too likely to spread. No wind, and the yard within the compound was broad and clear.

He opened the street-gate as if he had right. City watch had been pounding on it, unanswered. The porter was gone.

"The devil-worshippers in there meant to sacrifice the boy," he said. Great Gods, what was he trying to stir up? "They set their own damned fane on fire. Where's the nearest physician?" Blank, worried stares, maybe for their smoked and blood-stained looks, maybe the boy's coughing. His Taren slipping away into pure old Praitannec, so they probably only caught one word in three. He flung the gate wide, and they poured in, being human and curious as well as charged with the safety of the city, and he and the redhead got themselves sifted to the back of the growing crowd in the street, and out, and away.

Tightened his grip, when his captive would have slid free of him.

"No," he said. "You come with me."

Limp acquiescence.

"Name?"

"Ailan."

"Good. Come." Kept hold of that arm all the way back to the inn, though Ailan offered no resistance. Had learnt not to, probably. Learnt to wait, and flit when the chance offered.

"The fire won't take them all," Ahjvar told him. "Some are bound to survive, and they'll be looking for you."

Silence. Tension, in the body he dragged along, walking faster than the young man found easy. A sort of shrinking, as if Ailan would make himself smaller.

They climbed the wall into the innyard, Ahjvar boosting Ailan up, steadying him down. The stablehands were asleep and the watchdog's beginning growl was silenced when he murmured, "Hush now, you know me. I'm no enemy to your house." Nabbani words, but the words weren't what mattered. The dog sniffed and licked his hand, wagging her tail.

Wished sleep on the man and woman up in the loft, silence on the beasts, especially the camel he had come to call Scorpion. She was over-prone to grumble. Spider was more easy-going. Got them saddled out in the yard more by touch than the faint light of the lanthorn burning at the inn door, got his gear loaded. Back hurt, pulled, sharp and flaring.

"You're all blood," Ailan said faintly. "Your back." He still needed to smother an occasional cough in his sleeve.

"Won't kill me." Deal with it later. Didn't feel too bad.

Got Spider to her knees, shoved Ailan up among the baggage. "Just hold on," he told him. "I'll lead her."

"I can't—I've never—"

"So tonight you learn. Not leaving you behind for them." Spider heaved herself up, rocking, unfolding. He led both camels to the gate, unbarred it, closed it behind him. Pulled himself up Scorpion's great height and lightning flared over his lower back, so he lost his breath and his ears rang as if he might faint. Cold hells, no, he was not being taken in one of the Five Cities again, ever again.

Pushed the camels faster than they wanted to move in the night, finding an edge of light from somewhere, a greying . . . cat's eyes, god's eyes in the dark. Faint, distant scent of smoke, beyond the city's normal lingering tang. Faint, distant murmur of sound, not enough to alarm this neighbourhood, and yet there, when he listened for it.

City gates, and the bridge over the Noreia. Torches burning in iron cages, and the watch, wakeful. Hearing their approach already, coming out from the guard-house, two men and a woman, leather jerkins and broad spears, not expecting real trouble, but . . .

What in him plotted the swiftest way through, right side, left, saw them falling, was wrong, was what he would not be, and the crossbow was still in its waterproof wrapping, which had been a choice, back at the Heron.

Didn't mean he was going to stop and argue with them till daylight brought the hour of the gates' opening, though.

He'd been taking back the wizardry that had once been his, slowly, so slowly, over the years. Disentangling it from the fear, the history behind him.

He would rather have made a dance of this, weaving a patterned knot, sword in hand. Paced it out in his mind instead, felt it in breath, in heartbeat, in the blade's edge cutting the air . . .

Wind. Breath of the typhoon off the sea, sweeping down the broad street, gathering dust, rattling shutters and latched doors. Torches were snuffed out. Roaring. Rain, sheets of it, pounded, mowing like a scythe as it swept in wild gusts, wind-driven. Something shrieked, tiles lifted, falling, shattering, timbers cracking—gates twisted and that shriek was metal pulling clear. He whooped, rush of—damned, sheer delight, like

the dogs racing, barking, tumbling in the first snow of autumn. Wished
Ghu were here, now . . . Voices yelled, faintly, lost in rain and wind-roar,
figures scrambling for shelter ghost-mist faint, and the camels in panic
ran, were halfway over the bridge before he had Scorpion under some
control of the nose-rein again, but at least the sides were high and the
storm died behind them in a rising fog.

Laughing insanely and cold hells that made him hurt, but he couldn't
stop.

Hair wasn't even wet. A waking dream, most of it. Not all. They
might find a few tiles down in the morning. And the city would need to
replace its riverward gates.

Ailan was still aboard the camel, clinging for his life. Sensible. The
ground was a long way down.

Sobered, Ahjvar set the camels to a more sensible pace. They needed
to get off this road, which headed for Two Hills, find the hill paths that
might wander a way back up to rejoin the northerly route of the caravan
road while missing the obvious road itself. Put some miles between
themselves and the city.

Figure out what he was going to do with Ailan. That, too.

Ahjvar found his way by something that was instinct as much as
ancient memory, feeling, almost, by sheep-paths and country tracks, never
certain where he meant to go till it opened before him. If he thought,
tried to search memory, to reason, he lost his certainty. Stopped a couple
of hours before dawn, when he noticed Ailan was having trouble staying
put, nodding, sliding, jerking awake. They were down in a narrow valley
then, a rocky place, no human souls near, no distant village smoke fla-
vouring the wind. Ailan fell in his eagerness to be down, not waiting for
the camel to kneel, but he didn't try to bolt off into the darkness, which
Ahjvar half expected. Crouched out of the way with his arms wrapped
close about him, shivering. Night blind and terrified.

"We can't make a fire," Ahjvar said. "I don't know that anyone will
follow, but we don't need to help them along if they do. Probably depends
on whether or not the survivors of your priests blame the fire on us."

"Not my priests."

"Good to know." He didn't offload the camels. Told them to stay, as he might the dogs. As Ghu might, expecting obedience. They settled into sleep at once. He went to drink at the shallow stream that chimed between the stones. Ailan, warily, followed, stumbling. Ahjvar washed his face, wincing as he bent to the water. Shirt was stuck to his back now.

"Get some sleep," he ordered. "I'll keep watch. I wouldn't sleep anyway." Not with a stranger lying near and the possibility of hunters behind. "We'll be off before the sunrise."

Ailan didn't answer, but he did lie down, curled up, making himself small. Defensive. Or just cold. Ahjvar rooted in the baggage, which tore the scabs again. Set his teeth against the pain. Stripped off his coat and shirt while he could, though, and felt around, teeth clenched. A cut of several inches, deep, but not, he thought, into anything that should have been immediately fatal, had he been mortal natural man still. Hit ribs and didn't make it through. Bad enough. Ghu, were he here, would be muttering about sewing him up again. Wasn't going to draft Ailan for that. Likely heal by morning, anyway, if he could just leave it to do so. That wasn't any gods' blessing, the way he recovered. The curse a goddess had woven with her heart, hatred in it, stolen by Ghu and made his own.

Necromancy.

Of a sort.

He found a blanket and threw it over Ailan, who grunted thanks. It reeked of camels. Since Ahjvar was started, he refilled the water skins, then used the ruin of the shirt to wash his back. Ended up soaking his trousers, of course. Enough of cleanliness.

Restless. He sorted out his long coat of black-lacquered scale, the armoured boots and gloves and his helmet too, with its crest of ribbons, black and sky-blue. Ailan slept, and woke to cough, and slept again.

If they were going to be fool enough to come after him . . . let them have second thoughts. Nabban was not something the Taren Confederacy wanted to offend. It might save having to kill, if anyone official did catch up, if he looked what he claimed to be. *Rihswera* of Nabban. God's champion, god's sword in the world, with an ambassador's sanctity.

Also, crossbow quarrels bloody well hurt.

Ahjvar never did sleep, but he lay down shirtless on his front, head on folded arms. Waiting. Listening. Feeling the night around him. Autumn noises. Crickets. Two owls, call and answer. Foxes.

The air smelt—not like home. This landscape had not been home in a long, long time. Smelt like childhood. The right trees. The right grass. Even the crickets sounded—right. Different crickets in Nabban, different song. He'd never really noticed before.

It wasn't right, though. Nothing was. As if his shadow were rooted elsewhere . . . Felt as though he might fly, like a swallow to her nest, if only he turned back to face Nabban. Pulled home.

Touch on his skin. Back of the neck. Down his spine. A hand lying over the wound, till the ache and sharp flare of it eased. The slow rhythm of a calmer breath, warm, stirring his hair. Body lying pressed alongside his own.

Dreaming. Almost.

When the night began to thin to grey he stirred, no catch in the muscles of his back, no pain. Found his spare shirt and dressed before he shook the young man.

"Time to wake."

Wan and shivering, coughing in the morning chill, but he didn't sound so bad as he had in the night. Ahjvar should feed him as well as the camels. Not much to offer either. He turned up some hard biscuit. Ailan made no complaint.

"Getting to the market was the point of going into Star River Crossing," Ahjvar said, watching as Ailan gnawed at it, with water in the battered silver cup that had been fine, once, some gift to the god from the lords of Choa, but they lived in a cave and wandered on horseback or by canoe and fine didn't last undented long. Silver endured the road better than pottery or wood, and could be sold at need. "Your own fault there's nothing to eat. You any good with a sling?"

Wide-eyed look. Astonishment that he would even ask. "No."

"Me neither. I'll see what I can buy on the road, if we meet a caravan. Best we avoid the villages, not leave much trace of ourselves where bored people will talk."

"Oh." Ailan tried soaking the biscuit in the water.

We. Where was "we" in this?

"You're not actually very good at seduction," Ahjvar observed. "Maybe try something else to earn your bread?"

Ailan shrugged, contemplating the soupy mess the biscuit had left the water in. Drank it. "Do what I have to do," he said then, turning the cup in his hands. Wondering what he could sell it for, Ahjvar suspected. "Have, since—a while, now. Don't need to be good at it. Always someone'll buy you in the end. They're not out prowling by the gates in the twilight 'cause they want a friend." A shaky sigh. "Worse at thieving than whoring. Obviously." Spread his right hand, with the old character that could be read "thief" seared into the meaty root of the thumb. Offered the cup back, defiant of that brand.

"Rinse it. Goes in that goatskin bag."

"I'll hang if they take me before the magistrates again. Probably whether I've done whatever they say or not. The law-speakers, they're s'posed to speak for you but they don't care, not if you're poor. Nobody brings in a diviner to say whether you're lying or not. At least selling yourself's not against the law, if you put your name on the books and pay your quarter-tax." Ailan washed the cup, dried it on his gown, which might undo the good of washing. Crept up on Spider, peacefully chewing her cud, as if she were a fanged demon, and packed it away as ordered. "Had to borrow to pay that, last quarter-day. Moneylender pretty much owns me."

"You could have left the city."

"To do what? No trade. No kin. Never been outside the gates in my life till last night, that I remember. I s'pose I must have been once. I wasn't born there. I went to the sanctuary, once, kept a vigil. Asked. Nori said I wasn't hers, not from the city, not from up the river. All she could tell me. Told me I'd be better off leaving, wouldn't say why, or couldn't." He shivered, clenching his hand closed. "Don't know where my mother came from, why she ended up selling herself at the gates. Except she'd known something better once. Everyone says that, don't they? But I think it was true. She spoke—well. She could read. Don't know who my father was. Don't suppose their families'd claim me, either of them, even if I did know where they were. And leave to do what, anyway? Spin? Herd sheep?"

"Worse ways to earn your bread."

"Who'd think I was worth teaching?"

"You never know. Wouldn't end up dead in the mud of some back alley."

"Like my mother? Worn out and stupid with poppy-smoke, beaten to death arguing over a half-lily's worth of copper? No. I was careful. Thought I was. You can tell who's just wanting flattery and a bit away from what's at home, who's travelling and lonely and wants someone to listen to them almost as much as a willing body in their bed for the night. Who's . . . bad. I thought I could. Thought I'd learnt. Timon was so . . . I could have paid off the moneylender, paid my next quarter-tax, still had enough to live a few weeks without working, on what he said they'd pay, and only to get you into the mission-house, into that room. Wouldn't even have to get undressed, he said. Look—" He met Ahjvar's eye. "It wasn't—he said you were—he said you weren't human any more and weren't even alive. Not . . . not a live person at all. He said it would be a mercy, not murder."

"You'd have ended up dead. Like them. Tell me about your priest."

"Timon." Ailan swallowed. "They're strange, the red priests. They come to the city last year, opened that mission. I go round once in a while. They keep a kitchen; they feed you for free, anyone who comes in. Porridge, soup, not much, but that's something. Talk at you about their All-Holy, about the road to the Old Great Gods being destroyed by the devils, about how our souls will all be lost when we die, how their All-Holy's the only bridge to the heavens. Some people started going to their daily prayers, forswore Nori—" He meant Noreia, Ahjvar presumed, the goddess of the river, who interacted little with her folk the length of her valley, so often at war with one another through the years. "—and promised themselves to the red priests' All-Holy, got the tattoo. I never did. Don't like the way they act—the priests. Like they're masters and we're all servants, or children, maybe. Expect you to do what you're told. Priest Timon, he knew what I was. He started coming down to find me by the bridge. That's where I am, mostly. A couple of months ago, maybe, the first time. It's one of their sins. They've got so many. But he was—he came looking for me a lot. One of the lonely ones, you know? He never hit me. Only once in a while he'd get angry, bring a jar and drink, and then he'd cry because he was weak and deserved to be damned and cast out by his god. He was so—happy, about this. The Holy One showing him the way to redeem himself." Low-voiced, he added, as if he had to make it real to himself, "I killed him. He wasn't too bad, really."

"Wasn't too bad" seemed a bleak thing to mourn, if Ailan were mourning. Ahjvar couldn't tell. From what he saw, the priest had been trying to murder him to keep his own little secret, amid all their performance of the devil's wizardry.

"Wasn't too bad" echoed things Ghu had said. Ahjvar wasn't the only one who had had an occasional dark night, over the years.

"Your priest was trying to kill you. Remember that. There's no guilt in having defended yourself. No murder. Here. Up. We need to be moving." He kept a leading rein on Spider. Deal with teaching the man to actually ride once he decided what to do with him. If it came to that. Would need to find a proper saddle, not the pack-frame . . . Keeping him? He didn't want a youth at his heel. A city-bred failed thief, failed whore, failed tool of his enemies . . . Absolutely did not. Who in the cold hells ever would? "When did he start talking about me?"

"A week ago, maybe. Been watching for you. I wouldn't have picked you out to go after on my own, that's for sure."

"One of the bad ones?" Ahjvar suggested, looking back.

Ailan was concentrating on trying to balance without clutching at either the camel or her burdens. That got a glance up, even a flicker of humour. "Yeah. Sorry."

"What did he say?"

Ailan settled for one hand on a strap. "About you? His god had blessed him with dreams, a chance to serve, prove he was worthy. Atone for his sins, because the All-Holy knew how corrupt he was, breaking his vows. Blessed him, because he saw a way and I would be blessed, I could serve too. Easy, nothing to do I wasn't doing already. Just find this traveller who'd be coming into the city by way of the eastern gate, a big blond man who looked like a tribesman and talked like a Nabbani out of the empire—'cept you don't."

"Would you understand me if I did?"

"I don't know. Probably not. I don't speak much Imperial."

"Well, then." Any at all was—surprising, really, in an uneducated man.

"He said, a man who liked—sorry, not just men, but pretty young men—"

Ahjvar snorted.

"It's what he said! All I had to do was get you to the mission-house, tell you it was where I lodged, that back room—take you round and in that side door, say I was a servant there or whatever, tell you anything to get you over the threshold, and once you were inside, I could go, I wouldn't have to do anything more. I asked why, said I wasn't being party to robbery or murder, whatever he intended. I did, Nori my witness, I swear it. I thought—I thought probably they were Westron spies, trying to trap some enemy, a Marakander spy or something. I said they should hire an assassin. That's when he told me an assassin wouldn't be able to do anything, that you weren't a human man at all but a necromancer's creation it was their holy duty to destroy. The sixth-circle priests—there were three of them new-come from Marakand—had powers like wizards, they'd be able to do it. He said their All-Holy had blessed them with the knowledge." Laughed, too shrill. Agitated, his speech had echoes of someone who wouldn't have expected her son to need to find his liveli-hood up against the wall in some back alley. Or to die that way herself. "They were really wrong in that."

"It might have worked if I was what their master thought. Maybe. I don't know Westron wizardry. They didn't strike me as very skilled or talented in themselves, as wizards go."

"You're a wizard?"

"Yes."

"You don't look like one."

"No."

"What about—the rest of it?"

"Better you just think what you guessed first was right. They were Westron spies out to destroy an enemy. There's some truth there. I'm a priest of the god of Nabban. The nameless god, or whatever he calls himself now, away in the west beyond the deserts, is our enemy."

"You don't seem much like a priest, either."

"No." Ahjvar considered. Offered, as explanation, though why he thought Ailan needed one . . . "Used to be an assassin of Gold Harbour." And Noble Cedar Harbour, and Sea Town, and . . . A smile he knew full well was predatory. "The best." Conceded, "A long time ago now."

"Oh." Ailan rode in silence a while. "I can't go back, can I?"

"Wouldn't advise it. I doubt the fire killed them all. They'll question you, now he's dead, if people knew about your priest—"

"They don't. He had to sneak around. If they'd caught him—I don't know what he told the others about how he knew where to find me."

"Sounds like all he'd have had to say was he had a holy dream."

Ailan actually snickered at that.

"I wouldn't stake my life on that, though, if I were you. Do you want to go back?"

Scared. Scared both ways. Wanting both, too, Ahjvar saw. Maybe not his, that understanding. A trap that had held the man and maybe this was its noose loosening, and maybe that was only in order for the club to descend on his head . . .

"You can't go back, Ailan," he said. "People saw you talking to me at the Heron. And then I break down the city gates after someone kills a house of priests, even if they aren't Star River Crossing's priests. . . Even if the magistrate's runners don't want to talk to you, there'll be other red priests around, or the converts . . . If their god talks to some of them in dreams . . ."

"Yeah."

"Caravan?" Hand the young man over to someone heading safely east . . .

"Me? What would I do?"

"Learn."

"Like they'd take me. I'm useless. Not any decent gang-boss, and the others . . . what d'you think they'd want me for? Just more of the same and no getting away from them, day or night. No."

Ailan was probably right, at that. If a caravan gang took on a hand new to the work, it was likely someone's son or daughter, niece, nephew, cousin . . . Someone who could at least handle beasts. Someone fit to work. Ailan was all bones and nerves. The honest wouldn't take him; those who made themselves godless by how they used others—few enough, but folly to pretend they didn't exist—wouldn't have any good use for him.

"You could go down to Two Hills." How, if the youth had never been out of his city since he was a baby? Two hundred miles through the tributary lands, villages not over-fond of vulnerable city stragglers, where they feared the power and often tyranny of their city clan-father lords—well, that was how it had been in his day, who knew, now—but regardless, a long way afoot with no money. Send him off to beg his way alone? He would likely come to worse faster than he would whoring at the city gates. He wasn't fit enough for a decent day's journey afoot anyway.

Not Ailan's fault. He'd never had to undertake such a thing.

Ghu had fled worse. Faced worse. Far younger. Survived.

Chance kindness. Good folk along the way, as well as the users, the self-interested, the abusers.

Yes. And so.

No, no, no. Not Ahjvar's problem. Not his responsibility. The damned man had been working to get him killed.

He looked back again. Ailan was rubbing fingers over the heel of his hand, coppery head bowed. That brand was as much a bar to any honest apprenticeship or servant's position in Two Hills as in Star River Crossing.

Ailan looked up, caught him watching. "What's Marakand like?" he asked.

"No." Not a very convincing refusal.

"I don't mind working." That better accent was back. City. But clan. Some lost daughter . . . "I'm not lazy. It's just—who'll hire a whore's bastard? I'm *not* lazy. I could—I can cook. I mean, everybody can cook, can't they?"

"Ghu claims I can't."

"Who's Ghu?"

"My god. My . . . everything. I leave the cooking to him."

Ailan frowned, apparently considering someone who left the cooking to his god. Shrugged.

"So you need someone to cook, then. And I can, I can . . . feed the camels. What do they eat? Grass?"

"Your fingers, if you're not careful."

"I don't mind if you—if you did want company . . . I mean, I thought you were some kind of dead thing made to look like a man, that's why I was so scared, there in the Heron, why I didn't—"

"*No.*"

Ailan let out a relieved breath.

"Idiot," Ahjvar muttered.

"Want to go somewheres else," Ailan said, more to the camel than to him. "Be someone else."

Whoring till no one wanted him, and then begging, if he wasn't driven to theft again, and hanged.

"Are you a thief?"

"No." Resignation, not indignation. "I took a purse off a woman once, while she was sleeping. I thought—I don't know, I thought I could just—run. Not sure where I was going, even. Three years ago. I was stupid. Young. The runners had me before I was out the gates. Whipped and branded the same day. Don't suppose I'd do any better now. Not with this hair. It's the ones you don't notice till too late get away cutting a purse in the street, isn't it?"

"Wouldn't know. Never tried it." Never had to. He'd taken to murder for and of the clan-fathers and -mothers instead, when he'd lost his place in the world. "I'll take you to Marakand. Better than leaving you behind for anything that's after me to find. If they connect us with the fire, they'll send the magistrates' runners out, and the guard of the city clan-fathers, probably—"

Ailan cringed at that. Some things hadn't changed in the Five Cities, that was clear. The private soldiers of the ruling families were the ones to fear.

"—but I'd like to see the city-bred man or woman could catch me in these hills."

Or the clan soldier who could stand up to the Leopard. None had yet. With or without a wizard to back them.

And best to have some things clear between them.

"That 'no' was for always, not just tonight. However pretty you might be. I don't like . . . anyone. I'm Ghu's, his alone."

"That's a new kind of priest." A lightening, a gurgle of laughter in the voice. Life hadn't broken him yet.

Ahjvar shook his head. "Just don't—don't touch me, all right? Even in the ordinary way of things. I don't like it. And I have nightmares. Not often. But when I do, they're bad. I might not know where I am or when, or who you are and you might get hurt if you're within grabbing distance. All right?"

"All right."

Is he pretty, do you think? Echoes in his mind. His own thought, shaping how Ghu might tease. Or maybe not. More than memory, that voice. Almost. Scent. Warmth. Mass of a body so real it would be shock to reach, to touch and find he was not there.

One man, was the answer, regardless. It always had been.

CHAPTER XXV

W hen the god came out of the hills, the caravan-master Zhung Zichen was laughing, sharing a cup of tea with the border-guards in the beaten-earth forecourt of the tower, all formalities done, his gang and the homeward-bound merchant he escorted— a distant cousin by marriage—duly noted, goods itemized and those which should be taxed all debated and settled. It was the border-post's captain who first noticed the god, coming sidelong down the steep hillside above. He sprang down to the levelled ground about the fort and came towards them where they sat or squatted about the brazier. The captain rose to his feet and bowed, and in the spreading silence merchant and servants, caravaneers and soldiers, did likewise.

Zhung Zichen had never seen the god, but he did not need to have seen him before to know him. Perhaps, at will, Nabban might walk among his folk unknown and unremarked, but he did not choose to do so here. There was no doubting him. He bore the weight of great mountains and deep waters; he held the light of the sky.

Three travellers with the caravan were not of the merchant's household. They had joined at Sea Town in the Taren Confederacy. Philosophers, they said, wishing to see the east. A scholar of Marakand, the man Opran said, and two clerks of his household, and if the caravan-master did not quite believe that, still, he did not hold himself accountable for the untruths of others. That was between them and their own gods.

Not sociable sorts, Master Opran and his clerks. They had kept themselves to themselves all along the southern desert road, through the mountains to the freecity of Bitha, where Zichen had thought—hoped, perhaps—they might remain. There were scholars in Bitha. But no, they would continue. They wished to come to the City of the Empress.

A scholar, in Master Zichen's opinion, ought to take more interest in the world about him, and less in his prayers. But that was not his affair.

The scholars did not bow, though they got to their feet where they had been sitting, a little apart.

The god regarded them solemnly, with his dogs one to either side, shaggy, wolfish dogs, one tan and black, one white and grey. They were not dogs, of course, but dragons, spirits of the wind and the rivers. The god—did the foreign folk take him for a herdsman of the hills, barefoot and plain? Did they not understand the truth of his eyes, which were black, and drank you to the dregs of your soul?

He should have questioned the false scholars more closely as to what they wanted in Nabban. He should have spoken his concerns to the captain. Zichen thought that, now. He should have given that thin-faced, sad-eyed girl selling bunches of mountain herbs by the shrine of the Bithan lake-goddess a few coins, regardless of the fact he had not wanted any herbs.

"You have Iri's death in your heart," the god said to the supposed scholar. He spoke the dialect of the road, not the language of the empire, and it took Zichen a moment to understand that by Iri, he meant the empress. "Turn around and go back to the devil you worship, now, and tell him Nabban is not his and never will be. This *world* is not his, and never will be."

The soldiers and many of the caravaneers had drawn their weapons. Zichen's sabre was in his own hand.

The god did not need their defence; he was a warrior; he had led an army to reclaim the land from the devil-deluded usurper Buri-Nai, and yet Zichen knew he would willingly lay down his own life here, now, to defend him.

Master Orpan stood with his hands clasped together before his chest, like a little child prompted to make some pretty speech to an elder, but his face was shining with sweat and he trembled. He lifted his head and began to sing.

A grating sound, high and sharp. It had edges like knives, like saws, like broken glass, and the words were not anything Zhung Zhichen had ever heard, even in the teeming Suburb of Marakand, where the caravans of east and west met and mingled.

He wanted to step in front of the god, to make of himself a shield, because these words, this music they wove, was death. One did not need to be a wizard to hear it. But he could not move. It burrowed into him. It froze his limbs, as if his blood grew thick as tar, arms, legs, pulled heavy by it, sinking to earth, and even his chest laboured to rise, to draw in a breath. He fell to his knees. They were all falling, and the merchant's clerk who kept her accounts was choking, wheezing, losing the body's battle to breathe . . .

"No," the god said. "Stop."

The wizard-assassin did not stop. He seemed emboldened. Took a step forward, hands spreading, reaching, as if he would take the god by the shoulders, a friend's greeting but the song was an open mouth—

The god said nothing, but he moved to put himself within those grasping arms, hand spread, laid on the man's chest.

A silence. Clean, cold air, mountain's breath in the lungs, and the assassin-wizard dropped like a stone, like a dead thing, which he was, Zichen saw. Dead and crumpled on the ground, while the rest of them drew deep breaths and stood straight again, even the merchant's clerk, though he looked an unhealthy colour and steadied himself with a hand on the wall.

Orpan's fellows hardly hesitated. One flung himself forward, knife in his hand, shrieking something incomprehensible. The god stepped back, and Zichen and the captain forward, and the man fell cut from both sides. The other was running up the road towards Bitha, but an arrow took him between stride and stride and he ploughed into the dirt, clawing as if he would still pull himself away, and then was still.

The god stood looking down at Orpan's corpse. "There are wizards coming from the Empress's City," he said. "They're being sent to all the border posts and the ports. They'll aid you in keeping the borders and watching for such assassins. Don't make the mistake of thinking all Westron folk have given themselves to the cult of the red priests and their false holy one. But missionaries, those red priests who come openly—those we turn back now as before, and the wizards will be watching for any with a particular bond to their god."

He went down on one knee, took up the man's limp arm, pulled up the sleeve. Frowned, as if he did not find what he expected. Opened the front of the man's coat, and then his shirt. A hairy chest like an animal's pelt, most unappealing, Zichen thought. And the greying hair hid what the god sought, what he pointed to, drawing the captain's attention. A small tattoo.

"That," he said. "Captain Hani An, that's the sign of the nameless god. They call him something that means 'most holy' now, but he's the devil Jochiz. The folk who worship the nameless god usually tattoo themselves with this sign on the wrist, we hear from Marakand, but it used to be that Jochiz tattooed his chosen servants over the heart. It's more than a symbol, or it used to be. A binding. And yet not all who bear it are willing followers of the devil. So—hear me. We do not do murder at our borders. We do not kill, merely because someone is marked with this tattoo, even on the heart. A person may be tattooed or branded against their will, or may give their agreement for many reasons, and hold themselves still to their old gods and the Old Great Gods and to do good by their fellow humankind."

"Yes, holy one."

"But we do not let them into the land, either. The wizards who come to keep watch with you will be diviners and truth-sayers and those who can stand against attacks such as this man would have made, we hope. And those strangers who do act against the land and the folk of the land, those, you may treat as any other who raises weapons against you or who would force the border. We don't think there will be many such. The Westrons have few wizards of any strength and he will mostly want to keep those close."

"Should we bury them, or will the wizards need to speak with their ghosts?" the captain asked, practical.

The god shook his head. "Bury them. There are no ghosts. I think their god is an eater of souls."

He got to his feet again, and his smile was like a blessing, warm like the sun on your eyelids, Zichen thought, when you wake on a blessed summer morning to the light striking through the window and know that those you love are near.

And while he was thinking that, the god was gone from among them and they were looking at one another, a crowd of men and women all a little dazed, a little renewed—he felt it and was certain the others must, too—in heart and in strength and in . . . yes, mercy, and love. He would be better. Do better. Resolved it.

He murmured a prayer for the peace of the Old Great Gods to come to even folk such as these, would-be murderers, as he and his gang helped the soldiers to bury them by the roadside.

Up the hill, a dog barked.

He would make a gift of the whole of the payment the false scholars had made for their protection on the road to the orphanage in his home town, when they came finally to Jina Province again, he resolved, and a share of his own profits besides. For the god, and a remembrance of what he owed to those less fortunate than himself whom he met upon the road.

CHAPTER XXVI

Ailan was asleep under the shelter of a bank of hollies. A little thin grass softened the earth there. The hillside, a mile north of the road, was stones and sparse soil otherwise, not growing much but campion and dry mosses. The young man slept like a puppy, dropping deep the moment he laid his head down. Exhausted. Driving himself hard. Fits of rebellion, of course, of protesting he couldn't, he was tired, he hurt, he wasn't someone who could learn these things—

"I've brought up worse brats than you," Ahjvar would say. "And mostly they were princesses. You're doing fine. Stop complaining and try again."

Patience he didn't know he had. An ability to stand back and not grow frustrated. Something gathered into himself, long years watching Ghu, who was patience itself, with children and beasts and madmen. Or maybe he had always had it and had never noticed before, till he was here on his own, with this stray soul who was only a frustrated, lonely, frightened mortal youth, and in need of what he'd never had.

Some vague shadow of fathering?

So the man could handle the camels—had a knack for it, once he got past his own fear. Had the patience and even the calm to deal with the beasts, but not with himself. Nonetheless, he learned. Could make a fire with flint and firesteel, and pluck and gut a pheasant, cook porridge and bannock once Ahjvar bought millet and oatmeal off a caravan-master they crossed paths with, one swinging down to Two Hills and Gold Harbour. He'd been tempted to pay them to take Ailan off his hands, apprentice him, after a fashion, if a silver cup would buy that. The gang-boss seemed a decent woman. But . . . he didn't.

Had he ever wanted a son? Could have filled that need with the princes and princesses who passed through their lives, if he did. Didn't think a man of Ailan's age should be so desperate for a father, but what did he know of sons or fathers? It had all been such a long time ago. Certainly hadn't been what he'd found with Ghu, not what either of them had been looking for. His stray cat. Ghu's . . . hearth, Ghu would say.

Ghu's world was a strange one.

Ailan could maybe make shift to defend himself, unarmed or with a knife. Maybe. Didn't learn so swiftly as Ahj expected, didn't seem able to feel where his own body was, his own balance . . . but Ghu had been Ghu and the sons and daughters of the imperial house had some training in such things before ever they came to the god and his man, so maybe Ahjvar expected too much, too soon. At least Ailan could walk softly, aware of where he set his feet, and keep alert, and look, and smell, and listen. Began to read the land, a little, the tracks and the wind. Not entirely useless.

Not skills for the city, though.

He was not training up a poacher, though. Nor yet a young assassin. *Horse-thief?*

Ghu's thought, not his own. Was it?

Ghu laughed at him.

Or maybe that was a dream. He dreamed waking, sometimes. It didn't bother him the way it once might have, but then, the dreams were better ones, these days.

Ailan could read, to Ahjvar's surprise. That came up, talking, one day. He knew the variant of the Nabbani syllabics used in the Five Cities and Marakand. His mother had taught him. He might make some caravan-merchant a clerk, once he learnt some ciphering.

No pursuit, or none that ever caught up with them. Maybe the fire had after all dealt with any of the priests who knew anything of them. Maybe Jochiz had lost track of him again, or was letting Ahjvar run, deluded he was unseen.

Maybe the devil was as mad as Tu'usha had been and acted with as little consistency, and assassins, some Westron version of the Wind in the Reeds, might come unheralded out of the night, with poisoned blades and wizardry against what held the *Rihswera* of Nabban in life.

Ahjvar didn't sleep much. He wished he could, because in his deeper dreams, when he truly slept, he found Ghu on the headland over the Gulf of Taren again.

They had passed below the lands of the Duina Catairna, though that was not the name. Just a backwater of the confederacy now, no king or queen, no hall or tower. He thought of turning aside, riding up to Dinaz Catairna . . . no town up in those hills, a pedlar said. Never heard the name. The king's hall had moved elsewhere, once the goddess Cataira-nach was gone, of course. The seat of Marnoch and Deyandara had been established near where whatever god or goddess had in the end chosen to take on the protection of that folk. He had never heard, never asked. Never wanted to know.

Tonight the mountains loomed close, jagged teeth against the stars. A faint smudging of the sky to the north, some rising smoke or fume. The Malagru, marching down to meet the Pillars of the Sky, grew restless. He had led them off the road, but in the morning they would return to it, to climb the stone-paved highway up the pass. Be in the city by nightfall, probably.

There was a chill in him. A reluctance.

He had drowned in Marakand.

The Lady of Marakand, everything of her, was gone. Felt nonetheless as if he braced to plunge his hand into fire. War and earthquake, since he had last ridden this way. His doing. Well, his had been the pebble that started that avalanche.

And this time?

The fire he had made burned bright. In Marakand, he would go to the ambassador's house. Not expected, but welcomed, as he must be, the god's own consort. A place where he might command, if he wished to. He did not.

Yeh-Lin was there, in the city. He could feel her, now. So close, there was no hiding any longer. They had lived too near, too long, and she had sworn herself to him.

No. To Ghu.

Sometimes he was not altogether certain whose thoughts he was thinking. It should bother him, and it did not. He was the god's champion, his sword . . . his eyes and ears and voice, to go for Nabban where Nabban could not.

Twelve years ago, he had made a voyage.

The diviners begin to dream dark dreams, and the shamans of Denanbak, and the Tigress of the Little Sister. His god, in his fey and dreaming moods, when he sits watching unblinking through the night, sees a fire rising in the west and spreading over the world, sees shrines godless and souls lost, torn away from their road, devoured.

Sees the tides of the world shifting. Rivers wander. Forests walk. That is as it has always been. They remember that the Badlands of the desert road to northern Denanbak were once a lake, an inland sea. But the spring comes later and later to the northern provinces; the snows are deep, starving the herds in allied Denenbak, in Choa Province and Alwu and the hills of Shihpan. The rains in the south fail; the little rivers dry, and die, and the rice new-planted in the paddies grows yellow, parched. The imperial granaries that stockpile reserves against bad years are depleted and the folk of the villages flock to the cities, seeking work that is not there, and beg on the roads, and murder their neighbours to steal their little all. Storms come out of season, and a city in Pirakul is washed away by typhoon, its temple fallen, its goddess . . . silenced in the sea, her holy well drowned.

Is this what was, or what might be? Now, here, Ahjvar does not remember.

This is as it was when the great lake died, a woman says, a goddess, standing stretched, her arms reaching to embrace the sky, broad toes digging into the earth. *Brother turns on brother, sister on sister, the white bones of the beasts bleach on the cracked earth.* She is a tree, not a woman, holding up the sky. *A piece of the land dies, and its death births new winds. Currents change, and the sea bleeds fire. My folk are dead, all dead, and the generations lost to the gods of other folk, and the gods themselves, have forgotten my name. But in the coming time the desert will flow to the sea.*

This is a tale told by the devil Yeh-Lin: a goddess who is a lost river, a lost river who is a tree.

A thing does not have to cross the borders to bring death and destruction upon them. Better it is prevented before it ever does. And a god of the earth has responsibility to the whole of the earth, not merely his own folk. Ghu says that. It is not a thought shared by any other god or goddess Ahjvar has ever met.

What disrupted, what would disrupt, the balance of the world, neither they nor the diviners and seers of the Imperial Corps can determine, but—it seems ominous, and not merely a few bad seasons, when ships and caravans begin to bring stories of lands troubled by unseasonable cold, or drought, or sandstorms, rivers dried or lowlands flooded. True tales, not foreseeings. The caravaneers tell that the sleeping volcanoes of the Malagru grumble and leak smoke once more.

Then there comes a great wave, striking the coast east of the marshes where once the Golden City of the emperors had floated in its lagoon. Ghu has dreamed, or felt its rise; the few seers dwelling among folk of the stilt-villages, the fishers and fowlers and salt-harvesters there, see his vision, cry his warnings, and many are able to flee inland in time.

Not all.

They hear, after, that an island in the southern archipelago, where the pearl-chieftains rule, has been torn apart in eruptions of a green and sleeping mountain over the course of a week, and nearly all its folk, save some fishers out in the great canoes, have died in smoke and burning stone and poisoned air.

It is as if the world shivers in fever-dreams.

It does not seem to be any devil's working. And yet . . .

The *Rihswera* is the god's sword, held not over the land but against the things that might come to threaten the land. And to that end, the protection of the land, perhaps the world itself . . . there are other weapons they might also wield. Perhaps.

The young too-soon-empress is only a princess in these days, and Yuan, too-reckless hunter of wild buffalo in the marshlands of the south coast, is emperor still, when Ahjvar finds himself on a pilgrimage through the lands of the Nalzawan Commonwealth, which occupies the east of the southern continent beyond the sea.

"Try not to annoy any gods," Ghu says, before he boards the ship at Kozing Port. "Or princes. Or Yuan will come to me to say that if I must meddle beyond the borders, could I perhaps not send an armed thunderstorm to do it?"

Not Emperor Suliasra Yuan's term, but his mother Ruyi's—*Can you not keep your armed thunderstorm at home, Holy One?*—when the irate ex-ruler of a small hill-kingdom of Pirakul had begun to send increasingly undiplomatic letters to the empress and high priestess of Nabban demanding compensation for the slaying of that king's god and his subsequent conquest and exile by a neighbouring queen.

"Have the emperor lend you an ambassador, then, if you want," Ahjvar says. "I won't complain." He has no especial desire to travel to the lands south overseas, particularly as it means a sea-voyage of well over a month even with fair winds, and whatever he tries, he still suffers seasickness as badly as he ever did. If godhead has to spread tendrils through him, so that he dreams dreams not his own—not that he minds, Ghu's dreams being far the more restful—

Am I dreaming now?

What do you think?

I think I should be keeping watch.

I think you do watch.

—he might wish his good head for the sea were catching as well.

"I don't want an ambassador. This isn't a matter for courts and emperors. Try not to make it one, won't you?" A grin warm as a touch. "And Ahj, this time, whatever you do, don't start any wars."

He hadn't that other time. Nor killed a god. Not really. Only a halfling god, anyway, born into too much of his father's power, which most deities who took it into their heads to consort with human mates had better sense than to let happen. Not his fault that while he was in Pirakul the darkest rumours of the tiger-cult and its sacrifices turned out to be true, there in the far reaches of the hills, or that the deluded godling had chosen to set his devotees hunting the man who had been, in another life, the Leopard of Gold Harbour. That the king who had profited from fear of the cult so long suffered at last the wrath of his neighbours, his protector gone, was no responsibility of Ahjvar's.

That isn't what he dreams tonight. If he dreams. He can see Ailan, sleeping, a hummock of blankets. Hear the old, familiar song, the night-lark. A night-hawk, too, squawking, less melodious. See the stars, the streaks of high cloud trailing over them, like the smoke of distant fires.

But he is carried there, then, twelve years past, and it feels like dreaming, not memory.

The Nalzawan Commonwealth is governed by a council of elected tribal elders and the hereditary kings and queens of those tribes. The folk of its various lands, the lush coastal forests and the green hills that make the north to south spine of the country, the grassy plains and the desert edge beyond, regard both their monarchs and their gods as a shared heritage, unusually. Priests and priestesses of all their many gods and goddesses might travel to study and serve at the Temple of All Gods in the capital Barrahe at the mouth of the goddess Sato's river. Some never leave. It is a centre of learning and scholarship, like a library of the north. Ahjvar gets out of teeming Barrahe as swiftly and quietly as he can.

I would have liked to have seen more of it, Ghu says. *A beautiful city. Iri should send architects to study its domes. So light, compared to Marakand's.*

I don't like domes. However light.

You're not an architect.

A pilgrimage is a thing most Nalzawans try to make at least once in their lives, travelling one of the holy trails that begin and end at the Temple of All Gods in Barrahe. It is a worship of the young, almost a duty, a widening of the world, a way of keeping coast and lush hills and dry, desert-edged plains all united and in understanding—a chance to flirt and court, make friendships and partnerships of lives and trade both, and return home travelled and allegedly wiser.

A scholar from the north might do so, come to learn about the Nalzawan lands and gods.

To travel with the pilgrims seems a way to pass through the land quietly, not wandering unwitting into the forbidden, or disturbing presences who might see a straying power, however minor, as a menace and a threat, as had happened in Pirakul and not only in the affair of the tiger-cult. Go humbly with the shield and cloud of a company of souls about him, walk the sacred lines that have been walked for generations, and he will be part of an acceptable pattern, whatever his folk and his land.

The difference between a spy and a diplomat is more in how you approach a foreign court than in what you do when you get there, Ghu says.

"That sounds like Rat, not you."

Wisdom of the Tigress, says Ghu. *Yes, her words, not mine.* He laughs. The goddess of the Little Sister has her own way of looking at the world. As goddesses go, Ahjvar rather likes her.

From Barrahe he travels up the valley of the Sato by boat on the broad, slow river, where in the wild places hippopotamuses are as great a danger as the crocodiles, the latter giants compared to the small beasts of Nabban's southern rivers. Sato never appears to bless them, though several pilgrims who belong to the folk of the valley speak with her in dreams. All up the valley Ahjvar feels watched.

She feared us. Ghu regrets this.

Feared him. This is dream, memory flowing in waking dream, and Ghu is with him, which he was not.

Ghu has all this in his own memory. He must. He holds all that Ahjvar is. This memory, the dream that colours it. But they share it now. They walk this road of pilgrimage together.

It is a path. A pattern. A dance.

A summoning, cast to the wind.

The wind blows out of the east, west to Marakand.

He is glad when the company leaves the boat and its crew below a waterfall higher than any he has ever seen, a thunderous pillar of furious white.

Ghu stands, humanly entranced, the boy again. For a moment Ahjvar even sees him, solid as the stone beneath their feet, hair damply greyed with spray.

A broad road of steeps and stairs angles up the side of the gorge through dense forest, mist-cool, which clings with roots and tendrils into every crack in the stone. Locals who make their living off the pilgrim-companies have come to carry baggage for them, and to marvel at the foreigner who has travelled so far inland from the busy port to visit the holy places of their gods.

As they climb away from the water they move into heat and out of the trees. They follow the river past the falls to where the hills open out and the high plains stretch before them. Another shrine, another halt. Forzra, the god of the last of the hills, does not bring himself fully into the world to bless the pilgrims, but later that night, the god wanders down to the yard of the pilgrims' guest-hall in the town. No one else feels the god's presence out in the high-fenced yard, not even the chief of their guides, who is a holy sister of the Temple of All Gods in Barrahe. Ahjvar leaves the habitual evening drinking of an oily-tasting tea, said to encourage dreams of the gods, to go out to him.

"What are you?" Forzra asks. Gods do not always take human form, though it is most common. He looks a man, young, strong, black-skinned, his eyes long-lashed, hair in many short ringlets. The god dresses as the folk of the plains do, only a striped cloth twisted about his hips like a kilt, chest bare. Ahjvar has been getting used to that in both men and women, though it is not a fashion he has adopted, feeling naked enough when the heat drives him to strip to the short gown and sandals of Nabban's south provinces, with all the ancient scars even that exposes, to pilgrim's eye or god's.

An attractive young man Ahjvar would rather not have staring at him with quite such cool assessment.

Certainly not now, when he can even smell Ghu beside him, the lingering faint scent of horses that is never out of his clothes, the indefinable mingling of man and pines.

"A servant of Nabban, travelling to visit some of the shrines of your land," he says.

"The Nabbani have become like the Marakanders, thinking nothing real till they have seen it with their own eyes and set it down in their words." Forzra leans on a staff patterned in fine scales, its head carved like that of snake. He speaks as if he addresses it, not Ahjvar, then turns it so the eyes, chips of glittering stone, seem fixed on him.

Or on what stands beside him, shadow not quite seen. If he reaches— he won't, because to touch and find nothing would be worse.

"Yes. I serve my god in this."

"And how do you do so?"

"Here, in your lands? I've said. I travel to visit your shrines and hear the tales of the land, and to carry greetings to any gods I might meet."

"And what else?"

Ahjvar shrugs. "Nothing that is any harm to this land."

Forzra frowns. "There is something in you like a sudden wind from the north. The breath of the storm that brings the first rains."

Armed thunderstorm.

I'm glad you're finding this entertaining, Ghu. Why? Because there are other dreams he would rather dream, and other memories to live in.

Such as? Breath on his ear. Faint and distant laughter. *Walk this path again. It brings us—*

Forzra addresses the staff again, thoughtfully. "I am not sure that I like this storm-front that you bring."

Ahjvar bows, though it isn't Nalzawan fashion to do so. "I serve my god," he says. "Nabban has nothing but goodwill towards your land and its gods and its folk. All your lands and gods and folks, here beyond the seas."

The god says nothing to that, only continues to study him, which he endures in silence, until Forzra gives a nod, turns on his heel, and strides

off. Corporeal enough to leave footprints in the dust. But his staff leaves
no mark, and then he carries none, something thick as Ahjvar's upper arm
slung over his shoulder . . . swarming over his shoulder, riding there, tail
twining his thigh. Snake embracing the god's throat, rising over his head
like an elephant's trunk to look back.

The snake, mottled black and yellow and gleaming as if oiled, is in
the guest-hall yard in the morning, when they gather for breakfast while
their hired pack-oxen and their handlers assemble. A sacred animal of the
god Forzra, their guide Sister Enyal says, and offers it an egg, which it
ignores. "A blessing on our journey. Don't disturb it."

I prefer dragons, Ghu says.

Dogs.

The dragons don't track mud into the cave.

The dragons don't fit into the cave.

*The dragons turn into dogs, and the dogs roll in the mud and track mud into
the cave. They miss having you to tease. I miss having you to cook for.*

He wants to reach, to hold. To be held. But he is by a fire, under a
bank of hollies a day's ride from Marakand. He is no devil, to ride the
winds home.

The snake is at their hostel the first night out from the hills, too, or
its sibling is, and Ahjvar does not sleep, but sits with his back against the
wall and a knife in his hand. After that, Forzra's lands are left behind.
What watches him then, if anything does, he is never certain.

They have left Sato's river at Forzra's town; its course comes down
from the south through the fading edge of the hills and will no longer
serve them as they set off towards the northwest. Few shrines this way;
nearly as few good wells, and not the most popular of the pilgrim cir-
cuits. There are only hill-gods of small semi-nomadic herding folk, their
shrines often no more than a tree or an engraved stone, with a priest or
priestess living nearby in some small thorn-walled compound to tell the
stories of the god and accept alms for the blessing, or goddesses of the dry
riverbeds that he calls coulees, their shrines rare rocky outcroppings that
will be islands when the rains come.

A few gods and goddesses do appear to bless them, some as man or woman, one as an elephant—

No, he says to Ghu's presence.

Not even a little one?

No.

—two no more than a stirring of the air, yet a presence even those without a priest's insight or a wizard's senses could feel. They are wary of Ahjvar but do not approach him, wanting him gone. He makes them uncomfortable. Small gods, wishing to be left in peace and not to draw the attention of powers they do not understand. Much his own attitude to them.

Though the holiday pace frets him, Ahjvar finds the open land, the long views, ease his soul, at least in the mornings, before the chatter begins to grate. The grasslands are, in their own way, as strange to him as the hills, coulees marked by stands of tall, bare-trunked trees that lift their heads like clouds, unexpectedly graceful giraffes, which he knows only from scrolls in the imperial library, reaching to browse them, and wild elephants far larger than those that work in Pirakul. They see antelope of several kinds, some wild oxen that look to be all head and shoulders, wary wild dogs, red jackals with a different song from those of the deserts he knows. Lions, which take his breath away. And leopards. He watches it all and wishes he had an artist's skill to paint it, especially the trees like solitary clouds and the elephants and the striped wild horses that they say cannot be tamed.

He knows a man would bring them gentle and willing to his hand. But it is only his own eyes can look on them, beyond Nabban's boundaries. And at that time, he regrets the wonder lost that Ghu would find, more than he could ever see. The words he sets down for the imperial library are blunt and plain things. He lacks the gift of his long-gone granddaughter for poetry.

But I did see. You made me a winter's worth of tales when you came home. And I see, now, with your eyes, your living it again.

The pilgrim-party spends its nights either in guest-houses maintained in the thorn-fenced dry-season villages, or in compounds that to himself Ahjvar calls caravanserais, hostels maintained for these pilgrimages and spaced for their slow and easy footpace.

So many voices, so much noise. Unending, entirely inoffensive, laughter and jokes and tales traded in several related languages; even the inevitable grumbles and complaints and frictions between people should be no cause for real anger. So many small fretting days, dragged down to the trudging of the white oxen. A lean and leggy breed, but still—he could easily outpace them, and not regret doing without the burdens they carry, the water-gourds no more than the twice-baked cakes. He stops sleeping, which is never a good sign, and is not so gracious as he could be in refusing the suggestion by one of his fellow travellers that they might quite pleasurably share their blankets for a night or two.

She seemed very nice, I thought.

Ghu . . . And reckless, because why should Ghu be the only one to tease, or for that matter, the only one to— *Would you have minded?*

Ghu seems to consider this carefully. *Perhaps.*

Good.

But if you did want—only tell me, is all.

No. No.

The daytime heat is oppressive. No worse than that of the southern provinces, but here there is no shelter other than the shadows of scattered stands of thorny acacia and baobab, the latter of which makes him think somehow of elephants, the same ponderous curves massive against the sky. He wraps a caravaneer's scarf over head and face. Day by day the grass grows shorter, more sere and sparse, and the temperature climbs. The wind blows unceasingly, gritty with dust. They are drawing near the desert, Sister Enyal promises, and the turning point of their pilgrimage, after which they will make a shorter journey back to the hills and follow the highway of the legendary wizard Nalzawa, founder of the commonwealth, through the hills to Barrahe. The end of the world, this land, for them. If there are folk in the desert, no land claims them. Beyond, somewhere, one comes again to mountains, and the city-states of the north and west, the land called Rostenga. Few pilgrimages come this far, to the holy place of the goddess of the first and last tree, nameless and folkless.

A goddess of seers and diviners. A goddess of silences.

Last tree before the desert, first tree of the desert's edge. Oldest tree, in the tales told in the north of the world, but first, oldest, that might be a translator's error. Goddess of the underground river, a devil once told him. There are still occasional trees, mostly thorn, but there is no sign there was ever a river. Not even the least of coulees.

Ahjvar has always assumed an underground river must flow into or out of the earth—he expects hills, a gorge, a cavern, not just the pale grass and yellow dust reaching, it seems, to the world's end in all directions, the sky burning above.

"By noon, we'll come to her," Enyal had said as they settled into the hostel the previous evening. "She's not a goddess who takes form in the world, but she has been known to speak in the dreams of those who most have need of her. Perhaps tonight. She may watch us even now, as we approach her holy place."

Nothing watches in the night, except what feels like the night itself, the natural world of these plains: insect, bird, rodent, hunter, all disturbed and wary, a single human straying. The hostel left sleeping behind him, Ahjvar stops and unslings the bundle he carries, the one bag he does not let them put on their oxen, though they laugh at him, insisting on carrying himself his sheaf of paper, his inks and reed-pens for his daily account of their travels. What else he carries, rolled in an old plaid blanket, he has never shown them. A thing of his god, he says when someone notices and asks what he has hidden there.

Ahjvar shakes out the plaid blanket, snatches the scabbarded blade as it flies free. Belts on his sword and two of his knives, digs in the bottom of the bag for his bracelets, which are nothing of Nabban but a king's gold from another life, heavy, with terminals shaped as snarling leopards' heads. They cover one set of scars, but that isn't the reason to wear them. Declaration, of what and who he is, for himself as much as the goddess. Declaration and courtesy, offering respect. Ambassador, god to god.

Feeling even more unburdened than when he left the crowded hall of sleepers and all their pressing, dreaming souls, though a sword at his hip should be no lesser weight than in a bag on his back, he covers the last miles, as certain of his way as the arrow once it leaves the bow.

Only with the help of the Old Great Gods were the seven defeated, say the songs of the north. *But the devils were devils, even in human bodies, and were not so easily slain, despite the aid of the Old Great Gods and only by the Old Great Gods were they bound, one by one, and imprisoned: Ogada in stone, Jasberek in water, Vartu in earth, Tu'usha in the heart of a flame, Ghatai in a burning mountain, Jochiz in the youngest of rivers . . . and Dotemon, who had been the Nabbani wizard and empress and tyrant Yeh-Lin, in the oldest of trees.*

The girth of the ancient baobab is vast, a blackness against the stars. Ahjvar can believe it the oldest of trees after all. He has slept in houses smaller. Roots deep, deep, seeking hidden waters, and thick branches reaching like a child's stubby fingers for the stars. The naked twigs sway, and the grass about him whispers suddenly like the wings of disturbed bats. Nothing else.

He bows to the starless darkness that is the tree, there being no other obvious focus for courtesy. "Lady of the tree, my name is Ahjvar, *rihswera* of the holy one of Nabban, and Nabban sends me to you to speak of the devil Dotemon."

He waits for some thickening of attention, some change in the uneasy wind, but the answer when it came startles him.

"Priest of Nabban, they call you, do they not?" Human voice, a woman's, not young, not old, and the feeling of a body near him, that impression of warmth, scent, breath. And she speaks Nabbani, with Yeh-Lin's archaic accent. "But what is *rihswera*?"

"A Praitannec title. The *rihswera* is the champion of a king or a queen. What the folk of the north would call the king's sword. Lady of waters, you've seen Dotemon? She came back here?"

"She did, yes. Forty-four rains past. She stayed with me through a year."

Two rainy seasons, greater and lesser, in each year. Not so long ago, then.

"Why?" he asks, because it might have a bearing on what he has come to ask. He hopes not.

"She wanted quiet, she said. Peace in which to think, and to empty herself of thought. She had been many years travelling in Pirakul. She said—" the voice chuckles, deep and rich, and says something in a southern tongue he doesn't know, and then in the speech of the coast that is the second language for everyone of the commonwealth, "she said she must sit and let the winds off the desert blow the cobwebs and the clutter from her mind, because they weighed her down and made her coward when she faced thought of—she did not say what."

"Do you know where she has gone?"

"No. Is she an enemy of your god, *Rihswera* of Nabban?"

"No." He hopes not.

"She spoke of you. She spoke of your god. Her god, she says. She spoke of him often, when we spoke at all. Generally she only . . . was. Beneath the sun, and the rain. She is able to sit. The devils were restless, and the wizards they seduced to them were restless souls. Yeh-Lin Dotemon has found stillness. I value that in her."

"You believe her true, lady?"

"Do you not?"

"By her deeds . . . I think so. Nabban does. He trusts in hope."

Yes, Ghu whispers.

"And yet he keeps a killer to run his errands? Do not deny that you are that."

"I am not—" He doesn't bother. "No." Denial and agreement. "We'll find her when it is time, regardless. Lady of the oldest of trees, I'm sent to ask you to free her."

"I have freed her, in defiance of all that the Old Great Gods asked of me when they laid her like the dead above my river, within my trunk, with a stone arrow in her heart. I freed her, though I had wound roots all through her within my own Gods-wounded heart, to hold her deep in her dreaming death. I freed her and I let her go into the world to see it with newborn eyes. Why ask?"

"Because either she lies, or she is still constrained by you. Leashed and limited. You hold a part of her still."

"I do. *Rihswera* of Nabban, why would you have her otherwise? The devils were not meant for this world. They do not move through it lightly."

"Yet we would ask you to free her, lady. A time is coming when we may need her strength unleashed. My god sees it."

"Nabban goes to war? Is it Pirakul you would have her invade again, or the jungles and the highlands south of you? I know your land from her tales of her own old sins. It was great and it was feared, in the days of her rule. Would your god make it so again?"

"No. Not war. We hope, not war again. Lady, we know the devils are free, and some have died, and some are hunted by one of their own. There will be war, maybe, between them again, war to tear and scar the world as they tore and scarred it long ago. We don't know. We hope to avert it. We hope Dotemon will be our ally. We know—my god has seen—that there is a darkness growing in the west, a storm brewing—beyond our horizon still, but coming. He wants Dotemon freed to stand with us against it." Though if it reached so far as Nabban again, it would be too late.

Ghu shapes him, he knows it. He shapes his god. He is a corruption, he sometimes thinks, as much as consort—

No, Ghu protests, urgent. *No.*

—and he knows that other gods, and the philosophers and priests of other lands, might say it. A god should not look beyond his bounds, should not reach, and act. They do, he and Ghu—

We do now. Ghu, how?

We dream in one another.

Typical cryptic Ghu, going poetic and elusive.

Idiot boy.

Oh, always.

—They will use what they have, to prevent that storm ever rolling over Nabban. He knows it, there before the goddess of the baobab. He knows it now.

Come with me, not to be my assassin, the man had said, long ago, and, *You don't kill for me, not like that.* But that was a different time, and in defence of the souls of his folk, Ghu, who is Nabban, will use whatever weapons he has. And if Ahjvar his *rihswera* be one, Dotemon is surely another.

Ghu says nothing. Ghu knows this, knows he has always known it.

"He used the devil in his wars before," the goddess says. "He allowed his first empress, the Grasslander Suliasra Ivah, to use her."

"No. The devil served as general and wizard. Of her own will, and as a duty to the land. She was not used. She served, as lords of the land do. She kept her oaths, and she kept faith."

"You believe—your god believes she will still do so? In her full strength, which he cannot match? He would trust in a devil to choose to stand with the folk of the earth and their gods against her own kind?"

"Yes."

"Certainty, or hope?"

"Lady, we ask. We trust her. She has been tried and proven." To a point. So far.

"Fighting fire with fire? A tactic, but what if the wind changes? Should I tempt her, or let you push her, to be what she once was? Think— she was the tyrant of Nabban. Perhaps she still covets it. It is your land and its folk will suffer if your trust is misplaced."

"You think Nabban, he and I, would not suffer, if she turned against us, first and before ever his folk and his land? She knows us, and what we could and would do against her, however doomed that might be in the end. She would not leave us free to act against her. We don't offer our folk as sacrifice to our trust being misplaced, without offering ourselves first."

"I do notice you say 'we,' now, and not 'my god.'"

He keeps his silence.

"Do you speak for him, or he through you?"

He shrugs. No answer to give. To him, it makes no difference.

"Priest and champion. That is not what you are but what you do. What you are, your nature . . . There is the hand of a god on you and the breath of a god in you, and his roots run through you, blood and marrow, river and stone. You unsettle the winds of this land and the currents of its water. You are—a wrongness."

He is not going to apologize.

"You should take yourself out of this place, *Rihswera* of Nabban. Go back to your own land and stay there in peace with your god."

No arguing with that. He craves the solitude of two, not loneliness.

Ghu says, *I'm sorry. I miss you, every breath.*

The wind off the desert is hot. It gusts about them suddenly, and dry twigs rattle together. Some fall.

"Dotemon," he says. "We ask that you release her."

"Are you come to threaten me, if I do not accede to Nabban's wish in this?"

"No. But we need . . . he says, he sees her free. He will . . . I don't know. I don't know what we might do, or what you might do to prevent us. Or might try, to do so. Do you think you would succeed? Better we neither of us have to find out, don't you think? Gods and demons have died trying to hold the devils bound. None succeeded in the end. We need Dotemon, unleashed to do what she may."

"And when all the north is laid waste in another devils' war, will you come with the survivors of your folk to beg refuge?"

"I would be dead with my god. It's another devils' war we fear and try to find some way to prevent."

"So you say. Sit, priest of Nabban. And find silence. Wait with me for the dawn."

He settles with his back against the smooth bark, sword across his lap, and watches the rising stars until they begin to fade in the swift lightening of the southern dawn.

The goddess stands only a few paces distant, watching for the sun. The ground about them is a litter of broken twigs, dead leaves.

The tree is not dry-season bare. The tree is dying, or dead.

The goddess turns to look down on him, a face grave and beautiful, with broad cheekbones and a small chin. Shorter and stockier than most of the plains-folk, with full breasts, broad-hipped. She is quite naked, her cloud of iron-grey hair neither dressed nor trimmed. Her only ornament is a braided bracelet, cold black against warm near-black skin. She is quite humanly handsome, but she forms and wears the body as a shell, a dress to show respect and honour a guest, as he has armed himself and worn the gold. This is not she, not as the appearance of the god Forzra living among his folk had been the true expression of himself. This appearance of a woman was not something that the goddess of the tree has ever been or needed to be.

An underground river, Yeh-Lin had said. Did the devil think it so? They have met before, she and he—Ghu, not he, but now he remembers that vision as if it were his own. This is the goddess of the dreaming. This warned of—what would be, or had been?

The weight of a great and ancient lake, an inland sea, lost and remembered, and all the land tilts inwards to wrap around her, dizzying, folding up about him so that he feels he is falling towards her, to drown.

No. She does not intend that. She only is, existing, a weight in the world. As is his own god, but Ahjvar does not feel it so alien, being within it in himself.

A weight, still, even dying. Fading, as her waters, into the earth.

He bows low where he sits and straightens, waiting for the world to steady, as she seats herself across from him, legs folded under her, hands on her knees.

In silence, he can find the deep waters of his god, that stillness of stone, the light sparking out of darkness into bird-bright flight, all flowing wind and water. But the goddess does not keep her own meditation. He feels her brushing along the edges, listening, tasting, testing, and cannot help the jolt of anger, of outright fear, that gives him. He does not rise and pace, does not trace the lines in the air with the sword's edge, weave the dance, but he walks it within, sets *rowan* for protection, *almond* to forbid, *prickly ash* to counter what she works: her quiet insistent pressing to see beyond the surface of him. Too late, maybe, to keep her from seeing more than he would have her know, but she . . . backs off, or at least fades, no longer touching. The god's stillness is lost to him, though. It becomes only the waiting, the timeless watch, which might be for a death or a dawn or a changing of the guard, the stillness only of the drawn bow, of the breath yet to be taken.

He is not hunting. Remember that. It is the goddess who first breaks the stillness.

"I have seen what you are," she says. "I understand what it is I feel in you. Priest of Nabban, what has been done to you is against the proper nature of things. It is wrong. Would you be free of your god and the bonds that hold you?"

"No. *No.*" A deep breath, to stop himself bolting to his feet, reaching for some defence. He spreads his hands, lightly resting on the scabbard, not to clench them. "And do not you think to tear me from him. You will fail. Others have."

"I do not see how I might free you, yet, though if I sat long enough in silence I might come to see. I shall do so, if you would have that gift. This is an ugly thing."

"Yes, but it is not his doing. He only took what he found. I am his now, as I am—and of my own will. Leave us be."

"Is it you yourself who say so, or he?"

"*I.*"

"Do you know so? What is your own will, and what his? How do you know?"

"Faith," he says.

Oh, Ahj.

But it is as true an answer as any and less complicated than his own truth, which is that, for himself, still and after all these years, he does not find it matters.

Ahjvar . . .

"It is a terrible thing to keep a soul from its road," she says. "It is wrong. *Wrong.* But you are not of my folk. They are long ages gone, far-wandered and folded into other folks, following the waters. But if another god had taken one of mine to hold as Nabban holds you, I would have raised my folk to war to take them back and free that enslaved ghost to its road. Yes, even if it cost a thousand lives." She speaks as calmly as if she discusses the unchanging dry-season weather.

"I am not yours."

"No."

"And no slave. My will is my own."

"But how do you know?"

"You repeat yourself."

"And so do you. Faith is no answer, when you cannot step aside from him to see yourself clearly."

"Faith is my only answer. Love. Trust. But this argument is pointless. I'm no concern of yours," he says in Nabbani. "Lady of lost waters, you speak of binding and yet you don't answer me. Will you give Dotemon back to herself?"

"You have not said, servant of Nabban, what you will do, if I do not."

He shrugs. "I suppose, when the time comes, I will go to find her. I will tell her, as my god bids me, that Nabban would have her free to keep the oaths she swore him long ago. And we would all, you and we alike, await what came of that. I don't think you could hold her if she truly fought to be free. Certainly not if my god chose to aid her."

"You said you did not come to threaten me."

He shrugs.

The goddess shuts her eyes and sits so, long enough for the shadow of her to move, to turn to touch his knee, and he does not like to have even the shadow of her on him when she has spoken of taking him from his god, which is childish.

"Not for your threats," she says, opening her eyes at last. She speaks slowly, as if hearing and considering each word as it leaves her mouth. "Not for fear of Dotemon. Not even to have the corruption of you gone from my land while it is yet mine to protect. But because I dream as you dream, you and your god." She rises to her feet, ponderous, graceful, a weight like flowing stone. But she is water. "Take this, then. Make me free of her when you must, if you must. Yours, the choice, what you do."

The wind veers round, storm-wild, swinging through all points of the compass. Trees thrash, branches bend. Ailan wakes with a cry, but Ahjvar stays where he is, sitting by their fire. Walking memory. Dream. Reaches, then, a hand. Seizes the young man's arm, pulls him down, beside the fire under the bank of hollies, beside the fire under the baobab.

"Stay," he says, slow and slurred. "Nothing to fear."

Peace, Ghu says, to that wild-beating heart, and sets a hand on Ailan's head as he might calm a panicked beast.

Ailan settles into Ahjvar's forbidden side, close and innocent for once as a small child, frightened as one, baffled. Surely he thinks, will think, he is dreaming, when the morning comes. It's all right for him to be here. Ghu stands by Ahjvar. He can lean his shoulder against his leg, head to his hip. Feel the hand rest in his hair, fingers twining in it.

The wind settles into the west.

Young Ailan, who was not there, stares up at the naked goddess.

The woven ring of black the goddess wears about her wrist lands before Ahjvar. He catches it up, but when he looks to speak to her, the land is empty. Even the sense of her is gone, deep beneath her roots, into her waters . . . Only himself, the tree, the clear golden land to the horizon.

Ailan is only a shadowy shape, huddled into the side of the shadow-shape that is himself. Not here. Very far away, twelve years and thousands of miles.

Ahjvar rises to his feet and bows low to the thick skeleton of the baobab, sliding the bracelet onto his wrist. Silk sleek hair. He sets his hand on a long, ridged scar of the otherwise beech-smooth trunk. Once there had been bones coffined within the tree, prison and grave, and then a second birthing into life. Or a third life, maybe, or a fourth. She has remade herself more than once, Yeh-Lin Dotemon, starting when the peasant girl Nang Lin set off to find a noble patron and training for her wizard's talent.

We are reborn each day, and must make ourselves anew, the poet Yeon Silla wrote.

The pilgrim party is approaching. He feels them, the life of them, the intrusion, as if it were something he might smell on the wind. He turns to see Sister Enyal catch sight of him, come striding ahead, the white headscarf she wears over her priest-shaved scalp floating back like a banner.

"She called to you?" Enyal asks, foregoing the rebuke he expects with something like wonder in her voice.

Close enough. He agrees with a nod. The priestess's eyes go to his sword. "What have you done here?"

"Prayed," he had answered, then, and around him the dream is fading the land gone to shadows. He sits by the fire, a chilly night on the edge of spring, and Ailan is in the crook of his arm, as another young man should be, and is not. "Prayed. And been answered. I'll wait for you back at the hostel, Sister."

"Ahjvar . . . ?" Ailan, close within the circle of his arm. Shivering. "Ahjvar, I—was that a dream?"

"Was what?" He took back his arm, stood and moved away. Ailan stared up at him, all ruddy and shadow in the firelight. Hurt. Confused.

"I—I'm sorry. I had a dream. A nightmare. Sort of a nightmare? It—it scared me but it wasn't bad. You were there. A woman. She was a woman but in the dream I knew she was really a tree, and—Did I see your god? There was someone else and I knew he was your god. He was—he said—he . . ." Ailan shook his head. "I'm sorry. I wasn't trying to—not this time, I mean. I—" Incoherence trailed to silence. To get close, he meant to say. Which boundary he did try to push, once in a while, and Ahjvar put him off while pretending he didn't notice, which seemed the best tactic.

"It was a dream," Ahjvar said. "Don't worry about it." Added, "Sorry," himself, because he had dragged the man in somehow, or Ghu had, or—

The wind was gusting wildly, rattling the stiff leaves of the hollies.

Ashes swirled. Then stillness. But there was the feel of thunder gathering in the air.

She came like a dragon, a typhoon, a sandstorm howl of wind in the badlands. The hollies bent almost double. The fire went out like a candle in a draft. Ailan yelped and jumped to his feet. Camels bellowed but stayed put, hunkered low, shutting their eyes, heads down. Ahjvar shut his own eyes against the gust, rocked with it, but didn't move from where he stood. Rubbed ash and grit from his face as the wind died. Ailan scrambled over to him, the knife he had taken from the priest unsteady in his hand. He crouched, free hand on Ahjvar as if he were a rock to cling to, all warnings to keep himself off again forgotten.

"Dead king," Yeh-Lin said. "You called?"

"Did I?"

"I wonder."

"Someone did. And I believe you have what is mine." She held out a slender hand.

"No," he heard himself say. "Not yet." Echoes in the mind. Ghu.

"You deny me? Even constrained as I am, I could tear you from your young god's grip, dead king, and put you from the world. I could take back the empire that was mine and even your sweet-eyed horseboy in the full strength of his land could not in the end endure against me. Why should I serve him?"

"It's more interesting than the alternatives. We wouldn't want you getting bored. Also, you swore an oath of your own will."

"That."

"Don't be dramatic," he said. "Sit down, put my fire back together, and have some tea. It's nearly time for breakfast. Ailan, it's all right. This is—?"

"Scholar Daro Jang." She winked at him and bowed gracefully.

"Scholar Daro Jang, who serves the god of Nabban."

"Does she indeed?" Yeh-Lin asked, speaking Nabbani, Imperial, and as it had been two hundred years past, or longer. Her hair, loose and falling to her waist, still stirred in the memory of the wind she had ridden. "It seems we have established that I do, as you are still standing there. Oh well. Tea, you say. Proper tea or the tar they call such on the road in these parts?"

"That. You didn't bring any coffee?

"I was asleep in my bed, as a virtuous middle-aged historian ought to be in the small hours of the morning. A god boxing my ears and shouting for my attention does not immediately bring to mind the thought, ah, I should pack a little basket with a picnic breakfast, no."

"I wish someone would box your ears."

She laughed. At least she was not in her nightrobe. She wore a Marakander caftan, carried her sword on her back. Shifted it off into her hand, but only to throw it down. Ahjvar caught it by the brocade-covered scabbard before it hit the ground.

"I am Nabban's. Did you doubt? Did he? And that being the case, *Rihswera* of Nabban . . . What took you so long? I've been expecting you these past two months, and, since I have introduced myself properly to the ambassador at last, in all confidence, so has the ambassador. Lord Ilyan Dan has on my suggestion asked his housemistress to supply herself with the best Rostengan beans, and has found a tailor to produce a decent court gown in Nabban's colours that may possibly fit even your long bones, since you must of course present yourself to the senate, and the priests, and Gurhan the god, and I knew you would show up looking like something even the most desperate caravan-master would think twice about hiring. But—who is this?"

She folded herself to her knees—graceful, as her every movement ever was—and began to pile up the sticks of the wind-scattered fire. Smiled at the youth. Deliberate. Devastating. Wasted effort in the night.

Ailan was far too close. Ahjvar could feel the heat of him, pressing to his side. Moved off again. "A man."

"A young man, yes, so much I had observed. Have you acquired a son?"

"No!"

"Are you sure? He has rather a look of you, but for the pretty Nabbani eyes."

"Quite. He's—someone who needed to get out of Star River Crossing."

"Oh, indeed? And you brought him along out of the goodness of your heart?"

Ahjvar shrugged.

"I see. Well, that's between you and the young god, I suppose."

"Cold hells, do you think—"

She was snickering. Flicked a finger at the fire and watched the flames blaze up again. "I think nothing. He looks a charming companion. Perhaps I'll—"

"No."

"He's surely old enough not to need a keeper."

"Just leave him alone, old woman. Call him a page."

"He's too old."

"Not your horseboy, I suppose?"

"Nor my shield-bearer. Gods, he can hardly grab a knife by the right end." That wasn't fair. Ailan was vastly improving. "Call him whatever you want. My ward."

"I must introduce him to mine, though I fear she takes regrettably little interest in pretty youths. Or maidens, either. I'd worry less over her if she did. Does he speak Nabbani?"

"Not that anyone in Nabban would acknowledge. He's Taren. But yes, he claims he has a little Imperial."

"A very little, I think. For your god's sake, reassure him. He thinks we're discussing how to cook him for dinner, by the looks he's giving me."

"Weren't we?" he asked. "Ailan, it's all right, truly. She's—a wizard, the greatest of Nabban. She serves my god. She's—"

"Reformed," said Yeh-Lin, with excessive piety, hand over her heart.

"She's annoying, is what she is," Ahjvar said. "And she's not nearly as young as she's choosing to look. Pretend she's an embarrassing relative and don't let her bully you. Can you fill the kettle? *Jang*, tell me about these red priests."

"The army has crossed the Kinsai'av. I have that from the witness of one Moth, whom you might better know under the name—"

"We know Moth."

"Oh? She does get around, for a woman who by her own report spent nearly eighty years trying to turn herself into a glacier. I believe her humours are out of balance. Too much black bile, the physicians would say, although—"

"What? No. Never mind. Shut up about bile. What army?"

"Ah. Dead king, you are very behind the times. I don't suppose the empress has sent an army to follow you?"

"No."

"Pity. We could use one."

"What army crossed the Kinsai?"

"Jochiz had made himself god of Tiypur and is marching east. The Western Grass has fallen. The goddess Kinsai is dead."

So.

Yours. To die for you, idiot boy. Even for that. He will not reach Nabban.

CHAPTER XXVII

. . . winter comes on, the dying season of the year in which
the All-Holy conquered the Western Grass

Autumn declined towards winter during the month they travelled from the shores of the Kinsai'aa. At first they had travelled by night, when Mikki could ride, but as his strength returned they had begun to journey under the sun, hunting as they went. If Mikki was slow and sleepy, reluctant to wake in the mornings, that was—almost usual. He had told himself so. It was winter, and the nature of demons was coloured, somewhat, by the form in which the soul of the world had shaped them. He had used to sleep days at a time, those years when they had settled in Baisirbsk and the winter sun had barely crawled above the southern horizon.

Moth had been patient. She had not pushed. She held him when he twitched and whimpered in his dreams. When all he could do was pace in silence, and the hills and the sky faded, even the scent of them gone to rank reeking of his own body and human stench and smoke, a cage in the darkness of the All-Holy's temple or the endless jolt and creak of the wagon and the singing that was inside him somewhere, words circling, gnawing, rooted in his flesh . . . when he could not seem to lift his head even to follow the flight of a hawk or the darting fear of a hare, the water-flow passing of a herd of antelope, she was there, a voice, a clean scent, a rope he could cling to, to haul himself back. She sang, often, or chanted one of the old lays of heroes half-remembered, humankind and demon-kin in the old days before the seven came into the world—the travelling ones, the wanderer-heroes they had loved best, he and she both. In their former travels he had told those as often as she, they taking turns, sometimes, which of them presented themselves as the storyteller, the singer, and which hung back in the shadows, watching . . . They had hunted Ogada so, Ogada who had been her cousin Heuslar, slayer of her brother, of Mikki's mother, when first they took the road together.

He had been so young. His mother would have said so, though the cousins he had sailed with when he was truly a young man had grown old and white-haired and taken the road to the Old Great Gods by then.

The Undrin Rift twisted its way between the northerly reaches of the Red Desert and the Black, and followed the course the Shikten'aa might once have taken, carrying meltwater from the mountains to the northern sea. Ghost of a river, cut deep. Up in the desert it was all shattered, knife-edged stone. Where it sliced through the faded yellow grasses here, it was still a region of cliffs and ledges, dry terraces. To the north it broadened to a valley, and the river began to come to life in pools and sloughs and swamps, acres of cat-tail and loosestrife. Clans of the Great Grass grazed their herds in the summer meadows there, and held the hills against intruders, be they raiders from other clans or peacefully passing caravans. He and Moth been there before, long ago.

These cliffs were less contested, but a bad road for horses. For camels. For anything short of a goat, really. There was a track, or there had been, long ago, when Ulfhild Vartu had ventured on some expedition into her enemy and husband's lands of the Great Grass.

Moth had flown it first, making sure it was no false trail they followed, something that might fade away and leave them hanging over a sheer drop. Passable, she said. But she had sounded doubtful. For a bear, the narrow way was perilous. Mikki went head low, rocks rubbing his flank in some sections, each paw placed with care, following where Moth led the horses. She had said she would rather have taken the horses down first and flown back to follow with Mikki, but he had not waited. Had not argued. Simply been there, behind her.

Black ice slicked the stones in small patches where the morning sun had not fallen.

Not a child, not a damned invalid. He had been, he knew it. He was just . . . not ready to be out of her sight. To be where the wind might not bring him the scent of her.

"I sent you away," he said.

It had been burning in him, growing, a pain he could not spit out.

She stopped, there on the crumbling track. Tied the lead reins up, first one, then the other, where the horses wouldn't tread on them, careful deliberation. Came back, edging past the more excitable spotted horse. Sat down, there at Mikki's feet, Keeper hitched over her lap, her back to stone and some creeping thing with tiny leaves turning red hanging over her. Below them the stone dropped away, not quite cliff, loose and betraying, to any great weight that set a foot there. He sank down, head on his paws, where he could see her face. She set a hand on his neck, fingers digging into his ruff. She was looking for those scars again, as if she feared they might have torn open. As if she had to remind herself, every time she touched him, that they were there.

He wished she wouldn't. They were scars. Hardly the first he'd won.

"I left you," she said.

"I knew why, *minrulf.*" It came easily, and then it hurt, like seeing a place long lost in time, trees and years long fallen, half forgotten. Taste of the word on his tongue. Tears burning in his eyes and he did not think he'd ever wept before, not in his daylight form, not the bear. Could bears even cry? "I knew why. You were wrong. You should have defied them. The Old Great Gods to turn against a demon of the earth—they would not. They could not. I would have told you so. It was a lie, their threat against me. It was, my heart, it always was. But you left. You flew away. And so I looked for you. *Years*, I looked for you. Holla-Sayan came, too, a while. After his wife died—I was still looking for you then, and he and I went up into Baisirbsk. The homestead was gone by then—"

"I burned it."

"I know. It wasn't the first time I'd been back. But the ruins of it were gone to the forest, then, and the winters were growing heavier. Late frosts and early, they said, year after year. The folk at Swanesby were talking of leaving, going to seek new lands on the Amunn'aa. So I went down across the Great Grass, and nothing, nothing of you—no songs, no whispers on the wind, no scent, no rumours on the road. And I left Holla. I think he went up to Lissavakail for a time, and down to the south, to the sea where the lotus blooms. And I went home."

"I'd gone to Pirakul. Beyond Pirakul. To the eastern edge of the world."

"Why?"

"To see what was there."

"What did you find?"

"The western edge of the world. Trees. A land that perhaps the ships sailed from, to come to the Drowned Isles, long ago. I don't know. But I didn't find Jasberek. Then."

"Lucky for him."

"Maybe. Not in the long run. He came to find me, did I say?"

"He's dead?"

"Ya."

"I'm sorry."

"He tried to take Lakkariss." She shrugged. Said nothing more, beyond. "So? After you left Holla-Sayan?"

"But then you did come to me, when I'd gone home to wait, and . . . you would not give up the sword. Not give up what they had set you to do. To kill for them."

Her fingertips had found the scars. Followed them, as if nursing her own pain.

"I sent you away so I wouldn't see you serving that."

She would not leave the scars be. He jerked away, head snapping around, jaws closing about her arm.

Stop that.

They held so a frozen moment. Then he let her go. In silence, she rose again, edged back past the horses, chirped to call them on, not bothering with the reins now.

He followed. Angry without words. Not where he had meant to lead them. Not what he had wanted said. Couldn't find what, now, to say.

"Loose stone here," she called back.

It rattled beneath the horses' hooves. Something fell away, long, skittering plummet.

A yellow land, pale, with darker bands, tawny brown, running through the layers of stone. Sharp-edged where frost had broken it; smooth where time had rubbed it, or running water. A dry land, with the breath of the high desert in the south wind that sucked the moisture from eyes and nose and panting mouth. Something of the deserts reaching down, following the ghost of the Shikten'aa, hungry, to drag the Grass into it . . .

It was only a dry autumn wind. Nothing more.

The cliffs descended in shelves and drops and slopes. Not some single feature, but a region, a land, almost, in itself. Creatures lived here. Little scurrying things, and foxes and snakes to prey on them. Birds.

Disaster, almost, when a sparrow whirred away under unsteady Lark's nose. A hind foot slipping. Moth had him by the bridle, coaxing him back, calm—Mikki crossed that crumbling section of the path most warily, and Moth was there, tense, silent, as if she might take him by a handful of fur, tug him on, what slight weight she had against his bulk a useless anchor. He found solid footing again with a huff of breath. Nosed at her, wordless, pushed her on ahead.

She went, but thumped a closed fist on the top of his head, gently. Eased something between them.

Great black span of wings, circling against the sky. Eagle. Two of them. Something moving below, pale dun backs. A herd of kulan following a thread of green. Mostly barren stone and sand down there, but pools held water, and there were shadows of sedge-grown channels, greened by rain or seepage rising from below.

A change of angle, as the way they followed faded out from under their feet. Twisting to face into that south wind, and dropping down, onto a broader way, a layer of that darker stone. She could have used another human body then. He wasn't much use, though the horses were easy with him now. It had taken them longer to settle into acceptance of the scent of the devil.

Trying to turn them in such a narrow space, trying to lead them down, that leap below . . . turned, they wanted to go back, to follow the track before their noses, up.

Patience, she was, and calm, a rock of it. He squeezed around, not quite slipping over, to put himself between Lark and Fury, to keep Lark where he was, till Fury was down in a sudden rush and scramble. Moth praised him, Westgrasslander words, stroking his sweating neck.

Reminding him of Holla-Sayan, managing horses. Not something he had often seen in her. Too often forgot she could be. Something Ulfhild had been, that Vartu had rarely needed. She was so offhand, with Storm. Talked to him like a dog, like a contrary human. But the necromantically revived bone-horse hardly behaved as a normal beast anyway. To listen to her tales, he never had, even when he was a living creature.

She talked to Lark now as she had talked to Mikki himself, those first days after they crossed the Kinsai. Gentle. Careful. Very certain, too, that he would do, could do, what she wanted. Come a little forward. There. And down, easy, there, look, Fury's gone ahead, there, come . . .

Laugh or growl. *Going to talk me down too?*

You stay where you're at till I've got him out of the way.

Lark plunged, a rush, a skidding on the stones.

"Steady now, steady!" She was between the horse and the tumbling slope, fool, leaning into his shoulder . . . Mikki was prepared to fling himself down after, to grab her, if they slipped, teeth in whatever it took . . .

Of course, falling, she might fly. He and the horse would not.

The horse calmed. Snorted. Pushed on after Fury.

Moth waited until Mikki followed.

The afternoon wore on in the descent, but that had been the worst of it. No discussion, when they came, finally, to the valley bottom. "Camp," he said, and Moth, after a quick scan around, nodded. The horses rushed to where a trickle of water formed a reedy pool, sending a scatter of blackbirds into the sky.

Firewood was all small stuff, twigs and brush. No trees, even though this ought to have been a sheltered place, and it was not so dry as he had imagined.

No fish in the pool, though. He prowled away, came back with a marmot, went back to dig out another. Little enough. Moth had the fire burning and was baking bannock on a stone.

"You want those cooked?" she asked.

"You do. You're too thin. You don't eat enough."

"*I* don't?"

"Get me an antelope, once we're back up in the grass."

Advantage of having no hands. He got to laze on the sun-warmed rocks while she skinned and gutted the marmots, threading the livers and hearts on a stick of green willow. The sun itself was lost to them; they were in the dusk of the high walls, now, but the eastern cliffs glowed golden.

Going up, once they crossed the broken land between, should be easier, surely.

She jointed the marmots and since they had plentiful water, for a change, set them to seethe.

The faintest touch of a goddess lay over this land, an echo more than any true awareness. Shikten, Skitan sometimes, in the north. They had known her of old, in Baisirbsk. So far up her course, she might be almost a different being, far from spruce and birch and moss, far from the vast silence of the ice. Nothing gathered either to welcome or challenge them. A lonely place, the Undrin Rift.

Warmth was fading from the stone, shadows deepening. Moth was on her knees, feeding the fire beneath the kettle.

"Soon as you have arms, you can go find me some more wood," she suggested.

"It hurts," he said, nose pressed to her neck. "It hurts, but I'm better, I am. I'm—I just need you here, not—not fussing."

"Was I?"

"For you, princess, yes. You treat me like a wounded dog. I'm not going to—to fall to pieces."

"Or bite me?"

"Sometimes you need biting."

Tell me, she said, and sat back from the fire. Challenging. *He hurt you. I can't see it. I can't help.*

You do. Just being here, you do. Like getting Lark down that rockface. Were you going to hold him, if he slipped? You made yourself his shield, his anchor, and he trusted the way would be there.

"This was entirely the wrong path for horses. The winters and the spring rains wear the rock away more than I realized."

"Over centuries, yes, they do. You of all people should have remembered that. But there's an idea, we could turn mapmakers."

"Mikki—"

"I was in a cage," he said, lowering his head to rest on her shoulder, hairy cheek to her ear.

"Yes." She wrapped an arm over him. Restrained herself consciously, he suspected, from compulsively seeking the scars, to reassure herself he was still whole.

He drew a deep breath, long. Felt it. Clean air, sand and stone and water beneath the sky.

"I couldn't breathe. In the cage. I couldn't feel—the trees. The earth. The forest. My heart . . . it was torn away from where I would have it be."

Demons hid their hearts, human songs declared. Left them behind in their own place, and so unlike gods, they could wander, and yet always be one with their land. It wasn't so . . . straightforward. If his heart, a soul-heart, was buried, it wasn't in a place.

He had known she would find him.

Yet the songs caught a glimmer of the truth, faintest reflection on water.

"I was chained. To him. I could feel him, all the time. As if he were . . . a tick, feeding on me, but the size of a mountain. A mouth, buried deep within me. Is that what it is, to have two souls?"

"No. Cold hells, no." She was silent a long while, as if she considered. "Not for me, at least. I don't know. Holla-Sayan might have said differently, once. I don't know. But no, never. We are one, Ulfhild and Vartu. I am one. We always have been."

"Good."

There was more he wanted said. Much more, perhaps. What did it all come down to, though, but this? Arm, arms about him. Warmth of her, human warmth, and the heat and the cold of the fires that spun life over old bones. A lonely boy's dreaming, weaving stories around a figure in a tale who cast shadows, such shadows, beyond what the words had ever said of her. Born by her grave, he had been, in the many-chambered tomb that had been old before a demon chose it for her den and it was used to bind a devil down. He was meant for her, he'd always thought, felt, which was that boy's lonely dreaming, nothing more, and yet . . . and yet. He was needed. He never doubted that. And in that—

Something vital, still unsaid.

I knew you were coming for me, he said. *I knew you would find a way.* And aloud, "So, princess, how do we get Lakkariss back?"

She laughed.

"Beornling, I love you. I do. Let him keep it."

"Vartu . . ." He sat back at that. Sunset, too, overtaking him. The wind might still be from the south, but it was cold, now, raising goosebumps on naked skin.

"Why do you think it took me so long to come to you?"

"Tell me." He pulled her to him. "Leave the fire to look to itself a while."

She'd been so careful of him all this way, and he was—not needing that, now. He might, again. It came and went, the weight of the chains remembered, the cage, the suffocation.

Not tonight. He got her out of her swordbelt and byrnie and she was laughing, Moth, laughing again, like a girl, and making him do all the work of boots and ties while she clung close, mouth finding the places that made the breath come quick, ear and nipple and back to his mouth, hungry, both of them, as if they had been starved.

Near on two centuries. Mikki supposed they had been.

No cold reaching air of Lakkariss laid by them, either. Time enough to ask about that later. Maybe. Time, now, to let all worries go by. For a while.

The fire would die down before the soup-kettle boiled dry.

PART THREE

CHAPTER XXVIII

. . . a new spring, a new year, and the armies of the All-Holy
advance on Marakand

From the Chronicle of Nikeh gen'Emras

*T*he Army of the South swept over Serakallash while the sept-chiefs were still trying to negotiate a fee for its use of their wells. *The fighting lasted a day, the winds and the sand aiding the defenders, who had hoped against hope that they might turn the army aside and drive it to pass on. By sunset, however, the goddess Sera had disappeared into the depths of her spring, the chiefs had knelt to Prince Dimas and submitted to the All-Holy, accepting hasty instruction in the catechism and initiation on behalf, they said, of their folk, although the chiefs and warriors of the Herani sept had defied this decision and fled the town, after murdering the red priests of the mission-house.*

The bodies of all the Herani remaining in the town were presented to Dimas, as part of the surrender. They were laid out, men and women, in the courtyard of the burnt mission-house. The Herani were few in number. None remained alive.

In his mercy, the sept-chiefs asked, in the All-Holy's great mercy shown through his princes and primates, let no further vengeance for the murdered priests be taken on the folk of the town.

And Dimas was merciful.

And if the dead Herani seemed more to have fallen in battle than to have suffered execution—well, they had barricaded themselves into a warehouse, had they not, and been extracted by their own fellow-townsfolk only with hard fighting. And not one cried out, my son, my daughter, my father, my mother, when Primate Ambert ordered their bodies buried in an unmarked pit in the desert.

And not one said, Herani? Who are the Herani? Why are they not included in the song of the tally of the septs? Not one whispered in a Westron ear, "These men, these women, died in the fighting in the streets."

In the days of Ghatai's conquest there had been sept-chiefs who willing served a conqueror. In this time, for the little while it mattered, there was a unity of purpose. In this time, they held true to their goddess, in hope and in faith.

Dimas did not turn aside to climb the road into the mountains. He left a force to occupy the town, under the Knight-Commander Balba, and continued his march, while Serakallashi conscripts—converts almost over-eager to serve, rather—razed a number of houses of the Rostvadim sept and built a fort with high stone walls on the ridge at the north-eastern corner of the town, scowling down over the road.

A curse blighted the town, it was whispered in the markets, set on the very rock and water in the days when the devil Ghatai ruled them and left the heads of the sept-chiefs to rot in the goddess's holy waters. Few children were born to them. They were a dying folk. The priests had promised that the All-Holy would bring blessings, and the women would bear children, and Serakallash would grow great again and rule the Red Desert.

The goddess of the spring appeared to have abandoned her folk.

But in Lissavakail, in the mountains, the children of Serakallash were fostered among the folk of the high valleys. In the far pastures of the desert edge, the children of the septs lived with distant kin, and in the months that followed those who were found and taken to the school in the fortress were few.

They, and the townsfolk, were taught their catechism and initiated into the cult, tattooed with the sign and the blood of the All-Holy.

But the sacred ink, carried with the army over the mountains, thick and dark as tar, was mixed with water from Sera's holy well. A symbol, an old foreign woman who was said to be the desert-born aunt-by-marriage of one of the Battu'um sept-chiefs said. A symbol of how the All-Holy had conquered Sera and made her folk and her waters his own.

If it made the Serakallashi happy and compliant, let it be so. Knight-Commander Balba had other troubles to deal with. The old woman with the sketch of feathers tattooed on her cheek oversaw the preparation of the ink before it was sent out with the priests and their needles. She was most gratifyingly eager to be of help, and murmured prayers of blessing over them, calling on the Old Great Gods to shed their purifying light on that darkened land.

The sixth-circle seers meanwhile warned of traitors within the town, apostates who had never truly converted in their hearts, but the place had long been ill-omened for those with wizardry in their blood; all the market-gossip told so. Its only wizard-born left, by and large, for happier lands farther east. Everyone agreed this was so. It was even whispered that the curse that left them so few children took also its toll on those born with the wizard-talent. Certainly the priests and priestesses of the sixth circle were ill-fated in Serakallash. They wandered into the desert night, or walked into dust-storms, hearing the voice of their god summoning them, they said, and sometimes, raving, wild-eyed, they called damnation down on those who tried to prevent them. Sometimes they simply dropped dead in the street, with no one to witness.

The Serakallashi were an angry folk, and the ferry-folk of Kinsai both angry and inventive. They turned the waking and the dreaming minds of the Westrons against themselves, and waged a war of small and gnawing fears, which, as the worm in the roof-beam, weakened them almost unawares.

Knight-Commander Balba led a force into the mountains, but was turned back by storm and snow. He chose to leave the mountain-folk be through the winter; they were going nowhere, and his efforts must be to keep the road open for the caravans carrying grain and fodder and mutton-fat from the storehouses of the Nearer Grass to supply the armies through the siege that was expected when they came to Marakand, which was difficult enough. There were raiders in the Black Desert and storms of both sand and snow in the Red. Rumours swept through his soldiers of creeping death-worms, the colour of the sand, which would emerge from the dunes and spit poison; the touch even of their shed husks was death. Patrols did not venture far from the fort, after the first few failed to return.

In the early spring, as the waters poured in torrents down the valleys, Balba

tried again, but discovered that the road that should have led to the town of Lis-
savakail and the temple of the goddess Attalissa disappeared beneath the surface
of an unexpected lake. His scouts reported a river dammed between high cliffs to
the west and the dam guarded by a single watchtower.

Commander Balba prepared to lead an expedition to seize the mountain
watchtower and destroy the dam, opening the road to Lissavakail and the wealth
of the mountain mines. A small company. The warrior-priestesses of Attalissa
were legend, he said, not a truth to be feared.

Not like the death-worms of the sands.

Perhaps Prince Dimas had taken his wiser commanders on to Marakand.

The air was heavy, hot, and they did not even have a wizard's light to
find their way. Not that there could be any turning aside, or any hazard
left to trip over that they had not left themselves. Jolanan was sweating
and not sure whether it was the close air or the darkness itself that was
so stifling. She felt she could hardly breathe, as if something squeezed her
like a giant fist about her ribs with every inhalation. A good horse under
her and a lance cradled in her arm . . . here she was a beetle under a stone,
waiting for someone to step on it and crush her.

Tashi, beside her, touched her arm. "All right?" A whisper. A breath.
The streets were too close above them.

She took a deep breath, aware, then, how her heart raced; she was
almost panting. She had avoided the tunnel, had always been in the warehouse, carrying the baskets of rubble, filling the emptied grain-bins, first,
and then raising the floor, layer by layer, till there were a few places where
the tallest men had to duck under the beams of the attic floor above,
where they ate their cold meals and slept in their exhausted shifts, lying
alongside one another, men and women, friends and strangers, so many
dust-coated corpses laid out, awaiting burial—

She wrenched her mind away from that thought, wiped her hand on
the skirt of her coat, crawled on.

"Yes," she told the young miner. "Sorry."

Hand touched hand. She didn't suppose even the miners, folk of villages from the territories of both Lissavakail and the Narvabarkash, felt at home in this utter dark.

This was blindness. This was the axe taking both her eyes.

"Steady," Rifat whispered, ahead of her. "Low place here. You'll fit, but keep down. Just keep going, don't panic. It's not far."

Was her fear so obvious?

They had been warned of this low place, where the digging had hit stone the miners said should not be cut away, for some mysterious miners' reason. Twenty paces long, Tashi had said. Not far at all, if you could stand upright and pace it. Crawling on your belly like a worm, with a mass of stone over you, a town, streets, buildings, weight pressing down . . .

"Sera is with us," Tashi said. Not his goddess, not hers, but she took a deep breath and repeated it, voiceless, but shaping the words like a prayer in her mouth. Sera is with us. Horse-goddess of Serakallash. Lady of the undying waters, who had survived a devil's conquest and been born again from a stone. Whisper of wind past her. The presence of the goddess.

Sera, and Attalissa and her brother Narva of the deep mines, who sent them here. And memory of Jayala, give her strength. She touched her temples, her cheeks, feeling not for scars, just touching the tattoos. She was of the Jayala'arad. She had fought wolf and bear and devil's scouts alone. She had ridden into battle at the Blackdog's side. She was not afraid of . . . a little dark, a little close space. She would not be.

"I'm beside you," Tashi said.

He always was. Jolanan was not certain how she felt about that.

Plenty of room, they had been told, those who had not yet been down the tunnel. You don't want to rear your head up, or your rump—a bit of weary laughter, a bit of poking at the stouter among them—but you won't get yourself hung up, even with your gear. Just go carefully, no more than two abreast, don't shove the person ahead, not everyone's easy in the dark, just keep going and we'll all get through fine. Everything's solid, everything's propped and braced where it needs to be propped and braced, the folk of Narva know what they're doing and the gods are with us.

Grit pattered down on them. Something happening, up above. It was night. Nothing should be passing in the streets. The earth itself, moving . . . no. Nothing to worry about. Rifat and the priestess with him were gone, an emptiness she could feel ahead, and Tashi's hand brushed her face, reaching back. Jolanan drew a deep breath, started after him. The hand that still clutched her ankle released her. Someone else taking a breath, nerving themself.

It was hard, crawling. Like swimming, legs splayed. Pushing with elbows. She kept her eye shut. Opening it made no difference and her face was covered in dust. It gritted between her teeth. Her breath huffed in her ears. Coat caught. Something tore. Sabre's weight still there, all that mattered. It was his, Holla-Sayan's, a good weapon, heavier than her own, the blade much worn, the scabbard scarred. She had given hers to a boy of Serakallash, a caravanserai-mistress's son who had no weapon of his own. His parents and elder sister had been killed in the fighting when the town fell. That might be him behind her, young Sayid Sevanim, with Sister Dorji. Like Tashi and Rifat, he and Dorji stuck close. As if she were someone to follow. Her own little band of raiders. If all failed, they could steal horses, take to the wilds . . .

If all failed, they would be dead. And probably before the sun rose.

Twenty paces? Cold hells, she had been squirming through this crack for far too long, quarter of a mile, surely, and the rock was growing heavier, lower, over her, the ground beneath shifting, loose. She gasped, clenched her teeth. Felt someone tap her foot. Sayid or Dorji. She had stopped. Been lying still. Old Great Gods. Please. Hand seized her wrist.

"Nearly there, Jo."

Tashi. She surged towards him, heard something whimper. Herself. Crawled out into his arms, his hand on her head to stop her braining herself, trying to get up to hands and knees too soon. Shivering, kneeling there with her face pressed to the gritty leather of his jerkin.

Have to keep moving. More behind. Make space. Not leave Dorji and Sayid in that tight place. Sayid was like her, child of big skies and long horizons. Her mind shaped the thought but she couldn't make herself move till Tashi tugged her on.

Got control of herself. This was nothing. This was mere darkness. Fear of it only served their enemy. The tunnel was broad and high, high enough to crawl, broad enough not to bang shoulders and hips with Tashi, though they kept close enough they were touching regardless. Crawled. And crawled. She wasn't the only one found terror in that close, low passage, she was certain. Sayid, when he emerged behind her, was muttering, "Sera with me, Sera with me, Sera my shield and my strength and the spear in my hand, Sera with me . . ." the words all broken, rapid panting, while Dorji kept murmuring, "Not far, not far now, not far," as much to herself as to him.

At least they wouldn't be going back that way.

The assembly area had been the easiest part of the tunnel. They were a small party—and Old Great Gods, she wished she hadn't felt obligated, for the honour of the Western Grass, or because Rifat had, or Tashi—whatever had driven her—to volunteer to be part of it. But sixty men and women seemed too few, in their planning, and far too many, crawling up this tunnel. Sixty-two, they were, beginning to sort themselves, standing, straightening backs, checking weapons, moving as swiftly as they could left or right, hands on a guide-rope, knowing their company. Cellars. Storerooms, once, of two cousins of the Rostvadim sept. Not even a whisper, now. They found places by touch, in their pairs. No spears: too awkward, too dangerous. Sabres, some of them, Serakallashi and ferry-folk of Kinsai. The sisters of Attalissa carried short-swords, the men and women of the mountains axes or long-handled hammers or clubs. And the wizards, Rifat, two others of Kinsai's folk, and Sister Pehma, who was wizard as well as priestess and commander of the tunnel expedition, bore baskets with fire, of a sort, sealed within clay. A secret of the folk of Kinsai.

Still no light. They could not risk any open flame down here and there were a few surviving priests of the sixth circle in the fort; the making of wizards' light might be detected, Pehma thought, though the wizards of Kinsai were dismissive of the Westrons' understanding of wizardry. Leave that for the last moment. Which was now.

There. A soft white-gold glow grew with a word from Rifat, echoed by a man in the other cellar. Almost blinding, though it was so very dim. Those who had shuffled into place facing the wrong way realigned themselves.

The wizards were the first up the ladders, two to each. Cautious, still. No furious rush, not yet. A careful lifting, shifting. Cool air flowing down, heavy with the scent of horses.

Time to move. She and Tashi were the nearest to Rifat. Up, into darkness. Stronger scent of horse and manure and dust. As promised, they were in the block of stables within the fort, where the horses of the knights were kept. Restless beasts. Snuffing and blowing at the strangers crawling like marmots from a burrow. Jolanan went, the smallest glimmer of wizards' light drifting to follow her as Rifat saw her intent, to where a man slept in a hammock hung by the door. Knife ready. But he held up a hand and rolled himself out, tall, lean Serakallashi, horse-tattooed face. Nodded to her and removed a sabre from beneath a heap of straw. Grinned, white teeth catching the light.

Dead man folded into the corner. His fellow in this watch on the stable.

The other trapdoor was out in the courtyard, but hidden close by the wall, where sand always drifted thick. Tashi and Rifat came to the door by her side.

The watch in the corner towers looked outward. Why should it do otherwise?

Boredom, perhaps. Some chance careless sound, though she had heard none. The wizards' lights were out, people only following close on one another and enough light from the full moon—they had planned it so—that they needed none in the courtyards.

A cry from the nearest tower. Rifat stepped past her and Tashi, loading a sling as he went. For a moment all was still, save for the whisper of the whirling sling in the air.

The top of the tower exploded into flame.

No need for command. They went, then, with a rush and a roar. Too late for silence. The burning tower was one that looked outward to the desert, not over the town. It might serve as distraction.

Two gates. She led the charge on the one that opened on the town. The soldiers posted there were a handful, overwhelmed as they rushed out of their guard-room. Only two on watch above and Sister Pehma and a trio of priestesses were up the stairs and dealing with those as Jolanan, with Tashi and a pair of heavyset mountain men, wrestled the bar of the gate free. Many hands hauled its leaves wide, and more fires broke out, Rifat and others, now, hurling the fire-globes into doorways and unshuttered windows.

Red light and whirling shadows, rushing figures, voices crying out on their gods. Soldiers of the All-Holy threw some internal door to make a brief bridge over flame and poured from their barracks, but the outer gate was open and hooves were pounding, pounding up the moon-silvered ridge-road out of the desert night.

Warriors of the septs from the far pastures. Not only hooves, but the softer thudding of the camels. Tribesfolk of the further reaches of the Red Desert, and of the Black. From the town, they swarmed afoot, spears glinting in firelight, and the wind blew with them, the fires climbed to pillars, to the flickering forms of horses, rearing, dancing, racing. Two buildings dark, still: the stables, and the squat square tower that was the dormitory and schoolroom of the captive children.

The shrieks of those still within the burning buildings was terrible.

The soldiers who had escaped did not flee, not then. Some officer kept them under control. They formed a close company and tried to break for the gate into town. Sensible, maybe. Seize some smaller defensible place, try to get a message away to the garrison of the Lower Castle on the Kinsai, or wait for Knight-Commander Balba to return victorious from his expedition into the mountains. They met with a shock and a clashing of steel. Armed, but few in any armour. Few enough, in all. They had marched out two days ago, now that the snows that had sealed the mountain road had melted, to take Lissavakail.

Jolanan was not used to fighting afoot and missed Lark's height, that feeling that she and the horse were one creature, a thing of mass and movement, a dance. Tashi had never fought for his life before. He swung his club with ferocity, yelling, but didn't see what moved around him, how his rush took him into the enemy, left him surrounded, and she yelled and went after him, shielding him. They were beset, turned back to back, and she had no shield to her blind side, could steal frantic glances, swing wide, but she realized Tashi was watching for her, trusting her to take the other two quarters, ahead and aside to the right, and so she kept those clear and the Westrons fell back from them, leaving the bloody dead.

Serakallshi face, horse-marked woman, leaping over a body, spear thrusting. And more, and more, and camel wheeling around them, a dark man, braids flying, crying something in a speech she didn't know, and she and Tashi leaned on one another. Gasping, the miner was, chest heaving. She, too. He wiped his face on his sleeve. The courtyard swirled with people, with torches, now, small embers against the burning buildings. Horses were whinnying, a child crying, but not in pain or even terror, only confusion. Someone had them safe, she thought, or that was the plan; they were to be hurried away out to the hall where the sept-chiefs met, where several elderly wizards of the Lower Castle of the ferry-folk, armed with tattooing-needles, were changing the design of the initiation tattoo into some pattern that, they promised, would undo the binding meant to steal their souls, if what they had quietly tried to work on the ink itself in the first days of the conquest had failed.

Which only the dead might know.

Perhaps thinking it did not bind them had been a comfort to the living, at least. There were Serakallashi dead in this yard, and certainly no one who had remained in the town had escaped tattooing.

Archers still shot from the flat roof of the central hall. Sisters of Attal-issa shot back. Sera strode among them, a tall woman, desert-brown, her hair, red as the sands, streaming back like the mane of a running horse. She stopped at Sister Pehma's side. The earth trembled. Jolanan clutched at Tashi to keep her balance.

The roof of the burning hall collapsed. The walls fell.

Spring, the wizards of Kinsai had said. Hope grew, in the spring.

Hope was a small thing. The All-Holy might yet look back at what happened in his rear. A small thing, but sharp as a blade.

"You're going back to your own folk," Tashi said. His voice was hoarse, smoke and dust and probably a craving for water as desperate as her own.

"Yes."

His hand was on her face, brushing back her hair, which was free of the thick braid she had put it in and stinging her eye, prickling her scars. She had lost her headscarf somewhere after they left the stables.

"I know—" he said. Dropped his hand and looked away. Not even dawn yet, though the moon was sliding down in the west. Not even dawn, and there were fire-tubes launching red and green flowers from somewhere to the south. Painting a victory on the skies. Signalling to those who watched in the dry hills. The sounds of people, voices loud. Singing.

Too soon, she thought. Too soon, too late—

"I'll come with you. To your land. Your folk. If you want me to."

"Leave the mountains? Your god?"

Tashi shrugged. Fingered one of the beads of turquoise he wore at his ears. "I can carry Narva in my heart, wherever I go. Travellers do."

"The Western Grass is a ruined land. Occupied. Even if Reyka and Lazlan have survived the winter—most of our gods are dead."

"If you're going, you shouldn't go alone."

She took the hand he had let fall, touched it to her lips. Taste of mud and sweat and blood that was probably not his.

"Tashi." Tasting, too, his name. "I don't—I'm not promising anything. I can't yet. I just don't know—" Know what? Herself, maybe. But—she would miss him, achingly. As she missed Holla, still. "Can you ride?"

"They're coming," Attalissa said. Iarka only nodded. She should not be here, but she had ignored the old women—cousins in this degree or that, for the most part—who wanted to hide her and her precious belly away. Precious baby, not belly, and she was an active one, now, pummelling Iarka from within, as if she were angry. Rose, Iarka called her. Little Rose, because . . . Rose. Not lovers, the two of them. Only the best of friends and . . . yet it was Iarka and the surgeon Rose whom Kinsai had called to her, of all the couples she might have asked; them she had asked, to do this thing. So they had lain together in the river and found they might have been lovers after all, that between them there could be not only friendship, but passion they had never suspected.

A strange and heartbreaking thing it had been to realize that.

So the baby was Little Rose, whatever other names she might come to carry, and she was angry now, but she would grow to be wise, and a healer, like her father, of hearts and souls.

Assuming Iarka did not get herself skewered with a Westron arrow first. That thought did make her duck down again, safe—safer—below the line of boulders that looked some natural tumble of the mountains, but was not. A parapet, of sorts. Notches for archers. Caverns, behind.

Below, the lake. Not the Lissavakail, the lake of Attalissa. The new lake, which had so taken her aback, exhausted, grief-stricken as she had been, when it barred her way to the sanctuary of the goddess's town.

Ice still held it, though the snows had melted, save on the unmelting heights, and the rivers and brooks had thawed.

A bad winter, it had been. The worst in living memory. Attalissa, and Narva of the further valleys too, had gathered cloud and storm about them, but they had only shaped, a little, the direction of the storms, not spun them from nothing. The ice of the still lakes was thick.

"You should go back now," Attalissa said.

From her, Iarka didn't mind it. It wasn't fussing; it was just an opinion.

"I'll stay by you."

"Hm."

She needed to be here. She needed to fight, and if the cousins couldn't see it, couldn't understand—

She was fed up with them, dearly as she loved them all—most of them—some of them—seeing not her, but the baby, and not the real baby, her baby and Rose's, but some idea, some—hope.

Which was all of theirs, yes, but—it was also Rose, Little Rose. Who kicked her in the bladder just then.

Attalissa's mouth twitched at her grunt, the hand to her belly.

"If you can't keep me safe—what use hiding back at Lissavakail?"

"A head start, running for the Narvabarkash?"

"And where then? I'll be waddling, not running, before too many more weeks pass."

She wore armour, a shirt of scales made for some rather stouter man.

"Hold till my word," the grey-haired Spear-Lady, commander of the sisters, said quietly, and the word was passed from one six-woman dormitory, as they called their patrols, to the next.

In the watchtower on the north side of the lake where the road plunged under the ice they did not hold, but they were not asked to. They shot, picking off officers where they could. Arrows, lead bullets of the slings. A mere handful. The commander of the Serakallashi garrison did not command from the van, but midway back in the column, easy to spot. Only he and a score of knights were mounted. Before they came within range of the tower there were Westron soldiers smashing its one door, pouring up the ladders within, no doubt, pushed from behind, those in the lead reluctant, wary, if they had any sense.

The half-dozen sisters who had shot from the roof were meanwhile descending by ropes down the further side, scrambling away into the cliffs, leaving the tower deserted.

Cowards. Iarka took a grim pleasure imagining the Westrons' first thoughts. Cowards, and then, perhaps, a growing apprehension. Though these were all of the Army of the South, they would have heard the tale of the destruction of the Upper Castle. Yes, there they came, in haste, not lingering to hold the empty tower. One running back down the road to report to the commander, but the vanguard was already on the ice.

The tower failed to collapse or offer any other threat. No ambush broke from the mountainsides. A pair of rash Westrons tried to follow up the cliffs.

They fell, dark figures dropping like a lammergeier launching from its nest, limbs spread, failing to unfurl into winds and rise. Perhaps a thrown stone or two had helped.

The edges of the lake thawed where they were sun-gnawed, fringed with dark shallows, but the ice beyond was still thick and clear, where wind had swept the snow away, pale where it lay packed into a rough crust. Balba had left it almost too late. They had begun to fear he would await a later season and attempt the destruction of the dam, though he had few wizards and fewer engineers, by what the Serakallashi reported. The former had been quietly hunted by Iarka's kin and the latter taken on to Marakand by Prince Dimas. Though Attalissa's folk could likely have defended that narrow, precipitous place better than this broad expanse of ice. To merely hold a line was not their intent.

Nerves wound tighter and tighter, as if someone turned the crank of a windlass. All up and down this steep side. Would the ice hold? Balba was known a fool, but not all his under-officers were so. The van had spread out, and men walked cautiously. Not mountain folk, not winter folk. Iarka saw not one having the sense to carry his spear crossways so as to catch himself should the ice give way beneath him. But once they passed the halfway point without disaster they signalled back, a waving banner, and the rest came on in closer order. Good, that was good.

"Not yet," Spear-Lady murmured to some young woman who let out her breath, drawing her bow.

The goddess at Iarka's side watched with the intensity of a cat at a mousehole. Snow-leopard, maybe, eyes fixed on the shepherd's flock in the valley below. Grim. No smile, no pleasure in what she anticipated. Well, no. And no god should take pleasure in death, even that of enemies. Iarka rubbed her hand over her belly. Cold bronze plates. No comfort.

You hear, Little Rose?

Closer. And closer. Too close, surely. Balba himself was well out, halfway over.

A crack that echoed between the mountainsides. Even Attalissa looked startled. Horses shied. They rode too close, too great a weight. They were fools. They hesitated, which was further folly, before they spread themselves. Nothing happened and Balba stood in the stirrups, waving them on.

The rearmost company was starting onto the lake, but the van was almost to where water lapped over the ice again.

"Now," Spear-Lady cried, roared to the echoing heights, and Iarka with the rest drew aiming and loosed, and laid the second arrow she held and loosed again, and with each she made thought a curse, a second strike. *Die, in Kinsai's name.*

Some few of the vanguard made it to the shore, but none up the cliffs. Caught without shelter, they shot blind at movement guessed at behind the parapet, threw spears meant for thrusting.

Attalissa bowed her head. She wavered, no longer a woman, breathing, sweating, scuffed and wind-tousled. A shadow, a reflection as if seen on lake water, a girl, a woman, layered faces, young, white-haired, indigo-gowned, bronze-armoured, wearing a striped caravaneer's coat, hair cropped short, veiled in blue, in a net fringed with golden coins, long hair in a caravaneer's braids . . . A thing that was not woman at all, not a shape but snow and wind, green valleys and dark deep water . . .

The ice shivered, and—did not crack. Spring took the lake. A fog rose, billowing, and the ice went opaque and rotten in a breath, the work of days of warming air.

The cries were terrible. They did not last long.

Two of the horses made it to the shore.

Some of the men, too, of the rear company. They milled in confusion on the far shore, until arrows and sling-shot began to hammer on them from above. Rather more than the single dormitory that had held the tower was there. The Westrons began a fighting retreat, but there were sisters with spears and swords on the road behind them. Iarka did not see the end of it, as they made a rush for the north, but none came again to Serakallash.

The near shore was cleared before long, spearwomen descending. The soldiers of the All-Holy did not accept any offer to take their surrender.

Iarka waited it out at the goddess's side. That much sense, at least. Felt herself remote, floating distant, above the death. Felt the deaths as she never had, saw them. Saw the lives, burning bright, flicker out in pain and confusion and, among the Westrons, growing terror. As they were snatched away.

This is what we fight. This, even more than invasion, than conquest, than slavery and death of the body. This theft of the soul.

Iarka wasn't sure it was her thought. She wasn't sure it was Attalissa's, who stood at her side again, a human woman to all seeming, but for the light that burned through her, the sense that she was water and stone and shimmering reflection of the high peaks.

"We must open the sluices with care, once we hear from Serakallash and know that it's safe to clear our road again," Attalissa said. "We don't want to send all this down in a flood."

Iarka nodded. She would have liked to feel some joy in this. Satisfaction, even. She had thought she might.

A victory, but not her own.

Serakallash, Lissavakail—so they pushed the weight of the All-Holy aside a little. Broke his supply line of the road. That did not free the Western Grass, and did not free the shores of the Kinsai'av.

Lightning strikes, and strikes again, and again, and in the end the forest blazes. The voice was one she had heard in her dreams through the winter. A voice, sometimes near, sometimes remote. A woman's voice, speaking as if to itself, conversational.

Go back to your river, child of Kinsai, mother of Kinsai. That wounded land will be a long time healing. It will need all the care you can give it.

And what of Jochiz, who had devoured its gods? This was no victory. This was only a small yapping at the heels of a great beast, which would turn and strike them down, hurl them broken aside, once it had dealt with the larger prey before it. And when he had Marakand under his heel, and had swallowed Gurhan, would he turn back, for the gods of the deserts and mountains, or roll onwards, growing and growing, and draw all the world in to him?

She dreamed it so, sometimes.

In her vision, there was a shape against stars, though the sky had been blue afternoon. A sword, and it was—absence of light. Frost edged it.

Iarka blinked it away. The Blackdog was lost to Jochiz and so was the Northron devil's sword, and she did not know who spoke in her dreams.

Crisis passed, the baby resumed pummelling her in the vitals.

She most urgently needed to find a discreet corner to squat in, before the brat burst her bladder.

CHAPTER XXIX

. . . a few days past the full moon following the spring equinox; Serakallash is rising, the Western Wall of Marakand is besieged, and Yeh-Lin, riding the winds, descends on the Western Grass

From the Chronicle of Nikeh gen'Emras

*T*he Upper Castle of the folk of the goddess of Kinsai was destroyed by its own defenders, and it seems likely that many of the All-Holy's high officers who had overseen the conquest of the Western Grass died there, though the All-Holy himself and those closest to him survived its collapse. When Jochiz led the greater part of the Army of the North on to the Great Grass, the occupation force that remained worked, it was said, night and day, to bridge the Kinsai, quarrying the hills of the eastern shore. Many West-grasslander conscripts died in that labour, and many eager Westron believers as well. The Lower Castle below the Fifth Cataract, occupied by a smaller garrison, for the lands west of it over the Kinsai were marshy in winter and less useful a road to the east, was gutted by fire some time after the ferry-folk abandoned it. Whether that fire had been mischance, or the work of some spell laid before the evacuation, or even the hand of a daring and desperate West-grasslander, I have not heard. No attempt to bridge the river was made there in the south. The governor of the land, the prince of Rigo, ordered instead a wooden watchtower to be built on the western shore of the river below the Fifth Cataract, and made his own headquarters at the fortified bridge to the north of the First.

It was a winter of hard frosts and deep snows on the Western Grass, such as had never been known in living memory. Many folk and many herds knew hunger, and occupier and occupied alike suffered and died of lung-fever, not only children and the old, but adults in the strength of life.

Yet still the governor plundered the stores of the land, and conveyed even much of the seed-grain east in the army's wake, to supply the intended siege of Markand.

The Kinsai'av was below her, and the Western Grass stretched out beyond, a sea of rolling, grassy swells. The dead king would be sarcastic, should she take up assassination. Better to leave such matters to the professionals, yet it was a long way from Marakand to the west, if you could not ride the winds. And she thought the city had greater need of him.

Nabban had always wanted to reach the western ocean, though. Following the sun, he had said of himself. He would have liked this land, too, she thought. A place of sky and grass and small stony waters. He might have been glad, had Yeh-Lin brought Ahjvar with her.

To see through his eyes.

It did not seem right, to use the dead king as his god used him. She, Dotemon, would never think it right, no matter how much she, Yeh-Lin, found herself . . . envying that love, that gave and held and trusted and did not betray. A wistful sort of envying. But perhaps conviction of wrongness was born of her nature, something deep, too deep ever to change. A *knowing* that a soul of the earth should not be bound so; it should die out of its humanity, and yet carry that, too, and flow onwards . . .

Which was what brought her west, yes, but this small matter first. And if it turned the attention of Jochiz from Marakand a little, and yet from his heartland as well, all the better.

The river swirled over the ruined foundations of the Upper Castle. A strangely desperate act, the self-sacrifice of its last defenders, who might have fled with their kin days, even weeks earlier. They had delayed Jochiz's plans not one whit. She had never thought the ferry-folk fools. She did not believe she should think so now. The great destruction, the great sacrifice—there had been purpose, there, beyond a gesture of futile defiance worthy of a fool Northron. She hoped some day she might learn what it had been.

The new six-arched bridge over the Kinsai'av was a fort in itself, the roadbed passing through a fortified tower at either end, with another pierced tower over a pier in the deepest part of the channel. The artery between west and east, pumping the heart's-blood of his own land away and draining the Western Grass to keep his armies fed and clothed and otherwise supplied. Built in stone quarried from the eastern hills—not a good or lasting stone, she did note. Not something she would have had her masons and engineers use for anything but rubble fill, if that. Interesting, for what such work said about Jochiz and his intentions. He did not, as the builders of the castles had, plan for the centuries.

He never had taken pride in the elegance and good of a thing for its own sake.

The western tower was well within a larger curtain-wall. Stonework in places, earth and palisades in others, all rough and hasty, already frost-heaved and crumbling, with another gate-tower and lesser ones as well, anchored on the river.

Given command over an offensive strike against the Westrons here, she would find some of those Northrons who brought their river-ships to the Bakanav by the portage from the Varr'aa, and have them sail down from At-Landi to attack from the river while her engines struck at the gates of east and west . . . but she would not have let Sien-Shava Jochiz down out of the Karas in the first place, she would not have let her people remain a folk of little scattered clans who could not rise and act as one, she would . . .

Well, yes.

Jochiz had slain gods, in this land. He did not play by the rules of humanity any longer.

It was not General Nang Yeh-Lin who looked over the bridge from on high, dropping lower, the winds that wrapped and carried her a roar in her ears, a raging torrent of air.

Dotemon came down on the roof of the central tower, arms spread, sword already in hand, trailing scarves of cloud. The river below rose in a confused fury of whitecaps and settled again. No one to greet her. No watch kept here, but from the western tower there was a cry. She gave the sentries there a cheerful wave.

The setting sun hung low over the horizon. If she were the lord of this keep . . . Humming to herself, Yeh-Lin started down the stairs, and not with the grave, grim caution the dead king would no doubt advise. Not quite skipping. She had always favoured the swift strike.

Her mirror had told her that her quarry favoured this tower. Further from the noise, the dust, the soldiery of the garrison. A most beautifully appointed hall, where he and his lady held court as princes. And surely this was the hour to dine . . .

A glance out an arrowslot to the west warned of soldiers running, five of them on the bridge, halfway to the tower. She thrust open the nearest door. A plainly dressed woman within the antechamber was folding linens, and the bedchamber beyond empty.

"Were I you, I should head for the shore," Yeh-Lin told her, speaking Tiypurian. She continued on her way. Shouts below. She leapt the last few steps to the next landing, kicked back a wide door. Ah, the dining chamber, as she had seen. A white-draped table, polished bronze mutton-fat lamps in the Westgrasslander style, plentiful meats . . . a woman in a priest's gown stood at a lectern, reading aloud from some heavy tome. The wisdom or the prophecies of the All-Holy, no doubt. She looked up, mouth open on a word half-formed. Footsteps pounding the stairs. Yeh-Lin shoved the door to behind her and set a word on the latch, which would hold it as well as the bar it did not have. Guards to either side— she swung left, then whirled to the right, three strides into the room as they fell behind her and she leapt to the table, danced down it avoiding every dish and lamp—let us *not* put our feet in the butter—sweeping, slashing, left and right, faster than mortal woman might move. A seer of the sixth circle leapt away, overturning his chair—all the high officers of the fort were here, it seemed, a piece of good fortune for which she would not thank the Old Great Gods nor yet Nabban, whose disapproval of this dance she suspected—she wrapped the wizard-priest's rising words in her hand, a twist and they were taken from him. He gabbled silent, pop-eyed, and fell clutching his heart, which was not actually her doing but his own terror. The reader flung her book and seized up the heavy lectern, whirling it. Quick-witted, at least. Yeh-Lin dropped her with a word that turned to a dart of fire and left a black scorched hole in the breast of her gown.

Smashing wood. Axe to the door.

The governor of the Western Grass was said to be styled the prince of Rigo, one of the lesser towns on the Tiy, several generations old in the worship of the All-Holy. A fortunate man in that he had clearly not been foremost among those who had seized the Upper Castle. On his feet and a knife in his hand, his wife thrust behind him, but likewise ready with her knife, teeth bared and panting with her fear. Not, today, so fortunate, either of them.

She swept the head from his neck as the crossbow's string slapped behind her, burnt the unseen bolt in the air with a word spat out that human tongue could not have uttered, felt the air edged in cold. The lady of the fort lunged over her husband's body, fallen half on the table, flooding it dark, and Yeh-Lin split her skull. The soldiers who had forced the door were running as she turned, fleeing swifter than they had come, and a puddle of melting fat was burning, blue-edged, where a lamp had been overturned.

Yeh-Lin snatched up the prince of Rigo's head by its short forelock and walked back the way she had come, letting her trophy drain. One or two still lived. She left them. They did not matter.

They mattered. Nabban would surely say they mattered. Even these.

She had forgotten how messy a thing the head would be. Leapt down to tug off the cope from the man whose heart had failed, to bundle it in.

Ahjvar would no doubt criticize the lack of elegance.

No souls. There were no souls left in the room, save the two still living, cowering into a corner, clutching one another. Serving folk.

She paused. Looked back. "The bridge is doomed," she said. "Your god is a lying devil and the Old Great Gods have cursed him. Run, now." And she nudged them, found the shape of fear. No need to kindle what already burned high; she only set the drive in them: *flee, flee this place.*

They squeaked. They fled.

She could not, reaching further, tell servant from soldier. But every soldier who died was one less to stand against the Westgrasslanders, yes?

She retraced her steps to the tower roof. The sun was lurid in the west, touching the horizon now, staining the sky, smeared cloud.

She had not enjoyed that as she had thought to. Justified, surely. But—helpless as a basket of kittens, and their souls torn away from the road that would have taken them.

What would you have me do? Fight them one by one, and pretend to humanity so that they might have the illusion of a chance of survival? They are justly condemned. They stood by while he sacrificed children to shape the deaths of gods. If I brought them in chains to Nabban, they would kneel for the executioner's axe and you would bow your head and say, yes.

Nothing answered. Nothing argued.

Would she have had Nikeh see that?

Enough. She stamped a foot on the tower's roof, then sprang up to the crenellated parapet.

"This is the untamed Kinsai'av," she said. "And what the Warden Kinsai's son decreed for his castle, I for this bridge, which constrains what should not be constrained, and binds what should not be bound, and exists only to feed death. *Let it fall.*" Whispered the last, not wizardry but devil's will. She felt the force of the world in the words, the inevitability.

Fed her own life into it, just a little, rather than let it sear the world, even in small things. Enough. Because . . . because . . . *What would you have me do?* A small weakening. It hardly mattered.

She turned into the dance, cutting the air with her sword, binding it in ribbons and hair, knotting the swift-flowing winds to serve, and leapt up and away.

A stone slipped away beneath her foot. Another followed. Splash. And splash.

And a roar, and the water churning white.

The camp of the Westgrasslander warlord was on a hill within a meander of the Bakanav, defended on the north by a ditch and bank. Sod-built halls alternated with corrals in curving ranks. Scattered north, east, west were similar camps, or perhaps the seeds of villages, settlements of those who had fled over the rivers, with what herds and flocks they had managed to drive with them, cattle, horses, camels, sheep. It was marshy land, not choice pasturage, outright swamp in places, and the camps were all on small hillocks above the spring flooding. Lands the guild-masters of At-Landi and the elders of the villages around and about it had agreed to spare them. Yeh-Lin doubted whether the Westgrasslanders knew themselves if they intended to stay.

She let herself down softly. The wind gusted wild, dogs barked, but the sentries on the rough wooden tower only snatched at their scarves, looking outward. Fog coiled off the river and the standing water in the fields. She combed fingers through hair, shook her coat of armour straight, and took up the stained bundle she had set at her feet again.

"Gods bless the hall," she sang out in the language of the western road. Her Westgrasslander was rather out of practice, to put it mildly. "A messenger from Marakand."

The door—a cowhide curtain—was already being pulled aside as she approached. Firelight within silhouetted those who barred the way, squinting uncertainly into the night. Armed, both of them.

She held up her free hand, cupping pale light.

"How—?" the man of the pair demanded, looking beyond her for escort.

"Arpath!" the woman called back into the hall. "A wizard—get over here!" And to Yeh-Lin, "We'll have your name and business, mistress."

That was fair enough. Yeh-Lin bowed. "Yeh-Lin Dotemon. Servant of Nabban—the god and his land. I've come to bring your warlord a gift."

The man's eyes now were on the once-white cloth, his sabre in his hand. "What sort of a gift?"

The woman was repeating, "Dotemon?" under her breath.

More figures coming to the door, and there were people behind her now, drawn by the voices. She did not look around.

"The prince of Rigo," she said to the man. She smiled over his shoulder. That, she thought, was Reyka herself. A tall, grey-haired woman, with a lean man very like in face at her shoulder. "At least, such as is left of him. A mere token. The greater part of the gift is down the Kinsai'av. Or perhaps I ought better to say, under it. Jochiz's bridge is broken and the commanders of the fortress have gone down with it. Though I did not stay to break down the gates of the fort. Perhaps, looking back, I should have done so. Still, if you can find boats and water-folk of some sort in At-Landi, you may come at them from both sides while they remain in some . . . disarray. Headless, in fact."

"Arpath?" Reyka asked, of the young man at her other side. Wizard. A handsome-enough lad, but Yeh-Lin had never found the way some folk tattooed themselves for their gods particularly decorative, herself.

She had felt the wizard's tasting of her words. Smiled at him, let him see her, fully, just a moment. He took a step back.

"Devil," he said. Licked his lips. "She's—who she says, chief, but—"

"An honest devil," Yeh-Lin said. Her eyes found another man, not a tattooed Westgrasslander. He looked Nabbani, and not Taren. He bowed, when he saw her eyes on him, and his fingers flicked a sign. Ah. Awe in his eyes, when he straightened up, but no distrust. Near worship, which should be reserved for his god.

"Yeh-Lin Dotemon is said to serve my god," he told the warlord. "She's been long away from the land, but I've never heard she was unfaithful."

"I serve him now," Yeh-Lin said, and added, in Imperial, "Wind in the Reeds? You'd be one of the agents sent to observe the Western Grass a year ago? Your reports to the ambassador have been very sparse of late. I believe he thinks you lost to the Westron advance."

"Hani Kahren." A wary look flicked to an untattooed caravaneer who stood by him. Possibly she spoke some Imperial, or enough Marakander or Taren Nabbani to catch more than a shadow-servant of the empress's might wish. The woman did frown, as if puzzling over her understanding. "There weren't many travelling east over the winter, my lady. Or at all, with the Westron army between us and Marakand. And the autumn was—hectic."

"Indeed it was. I am heading west myself, or I would offer to take a letter. What of your partner?"

"She left with a caravan before the Westrons reached the Sayan-barkash. I stayed because—they're valiant riders and fighters, these tribesmen, but they needed a few who know real cavalry." A hesitation. "Did Hani Jin never come to Marakand?"

"No."

A brief silence. Then, only, "She was my cousin," he said.

No apology for freely interpreting his orders, though he was naturally apprehensive. And that was a very great difference between the horse-boy's empire and hers.

She found it rather refreshing, really.

"I don't question your choices. It's not me you answer to. Nor, ultimately, the ambassador. If you can aid this folk in heaving Sien-Shava Jochiz off their backs, you'll be serving the empress and our god and I think the gods of all this world more than risking your life to tell the ambassador what all Marakand already knows. It's not as though we didn't watch him coming. The city was besieged when I left. And I'm sorry for your cousin."

He bowed again, shook his head at the other caravaneer, who had begun to shape some question.

"Will someone," Yeh-Lin asked, switching languages once more, "please take this wretched head? I brought it lest you doubt my word."

The door-ward, if that was the nearest man's role, took the cloth from her, gingerly. She wiped her fingers on her thigh.

"So," she said. "I demand nothing, only suggest, Warlord Reyka. Were I you, I would not wait for a new commander to find his feet and decide that the Western Grass is a kingdom for the taking in his false god's absence, nor yet for a cabal of priests to do the same. I would muster what aid I could from At-Landi, send word to those allies you may have among the folk of the Great Grass, and ride to liberate your folk, camp by camp, tower by tower. Your strength is no greater than it was yesterday, and theirs, for all they have lost their governor and some of his officers, little less, but make the fall of the bridge a sign. Let the wizards and the bards speak of it so—they are still out there among your folk, the brave and the reckless, are they not? Even within the walls of the Westron camps? Say, a wind of hope blows from the east. Say, Sien-Shava Jochiz has ridden to his doom at Marakand. Say, the god Nabban sends west the devil who serves him, to strike at the heart of the All-Holy's power, and all the lands and their gods shall be free." Half she chanted it, shaped a poet's prophecy. It was not, but let it give them hope. She would not linger to do much more. To draw the attention of Jochiz to herself, rather than to what she hoped might be the beginning fractures of his too-attenuated lines—he could not live off the Great Grass, nor yet the Stone Desert—was not what she intended.

"Too many of our gods and goddesses are dead," the lean man by Reyka said.

"Yes," she answered, and heard herself say, "And yet, a god may come again." Blinked, distracted.

Not intending prophecy, no. But the mirror—

—was clouded, when she considered it, shaping in mind the shadow of what she carried, close within her clothing. And she would have it clear, there was only . . .

Grass blowing in waves, and the wind, and the grass was the river, and the waves ran endless and dark.

"The Old Great Gods be with you," she said, for what confidence that might give in her good faith, if the severed head and Hani Kahren's word were not enough. She bowed, and turned to find a crowd behind, men, women, boys and girls surely too young to be riding to battle, but their faces said they were not any longer those boys and girls they first seemed.

Gods lost, a land lost . . . She turned back. "And if no one has yet told you, there is a great and foul devil's magic in the initiation tattoos of the cult, worked in the ink itself as well as the pattern. It steals the soul of any so marked. They will never come to the Old Great Gods, never travel the road to their far heavens. Obliterate it. Blot it out, remake the pattern, scar it if you must. Deny him your own folk, and any of his you take living as well. And now—give me room. I call the winds."

CHAPTER XXX

. . . the last quarter of the waning moon, and the Western Wall is falling

A shape has been set. It has lain quiet, but not quiescent. Growing. Threading a way. Not a binding. An unloosing. A becoming . . . a map, Ahjvar would say, unrolling. A delicate thing, liable to destruction if discovered.

This is a pattern woven from a dance, the shaping of a sword's edge, the binding of the sacred twigs of wizardry. No matter that the dance was never danced, the sword never drawn, the twigs only small grasses, knotted, blessed with the shaping of Ahjvar's lean, strong fingers, swallowed, taken in, carrying what they wove. Growing. Thread by thread, weaving a way. Subtle. It must be subtle, slow, to unfold beneath the devil's gaze.

To lay a trail, to map a way—grass. Let the way be made in grass. It is magic, human magic, and that is how human magic works.

Ghu thinks so, anyway. He has never really understood. But there are many things he has never really understood.

A god might not move beyond his land, but a god, they have proven, may be carried. A little. In a dream. A touch, and now . . . he, they, Ahjvar who holds to him, is held by him in the bonds of an ancient curse turned to promise, have hold too of this pattern they have made, this promise, this path . . . and the walls that surround and blind and the chains that bind and the weight that crushes . . . are grown thin. Are stretched, too far, nearly too far, forcing through walls and wards, combed away, peeled back—image tumbles image, a poet's drunkenness.

They matter, even as a poet's elusive truth. They are all truth, and nothing but words for what has no shape of words.

In a dream, he might reach. Then. Now. Though Ahjvar isn't here, where the Blackdog hunts. Not now. Not yet. But the shape is set, and already he walks it (they walk it?) this lost soul—these lost souls.

Only let him (let them?) see, let the way he has made, they have made, he and Ahj between them, be understood. Let it draw the lost one home.

God might strain to reach to god—to reach to drowning man, fingers stretched, a reach too far, unbridgeable.

But he has a bridge beyond his borders. Heart within heart. The shape, the dance, the writing of the sword's edge . . . most tenuous bridge, finger-touch. Warmth. Not fire. Sun's warmth. Home warmth. Hearth warmth, embracing.

Let this be its time, the grass, the calling sky, the shape of a way.

Yes, now, with binding chains far-stretched, with that grim hold pared away by what the devil Vartu shapes as shield, god may reach to god, through god to man, to devil. May touch that threefold knot of souls and call.

In hope. Hawthorn. Cornel. Elder.

His brother's enemy. Long hatred, which Sarzahn did not feel. He never had—this enmity was his brother's affair and he did not understand, nor need to understand, its roots—but he had lost the warmth, the close embrace of his brother, as he crossed down out of the mountains, over the road. As if he moved into some thick and heavy place. With the waking noise of the Suburb about him, a stray dog, slinking in the last of the night's shadows, he had felt his brother's touch grow yet lighter, yet more remote. As if the seeping grey of morning might burn it off like mist on the spring grass.

It was bad that it should be fading, his awareness of his brother's touch. It was a shield, a shelter. His brother's arm about him, always. There was wizardry worked in Marakand, great wizardry, and woven through it ran other powers. A devil. A god.

It was a thicket of thorns, to bar the way to his brother, and he might yet slip through but they pricked and tore and shredded him, shredded the safety of his brother's embracing arm,

Rope, fraying. Chains, rusting. Wire, stretched and overstretched . . .

Some . . . thing . . . stirring, stretching. Dangerous.

Crossing the city walls—that had been pain. Like being born, he had thought, and wondered at it, because women surely bore the pain of birth, but did not babies howl? Scored, clawed, struggling, where once he had swarmed up walls and leapt down them. But he had made it through, as his brother wished, and once within the city walls he had breathed again, and rested, and snapped at flies and at something like flies, buzzing, nagging, whispering within him, which irritated ears that did not hear it.

His brother would soothe such voices away, but his brother was out of reach, or he was, strange to think so. A faint and distant presence. Alarming. Almost panic. Almost he had turned, to run back to him, to be sure he was not dead, lost to this world, his brother, his—

. . . my god and my brother, you are a part of me . . .

It was for him to lead the way. It always had been.

He would do what he had come to do, and return. He would be in his brother's sight again, safe under his hand, and all would be well.

No.

The woman was limp in his grip and the demon bear motionless, teeth bared, crouched to spring, which he would not. Sarzahn had only to bite—

And would she die? He thought not. Not so easily. His brother—had been waiting. His brother had thought he might follow, this time, where Sarzahn led, through what rents he made in devil's working, the unseen shielding thorns that walled this city. Jochiz had meant to join him in this death—

To ride you, possessing—

—to savour this taste of blood in the mouth. Together they could have unmade the weaving of her souls, devoured—

No.

Been devoured? He, too?

Where did that thought come from? It felt like his own.

He was lost. He reached, frantic, heart racing, a lost child though frozen statue-still, and found it, faint, but true, his brother's touch.

Sarzahn seized him, held fast to Jochiz. His safety. His rock to cling to, storm-battered shelter. He gathered himself to call, he would summon his brother, as he had when he had fought the dead man and been so inexplicably weak and failing, as if poisoned, as if his own bone and blood and nerve denied him—as if—

No. Turn away. Hear me.

Hear—

Not the devil. She did not move, did not speak, quiet and still as a puppy carried in its mother's mouth. As if that might lull him, turn him from his intent.

Hear—

Sarzahn, he heard, so distant, so weakened, it might have been memory, but it was his brother's voice, his touch, reaching for him. *My brother.*

And he snarled, with no words in it, but the word in his mind was, *Lie. Jochiz, that is a lie.*

His own paw, clawed on the earth, splayed wide, black-haired, black nails worn short from his running, from mountain stone, from—paw, hand, snake's head tattooed, it twined with the cheetah up his arm, needle's prick remembered, long, long work, building, building, smarting, aching, to something worse, to be endured . . . the ritual, the passage made, to be an adult and not a child, to be marked, declared for his god—Illusion. Dog's paw.

His god. Sayan. His name was Sayan.

Do you hear, at last?

The air smelt of frost.

There was nothing to hear, but the devil Vartu . . . listened. As if she heard a song he could not. Her blood was in his mouth.

There was . . . not a song. A taste of bitterness, and he choked, he felt it, flooding through him, what he had swallowed, it burned in lines, in hooks and thorns such as fenced the city; it wrote in him; it raced deep; it seared—

Not him, but what was in him. Hooks and thorns? Chains.

It burnt them all away.

He was blind, and deaf, the world torn from him, he from the world. Lost. Darkness. Void. No earth, no sky, no light, no wind, no warmth.

He howled.

Jochiz was gone and he was lost, as he had been lost, when Jochiz found him, when Jochiz saved him, his brother—

My god, my brother—

He was held. He was—not alone. Never. Not in himself. He was—

They were—

We. My god and my brother.

Sayan.

He.

I.

Here, now, in this place I make again between us—and the voices that cried out in his mind, in his heart, the voices that had never been silent, that had raged and called to him unheard, buried deeper than the dead within, they were not this voice, they were silent, too, and they listened, he listened, with all that was in him, in this fearful place of nothingness. *Like to like and what my own has woven, a bridge between*—*you hear me now. Like to like, by that bridge. Stand against him. Remember what you are.*

Vartu. Shape of a name, taste of it. His enemy. His brother's enemy. And he was Sarzahn, yes, and he must not trust, he must—his brother—

Was he your brother? A mild curiosity.

No. His—he found the shape of the idea, the thing it might have been, words.

Shield-bearer. Startled, considered that. The wrong word. Not a word of his people at all. The idea . . . not so inapt. Yes, *shield-bearer*, it might be. At his side. Following. Following into—

What was forbidden. What was—alien, overwhelming, they should not have, they should have debated, persuaded by other means—they had not understood—they had never dreamed what the world might do to them—

They sought to distract him. They sought to destroy. These voices, all of them—his enemies and his brother's enemies and he thrust the words away.

No, Sarzahn. Listen. Can you hear? But it was not Vartu who shaped those words.

In his dreams, there were always voices. They whispered, but the wind took their words.

What wind?

There was wind. Sudden. Fierce. Clean.

The wind took him. He staggered upright. He hurt, every bone of him hurt, and he tasted blood, and he smelt her, Vartu. They had fought—

They had fought the devil Tu'usha. He and she. Together. Allies. But this was not that, not rubble, not ruin. Not the hard victory, Tu'usha defeated. Not Vartu standing by him, battered, weary, wounded and heartsick, telling him something—she—he could smell her but he could not see her—he needed to remember that day, the pain in his head, his eye, the woman, not the devil, yes, the beautiful, lean, dark, weary woman sitting in the dust by the caravanserai gate—

Gaguush. Her name had been Gaguush.

Gang-boss. Lover.

Wife. Waiting.

There was, distant in the darkness, a faint light. A warmth, and he was very cold.

Sun slanted, setting, throwing long spears of light through broken cloud, bright on the grass, and the purple dark between. Wind ran in waves, wind became horses, running . . .

Sheep on the hills, blue cattle, broad-horned, in the valleys. They raised their heads to watch the wind-horses running . . .

He thought he saw the wind-horses, running, though they were a myth older than this land, these gods, a myth, a poet's fancy spun out of the rippling of the grass. He saw them, which no one ever had. Fleeting glimpse. White horse, and dark bay, running, running, running in darkness, silent, no ground beneath their hooves. They were with him here, in this emptiness that was where he . . . existed. Only that. Tall, swift horses of a breed he did not know, and they shed starlight, snowlight, like drops of water scattered fording some shallow stream. Fording the darkness, the night, the emptiness that was close and thick and smothering, muffling sound and sight and thought. He was the dog, chasing, hunting, through the darkness, to seize the horses and bring them down, because they were prey, they were enemy, they should not be in this place, and they ran, and ran, and kept ever ahead.

That was his brother's—not his brother's, his enemy's thinking and he must outrun it, must leave it, shed it, let the thorns of memory comb it away and if he bled, let him bleed himself clean—

He had been running so long. Hours. Days. He had been running, following, yes, days, and he forgot; he saw them and forgot and every time he slept, every time he shut his eyes, he was in that place again, and the chase had no end, but always the end was in view, a glimpse, a perfection he could not reach. The horses ran to it, and he followed, and there was something in the darkness that reached, that dragged, that sought to hold him, but in the wake of the running horses it could not hold and all the hooks and chains were torn away.

There you are. All of you. Go—go!

She stood between him and his enemy. In the darkness, she was a fire, cold and silver, streaked with scarlet, a pillar of fire spreading into wings of flame and her back was to him and her sword held against—the emptiness, and what lay beyond it. The thing that hungered yet for him reached, flung jagged grappling claws that held him and he slipped from them to run.

Her blood was in his mouth.

No. The taste of earth and grass and sun, and the horses, a sure path through what he could not see.

Darkness shrieked, and hissed, and commanded. It fell away, flung from this place by cold light and a sweeping sword.

But he was racing the horses, and must follow where they led.

The island of golden light and grass and the sheep on the hills and the blue cattle and the long low ridge of hills was so far distant, a small thing, run as they would they could not reach it, run as he would—a world held in a child's cupped hands.

Look, Pakdhala said, Trout said, Gultage said, *Look, papa, look, do you see? Now do you see, at last?*

Do you see the hills? Do you hear the black larks singing, and the killdeer cry? Do you smell the earth, the sun-warm clay, the grass bruised beneath our feet as we ride, the earth opened by the plough, the sweet rain laying the dust?

Do you feel it, opening for you, opening within you, unfolding . . .?

So close, the horses, running, running, and he could hear the thunder of their hooves, of his heart, exhausted, running, running, he had been running so long, chasing the horses, beautiful, wild, free, not enemy, not prey, only what he would be, and there was no scent of them in the air, only grass, and hay, and bitter greens, the taste harsh and choking in his mouth, his throat, and—

"Hawthorn for a god," a man's voice said, a stranger's voice, soft but with depth to it, a voice to shape song with, quiet and close. He spoke aloud, as if he stood by Sarzahn's shoulder. But he was running, running after the horses he could not overtake. Very matter-of-fact, the man's voice, though his words were meaningless. What language he spoke, Sarzahn could not have said. "And cornel for truth."

"Yes," said a voice which was his own, and he did not know why he said yes, what he agreed to, because the words meant nothing.

"And the white-flowering elder tree last, brother. Which is rebirth."

The horses—he was almost upon them, black-legged white and dark, dark bay, tall and fleet and scattering starlight as though they kicked up the winter's first soft snow—were running, running, and they plunged from the darkness, the emptiness, through into light and he cried out— howl, cry—leapt after them, desperate not to lose them, not to be left behind, into the golden light, into warm sun and green grass and the singing of the black larks. The horses leapt again into the sky, creatures insubstantial as an image on water, running, running, further and further, dwindling away, snow beneath them, or perhaps it was cloud, and a cold wind rushed past, carrying the scent of pines, and they were gone. Holla-Sayan was on his knees on the hill of his god, and his god was dead and not-dead, an unborn ache beneath his heart; the hill was empty of what should be there. He was weeping like a child for death first met, on his knees, and a sword lay against his neck, hot breath and a predator's fangs bared at his ear. His chest hurt, screamed its wounding, and even through the breast of his brigandine the hot blood was soaking, but the weapon that had dealt the blow had been spun out into chains and bindings, and now they were broken and gone. He bled, but the body—it knew what it should be, it healed itself, and Sarzahn snarled at the pain of it, the treachery of his lieutenant, of Jochiz. And still a sword lay against his neck.

"Is it you, this time, dog?"

But the devil did not wait for an answer, lifted the sword away and put her hand there instead, and then pulled him to her, arms around him, rocking him, and the bear huffed and nosed against him, licked salt tears; he was Holla-Sayan, cold and shaking and weak as if pulled from drowning, and he was held close within the compass of the bodies of his friends.

"Sarzahn," Moth said. "So. *Sarzahn.* Cold hells, Holla-Sayan, it's good to have you back."

It was . . . yes. But . . .

Someone missing. Someone lost. He remembered—

Intensity. Rare laughter, pressing close in the night. A weight and a warmth in the curve of his arm.

Jolanan. Her name. He remembered. But he was exhausted beyond bearing, beyond thought. Months struggling in the darkness, months lost, screaming, straining to hear the voice, the voices that were his own crying out his name . . .

He needed to seek her. He had hurt her. Siege and war and Gods-damned traitor Jochiz . . . he needed to find her. Tell her—what? Didn't know, what could possibly be said between them now. But needed, still—

But Jochiz at the gates of Marakand—

"Rest, brother," the god Gurhan said. "Rest a little. Ulfhild holds the city walls."

It was easy, to fall away into the welcoming darkness.

"Let him sleep," Moth said, and Mikki put an anxious nose to the man's face as he dropped himself down, falling almost, as if even to sit up demanded too much. Mikki huffed and lay down alongside him, for what comfort and warmth he might give. To watch over him. Holla-Sayan looked, in his human self, terrible. Dark as bruising all about his sunken eyes, and a grey pallor on him that made old scars stand out white like snow. The bloody wound in his chest did not help, though it looked to be healing. Hair all loose, knotted in rat's-nests, and greying at the temples, which he had not been.

"Will he be well?" Mikki asked, trying to speak low, but the rumble of his voice made Holla stir. Only to press up against him, though, back to his ribs. Comfort, maybe, he took from that. Trust. Touched his muzzle to the man's hair.

"Will any of us be?" Moth asked. "Ya, I think."

She stroked his head, touched Holla-Sayan too, a caress as if she left a sleeping child, and went back to her runes and her warding. Adding signs. Singing, soft and low, to wind them into the whole, building, breath by breath, another layer into the defences of the god.

CHAPTER XXXI

. . . the moon is just past its last quarter, and it nine days since Yeh-Lin left Marakand, riding the winds to Tiypur in the west

A hot supper. A proper hot supper, and a bath, or a bath first, a bath and hot food and sleep in a bed and most of all, no fear, no watching, listening, alert at every shadow, every sound. Would they go first to the ambassador's house, or to the god's hill? The priests would have something hot for their supper, that dish of eggs and vegetables and cheese, perhaps, all wrapped in pastry, a Marakander speciality, or just the everyday sort of meal of broad-beans and vegetables cooked together in a crock, with a bit of meat, rich with garlic and oil. Or if the ambassador's house, and in time for the formal evening meal that all the household took together, as was Imperial Nabbani custom, then there might be a variety of foods, meats and vegetables and noodles, with spicy sauces to dip into, or a simple meal of rice with fermented vegetables and salt-fish, or perhaps the dumplings Ahjvar was fond of. But he'd be happy with a skewer of roasted goat and onions from a market-vendor's stall. Anything hot and savoury that he could eat without fear. Ailan was lost in thoughts of food, the scent, the taste, trudging in a dream. They had eaten little in the last three days. Ahjvar, he thought, had eaten nothing since the day before. He hadn't set out expecting to feed two, and they had travelled far more slowly than the *Rihswera* would have done on his own, even without dodging pursuit, though no hunters had overtaken them since the gully of the waterfall.

Ailan had actually taken thought to carry some supplies with him, when he followed, but not nearly enough. Another lesson learnt.

Smoke. He could not see the city, but he could smell its smoke. See how the air smudged a little, to the south. Something he would not have noticed, before he went into the Malagru. They were close. Could not let their guard down, even here, but it was hard enough to put one foot in front of another. There was a part of him that wanted to stop, to huddle down and say he was done, he was dying. Stupid. He'd been hungry as this before. Worse. He'd scrounged through refuse heaps by the market square, snatched for rotten fruit, shoving beggars—other beggars—aside. Cried when a stray dog as starved as he snapped a burnt crust from his hand. That was before the red priests and their mission-house and the soup and porridge they offered. They'd done some good in the world, and he'd burnt them down. Hands on this throat, choking. Evil. Charity a mask for evil, charity a thing muddled with their need to win souls for their god, good a means to a foul end, and murder, and . . . he hoped it might be the pastry with the eggs and cheese. He thought that was perhaps his favourite.

He should learn to cook. There was no reason he could not learn to cook, as well as use a sword. He would certainly make no scribe. Nikeh left him in no doubt of that. His head ached strangely but that was being hungry, and he was not starving, in no danger of it; soon they would come to Marakand, down a track along the cliffs, to cross the road and walk to the gates without fear, and—

He walked into Ahjvar's back.

"Sorry." Steadying himself, a hand braced against Ahjvar. He looked around for cover, shocked into wakefulness, terrified how hazy his thoughts, his awareness had grown. Thorns growing all about them and he didn't know where the threat was.

"Ah, cold hells!" Ahjvar said, with his head flung up as if listening to something distant. And he dropped to his knees on the stony ground. Ailan crouched by him, reaching for an arrow, looking around wildly, seeing nothing.

"Get me wood," Ahjvar said.

"Wood?" he repeated. But he didn't ask why, that was something understood, ask questions after, not when Ahjvar spoke like that. He was already scrambling up over the rocks. There was a litter of dead twigs under the thorn trees. "What kind of wood?" He could maybe hack some bigger branches away with his knife but Ahjvar had sounded so urgent.

"Anything that'll burn. Now!" Ahjvar was scratching lines on the stones with the point of a dagger. Writing, not Nabbani characters. "Alder for flame," he said, Praitannec words and all the Nabbani overtones slipped away. It was beautiful. It did something, inside Ailan, as if the sounds were a home for him. Maybe his mother had spoken so, maybe his father, if ever he had one. Even when he didn't know the words and had to guess, or ask, they gave him that feeling.

"Yew for a devil. Hermit's pepper for binding."

Ailan was gathering the broken twigs even as he listened and tried to watch, to understand what need drove this sudden spell-casting. Thorns jabbed, stuck into him, but if he used his hands lightly they did not strike deep. Swept them into the skirt of his coat and scrambled back clutching it up.

"Good," Ahjvar said, and piled them all in a loose heap between his three—symbols? words? Laughed, even as he did so. "Hawthorn. Kingship and a god both. But we want myrtle." He wrote in the air with the dagger, and Ailan could see the lines, like frost, tiny flakes of it, sparkling a moment before they melted away in the sunlight. "Myrtle sets free."

The pile of dry thorns burst into flame, snapping and spitting, and Ahjvar rocked back a little on his heels, in time to keep the swinging braids of the hair before his ears from being set alight. He pulled one of his bracelets off his wrist, not the heavy golden ones with the cat's heads terminals, but the thin black braid of silk.

Not silk. He threw it on the fire and for a moment it lay there, untouched, but twisting, as if it were a live thing, and a white smoke coiled up. Then it burst into flame as well, a dirty grey smoke then, stinking. It was hair. Ailan had wondered, to tell the truth, if it were his god's hair, some lover's token, though it seemed a bit irreverent really.

It was over in a moment more. The hair turned to white ash, a braid of it clinging to the swift-burning thorns, and then it broke and sifted away, and the twigs too were crumbling, falling into nothing, consumed.

"Take care, old woman," Ahjvar said in Nabbani.

They watched in silence a little longer, but the fire died quickly, no charcoal remaining to smoulder, nothing but ash, and the characters Ahjvar had scratched on the stones turned from the white marks a rain would wash away to rusty stains. Ahjvar got to his feet and scuffed a foot across it all, scattering ash, flinging the stones aside. Offered Ailan a hand to pull himself up.

"What happened?" he asked, shrugging on his pack again. It was far too heavy, empty though it was. The sword. He took up his bow. It didn't seem as though Ahjvar were going to answer. He was already picking a way down another steep slope that looked something only goats should dare.

But he stopped and looked back. Waiting for Ailan to find a way down to him.

"The old woman . . ."

"Yeh-Lin," Ailan said, as they went on. "Has something happened?" And on another thought, "Is Nikeh all right?"

"I don't know. But Yeh-Lin was . . . her wings were clipped, a little. All this time. And she needed to be free."

"Is that bad??

"Yes."

"Is—has the city fallen?"

"I don't know." Ahjvar frowned. Held out a steadying hand, stopped where he was, a narrow place now, squatting down to study the way below. Ailan sank down beside him, grateful for the rest, so soon. "She's—far away, Ailan. I don't know what's happened in the city." He pointed, marking a route. Hunting signs, not words. Secrets of the Wind in the Reeds, the unseen agents of the empire, which possibly even the *Rihswera* of the god should not be teaching to a godless Taren whore.

But he obviously thought he should. Practice, always practice. Ailan still didn't know for what. Maybe Ahjvar didn't either.

"If we don't get back before he takes the Suburb, we'll have a battlefield to cross," Ahjvar said. "The Western Wall has fallen."

Yew. Hermit's pepper.
    Myrtle sets free.
And in the crystal cave beneath the ruins of the ancient temple of Grandmother Tiy, Yeh-Lin reached. She stretched, as if she stood straight at last after years stooped under a ceiling too low. Unfurled, self into burning, screaming, rotting self—

—and it was not enough.

There was poison in the scraping, gnawing bite of the legless newts, poison in their slime, their skin, their blood—poison that was of Sien-Shava Jochiz, the venom of his words, of his intent, a song sung and set against her and it flowed deep in her blood now, turning her marrow to ash and rot and—

She could not hold it. She could not remake herself; flesh and blood and bone, he corroded, he devoured. He tasted her soul, would drink her light, swallow fire—

Fire was what she might be, and cold light, and she flung wide wings of it, swept the creatures from her, crumbling into ash, hissing as hot ash fell into cold water, clouding it.

This time, they were not reborn.

For a while she only breathed, leaning on her sword. Fast, shallow, deliberate: a rhythm, a chant of it, counting. One. Two. One. And out. Control. Shaped what she could. Vision. The grip of her hands. The strength of her limbs, yes. She stood. She saw. She breathed.

She hurt, damnit, and her mouth was full of blood. She spat. Black blood and bright scarlet and there was a light that was not of her making, a fire, rose-tinged, growing, the crystals encrusting the walls brightening to something like daylight, nearly, or at least a dawn, and light rising on the water, the hollow in the black altar-stone, filled with blood.

He moved. Wherever Jochiz was, before Marakand's gate, whatever he faced there, his need turned this way.

She . . . dying?

She had not thought a human body could endure such pain, and her daughter's had been a birth that neither of them would have survived had not the foremost wizard-surgeons of the empire been at the emperor's command.

A part of Jochiz moved here. She . . . could feel the echo of his presence, like a scent, a whisper. Could hear nothing. The ringing of her own ears. Smell nothing but her own blood.

His blood.

It stirred, and the light, too, stirred, slow and sluggish. Waves, heat shimmer, patterns of currents in the depths.

He will make himself a god, Vartu had said. *In the end, when he has gathered enough souls—when they are such a weight and power in the world—he will take them into himself and become a god of this world.*

And now Dotemon had come threatening into this place, this womb pregnant with a fusing of stolen souls, and Jochiz was at the gates of Marakand, where Vartu waited, and she might have lost the soul-hungry sword that the Old Great Gods had forged from a shard of the cold hells to destroy the seven in the world, but Vartu was still, for all Jochiz might tell himself otherwise, something to fear. Even with Lakkariss in his own hand. Something, at least, to require his full attention, and—

He gathered himself here, a soul divided, an entwined and doubled being spread, reaching, across half the road of the world. He meant to destroy Dotemon, to not leave her even broken, failing, a ruined body that could no longer contain what it bore, dying at last out of this fascinating, wonder-filled, delightful world, at his back, in the heart of his . . . unborn godhead.

Everything must end sometime, somewhere.

She was on her knees. She had not realized she had fallen. Yeh-Lin pushed herself up with her sword. It was a good sword. An emperor's

sword. They said she had not loved him, a young mistress risen to wife
and widow, regent and usurper and tyrant by wiles and wizardry.

A lie. Partly a lie. She had . . . been fond of her emperor, her ageing
husband.

Strange to think of him now, a man so long dead.

His sword in her hand.

She felt a coldness forcing its way into her. Like a hand, reaching for
her heart, to crush, to seize and tear.

Tendrils of rose light spreading over her, wrapping her. It was not
the failing body imagined it was cold, imagined new pain of ice. The
tendrils pierced her, they grew into her through the wounds of the creatures Jochiz had created in the perversion of some small meek thing of
the dark caves.

He savoured this like wine.

"You always were a sick bastard," she remarked to the cavern at large.
"Hravnmod should have told Ulfhild to take your head when first you
came to his hall, guest-rights be damned."

All that she was, Yeh-Lin and Dotemon, will and body made one,
flaring into the fires of her soul, spilling out, so she became a thing of
light and shadow, stretching wings and tongues of flame, and the sword
she had sworn to Nabban sweeping down, as if her enemy knelt bound
before her, executioner, which she had never been, for all the heads she
had taken.

One last time. And Nabban strengthen her arm.

She poured herself out, the blade a channel. The blow resounded, not
steel striking stone but the sound of breaking glass, and the black stone
did not so much split as shatter, spilling the blood into the water.

Not only the black altar. A rain of quartz-dust, of grit, came sifting
down the walls, falling from above.

The light that crawled the water like mist flared wildly, breaking
apart into a thousand, an uncountable flock of lights, flung like birds, like
sparks roaring from a bonfire from wall to wall to wall amid the pattering
rain of falling flakes of stone.

She heard his howl of outrage, his scream. She felt it, reverberating in her bones, going weak and flawed as the quartz that had imprisoned the souls, threatening the same dissolution, and what were Yeh-Lin's bones but a vessel that had carried Dotemon all these years, to reach so many shores . . .

He was fallen, wherever it was he stood. Weak. Mortally weak, Sien-Shava drained of his life's blood, fed into this place, bleeding after bleeding, a sacrifice of self in the Northron manner but taken to madness—

Larger fragments of stone, beating on her, the sound of rain. Hail, plunking into the water. No longer the quartz but the stone roof of the cavern, and she was losing her way, her dust to be drowned here, in this pollution of poison, this venom of malice that ate still her steel's edge and her flesh, but the souls, the stuff of them—there was nothing of selves left in them, what ought to be the slow healing and flowing of the river, of the road, to peace, denied them in an abrupt theft, an ending in pain. But at the least they should not be lost to the world and the life of it, drawn away, flickering, the river—in this place, where once Tiy had been their guardian, their last conductress to the peace of the Old Great Gods, it was still river that felt the right word—to join the great soul, the great life, of which they had been born, from which all came and to which all returned—

But there was light in the darkness, the blood-black water rising, reaching, the seething, flowing light of Old Great Gods—

Nothing with any right to call itself God rose here.

Jochiz was here, in Sien-Shava's long-drained blood, and he reached, he opened himself wide to what he had bound here—

She felt the pull. The water, the freeing gate through which she might pass—but it was not the road to the heavens, the river to the underworld, the long and healing west of the soul. It was the fire roaring, drawing in all the air and every dancing mote that rode it; it was the maelstrom, swirling, swallowing, pulling down to drown and no strength to swim free, masts, oars snapped, doomed—

Yeh-Lin might, Dotemon might, pull herself free. Cling to the anchor of her bones, cling to pain, embrace it as a lover, a mother, a saviour. Cry out wordless, *Nabban, hold me fast,* root herself in stone and earth.

But he drank the thing the he had made here, Sien-Shava Jochiz did; he took the souls, the generations immured here, lost even to themselves, he devoured them—

The world in him. A piece of it, the stuff of the world's great soul, the stuff of godhead, the earth's own truth—

It flooded him. She saw him drown, in what he would drown, and she dared almost to hope, to see the life of the world take him, dissolve him into itself, to swallow in turn what was soul of the heavens and did not in the end belong in this place—

She was ignored, briefly forgotten. A small thing, in his drowning. Fires wild, raging. A heartbeat stuttering.

An anchor, dragging loose. Hers. His, as well. His, that faltering heart, that unravelling web. Sien-Shava, abandoned, weak. Dying.

Jochiz felt it. And was gone, back to the vessel that held him, back to Sien-Shava, filling him, overfilling, bloated, unsated, with all the souls he had swallowed . . .

She was left to silence. Darkness. Stillness.

Not silence. Yeh-Lin could hear her own breathing. It sounded— rather dreadful.

Her life a long road and it would not end here, she would not let it. A long road. Good, bad . . . if she might weigh her deeds, good against evil, virtue against sin . . . There was no atoning but in the life lived, and that—must end.

Nabban was a free land now.

Nabban was . . .

She wanted to go home.

Nothing more she could do.

She did not want to leave herself in this place.

She hurt. There was little left but hurting, and Dotemon was . . . fraying. Pulling away, from what could not be endured. From what could no longer hold her.

She was Yeh-Lin. She was Dotemon. For a little, just a little, hold together. She was the Dreamshaper. She needed, now a dream.

Mirror. Still with her. And strength, to grope for it. To make a little light, a faint memory of the moon. The silver was mottled, patchy with black corrosion. Her blood stained it when she took it in her hand. Was it her hand, that twisted thing, pitted, red, raw?

It shook, and the mirror trembled.

It was fifty miles from the Western Wall to the city walls of Marakand; the gates of the pass had fallen that very day, Ahjvar said, after a little. Maybe he could see things, have visions, even while they scrambled down rocks, into yet another narrow cleft of the sort Ahjvar too often treated as plain and easy roadway. But it seemed they were in no real danger of coming to a battlefield. Abruptly the Suburb was there, west of them, quiet and ordinary, or as ordinary as Ailan had ever known it, and the city walls rising high, the buildings of the city climbing behind them, plastered white, gold, pale pink, bright blue, washing strung on people's roofs in the sun, just an ordinary afternoon. The gates in their towers still stood open.

Battle would come to them. He and Ahjvar were hurrying towards it.

Why? They could go east, go back into Taren lands. Go down to the coast, find a ship, sail far and far away, back to Nabban and the god who did the cooking for his servant, and what would Ailan do there, anyhow?

He might leave on his own. Run away. He could, now. He thought he might. Might survive, that is, on the streets of Star River Crossing or Two Hills. He wasn't a body waiting for someone, some night, to batter it senseless, to die and be thrown in the river. He could survive, now. Do something. Be something. Some knife hanging about on the fringes of a gang, some use as a thief, maybe, small and slight as he was and climbing a wall, creeping over a roof, seemed not so difficult a thing to contemplate. Killing . . . The ones that hung around the north gate, they'd give him some space, some respect, now. They'd let him in, what he'd become. They'd be afraid.

He liked that idea.

No, not really. He didn't like that person he was making in his head. It wasn't him.

You didn't run off and abandon your brother.

He was going to die, wasn't he?

At least he'd die like a good man. The sort of person his mother had used to sing about.

The city was probably not ordinary. In times of peace, there would be more children running about in the green forest-garden of the Ravine, which coiled halfway around it. They had begun felling the trees there months ago; it was a wasteland of stumps, a wound. In times of peace, there would be caravans come from the west as well as the east, and the markets busy and loud and happy. Not riders on tired ponies coming from the west, bearing, by their faces, no good news. Ahjvar hailed one, showed some token of the ambassador's house.

The Western Wall had fallen and the army of the All-Holy was surging on. The All-Holy had destroyed the gates with some great wizardry. The girl—and she was a girl, almost a child—was grey with exhaustion. Maybe they would hold at the Shiprock, she said.

"Maybe," Ahjvar said, and in his distraction sent her on with the blessing of his god. "Nabban be with you."

"Yeh-Lin's not at the Shiprock, though," Ailan said. It wasn't meant to be held, whatever those not in the secret might think.

"Wizards are. Come on. Last bit of hiking for the day." A crooked smile. Ailan had sunk down on his heels. He used Ahjvar's arm to pull himself up, not thinking. But Ahjvar didn't pull away, just gave him a pat that was more of a thump on his shoulder. "Good lad."

Did he know what Ailan had been thinking? But he hadn't meant it, even to himself. He was here. He was this person, who was here.

They continued through a corner of the Suburb. Caravans there. Not just caravans. People. Families, children. Camels, ponies, asses, carts. People on foot, with bundles and baskets. Word came faster than the couriers on their ponies. All it would take was one diviner in a neighbourhood . . . it wasn't cowardice, to get your children away, but if those who could fight or help those who did all fled . . .

He wondered which he was. How long he would really last in the press of battle with a sword in his hand.

Through the Riverbend Gate. Ahjvar didn't linger to talk to the street-guard on watch there, or ask for the captain of the gate to get more official news. He strode on as if he hadn't been climbing and hiding and walking for days on little or no food, and Ailan had to push himself to keep up. People got out of their way. He remembered how Ahjvar had looked, riding in to Star River Crossing. A caravan mercenary without a caravan, carrying some whiff of the desert with him, barren places and harsh winds, and menace. Like he was a hawk and they were all mice scurrying about beneath him, and maybe he wasn't hungry just now but later, he might notice them . . .

They were looking at Ailan that way too, the people in the streets, plain ordinary Marakanders. Giving way, as if he were something dangerous.

He liked it, and then he didn't think he did. Gave a pretty girl with her hand through an old man's arm, tugging him away, a reassuring smile. He hoped it was reassuring. She didn't smile back at him.

He thought he could probably eat any number of mice right now.

He walked into Ahjvar again, or would have, except that an arm was there to catch him.

"Sit," Ahjvar said, and pushed him down on a bench outside a teahouse. He went away, not into the shop. Ah. They were by the little Riverbend market. Had Ahjvar spotted someone, some agent of the ambassador's . . . but he was coming back, and he had—the man was a god—a stack of flaky pastries wrapped in grape-leaves. He dropped them on Ailan's lap, lifting off the top one himself.

"Eat," he said tersely, and went into the teahouse. He was back before Ailan had wolfed down more than two of the pastries—egg and dried mushroom, salt sheep's cheese, spiced olives and spring greens—as if there wasn't a war on at all, as if they might never be huddled starving behind their walls, but of course they had all the Taren Confederacy behind them, if only the clan-mothers and -fathers resisted being bought by Jochiz . . . why did he have to think of such things?

Because Ahjvar did. Because he wanted to be the kind of person who thought about things and understood them himself. Someday.

Ahjvar sat beside him, sword propped against his thigh, long legs outstretched. Handed him not the dainty cup favoured by the houses that served Nabbani-style teas, delicate and perfumed, but a hearty mug that smelt of smoke and cardamom and cream. Caravan tea, or a city version of it. Ahjvar took a long drink from his own mug, and another pastry.

They split the last, returned the mugs. The briefest of rests. Ahjvar led on as if it had been hours, with a good sleep thrown in too. Ailan was feeling more and more that the day was a dream that would never end, but at least he wasn't sick with hunger, or staggering, or wanting to whimper like a baby.

He had thought they must be going to the ambassador's house in the Silvergate Ward, but Ahjvar led the way into Palace Ward instead, so it was to Gurhan's hill they were going, which meant climbing all those broad stairs up the hill beyond the palace plaza to the library and senate palace, and up the paths in the forest beyond.

His knees might possibly turn to some sort of floppy leather hinge, like a puppet with someone who didn't know what they were doing managing the strings.

Now that he was fed, he just wanted to lie down somewhere and sleep for a week.

The plaza was a great open square, a place of public gathering and political debate and festivals, paved in slabs of white marble. Mosaics of stone and glittering glass told stories in panels all along the walls that surrounded it: the two goddesses and the god of the city, the deaths of the goddesses, the heroes who had led in the war against the devil who had once ruled the city and sacrificed its wizards to a lie, ordinary folk of all walks of life, heroes just as much as the men and women every child could name. . . a great black dog with green eyes that glowed, catching sun.

All the wood of the clear-cut ravine was stacked there now, firewood and timbers for the siege they knew must come.

To the south, broad, shallow steps rose to the complex of buildings that was the great library, and the senate palace by it. All white columns and domes gilded or copper-green, broad arcades and galleries. But tracks led beyond, plain forest tracks, winding softly into the green dim holiness of the god's hill. Ahjvar was walking faster; Ailan had to make little jogging dashes to keep up. It was not nearly so crowded as any of the markets they had walked through, but still people hurried by, heading to or from the library or the palace, or they sauntered in chattering gaggles. A puppet-theatre had been set up by one of the woodpiles, drawing the more leisured. Ahjvar didn't bother going around even that. Strode his shortest way, like an arrow shot from the gateway where they'd entered across to the great steps. Worse rudeness than his usual assumption of space. A woman weaving wreaths from baskets of spring flowers had to snatch at her goods and scuttle back on her knees. Ahjvar went as if blind.

"Sorry," Ailan gasped, and gave her a little bobbing bow, scurrying after him, skipping over a scatter of cherry twigs white with bloom. "Gods bless, mistress, sorry." Another dash to catch up. "Ahjvar!"

He didn't look around. The skin-crawling menace of him was strong, now. Ailan had thought he had just gotten used to it, the threat that Ahjvar carried in his tension, his watchfulness that never relaxed, but this was something more.

He'd been in the presence of a god. He'd spoken with Gurhan, shared tea—brewed by the bear-demon—with him. This was—like that and not, it was the opposite, it was not calm and quiet and the feeling that the world was *right*, deeply and beautifully, it was some jarring wrongness in the world, it was—

—every play told it so. Black and gold mask, black for a ghost, the dusting of gold for his holiness, the touch of the god on him. The *Rihswera* of Nabban was a dead man, a soul captured from the road and bound to a body that should long ago have gone to dust and—he had been some evil thing, before. That wasn't in the plays, usually, except the hint of it.

The god had taken him away from some evil, saved him—bound him, because love and wanting alone could not keep a dead soul from the road to the Old Great Gods—

And then Ahjvar stopped, and fell to his knees. Head down, hands braced against the pavement. Muttering under his breath.

"Ahjvar?"

People looked around. Nobody came over to see what was amiss, which was the sort of thing Marakanders would do, he was certain. They were mostly a well-meaning and generous folk. But they were afraid, and they didn't understand why, he saw that in their faces. They wanted space between themselves and whatever it was they felt that they did not understand.

He wanted space himself. He wanted to back away, out of reach, out of sword's reach, wanted not to suddenly feel it was a corpse that he had—wanted, yes, desperately, those first few weeks. When he hadn't understood he could even have other ways of needing a person and being needed.

"Ahjvar . . ." Ailan put a hand, carefully, on Ahjvar's shoulder. It was shaking as badly as what he himself had tried to hide in the Heron. His hand. Ahjvar's shoulder. Both of them shivering, as if they had come into a pocket of dank winter. Ahjvar didn't lash around, seize his wrist, which he more than half expected. Didn't move. But then he reached up and put his hand over Ailan's. Warm. Hot, even. Not a corpse-hand.

"Stay with me, Ailan," he said. "Watch my back."

Against what was he watching? He wasn't going to get an answer if he asked. Ahjvar was sitting up now, hands resting on his knees, head bowed, eyes closed as if he had just fallen asleep, or as if he prayed, maybe, in the quiet of his mind.

But maybe it wasn't a very quiet mind. Ahjvar breathed as if he were running.

And he didn't have his armour. He hadn't worn it, going into the mountains. If something came, he had only a leather jerkin with a few steel plates to reinforce it, and no helmet and no shield either, and Ailan even less.

Ailan took out his sword. He couldn't see anything threatening at all in the people about, going around them the way respectable people in Star River Crossing would go around a beggar, a ragged whore. Or a muttering madman. Ahjvar was whispering something, under his breath. Praitannec, Nabbani, he thought he caught the cadences of both. Not Taren.

And it was against the law to carry a sword within the city walls, unless you were an officer of the street-guard or a licensed guard of some very high official. Even the household guards of ordinary senators only carried cudgels.

Ailan had a badge that said he was of the household of the Nabbani ambassador but he'd used it to close the neck of his gown; it wasn't on his coat where it should be, visible. Well, they'd know Ahjvar, any who came to arrest him. There weren't that many big blond men in the city who were Taren tan rather than Northron ruddy.

Ailan turned slowly through a circle, sword held across his body. Nothing. No one even looking their way but with the sort of worried curiosity he'd expect. He tried to be calm, to have that self-assurance that Ahjvar wore like a scent. Breathed deeply. Slowly.

Didn't work. His heart was racing, hands sweating.

He grew cold in the wind. Shadows raced over, little clouds out of the west. Nothing happened, except that Ahjvar lifted his head. Ailan didn't think his eyes were seeing anything in this city. Certainly not Ailan. He moved aside again, circling, keeping always his back to Ahjvar, to see what might be coming at them.

For what little use he might be.

Moonlight, Yeh-Lin cast on the mirror in her shaking hand. Faint. Watery. On her knees in the water. Clouds marred the mirror. Marred the ruin of it. Beyond, might she reach, might she at the least touch, hear a voice, a kindness at the end—?

He was stillness, calm water, ancient stone. He was deep current, a river that could not be stayed. He was—too alien a thing. A god of the earth. He was earth, and she was . . . what she was, and she was so very far away, in space, in the miles of the caravan road. Too far in nature. But the dead king was fire, and the dead king was flesh, and he was bone, and he was soul in a vessel made and remade to carry him held in the world he should have left, he was—

Fire. Not death in fire, which he carried, scar in his soul he still could not shed. But the truth of him that Nabban saw, or had led him, perhaps, to become—he was warmth, was light, was passion and the dawn after the dark night and she could know him, reach him, kind reaching to kind, the denial of the road, the once and should-have-been dead in life. And she could taste in the air, have the scent of him, of what he was, the great singing chord struck loud and glorious, could reach and grasp as if she drowned, and flung a hand, and found her wrist seized, and drawn into a hold that she could know would never fail her.

"Dead king—Ahjvar."

She walked in dreams. Always she had. Knelt now, not in corrosive water, in the taint of Sien-Shava's curdled blood that floated in the water like vomit, reacting to the poison his own devilry had made. In a place of stone. White and cold, beneath her, and she was beyond shivering, numb, with that drugged numbness that said the body still felt, the nerves still shrieked, but the mind was severed from them, hearing only the faint echoes of what destroyed it. A mercy.

He was warmth, and his arms were around her; she was pulled hard against him, safe as she could be.

Incorrigible Yeh-Lin, Dotemon observed, even now. She could not say she had not dreamed this, in the ordinary way of ordinary woman's dreams.

"Ahjvar . . ."

"I know," he said. "I know."

Necromancy, she had been willing to call it, once, and not so different from what his disturbed goddess had done to him. Not now. Maybe it never had been. She could see, now, what she had not. Perhaps as what was mortal frayed away, and what was human, and what was soul of earth, all unravelled from her, what was Dotemon saw, with the truth of vision that was askew from this world, this matter, this plane. They . . . flowed within one another, he and his god, soul and soul, lay heart in heart. Chains bound him, reins of light, shackles of adamant, a soul chained to a god's hand—she had seen it so once for all he embraced it and for all the promises they claimed between them, but it was not . . . not chains but the flowing pulse of a life shared, an interwoven, entangling web of soul. He wore a collar that was spun of sky and sea, and it was no symbol of bondage but a pattern made, a symbol and a tool, a wizardry that partook of god's will. A tracery that carried something of them both and what between them was one, that made a road to run the miles between them which a god could not, in the nature of the world, pass over. A sacred way between the god to what was of the god in the man? Nabban beyond Nabban?

Oh, let it be a path at need.

This place . . . not a marble pavement but a field of snow. White, cold beneath them. Then it was only a nothingness, the faint idea of *white* and *cold* and she was too far gone to see more, perceive more, make more in this dream to hold them.

"I want to go home," she said. "I want to see him. I want—not to leave my bones in this place."

The water was cold and foul. The white field was a place of dreams and she had lost it. Ahjvar knelt with her in the cavern, in the dirty water, and leaned over her, shielding her with his body from the falling rain of crumbling rock-dust.

She was not here to cuddle with the dead king, though pity was it could not be so and Dotemon might feel that pity, might stand aside from pain, now, all their close-knit union uncoiling, dissolving.

For a moment she lost that sense of herself, was only a child. Less: a small and broken animal, gathered close. Found herself again, Yeh-Lin, Dotemon—Yeh-Lin Dotemon.

"Vartu," she said. Her voice was very weak, not her own, slurred and stumbling. Maybe she only dreamed she spoke. *Tell her, I failed. Jochiz has devoured the souls he has stolen and hoarded all these years and made himself a thing greater than the gods of the earth, and since he has devoured gods and goddesses on his way, too, I do not know—don't let him take Nabban, Ahjvar, save him, somehow, not that end for him, not for Ghu, not him, please . . .*

Even Dotemon's thought grew weak, unravelling from her.

Ahjvar was warm, and clean, all honest dust and sweat.

"Hush," he said. "Yes." And she was not certain now who spoke. The wind was cool, and clean, spring-fresh, sap stirring, snow's retreat, and there were pines in it.

A whiff of horse, drawing near.

Even a splashing, and a horse could not walk the shard-spiked bottom of this pool, must not, warn him—

No, she only dreamed.

"It hurts," she said aloud. It sounded like surprise she had not meant; only a little whimper, was she not allowed? And, "I don't want to die here. I don't want to rot in this place. I don't want to leave my bones here in the filth he has made, in this darkness. I want the clean earth, I want the sky, Ahjvar—I want to go home, let me go home, Nabban—Ghu, please, let me come home—"

Whisper, pathetic, child's whine, and how she hurt; it deafened her, blinded her, and this was only dreaming. The winds would not carry her; she had not the strength to call them, or the life left to endure the riding. There was no road to the east.

"Shh," Ahjvar said and he kissed her, which drove the pain back a little, touch of his lips: forehead, failing eyes, what she had dragged back into being blurred again, bleeding, the worm's work reasserting itself. Lips, that were raw and oozing blood and poisoned slime. Kissed her, slow and careful, a lover's kiss, and it eased her, spread some clean quiet through her, a little.

"I did sometimes wish I had found you first," she said, and maybe that was her thoughts wandering death-drunken, delusion, into reckless truth. She thought he lifted her, and was walking. Through water, that splashed and echoed from a close stone roof, and still the crumbling empty crystals pattered down, and the stone to which they had clung. The roof would fall . . .

If she had found him, cursed and despairing—she would only have killed him, to set him free. And never known what thing she sent from the world, the hope of the land, her land, because what would his horse-boy have been without him? Running to the edge of the world, and denying the call of his dying gods.

"But then, I do not think I could have done for you, what he has done. Better you're his, in the end. For all of us."

Shadows. She could see nothing but shadows. Something moved, near.

"Good," he said, and she thought she caught a whisper, a mind's fleeting touch. They spoke together, not quite overheard, and she could not clearly see, only murk and haze now, and the moving shadows. The pain washed back, with the absence of his touch, his—did they drink her pain, to take it from her? Or only bless her with their breath, pour life into her, a little, a staving off of what must be? She did not think that was the dead king now, who kissed her forehead, blessing, pouring into her the quiet of deep water. Did not think those were his arms, his heart, under her head.

"I'm dreaming," she said.

Wind touched her face. Cold. Not the still, smothering wet air of the cavern. Sound . . . was wider.

"Dreamshaper," her god answered. "If you can hold this dream, we can ride it home."

"You cheat the rules, Nabban. How does a god ride over his borders?"

"In him."

"I am not in him."

"Oh, we all are. He is my bridge, my voyaging vessel, and we are all three and this dream you make—held within him. And Snow and wind and road and all."

Of course there was a horse, and he held her, and the white stallion Snow stepped out, light, easy, and the snow crunched under his hooves in her dreaming, and then he leapt, and he ran, in a dream between snow and sky.

He carried the fading of what was left of her home to Nabban, with the wind in the pines of the sanctuary of Swajui, where the cold springs flowed.

Darkness, but it was only the darkness of the night, and the stars were bright overhead through gaps in the boughs of the pines, which shifted and swayed in the wind. A warm wind, carrying spring. Water tinkled and burbled somewhere near, and the wind hissed in the needles. Like incense, the air. The ground beneath her. Soft. Years of falling needles. Warmth. Heavy on her, pinning her down. Weight of a quilt, only a quilt, filled with down, and she lay propped up a little, her head in his lap, his hand another weight, a warmth, a living-ness so strong she felt the shape of it, spread resting on her, thumb, a finger, touching her collarbones.

Took a breath. It seared her. Decided not to do that again, but the body wanted it, took another, shallow. It didn't seem to do much good. Wasn't much left to breathe with. Tried to start there, to build again what once she had been. She had been bone, she had been a desiccated corpse sealed in a tree, she had been . . . many things. Nabban, when he was only Ghu, had scattered her to bone and put her into the earth, as another man might have slapped her face, and three days it had taken her to find her way back then. What Jochiz had done, the malice he had shaped by devilry into the gnawing, scraping, sliming amphibians—it ate at her still, and she could find no way through it. Dotemon was uncoiling from her, and even human eyes might see, she thought—because she saw, now, tendrils against the sky, between her and the stars. Moving like water-weed, swaying with current. Could feel, still herself, two in one, still rooted, still held in what they had made between them, but the inimical world began to tear at them.

Soul of the heavens, of the hells, of the underworld that had once been the shape by which it was understood . . . none true, and all, but what was truth was that they had no place within this world, and they could not long sustain themselves here, naked, cut off from their own place, which was within them . . .

It was all very confusing to Yeh-Lin's mind. She remembered that it had not been so, when she was whole. When she was devil . . .

Mystics, philosophers, even rhapsodists who should have contented themselves weaving tales, had driven themselves half-mad, meditating on the recursive truths of the cosmos and the nature of the Gods. Perhaps they should have put their minds to other things, or drunk less hydromel brewed from the bee-maddening rhododendrons of the coast.

She hurt, and there was nothing but the hurt, no sight no sound no warmth no wind, and then she dragged another breath.

"Let us go," she said. "I can't—" A moment of clear thought, of vision. Of urgency. "Let us go. He needs you. Go to him. Now! Take him, run, hide. Save yourselves. Jochiz—"

"Hush. Yes. Don't worry."

"Please, Ghu."

"Yes," he said, and he bent over her, kissed her mouth one last time, touch she barely felt, drowned in her pain. "Safe journey on your road, Yeh-Lin."

The road was a river, the great Wild Sister, who was this man, a rushing current, and then a wind, sweeping down the mountainside and it called, and what had been Yeh-Lin shed her ruined body and her pain to leap to it.

Dotemon twined into a column of fire that lit the grey trunks like the moon that was yet to rise, and spread wings of light. Hesitated. But she—it—could no more live long in this place than a fish on stone.

"Stay," Ghu said. "Do you understand what you've sent her to?"

I? The dead go to the Gods. I did not send her. Your blessing on her.

What else could I do? The road is broken, Dotemon. They go—do they even reach the Old Great Gods? They don't return.

They never did return, Dotemon said. The God did. It was an Old Great God filled the space between the trees, that lit the pines with the nacreous colours of the northern sky-dance. *Not as you mean it. Not as . . . selves, into self renewed.*

No. I never thought so. He shrugged. *I never thought on it much at all. Save to keep Ahj from it.*

You thought as most folk of the world think, the heavens a place, an ending. But we are the guardians. We welcome. We hold. We remember. We do not keep. In the end . . . soul fades to soul. Death to birth. The great mystery of mysteries. But we hold all in our hearts forever. It is what we are.

Something holds them now, forever. Holds the souls from the great soul of the world that should take them back. They never return to the world. To us. To the life we all are. Lost children.

That is a lie of the All-Holy's cult, that we broke the road against human souls, to sever them from the Old Great Gods in the Heavens. Jochiz is the stealer of souls, the destroyer, who tears soul from the world itself and devours it. He will make himself the soul, the god, of the whole of the world, unchecked. My failure—

You did what you could. But Dotemon, I think there's a core of truth in his lie.

No. We never barred the road to human souls.

Dotemon—go to the road. To the heavens. Serve me, one last time? Be my scout. Find the truth. I know it's a hard road, a damaging one—you did it yourselves.

Yes. They had.

So make it your road of penance and atonement, as every human soul that travels it must do. Go, and find the truth, and return—find a way. Walk my dreams. Tell me what truth you find, and why the soul of the world cries out for lost children. He stroked the dead woman's hair, faded to iron grey, the truth of her. Old woman when she joined with Dotemon. *Maybe you can overtake her on the way. Share your burdens. You made your sins together.*

Not all of them, Dotemon said primly, Yeh-Lin's very intonation. Yeh-Lin might have laughed. Dotemon did not.

A wake. A remembering. Dotemon was not what it had been. Never would be. Something of Yeh-Lin within, always. Value that.

"Go," Ghu said. "I'll look to her as she would want. No imperial tomb. The clean earth. Go. Leave Jochiz to the storyteller."

A fey boy, dream-dazzled with truths half-seen before ever he was a god.

The heavens were within the Gods, and the hells too, and the Gods themselves . . . a mirror turned on itself, containing itself, light lit of itself. The devils—Dotemon, and Jochiz, and Vartu, and Tu'usha, and Ghatai, and Anganurth, and Ogada together, united at the last in anger, in vengeful defiance, had broken the way between the reality of the world and the Old Great Gods. Dotemon might seek the heavens. There was no certainty that it would find its way, or come unscathed to the Gods in the end.

And certainly no welcome, when it did.

But it was the only open road. It did not believe he could be right, that they had made it a trap and a barrier for human souls as well.

The god of mountain and river sat with the dead woman still held resting on his lap, but now he was an emptiness, a waiting.

Gone within himself so very far away. Seeking his other self.

Dotemon wished him well and sought the heavens.

CHAPTER XXXII

. . . the Western Wall has fallen

Nikeh saw Sulloso Dur stumble, fall several stairs, struggle her way to her feet, leaving blood smeared on the wall, and vacant-eyed, fall again. No rising. She gasped, no fury left to yell, and stabbed upwards into a man's belly. He came down onto her as she yanked her blade free, ripping the wound wider, spilling blood and the muck of his entrails over her, a heavy weight driving her backwards. She fell, flailing for balance, into a mass of her own comrades. Someone propped her steady and she found footing again; a Westron spear came thrusting at her but he was awkward in that close spiral and it struck her shoulder, armour turned it; someone seized it and jerked. That man slipped and they killed him, two or three of them, crowding close.

They were growing thin, those who set the pace of the retreat down the stairs, the rearguard. Draw lots, the captain had said, Marakander to the end, but there had been no need, enough had said they would hold it with her. Four patrols, all street-guard, a handful of others. Enough. Give the others a chance, give the wounded a little hope, that they might limp away, find some hiding place to await the dark or have time to . . . choose what they might, alone or with a friend. The message-riders would have gone when they saw the rockets; they had their orders, too.

A fury with an axe, a lone man well-armoured, had ridden a scaling ladder as it was raised and they had not managed to dislodge it before he had cut a space about him, holding it for long enough that others followed, and in that frantic time another slapped up and another, and first the wall-walk and then the tower platform grew slick and bloody and the fallen of both sides tripped friend and foe and were climbed over, on, trampled, and what did it matter, when the towers of the gate had fallen . . .

At least Sulloso had not hesitated, the moment they all picked themselves up again, things cracking and tumbling, tiles and coping-stones dislodged, the ruin of the trebuchet fallen. She had given the order and Lia had lit the fuses. Thank Gurhan's grace or Teacher's wizardry, the enemy assaults of burning missiles had not fired the rockets earlier. The signal had shrieked skyward and they knew now, up the pass, that all was lost at the gate.

There should have been more time.

There were no doors they could shut and bar against descent save with weak and makeshift barricades that didn't seem worth the time they would buy; the tower was meant to be defended against entry, not a gaol to hold against those within. A woman dropped away from beside her, and when she gave up yet another step Nikeh felt the soldier's hand crack beneath her boot. But the woman didn't move, cry out. Too far gone already.

No time to give those who died any blessing to free them to the road, even with the simplest gift of earth or salt. Their ghosts must endure, helpless witness, and hope the enemy at least buried or burned their bodies. Hope the enemy had no way to steal their lingering souls, as he did those of his own.

The Marakanders were thinning out behind her. Slipping away. Not cowardice. Orders. They reached the storeroom and moved with frantic haste, some of those who had faded away on the stairs ready, the door pulled to, a great table overturned in the doorway, hammers thudding, big spikes driving through age-hardened planks to nail it to the doorframe. Jars, crates—they threw whatever they could there, oil-jars shattered to foul the floor and wood and then someone broke a jar of flour and they threw the lamps and ran, the last of them, for the yard between tower and stable and barracks, as the air behind turned briefly to a fire-ball, as effective as any wizardry.

There was little hope, no hope, was there, that the wounded might escape, though the shadow of the wall did stretch to the north-east, now, and the day declined. Not swiftly enough. Maybe no hope for any of them.

"We have orders," Lia Dur said. Her voice was harsh, rasping and cracked. "It's not cowardice. Don't wait. Scatter, run. For your very souls' sakes. To the hills."

But they kept together anyway, at first, a straggling pack. Perhaps the Westrons had no orders to pursue, only to take the wall—but then looking back Nikeh saw them coming, archers, a man in armour with a sword, gesturing.

"Arrows!" she shouted. "Scatter, get to cover!" and that finally broke them. They ran, then, like rabbits, all of them, dodging towards what they could find, some goatherd's shed, a copse of hazels, the ragged edges of the rising cliffs, where fig and lilac and juniper grew in the cracks of the stone. Maybe half of them made it, maybe more. Some crawled wounded, crying out.

Nikeh did not look back again. She kept by Lia, waited when she could have outrun, grabbed her hand and tugged her on. Her eye was set on one certain seam of lilacs, where she knew it was possible to climb, keeping out of sight from the valley, high to a plummeting stream that sank into stones and vanished underground before ever it reached the pass. That would give them a route higher yet, and water, which they would be ready to bless by that time. Few of them carried any rations at all. They hadn't believed the gate could be forced, hadn't believed . . .

Jochiz was a tale. The devil Tu'usha had impersonated their goddess and ruled their city and they still did not believe another devil could come; it was so long ago, the kind of thing that happened when their grandfathers' grandmothers' grandfathers were children, not real.

Lia was gasping for breath, but they were in under cover now, and alone. Climbing, already high above the road. A glimpse of it, swarming with movement. The Westron army. They weren't going to pause, consolidate their hold on the wall? Not even any rest. Pushing on. Ants. Hornets. A mindless swarm.

Nikeh had no idea where everyone else had gone, if anyone at all had survived. She didn't think the Warden of the Wall had really expected anyone to. *Make for the heights if the gate is taken, each as best you can. Report to the captain of whatever city gate you can best come to, and hold yourselves under the orders of the Warden of the City.*

Words. Meant give to purpose. To give hope, because you did not say to the people you commanded, *We will die here, and we trade our deaths for theirs to come.*

She should have been at the Shiprock, in the squat whitewashed tower of the windmill. Teacher was meant to be there. But it was hardly a fortress of safety, not with the Westrons advancing like the tide.

She and Lia were running, sometimes, even now, crossing open ground on the hillside. Creeping through undergrowth, crawling, ever climbing, Nikeh choosing the way, keeping hold of Lia's hand whenever she could. Not even certain why, when it occurred to her she was doing so. A kiss on a rainy night, and warm arms she could wrap herself in, that was where it had started, and a shared bed, now and then. A shoulder to lean against. Never more, never anything said, the sorts of things you said to a lover. Not on her part, and Lia had stopped, when Nikeh never gave her words for words.

But she wanted, she needed to hold that hand. She needed not to let go.

Slow. So slow. Hours? Hours. The sun fell remorseless. Lia was slow, clumsy. Infuriating. Demanding of patience. Lia was no agile climber, no squirrel-lithe scaler of trees, but she was fit and strong and should be no more out of breath than Nikeh, and yet she dragged, and dragged. Up and down and over and looking back to see yards, not miles gained, and the ruin of the wall, and the Westron army below . . .

Lia slipped, a heavy tug on Nikeh's arm. She tightened her grip, knelt down.

Lia's face had taken on a grey tinge about the eyes, lips tight on pain.

"What?" Nikeh demanded. "Where, Lia?" Whimpering like a child somewhere deep inside her chest. Not slow, not clumsy, not exhaustion. Wounded and too fool proud to speak. Wounded—

Not Lia, no, not Lia Dur; she could not lose her friend here. Lia's arm was clamped across her ribs. No broken arrow, no blood, no great damage to her armoured vest. They were sheltered in this place, crouched among mountain boulders and juniper where the little stream spread and faded, one strand gurgling like a drain feeding a cistern in the winter rains. The sun was low in the west. They couldn't go on in the night.

"Got walked on, on the stairs," Lia said. "Hurts. Breathing. Sorry. 'S'alright. Getting worse, is all. Sorry. I can keep going. Don't do that. Just let me catch my breath."

Nikeh was unbuckling her, checking, feeling for anything swelling, feeling, watching, for the breath to be rising where it should not, but she seemed intact, ribs and breastbone, only her quilted vest under the armour torn by the rivets, and the skin under—Nikeh slid a hand up under her belt and Lia pulled a face and said her hand was cold, trying to make a joke—a little broken, sticky. Nothing to speak of. Rivets. A soft swelling that made Lia wince and flinch, but it was only battered flesh, not anything pushing from inside, nothing bad.

"Nothing broken," was Nikeh's verdict. "But you're going to be black and blue, if you're not already." Hated the words before she said them, but—"You have to just shut it out and keep going."

"Was," Lia protested. A gasp.

"Yes, I know." Nikeh started fastening Lia's buckles again. Kissed her, since her face was there close and she had thought for a moment— anyway, it was close. Lia laughed, the sort of laughter that was far too close to howling, and leaned cheek to cheek a moment before moving herself stiffly to hands and knees, to kneel on the water's edge and cup it up.

She went flat into it, face down, a boot on her back.

That the All-Holy had not seen fit to honour him with the lordship of Emrastepse was not something he must regret. The All-Holy knew how best he might serve. If he was not yet worthy, that was the way of it. Primate Ambert had spoken for him, but the All-Holy's wisdom was greater. Ambert had given him another opportunity to serve. A captive scout taken on the hills had spoken, eventually, of a Nabbani wizard of great scholarship overseeing some secret work further up the pass. The All-Holy had spoken of the god of Nabban as his enemy, an evil different from the small gods of the hills and goddesses of the rivers who in their ignorance opposed him, whom they ought to revere as they did the Old Great Gods. A great service to the All-Holy, to take this wizard, to seize or kill her and disrupt her scheme, whatever it might be.

And so rather than taking part in the assault on the wall Philon had taken a seer of the sixth circle, the only one who could be spared, and a handful of soldiers of Dimas's former household, and set out by the mountain tracks.

It went badly from the start. They were slow in working their way up the cliffside, missed their way and could not pick up a track heading east. Found themselves having to slowly and perilously descend a cliff where hand and footholds crumbled, when they found no way forward but one below. They weren't hill-folk, none of them but him. Folk of the plains along the Tiy, dizzy with heights, no understanding of stone. One man fell, bouncing and screaming, and then only thudding, rattling stone loose. Even back on safer ground, a goat-track Philon thought he remembered from earlier scouting, the soldiers were fearful, whispering that there were devils in Marakand, commanding its wizards, and thus the wizard chosen to command any great work would have a devil at her shoulder. They whispered, too, that Blessed Philon had lost the All-Holy's favour through his failure to defend Prince Dimas from the heathen assassins.

They whispered they would die on this mountainside and if they lived, be denied the glory of having taken part in the storming of the wall.

And so the day passed with little forward progress. Philon heard the bells, and much later, bells again, and the shrieking of some fire-signal launched skyward, though what it meant he did not know, only that if it was their own, he had not been told of it. But he had lost the All-Holy's favour, so perhaps he would not have been. Or perhaps the Wall cried for help.

On the mountainside, nothing changed.

They could not travel this treacherous terrain by night; not long before they must lie up and wait for light, and pray that the All-Holy kept them safe from hill-folk and demons and whatever else might prowl such wildernesses.

When the seer grunted and dropped, an arrow in his back, they scattered, all discipline lost, though Philon shouted that they must stay close, make a wall of their shields against their enemies above on the mountainside . . .

He could not see them. A flicker through the leaves, there, where wild olives tangled. More arrows. Cries. Philon went like a crab sidelong, down over scree, into junipers. Two of his own followed him, clumsy, but they made it, and he scowled them to silence and led them downwards again, into a gully where a tiny stream made noise enough to cover their clatter and gasping breath. It would also mask the sound of anyone following, but he saw nothing of pursuit. Distracted, hunting the others higher up.

Then sound, but ahead of them. He waved to the two soldiers to be silent and still, went ahead himself, down the twisting course between the stony walls.

Two Marakander soldiers, women, at the water's edge. Kissing, distracted. Young fools. The teachings said that women were so, easily distracted, more tied to their bodies, but he had never himself noticed much difference. Sometimes he wondered if the old prophets of the nameless god had had some personal grudge against the sex. Certainly the All-Holy, though he did not speak against the edicts that said women ought not to take up the sword nor hold high office, did permit a chosen few to serve so. Primate Clio, most notably.

Youth, though, that was folly.

Philon moved slowly, nearer. One of the women crawled to the water to drink. Wounded, he thought. She moved so. He sprang, knocking her down, into the stream, turned with sword in hand to deal with the other.

Small and slight and fast, a fine-boned, olive-skinned Westron face set in a mask of fury, bush of black hair curling from under her conical helmet. She struck while he still stared.

Hecta. In his last light of the sun he saw lost Hecta, whose ghost had faded trapped on the broken road, denied the gods by her unbelief, by his failure to break his silence, to do what he had been forbidden and speak of his truth, to convince . . . Impossible, that she should be here in his dying, to welcome him to the embrace of the Old Great Gods. Yet she looked on him. But she did not smile, and the pain, the pain, something dragged, and his arm, his heart burned, and he could see, could hear and taste and smell—home, the direction of home and he had only to turn and set his foot to the road and he would find his way but he could not, he was grappled with a thousand burning hooks and hauled, struggling, thrashing like a fish, into—into—

There was light, like the sun through eyelids. A pulse, a slow breathing that was not his own. It grew and grew until there was nothing else.

Nikeh yelled, sweeping her sword free, up as she rose on a knee and thrust herself to her feet, blade into him with all her weight and rising force behind it, the angle of his jaw under his helmet, armoured knight of Tiypur, and he fell back, overborne, though he was much the taller, a burly man, jaw grey-stubbled, brown eyes wide as his chest flooded crimson. She used a foot to hold him down, wrenching her sword free, and he did not thrash or squirm or react at all, only lay there bleeding a flood. No time to check on Lia. Splashing and cursing; she wasn't dead, and two more Westron soldiers were scrambling down the slope above them, neither with a bow or she and Lia would have been dead already.

Nikeh sprang to meet the nearest, dodging aside and tripping the man as he passed, wheeling back to slash across his calves, low, severing tendons. While he yelled and shrieked and tried to rise she flung herself after the other, a woman her own height, slashed and hit a horn plate protecting her back, but it was enough to make her stumble and by then Lia was there, her sword striking hard, and they had the soldier down, cutting, brutal and swift. Nikeh turned back to finish the wounded man. Such a relief, the silence. Watched the heights above, the scrub that promised concealment and might hide too many others. Movement.

"Lia . . ."

But then a man stepped clear, waved a bow in the air. A lean Malagru hillman, his hair in a topknot, bare-chested beneath a goatskin cape, his kilt the dusty colour of stone.

"Up here," he called. "Hurry."

They scrambled to him, Lia doing her damnedest to keep up, but when Nikeh offered an arm she took it, slithering down into another bit of cover together, broken teeth of stone and fig trees. A patrol of hill-folk stretched out above, making a slow way up a dangerous ledge. A few in armour among them, others who had somehow made it from the wall. Nobody Nikeh recognized on sight, though Lia traded nods of greeting with some woman who looked back once.

"There's a better path above, if you can make it up," the archer said. "I'm Orhan."

"Lia Dur of the third tower of the wall. Nikeh, apprentice to Scholar Daro Jang of the Nabbani Embassy." Lia spoke in breathless little gasps. Nikeh was not so sure no ribs were cracked. She put an arm around her.

"We can make it."

Orhan only nodded. "Come. Lia first. Follow me close. There's no true climbing. You'll be fine."

An encouraging lie.

Sunset, when the Shiprock came in sight. It was still miles distant, a prow of grey stone thrust out from the south into the pass, like a ship nosing from the fog. A height, but a mere toe of the Pillars of the Sky. The road made a sharp jog around it, passing through a narrowing gap. Why had the ancient builders of the Western Wall not set their defences there, Teacher had more than once muttered, as she and her fellow wizard-scholars of the library set their lines and their symbols all up and down its clefts and fissures.

Nikeh had been much called upon for her climbing skills, she of all the scholar-apprentices not fearful of the chimneys and the high ledges.

The windmill stood pale, its sails furled and motionless. Deserted, she suspected. The valley below seethed. Surely the better part of the Westron army. They must have marched without pause, leaving few behind to consolidate their hold on the wall. The action of a raiding band impatient for plunder, not an army, that must seize and hold and defend as it came. A plunder of souls.

They would be exhausted. They would have outpaced their supplies, be thirsty, hungry, wounded . . . ready to drop where they stood. Almost twelve miles, the distance from the gate of the wall to the Shiprock.

A victory might yet be snatched from this, if only the Stone Desert tribes had not all flitted away to the fringes of their wilderness, out of the All-Holy's path. But no. The god of the city was the great prize to be taken, and there was nothing any attack from the rear could do to prevent that.

Nothing she could do, either.

Their little band could go no further. Lia sank to the ground at Nikeh's feet, arms hugged around her body, grey-faced. Even the Malagru-folk were done. The shelter of rocks and scrub and shadow—it was little enough and they could certainly risk no fire. Water-gourds were passed around. Nikeh held one for Lia, made certain she drank. Salt white cheese, smelling high, and flatbread that had gone dry and hard.

"We'll wait for moonrise, then move on," Orhan said.

Nikeh squirmed out to where she could watch openly, lying flat within a seam of lilacs, their leaf-buds swollen, not yet opening, at this height. Orhan joined her.

"We should go up to the copper mines," he said. "I don't think—I fear we'll only come to Marakand to see it fall."

And his home and his kinsfolk would be north, the road, the Suburb, become a deadly river he could not cross to reach them, unless they got far ahead this night. But would Jochiz even allow his army that respite, or would he drive them on by night, with Marakand so close?

He'd come to the city walls with his folk dropping like foundered horses, if he did. If they were not already doing so. But perhaps he did not care. If he could single-handedly blast his way through the gates . . .

Secrets. Still to be kept. A Westron patrol might yet spring on them from out of some fold and shadow of the mountainside.

Or were the wizards all fled, or dead? Deserted, like Teacher . . .

No. Teacher served where she was sent, and her empress and god had sent her to be elsewhere. Whatever she did there, served.

Nikeh was only an afterthought.

Child, Teacher would say—almost she heard her—*you are never an afterthought. And since I am your Teacher, consider what you have learnt, and that there comes a time for every student to take what they have been given and go on ahead. Thus we move our knowledge through the years, beyond life and life.*

"I should bind Lia's ribs before the light goes," she said. "She can't keep up. I'm not sure she can go on at all. If you need to leave us behind, do so. Two can hide more easily than two dozen. Only leave us water and a bow and arrows."

Orhan nodded. Relief?

But still Nikeh watched, as the white tower flushed ruddy with the sunset.

Gone. Dead. Taken, to become a Westron lookout post—

She felt something run through her body, prone on the rocks. A shudder. Twigs quivered. Someone down in the hollow exclaimed, "Gurhan save, what in the cold hells was that?"

Dust rose first, in small plumes. Or perhaps smoke. There had been much fire-powder involved in the working they had laid.

"What is it?" Orhan whispered.

"Watch," Nikeh said. "Oh, watch. My Teacher was a great, great wizard."

She grinned. It was delight. It was a great, hot joy. Lia should see this. And Lia was there to see, teeth clenched, breathing shallowly, but crawling up beside her to look, and the whole patrol and all their straggling soldiers, everyone, and not all remembering to keep down, either, but the light was fading.

Dust, smoke, catching the sunset light, as if the air burned, a lurid and dirty red. She gripped Lia's hand, hard.

The Shiprock seemed to split open, as if struck by a hammer. Shattering. Sliding away in great rushing cataracts of stone. The windmill vanished in a growing cloud of dust, but for a moment she saw it again, a pale, tilted piece of flotsam, sweeping down, its round bulk still intact, a ship to ride the descending waves of stone. Had there been priests, seers, advancing up the steep paths to secure the vantage point of the mill? To look for the ambush that even a fool would have suspected, at this narrowing of the way? Had the primates and commanders been there, close by, to lead the army through, to whip them to order when the expected ambush came?

The sound came like distant thunder, growing, unending, wave piling on wave.

And then a silence. Only gradually, other sound. Crows cawing. An indistinct faint noise that might be a thousand voices crying out, praying, denying . . . It faded. Thickening darkness on the mountainside but still the cloud hung, murky crimson, a slow seething that filled the valley.

Might they choke on the dust, those not under the rockfalls.

Probably most had not been. A hope, that they might destroy the commanders. The wizards of the goddess Kinsai had tried some such thing. It was news of that which had made Teacher go to look so thoughtfully at the Shiprock.

She thought the wizards who had made the windmill their base had all gone up the mountainside to watch their work make good. That had been the plan. She had only to get Lia so far, and there would be help, perhaps even knowledge that might speed the healing of broken ribs.

Perhaps news of Teacher.

"That won't have crushed the whole of the army," Orhan said. "It can't have done." His voice asked her to assert otherwise, to tell him, yes, it was over.

"But the pass is blocked," Lia said. "Look."

The dust did thin. Shapes, as if seen through fog. A dam of broken stone, a new ridge, moraine, high and difficult. Fanged and savage. A reef, to shred this army as it crossed. It must come down the other side all in broken pieces, to be opposed in its fragments. And surely, even a devil would have difficulty in blasting his way through what a devil had wrought.

A thought she had not meant to let out where she could see it.

She put it away again, the way she did the weight of Birdy in her arms and his wet warmth soaking her, when that came into her head.

Where was the All-Holy, in that mess below? Beneath half a small mountainside of stone? Even Sien-Shava Jochiz must be—inconvenienced—by that.

CHAPTER XXXIII

Sarzahn was lost. Dead. Taken. Or made beast again, it was all one. Ripped away, a fool's defiance on Vartu's part—if that had been Vartu. There had been the whiff of a god about it, that severing as he reached too late to hold what ran through his hands like water. A god, and not the old power of the hills who cowered weak and helpless behind Vartu's shield. Nabban? He *dared . . . ?* And how? Vartu allied with Nabban, using him, somehow? He had never intended to show her any mercy regardless. Now—she would burn and he would swallow what was left of her, and the god of the hill as well, and come in the end to Nabban, and destroy him.

—he should have devoured Sarzahn so, not to lose him to this foul world that had made a beast of the wreckage of his soul.

Put Sarzahn from his mind. Vengeance for his loss would come, but not now. Now Jochiz had a city to take.

And the folk of this wretched army of his were cattle, mindless of any understanding, fit only to be beaten along their road when they baulked. Beyond reasoning with, many beyond answering even to the driving spur of faith and fervour.

The All-Holy had a captain of archers, who defied the knight commanding him, saying his men could march no further, dragged aside and strangled with his own bowstring, and strung up on a little stunted wild olive as a warning. The rush they had made after the taking of the Western Wall carried them only so far. They wanted to stop, to gorge themselves and drink, like beasts, as if the victory were theirs and not the work entire of their god—his grace, his blessing.

The weak, the wounded—they were left behind, to struggle on or perish in their shame and failure, he did not much care. They were a harvest, either way.

The less time Vartu had to prepare her Marakanders against his coming, the better. He would march them through the night till they dropped, drive them with whips outright if he had to.

"They need to rest, Holiness." A whine in his ear, a man riding at his side. He had been bleating on some time, unheeded. Primate Ambert. Jochiz turned a look of reproof on him. Forbearing. Did anger cast a light in his eyes? Ambert ducked his head, his horse reacting to a tension on the reins. Jochiz tasted his fear, felt the man's heart quicken. No doubt he would take it for the light of the All-Holy's divinity.

"They can't march all the way to Marakand, Most Holy. Even a courier takes a day to ride it. May we give them some promise of a halt?"

Clio murmured, "It would show wisdom."

Not Clio. She was dead. The other woman, riding at his side. The bright Northron horse, the cape of mottled silver sealskin.

"The gap," he said. "We take the gap, the place they call the Shiprock, and camp beyond. If we come too slow, they will hold it against us."

They already did, unless they were fools—something waited, he thought, a shadow to his seers and even his own vision. Nothing of any account, in the end. Let them fall here, let them fall at the walls of Marakand—so long as they offered themselves, and made his name a conqueror, a god, a force of nature whose great tide sweeping east could not be stopped, that the rulers of Marakand and the cities and the lords of the tribes and even the empress of Nabban should know and fear what rolled towards them, and abandon their gods. That their gods might know themselves abandoned, Nabban be rejected by his folk, deprived of the worship of the godhead he had stolen, mortal fool, claiming what he had no right to be, what was withheld from even the greatest of wizards, even those born of gods, a birthright denied . . .

Not for much longer. After Marakand—there would be deaths enough before ever he breached its walls; they would be slaughtered in the ravine trying to come at the walls, its bridges denied them. He would let his followers prove themselves there; he needed only the knights, the seers, the administrators of the seventh, his faithful commanders. The rest might die and be replaced, as Marakand abandoned its god for him.

Perhaps, at last . . . an anticipation to be savoured. Once Vartu was dead. Once Marakand was taken. It would be time, then, to prepare the greatest ritual of them all. Self, sacrificed to self. Heart's blood offered, heart opened, to take in what he had drained himself to bear, to nourish, to nurture to its ripeness.

The heart ached in his chest. Ached, all through him. Scars of his bleeding burned.

He grew tired. Weary, Sien-Shava's weakness.

Sien-Mor smiled her old, sweet smile.

She wanted something. She always did.

He rubbed an aching forearm, frowned. The company nearest trudged in silence. No hymns, no chanted prayers. Were they a retreat, a defeat?

"Let them sing," he told Clio. But of course she was not there. Sien-Mor raised her eyebrows. He looked over to Ambert.

"I shall see to it," the primate said, and turned his horse aside, summoning a lesser priestess to him.

Why this ache, this pain? Pain was the body's. It could be set aside, should be disdained. But it warned.

"You won't bring them to Marakand's walls even tomorrow," Sien-Mor said. "They'll die on their feet if you keep driving them."

He frowned. She was probing at him, taunting. She always did, in her sly and subtle way. Trying to assert that she too partook of the god their father's wisdom and his strength, which was not the case. It never had been. One womb, one birth, but her cleverness was only their mother's, a mortal cunning.

Ache. As if the wounds were freshly opened.

Ache. As if something burrowed into his heart, which beat steady in his chest, which pulsed in the sanctuary of his godhead—

Vartu—

No. Not she. *Dotemon.* It was Dotemon. Sly, mocking, ever-treach-erous—Yeh-Lin Dotemon, and she had crept undetected into the very heart of his mystery. She was there, she was within the cavern, within *him,* the sacred reservoir of his blood, she *dared,* she profaned his holiness, she threatened . . . *everything.*

"Does she worry you?" Sien-Mor asked. "She should."

But he was not listening. He dropped the reins on his horse's neck and shut his eyes not to see her. The ghost. The imagining.

Madness, his sister suggested. *Perhaps it was not your doing, what broke me. Perhaps we were always mad, the both of us.*

He shut his ears to her and fell away into a place where he could reach and shape, could make a death. Mere wizardry would not serve and he could not turn his back on what passed here in the pass, either. That might be their intention, to distract him from Marakand. Dotemon and Vartu, allied? Perhaps. Far more likely that Dotemon was sent by the god to which she pretended—it must surely be pretence—submission. A spider in cunning, Nabban was, hidden in the heart of his land and sending out his tendrils. Jochiz knew he should have gone to hunt the assassin, that offence of necromancy and abuse of divinity, in the moun-tains himself when Nabban's sword came after Sarzahn, should have left the army to its march—even Clio could not have gotten them lost, coming south along the edge of the Malagru. He would prune that arm of Nabban's reach away soon enough. And this one, Yeh-Lin Dotemon, this traitor who ought to have remained forever damned to the cold hells, he would finish her now. Did that slave-boy made god all unde-serving, profanation of the very concept of divinity, think Dotemon so great, so subtle, that one so mighty as Jochiz would not see what she intended?

Jochiz reached, found what he might, to shape, to ride—a small, soft thing, pregnant with potential, hiding in the damp gravel of a pas-sageway worn to a channel by floodwaters. It would serve.

He began to shape it, to put into it his thought, his will. His fire, to consume beyond any restoration.

Sien-Shava rode distracted, abstracted. Some work afoot. Sien-Mor could not tell what he did. Devil's work. She probed but could get no sense even of where he directed his attention. Such were the limitations of mortality. If that was what it was called. Ghosthood? She knew the shapes of things, but could no more manipulate them than she could touch or lift or taste. She relaxed her hold on her seeming, a little. Not too much, lest she be swept away, out of this place that seemed so—strange, now. The life burned in everything—human, horse, tree, bird, weeds underfoot. It all pulled at her, and her yearning to fall into it was strong. Free of the body, at last, at last. Free of the pull of the road, the summons she yearned, with all that she was, to obey, and could not not; fighting, fighting, a current that swept against her, a wind, an endless storm of sand, of ice, of timeless, hopeless journeying . . . Vartu did not know what she had done, summoning a ghost so, tearing her free of the nightmare struggle—and Sien-Shava had always held a little piece of her, even after her soul had sought the road. She had not been whole in so, so long.

How strangely clear, her thoughts. She had not shaped a clear, clean thought in so long.

Quite a few of her thoughts were of how she should like Sien-Shava to suffer—as though pulled again into the world, she took on all the grime of life, the pain and the hate of it, that she had put from herself. Or at least—it was there again, like a garment shaped of memory, of pain and guilt and sin acknowledged and shed like a caterpillar's last skin, left an empty shell on the twig once the butterfly had flown. She fit herself inside it, and it began to cling to her.

Must she then die, and make the journey, and cleanse herself all over again?

And it had been a long, long road. Beyond enduring. But one endured. It was necessary. Her sins were very great. She had never yet come to the heavens. What she thought she knew—that was only fragments. Tu'usha's memory.

She rode—she and the illusion she made of her favourite horse, the memory she shaped—as a chill breath, a drifting air. She hoped it was not Vartu that Sien-Shava so intently worked against. Miles, and more lost souls falling by the roadside. Did he mean the whole of this army to die? She began to think he did.

He screamed. He screamed most terribly, and clutched his chest as if struck to the heart, and slumped forward. Unbalanced, fell slowly from his horse, tipping, tipping . . . she might have reached to stop him, had she any physical form to bear such weight. If she had also wanted to. She smiled, and watched. He slid down the horse's side, crumpling on the ground. Senseless. Unmoving. Scarlet spread over the unnaturally dust-less white of his gown. Scarlet trickled down his wrists. His lips were very pale, blue-grey. Drained.

She had not thought anyone, not even Vartu, had the power to wound him so.

But alas, he still held to life, Sien-Shava, Jochiz, still himself, still live and in this world, anchored. Life flickered. His sycophantic folk swarmed about him, their cries like the peeping of a brood of chickens deprived of the hen's warmth. Lost, shelterless . . . witless.

Let them sort it out.

Too soon, the one called Ambert asserted himself to do so. It was not entertaining. They bandaged Sien-Shava's bleeding wounds, the gaping tear as if someone had tried to cut the heart out of him, which clove through the bone and should have killed any mortal man. But of course he was their god, and his heart beat still. Indeed, she had a glimpse of it, while a shivering surgeon and a frantic seer reaching far beyond his talent or knowledge tried to put Sien-Shava back together again. That, at least, was gruesomely fascinating.

They put him in a horse-litter between two steady mules and Ambert—really, the man was devoted beyond all reason—refused all cries, all pleas for a halt.

It was not the will of the All-Holy that they rest. They must take the defensible gap of the Shiprock, lest Marakand come to hold it against them. He shouted. He spoke with quiet menace. He denounced as cowards and apostates those who spoke against him. He claimed to utter the All-Holy's own words.

It was when he cried, vengeance, vengeance for the devil's attack that had laid the All-Holy low, that the commanders, and perhaps more crucially the common soldiery who stood behind them, were stirred. They must push on. Marakand must fall. This was only the first march, the first great stride, and if it faltered, the whole might fail.

It was not enough to have taken the Western Wall, which had never in human memory been taken.

They were already so close to the camping-ground that the All-Holy in his wisdom and foresight had decreed for them. The Shiprock was in sight, and the scouts reported no sign of any Marakander defences. Sien-Mor whistled a little tune to herself. Cheerful. Lilting. A Northron thing. "My brother lies in the cold, cold ground . . ." One seer frowned, looking around blindly. She chuckled, drifted over, dropped a chill kiss on his cheek, a whisper in his ear.

"You won't live to see the dawn, poor boy."

The scouts sent through the gap of the Shiprock reported nothing. No hasty fortifications, no archers on the heights, no engines concealed behind the windmill. Deserted.

The Marakanders were fools who had trusted entirely to their Western Wall, Ambert declared, but he did not believe it, and he ordered the tent of the All-Holy erected and a guard drawn up around it even as he sent the vanguard on beneath the cliffs, and dispatched parties with sixth-circle seers among them up the treacherous cliff-paths to investigate the windmill more closely.

A low camp bed. The black sword was laid by the All-Holy's side, and his own as well. They did not dare carry those elsewhere; their god was never without them. Sien-Mor drifted out again. Nothing had changed. The companies still marched. Ambert was determined to prove himself the All-Holy's most obedient and faithful servant—and successor? They would seize the broader space beyond the Shiprock gap for their main camp, a bridgehead from which they might march on to Marakand. The sun at their backs pushed long shadows up the pass. It grew dark, down in the narrow place, but the white windmill gleamed.

She began to be disappointed in the Marakanders. They should surely have seen the value of this place. Sien-Mor returned to her brother's side, as a faithful and devoted sister ought.

The All-Holy stirred and muttered, clutching his bandaged chest beneath the sodden bandages. His forearms, too, were bandaged, elbow to wrist, and those were soaked as well. He bled yet, not healing swiftly as he should, being what he was. Could not summon the will, or was there some thing that worked against him? Sien-Mor could not tell. So limited and limiting, humanity, even for a wizard. She reached—and Tu'usha was gone from her, even memory of what it had been, to be her, gone remote and dreaming. But perhaps that was her madness.

She felt quite sane. The healing of the road, even if the journey were uncompleted?

The physician was coming with more wrappings. They would swaddle him into a cocoon, and still he would bleed. He had, after all, a great reservoir of blood to shed. They prayed, priests and seers, stationed in ranks about him, voices raised in songs of pleading and praise. Praying to their god for their god's restoration.

"Poor fools," she told them, unheard. Crouched at Sien-Shava's side, considering him. Little she could do. Whisper into his mind. *You should die. Give up, flee away. You aren't anything greater than you ever were, for all your hunger. You might consume every god and goddess of this earth and every soul and still you will be nothing but a sick and bloated parasite, a tick feeding on what it cannot digest. Pregnant with sterility. The world will take back what you have stolen . . . what we have hidden . . .* The thought distracted her a moment. When she focused on him again, his dark eyes were open, fixed on hers. Ah, he saw again. She smiled, sweetly, as he had liked her to smile.

But no, he looked through her, beyond. His lips were still pale with the blood he had lost, and he shaped some word she could not decipher.

Twitched and thrashed, struck away the physician who tried to take his arm, knocking the clean bandages from her hands. Sat up.

It seemed to take a very long time. The world, slowed. A massive strength, gathering itself.

There was a rumbling, as of thunder. The ground shook.

"*You.*" He did not shriek. It was hardly more than a whisper, but it carried a rage she felt through to the bones that were so long ash. And what washed over her—she lost her hold on herself, scattered, dissolved almost to nothing, to shredded confusion of memory, of will—

He saw her. He knew her, at last, to be no dream, no delusion, not even a ghost, but a soul stolen from the heavens, a soul flown willing on the path laid open to it into the dream-delusion Vartu had sought to create, back down the thread her brother had always held, refusing to give her up even to death—

For a moment he was their father, a great silver seal rising from the curling waves, a great tall man striding up the white beach, and the air about him, the cloud building, the waves, the slow weight of a god's anger . . .

Lightning, white, burning. A roar, a crash that was more hammer-blow than thunder-growl. Blinding. Scent of scorched wood and cloth, flesh and hair. Chaos and wailing and a ring of dead, struck down as cattle crowded under a hilltop tree to shelter from the thunderstorm. The canopy of the tent flapped rags in a clear-sky gale.

Sien-Mor was already fleeing as Sien-Shava—whatever was left of Sien-Shava in the thing that had risen from the litter—reached. She was running, flying, crying out on the Old Great Gods to see, to stretch out a hand to draw her home—

No road before her, no deep well of safety into which she might plunge. No way back.

He closed on her, in fire, in the white light of the heavens and the molten heart of the earth.

She was only a small thing, in the end. A butterfly held in the hand, crushed to ash.

Nabban . . . The necromancer god dared think himself something greater than he had any right to be, to walk beyond the bounds of his land, to do what no god of the earth might, what only the god of the earth, god of all the lands, Great God of the earth might do.

Nabban stole the trophy of Jochiz's victory from him, made of the corpse from which Dotemon had been driven some heroic fallen vassal, to be honoured, entombed—she was traitor to her kind, she was *his*, Jochiz's own, her bones—she should rot and lie in the heart of his mystery and her soul be forever denied its road—

And to steal her the false god of Nabban revealed what Jochiz had suspected, that he did ride the soul he had withheld from the Old Great Gods, the bones he had kept from their right and proper grave, he rode the soul of his dead lover even into Marakand, which was Jochiz's, his sister's city, a place belonging to him and all the souls within it his as well and Nabban dared defy that—

There was only one god, one *God*, who might range the road, and it was not the slave-born mortal boy of Nabban, whatever trickery of necromancy he worked to free himself from the constraints of the godhead he had stolen. Base human mother, base human father, elevated beyond due by the senile desperation of a land's dying gods . . .

And Nabban had even taken Sarzahn his brother from him.

Jochiz left the army of the All-Holy to look to itself. They were lost to him, useless, until he could shape a new sanctuary in which to gather them. There were caves enough beneath Gurhan's hill, and the god—like would bind to like. He was become soul, the world contained within him, a creature who burned with its light. Very godhead lay now within him, he made it in himself through those he had carried, encysted, the gods of his army's march, and now he might—he did, he swallowed them, felt himself spread, and deepen, felt he might stretch and reach the horizon, reach into the beating heart of the world and draw it fully into himself, contain it all.

There was still a long road to the eastern sea, and there were still roads beyond, south, more easterly yet. But he could reach, he would, and with every land he crossed he would grow. Here he could dispense with the ritual, the sacrifice of the children made vessels, earth-soul to itself. He was god and he was God and he might take Gurhan so, and bring Gurhan's land into himself, and its folk and all, and spill out along the roads east, by desert and by sea.

And Vartu's defences—

They were nothing.

She was nothing.

But Nabban, he would deal with Nabban first. Since the false godling rushed so headlong to meet his doom and offered himself, in the body of his Praitannec king.

CHAPTER XXXIV

Ahjvar staggered to his feet baffled and blinking at slanting afternoon light where had been darkness, unsteady on even ground, balance expecting soft and rolling forest mould. Still hearing voices.

"Ahjvar," Ailan said, fervent as prayer, and reached a steadying hand for him, which he allowed. Understood again where he was, found the world solid around him after all. It hurt, as waking from a dream. Close almost to touching, and now he was fallen away.

And Yeh-Lin was dead. But taken, at least, from a grave in Jochiz's unholy ground.

"What happened?" Ailan was asking—repeating, he had asked more than once, his voice an echo, a confusion.

"What?" Ahjvar asked. Shook his head against a growing pain, a headache blossoming, thunder brewing and he did not need this, not here, not tonight. "Yeh-Lin—" he began, and frowned at the blue sky, nothing but a few white tatters of cloud trailing from the southern peaks, while the storm-megrim pressed and edged his vision with streaks of murky colour—

He lashed out and flung Ailan away as the sky split, or his head, white searing the eyes, slid aside from the descending blade, the man, the burning bolt of light that contained and was barely contained by the human shell, heard the thwack of the steel striking stone and the burning man in all his wrath and glory stumble off-balance.

No shield, no armour, no helm. Sword in hand. Ahjvar drew the heavy dagger to guard, went in with a sweeping blow that Jochiz, turning, caught and slid off his blade. Backed from the edge whirling up, spilling flame, the man himself still burning, as if a shadow of pale fire followed him. A flurry of blows, then, and Jochiz defending with a hand raised, no shield, no buckler, but the spilling light of him hazed and dazzled and Ahjvar knew when he had connected, felt the blow in his shoulder, the brief jarring resistance as Jochiz dropped his warding arm and turned away and came back low, swinging up, but then the devil was moving freely again, no lame limb, no hesitation, no blood, teeth bared in a grin that was fury. Nothing human in his eyes at all: hollows in a skull, windows in a lantern.

Fighting for his life at last, an enemy who did not need to match him with the sword but nearly did, and it would take only one strike, with the devil's strength and will in it—the devil's malice reaching into him, seeking a grip on what held him in life, to sever artery and muscle, sinew and bone, and the old, old weaving that Ghu had made his own.

Jochiz was vast, to some sense that was not the eye. A weight. He pulled the stone of Marakand to him. He pulled the god of the hill.

No rite, no song of binding and death. Only a reaching, the many waving tendrils, tentacles of some sea-creature, touching, clinging with a thousand barbs, pulling—and runes flared in light, and words rang hard, like silver strings and brass, in denial. But still the devil reached and the god of Marakand—frayed.

Jochiz blazed. Higher. Deeper. As if he expanded, grew, in dimensions unseen.

Laughed. Gathered himself, greater and vaster. Reached again to seize Gurhan, crushing the already failing runes, the priests and their prayers, the god's own resistance—a hunger, pulling. With no faltering of attention for the work of his sword.

Nothing Ahjvar could do. Jochiz might, but he could not, face two directions at once. He shut out Gurhan's pain, the prayers and the wizardry of his defenders, the cold hard edge that raised again a wall, a last sanctuary, about the god, now that the bounds of the city were broken. Legacy, something set to wake and hold, no active working in it. He had no sense of Moth at all.

Nothing he could do. Fight the battle before him, and endure, till—till something changed.

Yet Ahjvar forced the devil to give up ground. No place to corner him, no rough footing to unbalance. Nothing but the flat white paving and the vast open space. The folk who had wandered it fled to the far reaches —only Ailan, spare a corner of thought—Ailan on his feet again with his damned short-sword in hand standing off, as if he watched for an opening and would rush in to stab the devil.

"Get to Moth!" Ahjvar shouted, wherever she was, whatever she did—it gave the boy purpose and reason to run, to be saved from this—

Ghu, he thought. *To die for you, yes*—and could he drag the soul of the human Sien-Shava with him when he died, when that devil's sword took him as it must and ripped him from love and curse and life and all? Could he wind it into himself and pull it to the road and leave the devil broken, a damned and inhuman soul adrift in a world that could not sustain it, powerless, no more to threaten gods of the earth, no march on Nabban that empress and wizards and banner-lords and the army and fleets could not defend against, and the god safe in the land . . .

Or—*now*—and he was in, striking aside the devil's sword with the dagger and the heavy Northron sword had its opening, the whole of his body a prayer behind the edge, the whole of his body, his will, the dance, in *yew*, which was death, and he cut the head of Jochiz from its body, he did, he felt it, he saw, the startled moment, the brief searing pain, the terror—

—the flaring screaming light, flame white and marble-streaked, red, gold, and the head did not fall, the blood did not spray, the man did not fold to the ground, only the blade came whistling around and Ahjvar struck with the left-hand dagger what was not flesh and took no harm, though his own blow wrenched and twisted and something in his shoulder gave, lance of pain down his side. The dagger dropped from numb fingers—his sword again to turn and slide the devil's edge away as he moved back—but it struck hard and edge to edge. The blade of the leopard-headed sword shattered, shattered like glass to flying shards and the force sent Ahjvar stumbling to his knees.

Arm did not answer, to catch himself, his left, and he was reaching with his right, the forage-knife sheathed at the small of his back, the broad curved blade, recovered balance on his knees and was up in a rush, a sweeping slash upwards that he followed with the whole of himself, into the fire.

It wrapped him. It tore air from his lungs and burned the water from his eyes, stink of burning hair, the heat on the skin, and yielding firmness giving, the knife buried to the grip, the wet heat of it, the opened belly and the shriek that was human, the body he leaned into solid and its fires contained, staring, bloody neck-wound half-healed, and they were crashing down, with the god's knife buried in the devil's guts and the god's hand on it, the god in him, a clean cold certainty of stone and water and the green great breathing land, that would not lose him, lose Ahjvar, who was life and love and warmth and the only thing in the end that mattered to the man still in the heart of the god—life and love and his own beating heart. He ripped up and rolled away, the knife held hard, skin to leather-wrapped grip, blade and hand slimed with blood and filth to the wrist. To his feet and his left arm not answering and had he done it, broken that body past restoration, severed the devil from his anchor in the world—

—Tu'usha, Sien-Mor dead, body destroyed, had taken refuge in a goddess, a welcomed fugitive who betrayed and devoured her host and seduced a new human partner to carry her—

—Jochiz tried it. He reached for Ahjvar, hasty chains of wizardry, shapings of devil's will, no seduction but the mindless possession of enslavement was his intention, a vessel he thought to seize and deny to Nabban.

No, Ghu said.

Flexed left-hand fingers. They hurt, but they answered. Ache, deep in the bone of the upper arm. Better than what had been before.

Wizardry for the binding of a devil. It had taken the Old Great Gods themselves, aiding the wizards of the world, to bind the seven in their half-death, half-sleeping prisons. A wizard in godhead, a god in wizard's understanding . . .

They might try—

The devil was a mass to him they could hardly come to grips with.

Ailan had not obeyed Ahjvar. He moved behind Jochiz, slowly, sword held most correctly for a thrust to the devil's kidneys and if in that moment's distraction he, Ghu, *they* struck for that still-healing throat and carried in mind and blow the patterns of yew, and the male holly, and hermit's pepper for binding, and the great knot of sealing that was a pattern of the Great Grass—

Sien-Shava Jochiz saw, felt, something. He struck backwards even as Ailan lunged, straight and true. Not his sword the devil swept around but a lash of white fire that knocked the young man flying, rolling when he hit the stones, a black path coiled around his back and arms like the welt of a whip left in the thick wool of his coat, maybe the flesh beneath. He did not get up. But Ahjvar had moved, striking, not the throat, no, the heart, cut the heart from his body, some old, old magic there and the devil leapt away and flung his sword like a spear. It did not fly true. They stepped aside and were running in to take him when he slid the second sword down into his hand and brandished it, sheathed.

Even so it made a coldness in the air, a crack into winter. Or something very like. But it was a thing of the heavens, the hells. Moth's sword. They had seen it before.

It was only a blade and stone or steel, theirs was just as to be feared, now.

Jochiz maybe saw that in their eyes. He backed again to give himself room and drew the blade, dropping the wood and leather scabbard that any fool would keep to parry with, and the narrow black sword was obsidian, maybe, or ice, or glass, or steel with the gloss of polished stone, but all up and down its length ran a tracery of script in silver. A moss of frost grew on it, born from the air's touch, and delicate white feathers, turning to flakes and drifting down. They hesitated. Not for fear of it. In wonder at the beauty, the unworldly song of it, thing that should not be, could not be, existing in this place, this world.

Jochiz grinned, misunderstanding hesitation.

The sword was a blade, an edge, whatever it else it might be and might hold and it knew this, too, and in its forging was the severing of soul from soul, the unmaking of that alloy of human and Old Great God that was the bound devil in the world, and how little different was what stood before it, god and man in one—

Jochiz came at them and Ahjvar wanted his own sword, wanted reach, but they had what they had and it was their dance—

Though Ghu's best tactic, he had told Ahjvar once and not entirely in jest, was to hide behind Ahj when he could not get in close to cut throats, preferably from behind. Or hamstring them. He-they went down to their knees, sliding, rolling, came up with Jochiz slashed and pitching forward, but it was not enough; the devil held himself together still, though he could not, it seemed, burn again into fire. They held him from that; they might yet take him that way, and have a dead wizard sent to the road with all his great and many sins upon him, an Old Great God loose and lost, to fade, they might hope, and die, withering in the world for which it was not meant . . .

Gods he was fast, fast as Ahjvar, who was hurt, who was tiring. The black sword left cold in the air, struck, chill, to the marrow in its mere passing. Snatched the air from the lungs like deep frost on mountain height. Ahjvar swept up Ailan's dropped short-sword to his recovering left hand, but it was still they who were beaten back, giving ground each stroke, some searing pain, some new wounding they had not noticed. The black sword bit as keen as glass, hip, ribs, and blood new-staining their left hand, which was Ahjvar's own, to match the gore of their right, which was not.

Ghu within him might hold flesh and bone to itself, what had once been bone and ash, and yet now the fire was burning high in Jochiz again, a frame and cage, he was become, and there would be no tiring him, no matter how he bled when they struck into fire, into flesh.

"I never thought—" Jochiz said. He gasped. He fought for air. He bled. But still he spoke and pressed and the sword laid another touch, a bite of frost over the chest—

"—that I might kill a god so, hand to hand. And I have your name, Nabban, and your man's blood and what may I make of that, to take you and your land . . . and all the world lies open, once I am all that you are—"

"You could never be anything that he is or ever was," Ahjvar—it was most definitely Ahj, and a breathless snarl, and a lunge with the stabbing sword that made Jochiz reel back and fall—

—Jochiz fell, like any faltering human, flat and stunned and bleeding, heart-wounded, and the ice of the black sword came crawling up his arm like ants—

But he rocked to his feet again even as they swooped to cut again that throat, the shapes of death and binding a possibility, a hope, and they dodged back from what must have killed any man had it struck and for a moment paused, both alike, Jochiz and Nabban, a few breaths gasped.

There must be an ending.

I can take him with me. Let me go.

No.

You promised, Ghu.

I was lying.

You don't lie.

But he would, he would in this, not like this, not ever, to cut his own heart free to what should once have claimed it, what might no longer claim it, grown into something greater, deeper, god-soul enduring in the land—

He did not think Ahjvar, even truly willing, which he was not, might take that road any longer, no more than any god of the earth might fling himself to the distant heavens and say, come untangle this mess that your kind has wrought in this world . . .

And Jochiz laughed, lunging up, flesh, bone, spilling light. The black sword drove at them.

Thunder cracked over the city and she was on her feet, and Mikki, and the Blackdog startled up out of the deep stillness that had held him much of the day, a baying bark that trailed off into a confused snarl, looking around, uncertain. He was the man, then, a hand on Mikki's shoulders, braced, but weaponless, not even a knife.

"*Jochiz*," Holla-Sayan said.

The runes Moth had built all these long weeks flared and burned as if traced in lightning, and were gone.

Jochiz. All defences of the walls torn down, and Gurhan vulnerable. But Jochiz did not appear here among them, though the god stood by. Priests and priestesses from over the eastern ridge of the gnarled hill were running, some of them, the young and fleet, and street-guard with them for what that could do, for the cave and the most sacred sanctuary, as if by defending that they might yet save the god.

Jochiz. He was—

Old Great Gods damn—

"*Ahjvar*," she said, and her hand went to her belt, but her feather cloak was in the god's sanctuary. She was on her feet and running, and Mikki came crashing down the hillside after her, snapping saplings, and the Blackdog after him.

Gurhan was before them, but he said nothing, stepped aside from the cave's entrance to let her pass. The cloak was flung with their other few things, there on a stone, and she caught it up, a mottled softness that was too light for its size, stirring faintly like weed in water as it lifted into the air.

"Go to your folk," she told the god. "Be with them. Find your strength in them and be their strength. He will not have you, I promise."

Gurhan—Gurhan bowed, and was—not gone, not in this place. But no longer a visible thing, only rock and tree and the deep, deep stone on which the city was founded, and its waters too.

The light dimmed. Mikki, great bulk blocking the entrance.

"Moth," he said.

"Move."

"Moth—*Let him keep it,* you said. He has Lakkariss. He can kill you. You. Vartu. Both and all of you."

The ground beneath them trembled. Stone slid. A breath-holding pause, and again it shook, violent shudders. A tree cracked, up the western ridge, and crashed down.

"Gurhan," Holla-Sayan said, warning. "Jochiz—" He sniffed the air like a dog. "Gods, Moth, Jochiz is here in the city."

"Cub, move and let me go."

"I was ill. I was weary and heartsick still and I didn't ask, I didn't want to know and—and after I still did not want to know and I let it slide and told myself later, later, and it was always later. You were late coming to me. So late. You left me in his hands a year and more around, Ulfhild, my princess, my wolf, and you did not do that without great need. I do trust that. I do." His voice almost broke. "What do you mean to do?"

She said nothing. What could she? But she stepped into him, arms around the neck, heavy again with muscle, the deep fur, the warmth, the clean beast-smell of him, old oak leaves and earth, as if memory of the den lay in his pelt. Such warmth. Such strength to lean on, to lose herself in. To give herself to. Held, hard, to him, and if that was heartbeats, breaths of life for her, it was surely stealing them from the beloved of the god of Nabban and his faithful young man. But she held there regardless and felt the deep breath he heaved, the tremor that shook him.

She took his head in her hands and kissed him, closed her eyes, open-mouthed, tasting the heat of him, the breathing, thrumming vital life. The sweet warmth. The urgent hunger, to have, to hold, to press close and closer yet, to make two so close to one as bodies could be and yet be two, souls distinct. A worship, a wonder.

Broke from his hungry, desperate mouth—as if he might hold her there, forever—and he lowered his head, pressed his long face against her breast, and she held him still, face buried in his fur.

"You were the best thing ever in Ulfhild's life, Mikki," she said, muffled, and if her voice shook, what did it matter. "In mine. Now let me go."

He backed away. A step. Two. And Styrma, good Storm, flicked his ears and stamped and nodded.

"You were only ever a ghost," she told the bone-horse. "You've served longer in this world than any wizard's making should have endured."

Memory and an old skull, nothing more. He tossed his head and nickered.

"Oh, go and run where you will, fool beast."

Met Holla-Sayan's eyes. Said nothing.

She couldn't. She seized on Mikki again, holding hard, arms about his neck. Clung there, while he leaned against her, careful weight. Too long. Let him go and laid the feather-cloak to her shoulders. "You saved me, Mikki. You know you did. My dear heart, be well and never despair. Hold to joy. That gift you gave me."

"Moth . . ."

Look after him, Blackdog.

She flew.

"Ulfhild!" he howled, and reached after her, rearing up on hind legs. *Moth! No!*

She shut him out.

A falcon plunging from the sky. Moth struck like the lightning, a tattered swirl of silk and feathers and pale hair unfurling between them. Sword met sword and the obsidian did not this time shatter Northron steel. Ahjvar reeled back, ended up down on one knee, bracing himself on the short-sword, breath dragging in his throat, smoking in air grown winter-cold, dry and painful. Ice growing, spreading along the cracks between the stones of the pavement.

They kept some space between them, the two devils, but the black sword seemed almost to shiver, like a dog keen to leap. Did the silver lines shift and crawl? Change?

"I told you to keep out of my way. You and your beast. I hope you had some pleasure out of him worth your ruin. You should have kept running."

"Should we? Where did you mean to stop? How far? Nabban? Pirakul? The south? The lands of my far ancestors beyond Pirakul? We never ran. We only went to choose our ground."

"Is that what you call it?" Jochiz laughed. "In that case you took your time, Vartu."

She flinched at that; Nabban saw it.

"I'm here now."

"You did not have to be."

"Oh, but I did. Since the moment I woke in the far north, since the moment he cried out, the wolves of your necromancy pulling him down, I have been on my way here. Sien-Shava, I was putting myself from the world. I was sleeping . . . I would have faded out of all thought and memory. *You called me back when you took Mikki.*"

She glanced back at Ahjvar, through him, into Ghu. Briefest inattention. Smiled, even as Sien-Shava Jochiz lunged forward. Met him in a clash and flurry of movement, of steel, silk, feathers, that ended with them locked together, the black sword forced up between them, and neither blade to bite.

Ahjvar did not think the iron rings of her mail would turn the stone's edge; Ghu knew so.

Frost silvered her, whitened the dark hair of Jochiz, fringed his beard.

"Lakkariss," she said. "Shard of the cold hells and a rift to drag back what escaped. But we know that is a poet's tale. We know the hells so, and the heavens. A tale, and a truth beyond words. But words have shaped Lakkariss for this world. And words have reshaped it. Time I completed them."

Jochiz was already breaking free, shoving her from him, but she turned and stood ready, laughing, as he came on in another rush, using the edge this time, swinging. Moth lowered her sword and sang.

It cut the air. It resonated deep in the bones, and the stones beneath them shuddered. Words, maybe. They could not grasp the shape of them, not Ahjvar, not Ghu, not human ear nor god's understanding. Music, voice, thought, a power shaping, a thing that lived in itself—

The sword cut. That, they saw, even as they surged up again, too late, to do whatever it was they might have done to stop that blow. They saw the blood spray, the singer silenced, reeling back, and the silver script traced on the black blade turned crimson as storm sunset, drank, it seemed, that blood, that staining, burned in brief fury, and she was not falling but striking then, a two-handed blow that split his skull and she took her left hand free to catch Lakkariss falling by the blade, pinched it from the air and flipped it and stabbed left-handed then, and the air cracked in its wake and the song she had broken off echoed and re-echoed even as she fell, folding over, the silver lines running with Ulfhild's blood, with Sien-Shava's, smoking, frost in sun, burning into the air. They rose, words written in air. Souls? They made clouds, winter-fog dense, cold.

God's vision saw them die. Ulfhild, Sien-Shava, human souls torn away, dissolving into silver, into frost, no blessing, no road awaiting, though Ahjvar, Ghu, reached a hand, cried her name. Saw them die, Vartu, Jochiz, saw the fires annihilated, fed to the silver smoking frost, saw the flame of Vartu leap to meet what came even as it faded and Jochiz roiling, brief futile struggle to fight free. Lakkariss melting, ice in the sun, smoking, rising—

Saw them gone, bone to ash to nothing but rising mist and light, sacrifice of blood and soul consumed in the making—

The air tore, where frost and smoke, blood and silver and souls had in destruction made a way.

Darkness beyond. The black between the stars. The lightless heart of stone. That which has no name.

Heavens. Hells. Fissure growing wider. Road, he thought, Ahjvar did, felt the old pull of it, the shape, the need, but it touched and let him go; it was not his road, not any longer.

Road. River. Dark wind, roaring free.

Light. Darkness burned into white flame, into tongues of ice, into colours: silver, red, green, gold, blue, nacreous crawling light, spilling out, rising, streaking the sky. Twisting, clashing.

The roads of the heavens were opened and the seals of the cold hells breached. The sun was setting, and the Old Great Gods and the devils of the cold hells poured into the world.

On the mountainside, where the hill folk patrol camped fireless and cold above the ruins of the Shiprock, Nikeh cried out. Lia did. Orhan—a yell. Shielding eyes.

Something—distant, far beyond Shiprock. Light. White. Green, red, gold—cold light, bursting the night. Sound. Thunder. Rising. Rising, rising, till Nikeh screamed and it rose higher through her screaming and into silence and the ringing of her ears, the searing after-image of the light in her eyes, sight and sound one pain, ebbing, but she could hear how almost, the sound that was no longer sound echoed and re-echoed, washing between the mountain heights.

"Gurhan bless." Lia's voice was a child's whimper, high and thin.

"Old Great Gods defend us." That was Orhan.

Nikeh was silent then.

Over Marakand, the cold fire burned the sky. It spilled to fill the valley between the mountains.

She had dreamed a woman, once, whose body was washed through with such light.

"No," Ghu said. "This ends."

Ahjvar pushed himself to his feet. Ailan breathed, good. Life burned bright in him. He should gather him up off the cold stones . . . Ghu wasn't there. He had spoken himself. The world about was strange, over-bright, over-sharp, a construct cast in light like glass, like steel. The light of the Old Great Gods—so close, so distant.

Old Great Gods, devils. There was no difference to be made between them. And beyond, within . . .

A pressure, building. A river dammed.

A frantic flying storm of starlings, caged—

Now, Ghu said, and they reached, they spread their arms wide, inviting, and they reached—they were the world, and the world within them, god in man in god and the dreaming soul of the world finding its way to a voice that might speak, an eye that might see, at last. *Come home.*

Invitation, not command. There was—they stared into the heart of what was not a sun, what seared the soul and not the eye, and there were no words, there was no image to hold, only—there was the stuff of life, of the world, the stuff of soul, and some souls sought refuge in the Gods, and some were ready, eager, long, long held away, and these heard, and answered.

They opened themselves, a gateway, and the light poured into them, through them, he and Ghu, he and Ahjvar; they made of themselves a bridge, a road, a riverbed coursing with what they could not hold, being in the world and of the world, god made man made god . . . the world within the god, the soul that was the Soul, the great heart of all that was, that the Old Great Gods had bled away, little by little.

The soul of the world is a wholeness, and it is not whole. That which should be of it, in it, is lost. The soul, the life. Not Ghu's thought. Not Ahjvar's. Not words. An understanding, a plea . . . it found its way into them all, and Gods trembled with it.

The souls that sought healing and rest in the heavens. In time, they must return. They were a part of the world's own soul. The world was wounded, when the heavens folded closed around them and barred their return.

And the devils, too—severed, held apart. A deep wrong.

There should be demons born of the earth in Nabban. There should be gods and goddesses and demons reborn into the west.

The cold hells. Do you see? That was a whisper, a thousand voices, thoughts.

There was a shifting within the light, a stirring as of storm. An urge to deny? To prevent?

"Are we Jochiz, to be thieves of the soul?" Dotemon. Ahjvar's mind made it Yeh-Lin's very voice.

A terrible yearning, a pain. Hands, heart reaching to enfold, to hold self to self, to make whole what is sundered.

A division that should never have been made.

The severed self that seeks its restoration.

What is sundered must be whole.

The Old Great Gods hold the world, the souls of the world. The guardians, in their awe and their wonder at what the soul of the world makes of itself in its passage through its self-knowing lives . . . But they too are of the world, of the soul of the world, apart and containing . . .

But do not come into the world to walk among human-folk again. This is not your place.

Light faded.

Ahjvar was on his knees again, propping himself up with his hands on the stone, braced like a drunk.

It was still there, the one who had been Yeh-Lin. A last figure of light, almost a woman's shape. He couldn't have said how he knew her, it, from any other.

"Dotemon," he said.

Yes, the God said.

"Sort it out, old woman."

Do you think we move in the breaths you measure, dead king? Trust me.

And then Dotemon too was gone.

Mikki sat on the steps above the plaza, naked, human in the night. Ulf-hild's sword across his knees, finger tracing the runes on the blade.

There had been nothing else to save of them. Ash. Fragments of steel and bone. She had made of herself and Sien-Shava a great pyre, in the end. But her sword had survived.

"What does it say?" Ahjvar asked.

Past midnight, and the moon was rising over the roofs. Torches burned on the pillars of the library's long arcade. Down in the plaza, a patrol of street-guard passed, lanterns swinging, and then a pair of couriers on wearily clopping ponies. The senate palace was ablaze with light. Captains and wardens summoned; there had been much traffic early in the night. Quiet, now. There was a still an army encamped in the pass, broken and confused though it might be. Stories of madness, of the seers and highest of the priests struck down with apoplexy, left mumbling imbeciles, were coming to the city. Yeh-Lin's spies, abandoning the army for good, brought news. Work-gangs of Westgrasslanders were deserting wholesale and vanishing down into the desert, taking the better part of the camel-lines with them. Ambassador Ilyan Dan was in the senate. He had been sending pages out to the *Rihswera*, who would not come in to speak to them with the authority of his god. Reports, and requests for advice.

What could Ahjvar say that the ambassador could not put in better words? No slaughter of the broken and confused, the god-bereft and starving. Show mercy, and the truth of the gods. Gurhan was there, to say all that was needed. He had sent the latest weary child back with that word—whatever Gurhan says, Nabban affirms. His land. Hear him.

A great light from the sky. The Old Great Gods, descending at the last, to save the world from the devil who would have destroyed its gods. The folk who had witnessed, who had not been under their beds or deep in their cellars in terror—there was nothing but awe. Wonder. No understanding of what they had seen.

The way of humankind. Moth, Yeh-Lin . . . old tales. If they came into this, in after years, it would be as devils, destroyed by the Old Great Gods.

Not how it should be.

He just wanted to go home. God-bereft. No warm voice, now, in his head, no words not his own in his mouth, the feeling gone, that he was held, that a hand lay on, within, his own. Just an exhaustion that struck bone-deep. And he ached, throbbed, with wounds half-healed. Rags of his shirt glued to him. He'd shed his coat, too fouled and shredded to bother with.

He was cold, and his head ached.

He sat down by the demon. Pain there, unwounded, that cast his into nothing.

Ailan, huddled at a little distance on a lower step, looked up. Looked away. He should send the lad to the ambassador. A gift. Or at least order him to the Nabbani house to find himself a bed.

Touched the blade, one finger, drawing the demon's attention. Wanting to make him speak. To make the world real.

"I don't know the runes."

"Kepra," Mikki said, voice low, hardly audible. "Its name is Kepra. Keeper. She brought it from the Drowned Isles. *Keeper. The Wolf made me for Hravnsfjell.*" He turned it. "*Strength. Courage. Wisdom.*" Looked up, met Ahjvar's eyes. Stood the sword between them. The hilt was gilded, studded with garnets. A royal sword. "On the cross-guard, here, it says—a prophecy, a curse. She never told which she believed. She made jokes, that it was a charm against rust and breaking. *Until the last road, and the last dawn.*"

"Ah." He could think of nothing more to say. I'm sorry? He'd want to take a man's head off for that, were it him. Ghu would—not need to say anything. Only to be there, so that Mikki was not alone.

The Blackdog lay behind them, like a watchdog overlooking all the plaza. He stirred, sat up, and came down to sit on Mikki's other side, battered human.

"Make a song," he said.

"She was the skald. She should have been. Where her heart lay, always."

"The first time ever I saw you, you were singing. A wedding in At-Landi. Northrons come south on the rivers. Some cousin of Varro's, I think."

"Oh."

"Make a song of the truth, before it's all forgotten. So that she's not forgotten. What she made of herself matters."

What Ahjvar had been thinking. "Yeh-Lin, too."

"She went to the west—Moth said."

"He killed her there," Ahjvar said. "We took her home. She died in Nabban. But first she struck him down, even if it was not to the death."

They waited. He told them. A wake. A remembering.

Wondered where Nikeh was, and how he might tell her. Whether she had ever known Yeh-Lin's true nature.

"Moth had been writing the lays of the Drowned Isles, before we came south," Mikki said, after. As if it followed naturally.

It did.

"That was when we came to find Ghatai. She sent what she had done to the royal hall at Ulvsness. I don't know what ever became of them. I don't think she ever finished."

The night wore away in such small memories, passed slow between them like coloured stones, turned in the hand, while the moon rose. More messengers went out from the senate palace, and some of the wardens, soldiers about them. Faint noise from the city. Militias moving.

Mikki fell into silence. A deep breath that came out choked. Holla-Sayan put an arm around him. Ailan was asleep, coiled up on his lower step like a little dog. Like a dog, he whimpered and twitched himself awake, jerked upright on a cry of pain, looking around in nightmare terror. Found Ahjvar and sighed, which brought another whimper with it, and eyes squeezed tight a moment.

"Ailan." Ahjvar held out a hand. Ailan came up the steps, stiffly, face tight with pain, breathing too deliberate, shallow, and sat again, one step down. Lugging a bundle with him, something wrapped in his scarf. All the rest they'd had with them left in the plaza. Probably to be looted for relics of the presence of the Old Great Gods. The holy kettle . . . That had been a decent crossbow.

Ailan's shivering ran through him in waves. His teeth chattered loudly.

Ahjvar put a hand on his head. Cold. Pain. The burns were bad. Weeping. Bruises would heal on their own, but that . . . He shouldn't have left the man lying there all the night. His responsibility. His . . . *gewdeyn*. Spear-carrier. Follower. He could . . . feel the raw flesh, the blistered swollen matter that threatened a death-carrying rot, the screaming nerves. What wizardry might do, and god's blessing . . . in *mountain ash, cypress, white-blossomed rose.* Protection, healing, purification. After a moment Ailan let out a long and easier breath, leaned against his knee, like a little child, and his shivering eased. Ahjvar held his head there and let him lie.

And then Mikki was weeping, choking with it, howling, and Holla-Sayan knelt, holding him, rocking him. One might wish *elm* for peace, *cypress* for healing . . . but that was a long, hard road.

Friendship, most of all.

Could reach, find the Blackdog's mind. A strange turmoil there. A strange creature, no peace in him, under that surface of calm. Not anything Ahjvar could ease, or carry. Not anything Holla-Sayan was asking for help with. *You'll stay with him?*

Yes.

Gurhan, then, walking quietly, as if he had come down from his hill, though perhaps he had only taken physical form here, coming down the steps. Crouched down, to put a hand on the demon.

Weeping must end, and did. They held him, the Blackdog and the god of the city, until he could look up, wiping his face on his arm.

"Come back to the hill," Gurhan said. "Come into the stone and trees, away from here. Rest."

"Ya," Mikki said, with a kind of weary obedience. Looked at the sword still in his hand.

"Yours broke," he said to Ahjvar. His voice was gone to a thick croak, very quiet, too, but Ailan stirred and raised his head.

"I have it," he said, and he did, too, that bundle in his scarf. "Can a smith—"

"Doesn't matter," Ahjvar said. "I've Ghu's knife. For the road."

"Oh."

And what did it cost Ailan, dragging that weight in his condition? "But thank you. It was a good thought. When we get home, maybe the empress's swordsmith can try." He did not think the steel, the sword itself, could be saved. Did not think it would be wise to try, broken on that unearthly edge. But the ancient hilt, and a new Nabbani blade . . . well, maybe. Maybe someone else might carry it, someday.

Ailan had gained a little height, he was sure, and certainly some breadth across the shoulders, since he picked him up in Star River Crossing.

"You use a Northron sword," Mikki said. "Take Kepra."

"Mikki—"

"I'm no swordsman. Take it. A demon made it, the Wolf-Smith of Ulvskerrig. Take it to serve your god." Mikki pushed it to him. "Its last road isn't mine."

The weight was easy in his hand. Felt—like it belonged.

"Good," Mikki said, and used Ahjvar's shoulder to heave himself to his feet.

The eastern sky was thinning, stars growing pale. He was a bear before he reached the top of the stairs. The god of Marakand and the Blackdog went either side of him, close, just touching. Gurhan looked back once. Gave Ahjvar the shadow of a bow.

"Come on," Ahjvar said, in the Praitannec that there were only three of them left in the world to speak, now that Yeh-Lin was gone, and Ailan's was still hit and miss. "The ambassador's house. Walk that far, and then you can rest."

"Will they still come?"

"The Westrons? Who knows. But they won't pass the walls if they do. Leave them to the Marakanders and Gurhan's mercy, poor lost folk. Not our land. We're done."

He hoped. He wanted to go home.

Touched the necklace at his throat, but it was gone. Burnt away in the fires of Jochiz. Well, the binding that mattered between them was not something even a devil had broken, and if he carried no elusive road of wizardry any longer . . . there was still the long true road, and it ran east, into the dawn.

Something rubbing, inside his shirt, caught against his cinching of his belt. He searched, like a man chasing fleas. Seashells, ash-stained.

Laughed.

"What happens to me?" Ailan asked, low-voiced, "when you go home?"

"You want to stay here?"

"No."

"Good. The empress can use a man who speaks half a dozen languages and knows the lands between us and Marakand. Ghu can. A good man, and a brave one, who keeps his wits about him and watches the world."

"I only speak . . . three?" He was counting on his fingers, frowning. Not noticing, how the pain no longer hammered him down. "Does the Marakander Nabbani count separate from Taren?"

"I'm not done with you yet."

"Oh." Ailan considered that. "Good?"

Ahjvar put an arm around his shoulders, comradely, and because he might have pushed the healing along a little and turned back the tide of fever, but Ailan was still stumbling, nearly dropping. "Long road home. Good you learn the way."

In the sanctuary of the god's cave, Mikki had fallen into the deep sleep of exhausted grief. Holla-Sayan sat by him. Didn't want him waking to find himself alone. There would be more weeping yet, and anger, and the deadly dull weight that pulled one down beyond all caring. Gurhan went out again among his folk, with the priests and the priestesses. The voice of mercy, of reason. The army of the All-Holy, in piecemeal confusion, offered its surrender. Some parts of it. Rebellions of its conscripts and converts made small massacres among the red priests and the officers. Some of the faithful fled back down the pass from the imagined pursuit of an army of devils. But most were grateful to lay down arms. To be fed.

"There is a god in you," Gurhan said, and Holla-Sayan, who had slipped into a weary sleep himself, sat up. Afternoon, already. Sun bright beyond the curtain of leaves.

He met the god's eyes, considering.

"Yes," he said at last. "I know. I tried—*we* tried. I wasn't sure. Jochiz was working against him. We were desperate—Sayan and I. The dog, too. Sarzahn." It felt strange, to give it a name. Strange, but—welcome. "I thought we had failed, the dog and I. Lost Sayan even as we tried to hold him. But . . . I can't hear him now. Yet I think he called to me. I think he was calling, all the time I was lost under Jochiz's binding."

"You've swallowed him," Gurhan said.

"No. Jochiz was trying to. We needed to hide him. Sera of the Red Desert was carried to the Narvabarkash, sleeping in a stone."

"Or he has swallowed you."

"No."

"I do think so, brother," said Gurhan gently. "He may be sleeping in you, dormant and dreaming, but he is—not to be so easily disentangled as a goddess from a stone of her spring. What was Sayan is . . . alive within you. A potential, to be reborn. You are—"

"I didn't—"

"I do think it took all three of you," Gurhan said. "Willing. You are—when I look at you, when I try to see, what lies beneath . . . not a tangle. A braid of light. Like what Ahjvar and his god have become, I think. Man, the broken remnants of the one called Sarzahn—and the god, coiled within you. Waiting to wake."

"In his own land."

"In you."

A deep breath, then. He shut his eyes. Sarzahn was quiet. No pain. No rage, the dog's barely-leashed anger. Only . . . a settled certainty. In himself.

A wholeness.

And the sure knowledge. He needed to go home.

EPILOGUE

. . . over the months following the Battle of Marakand

They were waiting. No one said for what. Not all the folk of Kinsai would leave Lissavakail with the first caravan, and little of the library, though the chests were stacked ready in storerooms of the island temple. The first party went only to visit the ruins, to see what was left and decide what might rise again.

On the shores of a river bereft of its goddess.

Only Iarka grew impatient, but she had most urgent need to go. Restless, pacing, as if that would help. Swelling visibly, Jolanan thought. Seven, heading for eight months.

"I want to be in my own land by midsummer day. I want the river. She *needs* the river."

"We'll go," Jolanan told her. "The three of us, if we have to." It was on her way home. Find Reyka's band. Find Lazlan and Tibor. Find what had become of the folk of the Jayala'arad, the first to fall to the Westron army. News, swift messengers, down the caravan road. Dreams of seers. The All-Holy, the devil Jochiz, fallen. Destroyed, and much of his army with him, and its wreckage—to be pitied, Attalissa said.

No one thought the tribes of the desert were likely to view it so.

And if Jochiz had fallen—

There had never been any word of Holla-Sayan.

Rifat, always at Iarka's side, nodded. "Alone if we have to. But Attalissa says, wait, just a little longer."

Wise to go in a caravan. There would be brigands, lawless folk, desperate, even if the broken army of the west were not straggling home.

"Wait for what?"

"She doesn't say. I can't see. Can you?"

"No. Only—something. In the mountains. And I don't care, I want to be travelling, before it's too late. You're going to have to lug me along like baggage as it is. I hate this. I wish we laid eggs."

Which meant they all ended up laughing, a bit desperate.

Three, when the time came, or four? Tashi had followed and had stayed in Lissavakail, when Jolanan went up into the mountains again, not gone back to his own people in the Narvabarkash. She was glad of him. Five. Rifat's little brother Besni was not going to be separated from him again.

Jolanan left Iarka and Rifat and went out from the town, restless as much as Iarka and certainly more mobile. Tashi joined her, with a dog at his heels. They climbed up one of the steep paths that spread out up the mountainsides above the track that led around the lake and down to the desert. A view, there. Endless peaks rising, white-cloaked. The lake held blue below, green-fringed now with spring's advance. The town, stone-built and mud-plastered, tinged golden by the morning light. Washing blowing on rooftops. Tashi didn't say anything. Neither did she. Found a boulder big enough for two to sit and watch.

Restlessness stilled. Like waiting, watching the cattle. Tashi's hand lay by hers, and then touched, questioning. She laced her fingers through his.

Hardly surprised when she heard footsteps on the stony path behind. Looked to see Attalissa, a physical presence, striding up to them, dressed as one of her priestesses, but her hair swinging in a caravaneer's long braids. A girl in her teens, she looked this morning. Smiled and raised a hand in greeting, but then her gaze shifted beyond.

Jolanan looked, too, and Tashi. She got to her feet, letting him go.

Shadows on the mountainside, coming down where there was no path to follow. Big shapes, and dark. They didn't move like yaks. She squinted, shielding her eye against the higher snow's glare. Two. No, three.

Bear, wolf. Bear and wolf and . . . horse? Tibor not here to make stupid jokes. Honey-gold bear, and the wolf not a wolf but a mountain mastiff like the one that sat alert at Tashi's side, twice the size. The horse—heavy, feather-fetlocked blue-roan thing, oddly hard to see—there, then just shadows, and climbing easily as a goat where even a mountain pony should not go. They came down slantwise, stones rattling at the last, a rush, a leaping down to the path. Tashi's dog got to her feet, tail slowly wagging.

Attalissa ran to them like a girl, arms about the Blackdog's neck, face buried in his ruff. Silent, for all Jolanan could hear. Couldn't have said anything herself. Tashi was watching her. He stepped away a little. She didn't move.

Attalissa embraced Mikki, then, and stood cheek to cheek with him. If a bear might look exhausted . . . The dog shook itself, was Holla-Sayan.

He'd aged. Grey in his hair, just a little. Stupid thing to notice. Wearing it loose, not braided. She'd never realized how very long it was, free, curling almost to his waist. Never seen it so. Liked it. Battered as if he'd come from some long road, though his dusty caravaneer's coat was new. Unarmed—well, his sabre was at her side.

"Jo," he said.

She went to him then. Ran. Hugged tight and hard, and had to stop herself tearing open the horn toggles of his coat, groping within his shirt to find that wound, the scars, to assure herself the nightmare that came so often was—what, true, a lie, over? He held her so tightly— kissed her, fierce and passionate, and then softly, gently, and held her off. Watching over her shoulder. Then looking at her again. She ducked her head, couldn't meet his gaze. Couldn't find words. He tipped her face up. It wasn't hurt, there in his eyes. Wasn't betrayal. Just—caring. Kissed her once more, and she could give that back, passion in it, and caring, and—not even farewell. Only something whose time had ended, maybe. He held her off, touched her face, the scars. Smiled.

"Your horse got left in Marakand," he said. "Sorry. I think the Nabbani ambassador's claimed the pair of them." Nonsense. Because any heavier words might still break something.

"So you owe me a horse . . ."

"Not the blue roan. He's Mikki's. And a ghost. Of sorts."

"Ah." She could believe it. Almost. Jolanan took a deep breath, looked back, beckoned. "Two horses. Live ones. Good breeding stock. This is Tashi, of the Narvabarkash. He wants to come to the Western Grass."

"Gods bless," Holla-Sayan said.

The dog went past, tail still wagging, to Attalissa and Mikki.

Someone missing. She had her mouth open to ask. Holla-Sayan shook his head. A "tell you later" sort of look. She nodded, let go the hold she still had on him and went to Mikki. He leaned his head against her a moment.

"I'm sorry," she said into his fur. The words that could be so empty, save when they were honest. He didn't say anything, but he pushed against her a little, like a hug accepted and returned. Looked up, towering over her. She had forgotten how big a creature he was.

"Iarka."

She was riding one of the hill-ponies, Rifat at her side and getting glared at for his hovering, Besni, carrying a spear far too long for him, bouncing up and down the hillsides after them. Iarka reined in, rubbed the small of her back.

"Now we can go," she said.

"Now you can go," Attalissa said. "Blackdog . . ."

"I won't be coming back."

"I know, papa."

"Why not?" Tashi asked. Jolanan was glad someone had. She seemed to be holding his hand again. Well—that felt right.

"There's—a god in him," Iarka said, hand on her belly now. Shook her head. "And a devil still. How do you even get along with yourself?"

"Practice?" he suggested. "How's the baby?"

"She wants to go home. She wants the river."

"The caravan's waiting in Serakallash," Attalissa said. "Twenty of Kinsai's folk, to travel with Iarka, and four dormitories of sisters as well."

"More than we need."

"Take them, Blackdog. You've had enough of fighting, you and Mikki both. We all have."

"It won't be over. What's left of the Western Grass—"

"Is yours to reclaim, and yours to heal, with those who remain, and those who return. Folk and gods both. But you don't need to be fighting off raiders alone across the Red Desert, at least."

"No. Thank you."

They went back down to the temple, then. Jolanan walked between Tashi and the Blackdog. She felt lighter in the heart than she had in all this second life.

They came over the border with the sun setting, and the autumn winds carrying frost off the mountain peaks. Denanbak behind them, and not so swift a passage as Ahjvar would have liked, there or in the desert behind. Storms in the badlands, and one of the three baggage camels lost to a broken leg, but it was the expectation, all along the road, that they carried news from Marakand, that delayed them, gnawed at his nerves. Every chieftain's hall, once they were out of Taren lands, every god's shrine, every shaman or desert hermit . . . the *Rihswera* of Nabban did not pass so unmarked as he might hope, five, four camels and a *gewdeyn* he was trying to teach the ways of the lands of the road.

Too late in the day to make Dernang with any light left, and tired camels, and taking the tracks up the holy mountain in the dark—well, he would, but not with four tired camels and Ailan.

The guards of the border-post swarmed around, respectful, but wanting to know, wanting word—they had outridden any messengers the ambassador might have sent, or perhaps there had been early snows on the road through Bitha. Few took the road through the badlands. Now he remembered why.

A courier went, with what brief summary he gave, riding as if in a race for the castle in Dernang. He left the camels to the little garrison's stabler and Ailan to the cluster of young soldiers, mostly women, so taken with his coppery hair and exotic accent. Food, they were promised, and baths, and bed, and the captain wanted a more thorough repeating of the news, a story made of it, no doubt, for the dining hall.

Ailan was turning out to be very good at that sort of thing. He seemed even to enjoy it. Leave him to it.

Thought you'd be waiting?

I am.

Dogs, barking, running wild up and down the hillside in their frenzy of welcome, which turned into chasing one another into the sky, dragons tumbling the clouds and a wild wind with a kiss of snow in their passing.

He found Ghu further up along the ridge, where the ground was rough, tangled with stands of scrubby rhododendron and layered mats of juniper between the thin pines, which whistled in the wind. Stars streaked with cloud, more fitful snow in the air. A full moon rising, silvering all.

Home. Land and god and man.

They ended up under the pines, lying on their coats beneath the reaching juniper boughs, where the air was sweet and sharp with spice, wrapped and tangled in one another, hungry and urgent, holding hard each to the other, close and shivering with need in the night; the divided heart made whole, the soul's own home.

From the Chronicle of Nikeh gen'Emras

In the many-towered library of the ferry-folk of the reborn goddess Kinsai, on the black ridge overlooking the Fifth Cataract, there are books, a library to rival those of Marakand, Barrahe, and the Imperial Palace in the City of the Empress. Few even among the world's scholars and wizards were aware of just how extensive the libraries of Kinsai's folk were, before the destruction of their castles. Over many long lifetimes, they had built a vast collection of scrolls, bound codices, and unbound manuscripts. Histories, songs, romances, travellers' tales, works of philosophy and mathematics, the knowledge of the earth and the stars and the speculations and research of scholars—all that was offered, they were willing to take in.

What is little known is that in the early days of the two castles, the Lower that has grown into the twin towns of Kinsai's Crossing on the eastern shore, and Kinsai's Landing on the west where the causeway of the marshes begins, and the Upper, of which only a few worked blocks of stone remain to be seen in the clear waters of the river, wandering children of Kinsai journeyed into the west, in the aftermath of the wars of Tiypur's destruction. From those lands they carried away many relics of the dying empire, including books of history, of philosophy, of engineering, and the writings of the priests of the gods and goddesses, including the sacred texts of the priestesses of great Tiy, which told of the river and the journey and the rites of the dead.

I have spent many years in study of these, which are written in a script and a language ancestor to that of the west in which I was born, but the last rhapso-dists who preserved any knowledge of the ancient speech died in the years of the long tyranny of the cult of the false god Jochiz, and those who could interpret the inscriptions on the ancient tombs with them. Only in the ferry castles beyond the Nearer Grass were there yet scholars who understood, a little, of what they held, and even they were more concerned with preserving than with understanding. That, they believed, was to be the task of others.

I have made translations of the most significant of these into Imperial Nabbani, at the request of the god Nabban and his Rihswera, in memory of my Teacher. Others have set my words into the languages of Marakand and of the Nalzawan Commonwealth, for their libraries. In Tiypurian, I have written these my own histories.

Also, Yeh-Lin Dotemon was my teacher, and though she told me little, she taught me to read the ancient scripts, to read and speak and think in the ancient language of my people, that I might find what was so close to being lost. And further, I have had long speech with the god of the northern reaches of the Nearer Grass, who was once a man named Holla-Sayan, and was once the god Sayan, and is now called Hollasayan, and who also, in some part, contains within himself the memories, though not the nature, of the devil Sarzahn.

And Sarzahn was the great captain of the first rebellion of the Old Great Gods who became the devils.

Here I make, for those who strive among the tribes of the west to save and to restore something of what was good in our land in the days of the princes and princesses and their towers, who fight with words and with knowledge and teaching as surely as any warrior with sword in hand to defend truth and justice and what is good in the world, to deny oppression and tyranny and the lies of priests who yet serve the evil of the devil who would have made himself a god, a brief tale of the mysteries understood by the priestesses of Tiy, long ago, and the changes that came to the world even before the fall of Tiypur, and again, long after, when the tale of the seven devils came at last to its end.

If any story can ever be said to have an ending.

The Old Great Gods were born of that which is beyond the worlds, and contained it within themselves, and observed it in joy and wonder. This is a great and holy mystery beyond all human understanding. We are as children, striving to see what is beyond our horizon. But what is within our reach, is the understanding that the Old Great Gods were the guardians, who held the worlds—not the world of humankind alone—in their hands and in their hearts. Our ancestors understood them as the guardians of the souls of the dead, which is a part of the truth, but only a shadow of it. There were many beliefs in many lands, and all were true, and none, and changed as the ways of the lands and folks changed, but in the valley of the Tiy in the west, and later in all the lands of the empire of the many princes under the emperors and empresses, it was believed that the Old Great Gods dwelt in an underground realm of peace, to which human souls were drawn on death, making their way along a great river of healing and cleansing, and that in time, these souls returned to new life. In later times, indeed in our own time and for many generations before, throughout all the known lands, it was said that the realm of the Old Great Gods was in the distant heavens, among or beyond the stars, and that the souls of the dead made their way to the peace and comfort of those heavens on a long, long road, on which they were healed of the hurts of their lives, and learned to repent and in their hearts to make atonement for the sins of their lives. From this realm of the Gods, few folk taught that there was any returning. But most folk held that the souls of beasts—like those of gods and goddesses of the earth and the demons, returned into the soul, the life, the heart of the world, and were reborn of it, not as what they had been, but as water, which flows to the ocean and is reborn as rain and lives again its many lives.

The forgotten histories of Tiypur record that in the days of the empire, some among the Old Great Gods became fascinated with human individuality; they desired to preserve it by maintaining souls intact, not allowing them to merge back into the world-soul from which they had been born, as a child may collect pebbles at the seashore, taking them from the shore and treasuring them in a dark box, away from sun and wave, until they are forgotten. Others among the Gods wanted to enter into the human world to shape and guide it. And this they attempted to do, though the nature of the Old Great Gods was such that they could not long exist in their own form within the world, which was within them. They appeared as beings of light, brief enduring, or touched the world only through the dreams and visions of those they drew to speak for them, their acolytes, who strove to interpret their will and who rejected worship of the gods and goddesses of the hills and the waters to worship them as great and all-powerful mysteries. This was the first rebellion of devils; and there were many wars, for humans too often can admit of no complexity and set worship of the Old Great Gods against the worship of the gods of the earth, which had not been the intent of the rebels among the Old Great Gods, but was their crime. This all ended in disaster and the deaths of gods and demons, as Old Great Gods fought Old Great Gods through their followers among the lands of the west, few of whom had any true idea of why they fought.

It is easier to start a rockfall on the mountainside than to call it back.

The rebel Gods—the devils, those who had sought to partake of the life of the world by entering into the thoughts and dreams of philosophers and wizards— were defeated and sealed by the victorious Old Great Gods in the cold hells, which I myself have heard those who have spoken with devils describe as a physical place, as real as this earth about us, a world of ice and copper sun, yet that is a mystery and a poet's metaphor, a truth, but not the truth.

But after over a thousand years had passed, the seven devils of the stories every child knows escaped from the cold hells, led by Vartu and its—for the Old Great Gods are neither male nor female—beloved companion Jasberek. They tried a new way to exist in the world, binding their souls with that of a human, in order to live in the physical world, each sharing their nature with the other, mortal and immortal. This experiment was a great disaster, as the devils became entangled with human ambitions and sins and lost sight of themselves. Many wrongs were committed in the world because of this act, and much suffering followed.

And that is a story we all know, which led to a century of terrible wars, and the binding of the seven devils, and their awakening, and the hills and the waters again knew the deaths of gods and goddesses and countless human-folk, as had happened too in the days of Tiypur's fall.

And in the end, the devil Jochiz sought to become in himself the god and the soul of the world, perhaps even desiring to usurp the place of the world-soul that contains all. And the devil Vartu destroyed him and herself both, and shattered the seals of the cold hells, and the gates of the far heavens, and released both the imprisoned devils, which is to say the rebel Old Great Gods, and the souls of the dead who were garnered in the heavens, held lovingly, but for all that held against the will of the life of the earth, from flowing again to rejoin the world-soul from which they had been born.

And what may be the nature of the fate that awaits the souls of the dead now, we do not know, but those who dream deepest, the shamans of the birch forests of Baisirbsk, the mystics of the great desert between the Nalzawan Commonwealth and the Rostengan coast, the god of Nabban on his high mountain, in his deep river, say that it may be that the Old Great Gods and devils are reunited, and again hold the world within their heart, and that what is soul may linger long in their care, but flows in the end again to soul, to the world and the life of the world, when its time is ripe to do so.

And so we are all, every living thing, woman and bird, weed and hound and fish and spider, demon and god and the least worm of the soil, the stuff of life. We are the living, born and dying and reborn, soul of the world.

We are one.

FINIS